THE PARIS PACKAGE

STELLA BLED BOOK ONE

A.W. HARTOIN

The Paris Package

A Stella Bled Thriller Book One

ALSO BY A.W. HARTOIN

Historical Thriller

The Paris Package (Stella Bled Book One)

Strangers in Venice (Stella Bled Book Two)

One Child in Berlin (Stella Bled Book Three)

Dark Victory (Stella Bled Book Four)

A Quiet Little Place on Rue de Lille (Stella Bled Book Five)

Young Adult fantasy

Flare-up (Away From Whipplethorn Short)

A Fairy's Guide To Disaster (Away From Whipplethorn Book One)

Fierce Creatures (Away From Whipplethorn Book Two)

A Monster's Paradise (Away From Whipplethorn Book Three)

A Wicked Chill (Away From Whipplethorn Book Four)

To the Eternal (Away From Whipplethorn Book Five)

Mercy Watts Mysteries

Novels

A Good Man Gone (Mercy Watts Mysteries Book One)

Diver Down (A Mercy Watts Mystery Book Two)

Double Black Diamond (Mercy Watts Mysteries BookThree)

Drop Dead Red (Mercy Watts Mysteries Book Four)

In the Worst Way (Mercy Watts Mysteries Book Five)

The Wife of Riley (Mercy Watts Mysteries Book Six)

My Bad Grandad (Mercy Watts Mysteries Book Seven)

Brain Trust (Mercy Watts Mysteries Book Eight)

Down and Dirty (Mercy Watts Mysteries Book Nine)

Small Time Crime (Mercy Watts Mysteries Book Ten)

Bottle Blonde (Mercy Watts Mysteries Book Eleven)

Mean Evergreen (Mercy Watts Mysteries Book Twelve)

Short stories

Coke with a Twist

Touch and Go

Nowhere Fast

Dry Spell

A Sin and a Shame

Paranormal

It Started with a Whisper

For my mother, Mary, who prefers history to mystery.

CHAPTER 1

Steam billowed over the tracks in dark, grasping coils, obscuring the Venice train platform. The other tourists dithered about, looking timid and unsure at the darkness. But Stella walked straight through, coughing away the coal's metallic tang in the back of her throat as she looked for her husband. She spotted Nicky's gleaming blond head above the crowd, looking elegant and at home even in that dreary place with its dirty windows and crowds of smoking Italians. She walked toward him, skirting vendors hawking everything from Murano glass beads to pastries stuffed with mysterious meat. An impudent wind stroked her ankles below the hem of her curly lambskin coat and she lifted the fox fur collar to frame her face against the chill. Nicky didn't notice her even though the feathers on her hat stood a stiff twelve inches above her head, proclaiming her position and garnering attention wherever she went.

The crowd did notice Stella and made way for her, revealing Nicky dressed in his blue tweed suit and holding the enormous black golfing umbrella he carried everywhere as a precaution against the Venetian weather. Not that it did any good. The wet came from everywhere, not just from above, and glommed onto every surface, making Stella damp all the time.

Nicky brushed his hair back and Stella stopped walking through the throng to watch him, just for the pleasure of viewing him unobserved. She decided she didn't care if her father suspected quite often and out loud that her new husband might just be a pretty face. She knew there was more to him than that and, in time, all would be revealed. And if it wasn't, she'd dig it up with a pickax, if necessary.

An enormous man stinking of Turkish coffee and exotic spices Stella couldn't name jostled her to the left muttering, "Americano." She glanced up at him, wrinkling her nose in distaste and wondering how all Europeans tagged her as an American. In Paris, she'd replaced all the clothes her mother picked out in St. Louis. Why didn't they see her as French? When she looked again at Nicky, the crowd had backed up to reveal a red-faced porter with balled-up fists standing in front of her husband. Nicky regarded the angry little man with a bland expression.

"It simply isn't possible," said the porter.

"And why is that?" asked Nicky, tucking his hand in his pants pocket and sighing.

The little man flexed his fingers. His eyes never left her husband's face, but Nicky remained smooth and unruffled. Quite the picture of an American. Even Stella could see it was more to do with attitude than dress. His suit was purchased on Savile Row in London, along with his bespoke shoes and the umbrella. Nicky should've come off as British, if anything, but he didn't. Not even close. The little porter looked French, but his accent was off, so maybe he was Belgian like Hercules Poirot. It really didn't matter. He was arguing with Nicky, so Stella didn't like him on principle.

"Sir," said the porter, flexing his fingers faster. "It isn't possible."

Stella brushed past the Turkish coffee drinker, who sneered at her, and approached Nicky with a huge smile. She couldn't help it. The mere sight of her husband made her smile like she'd invented the expression. Nicky accepted her arm hooked around his, but he didn't shift his gaze from the porter.

"What's wrong?" asked Stella.

Nicky patted her arm. "Nothing, darling."

"Doesn't look like nothing." Stella swept a lock of light brown hair out of her eyes and tucked it safely away under her hat.

"Nothing is a matter of degree."

Stella bit back a retort. Her mother said a married woman should learn to curb her tongue and she certainly did. In all of Stella's eighteen years she'd never seen her mother disagree with her father. People called her mother a saint. Whether that was a reflection on her mother's character or what she had to put up with, Stella didn't know. She would like to be considered a saint, but feared she hadn't the constitution for it.

Nicky continued to stare at the porter until the little man took a step forward and went up on his tiptoes. He looked like he was trying to be intimidating and the notion of someone trying to intimidate Nicky almost made Stella feel sorry for him. He'd obviously never dealt with a Lawrence before. It wasn't an experience a person was likely to forget.

"Sir, I repeat, it is not possible," the man said, raising his voice.

"You certainly do repeat and so shall I," said Nicky, matching the porter's volume and then some. "And why is that?"

"As a representative of the line, I'm required to inform you that it isn't possible."

"Why?" Nicky bent at the waist so that he loomed over the little man, who took a step back.

"Sir, you must know why." The porter glanced at the gathering crowd, peering at him with interest. Then his gaze moved to a spot beside Stella and he glared. She tilted her head and looked at the tall spare form of Abel, their tour guide, who had appeared at her side. A dusky rose decorated Abel's high cheekbones, but he looked at the porter with a level gaze.

Nicky reached in his breast pocket and extracted their tickets. He held them out to the porter. "Care to take another look?"

"That is unnecessary."

"Then you agree that all three of our tickets are first class and unrestricted in any way."

"They are, but you must understand the situation," said the representative of the line.

"I understand nothing." Nicky tucked the tickets back in his pocket and his voice deepened. "Explain it to me."

"Sir, this really isn't the venue."

"It's the perfect venue. We have three First Class Tickets on this train. We are here. Our luggage is in our compartment. The train departs in five minutes and you won't let us board. Why is that? Please tell us." Nicky spread his long arms wide, gesturing to the crowd. The porter stepped forward and lowered his voice so that Stella strained to hear it.

"*He* isn't allowed in first class."

Nicky cupped his hand behind his ear. "Speak up, man."

The porter reddened further until he resembled an angry Bing cherry. He sputtered a bit, straightened his tie, and swallowed deeply. "Please excuse the delay. We'll be happy to have you board immediately."

"I thought so," said Nicky as he ushered Stella past the man. "Come on, Abel. We're in."

The train lurched forward as they made their way through the narrow corridor toward their compartment. An assortment of clicks, clacks, and an occasional boom visited Stella's ears. They were all lovely noises and made her heart beat to a special traveling time in her chest. But even better than the noises were the smells. Furniture polish, flowers, and leather mixed with a dozen different perfumes and colognes. The train smelled just as it ought to. It smelled like luxury.

As she reached the compartment, she heard Abel say behind her, "You needn't have done that. I could've sat in the club car."

"Don't be ridiculous, Abel. I wasn't going to let that pretentious little prig sit you in third class," said Nicky.

"Thank you." Abel's voice sounded a little choked.

"Don't mention it," said Nicky as he reached past Stella to slide open the compartment door.

Stella hesitated before entering. After spending weeks traveling on Italian trains, she'd learned that first impressions weren't necessarily accurate. The corridor might be beautiful, but that didn't mean there wasn't a dead skunk in the compartment. But Stella was poised to approve of anything that didn't stink and seemed remotely clean.

Nicky ushered her inside and then bent down to whisper in her ear. "Not bad."

Not bad indeed. Abel had told her that the Austrians were fastidious with their trains and he was right. The compartment was spotless with gleaming dark wood and polished brass fittings. Best of all, the seats were free of vile stains that suggested Stella might catch a communicable disease if she sat on one.

Stella placed her handbag on the seat without worrying about what she might get on it and pulled off her gloves. "This is very nice. Well worth the fight."

She hoped the comment would prompt an explanation of the argument, but he only responded by tweaking her chin and kissing her lightly on the lips. Stella wiped her oxblood-colored lipstick off his mouth with her thumb while Abel shuffled his feet and looked at the ceiling.

"I see the porter has left you a morning paper," said Abel, heading out the door. "I think I'll see if I can scare up a few more English editions."

Nicky glanced at the paper on his seat and said, "Good idea. The more, the better."

Stella sighed and rolled her eyes. "Yes, yes. More newspapers, please. We haven't had nearly enough of those."

Nicky grinned at her and picked up the paper with a flourish. Stella turned her back on him and peeked out the window at the gloomy Italian countryside zipping by. It was good riddance in her opinion. She never wanted to see another filthy train car or *Madonna and Child* in her life and Italy was lousy with both. A person couldn't turn around without having to admire a third-rate *Madonna and Child*. Just because a painting was four hundred years old didn't mean it was any good. Bring on Vienna with its bevy of old masters and the glorious Gustav Klimt. With any luck, her father's connections would get them in to see Klimt's Beethoven Frieze. She would have to send a telegram home and ask Father for an introduction to the Lederer family. She had no doubt it would be forthcoming. Her parents had seen the Frieze, even though it hadn't been exhibited since it was created in 1902. Her mother said the work was illuminating and led to greater understanding of Beethoven's Fifth. Stella had to see the painting. It was an absolute must.

And once she knew the Lederer family, other introductions could be easily arranged. Stella had no doubt that Nicky could be persuaded to stay in Vienna for a week or even two. Uncle Josiah was quite specific about which families to visit and she wouldn't let him down. Vienna would be an adventure and if Stella could have willed the train to go faster, she would have.

Stella settled on the plump green cushions next to Nicky, who ignored her as he made his serious student-of-the-world face and studied his paper. She ran her hand over the slick fabric and then down the length of his thigh. She waited to see if he'd respond. He didn't. His eyes remained on the newspaper article in front of him. Words like "mass expulsions feared" and "world conspiracy" jumped out at her, but she paid them no mind. Instead, she looked at his long legs stretched across their compartment crossed at the ankles. The gleaming wood paneling set off his smooth blond hair. He was her piece of precious art, a Michelangelo dressed in Harris Tweed, smelling of pipe tobacco and starch.

Nicky rattled his paper and straightened up, attracting the attention of a woman passing by in the corridor. She stopped short and gazed at him through the beautifully-etched glass with an intensity Stella had only observed on ravenous dogs before a platter of raw meat. It really was unseemly. The woman appeared to be elderly, at least fifty. Her eyes left Nicky when a porter approached and when she looked back in the compartment, her eyes fell upon Stella, who nodded and tried to look understanding. The woman reddened and straightened her furs. She looked ready to stalk off, but Abel arrived back at the compartment in that moment. Stella watched as he spoke to the woman. Although Stella couldn't hear him, she could imagine his soft polite tones in the lovely Austrian accent she'd come to adore.

The woman, instead of smiling back, frowned severely and stepped away. Abel gave her a sharp bow, pulled open the sliding compartment door and entered with a slight duck of his dark, well-groomed head. The woman hustled away, looking as though she'd smelled something nasty.

"Whatever did you say to her, Abel?" asked Stella. "Did you tell her to stop staring at Nicky?"

Nicky looked up with a jerk. A lock of thick hair fell onto his forehead and he brushed it back quickly. "What was that?"

"I said good afternoon to her, Mrs. Lawrence," said Abel, his expression long and sad, as it often was.

"You're supposed to call me Stella."

Abel brightened and nodded. "I forgot, Mrs. Lawrence."

"Stella."

"I'll remember next time, Mrs. Lawrence." His dark eyes twinkled and Stella wondered how the woman in the corridor hadn't found him completely charming.

Nicky waved a hand between them. "Said good afternoon to who?"

"Just an elderly woman in the corridor. She liked you quite a lot," said Stella.

Nicky shook the paper and went back to reading. "Don't be ridiculous, Darling."

"It's not ridiculous. It's a fact."

Abel sat opposite Nicky and Stella, leaning back on the thick tufted cushions. He opened his overcoat but didn't take it off. He never took it off, no matter how hot it got. He set a pile of papers beside him with their itinerary on top. Stella smiled to see his neatly typed plan written over and in some cases scratched out completely.

Vienna was definitely next. After that, maybe Salzburg. Then again, maybe not. Abel caught her looking at the itinerary and smiled back at her. In the two months he'd traveled with them, he'd learned to cope with his clients' sudden whims. Stella flattered herself to think that he also enjoyed them. After all, if she hadn't hopped off the train in Aquileia, they would've missed the beautiful mosaics at the basilica. Of course, it did take a full day to track down their luggage, but that hardly mattered when there were mosaics to be seen.

Stella, thinking of their one night in Aquileia, scooted close to Nicky. "What's so interesting?"

Nicky lowered the paper and folded it in his lap. He didn't look at Stella, though, but at Abel instead.

"It's quite a situation," said Abel.

"You've got that right and we're headed straight into the middle of it," said Nicky.

"What situation?" asked Stella.

"Let's hope our fears are unwarranted," said Abel.

"They're probably not," said Nicky.

Stella gave Nicky's shoulder a gentle punch and he turned to her with a jolt, perhaps surprised to find her there and listening. "Yes, Darling?"

"What are you talking about?"

"Don't worry yourself."

"You said there's a situation."

Nicky looked to Abel, who shrugged slightly and said, "It's to do with the Nazis."

"What have the Nazis to do with us?" she asked.

"Nothing," said Nicky. "They won't bother us."

"Why would they bother us, or anybody else, for that matter?"

Nicky glanced at Abel, who was shuffling his papers. Abel glanced up and something was exchanged between the men, a kind of understanding that eluded Stella.

"What's going on?" she asked again.

"You remember the shooting I told you about? It's got everyone riled up."

Abel leaned forward, his hands clasped under his chin, elbows on his knees. "It's not too late. We could still get off at the next stop."

"Get off?" Stella plucked her hat pin out of her ever so fashionable traveling hat, purchased in Paris, and jabbed three of its ten inches into the cushion next to Nicky's leg.

"God, I hate that thing," he said. "Why can't you use a less lethal pin?"

"Because it was Great Grandmother's and the pearl is flawless." Stella removed her hat and stuck the pin into the crown.

The train whistle sounded shrill and beautiful in the distance. Stella smiled. It was the sound of travel, of adventure. Anything could happen.

"As I said, it's not too late," said Abel. "A word to the porter and our bags will be removed forthwith."

"Why in the world would we get off?" asked Stella, careful to keep calm. She had a mission and she wasn't about to give it up.

"Because," Nicky paused, rubbing his forehead, "of what happened in Paris."

Stella looked at Abel. "You think we shouldn't go to Vienna because of a shooting in Paris?"

"Things have changed with the Nazis and they're much worse. Even if Von Rath doesn't die, there are bound to be reprisals," said Abel.

"Against who? They have the man. You said so yourselves. I don't see why we should change anything. All I've heard about for the last two months is your beautiful Vienna, Abel, and I intend to see it. The majority of Klimt's works are there and it's not a grand tour if you don't see everything."

Nicky placed his warm hand on Stella's. "I suppose you have your heart set on this."

"Of course, I do."

Nicky rubbed his forehead again. "Perhaps it will be all right."

"It will. Of course, it will. Vienna is a long way from Paris," said Stella.

"Europe is a very small place these days, Mrs. Lawrence," said Abel.

"Stella."

"Perhaps it will be all right," repeated Nicky.

They both looked to Abel to hear a confirmation, but Abel wasn't looking back. He gazed out the window at the gathering clouds above their car.

"Perhaps," he said softly.

CHAPTER 2

The train jerked as it began slowing for their stop in Vienna and Stella's handbag teetered on the edge of the seat before spilling its contents onto the parquet flooring. Abel bent over and delicately picked up several things as they slid around with Stella chasing them.

After gathering about a pound's worth of cosmetics, Stella started examining each piece for damage. She groaned when she found that her favorite rouge compact had a chip in the enamel.

"Can it be repaired?" asked Abel.

"I don't know." She ran her thumb over the jagged edge to see how bad it was when she felt a familiar flush, a prickle of intuition. "Maybe."

She pushed too hard and the chip bit into her thumb. She dropped the compact in her lap and examined the smear of blood it caused.

"Are you alright?" asked Abel.

"It's only a little—" Stella glanced up to find Abel, not looking at her as she expected but out the window to the corridor where someone was watching them. It wasn't Nicky, who was buried in another newspaper. A stranger stood outside their compartment. He wore a black well-fitted suit and had dark hair graying at the temples.

The first word that jumped into Stella's mind when she saw him was ordinary and the second was odd. He wasn't staring at Stella or at Nicky. Sometimes, even men stared at Nicky. The man looked at Abel like he was the only one in the compartment and Abel stared back, his normally sad face inscrutable.

Abel stood up, his hands full of Stella's items. He handed them to her without taking his eyes from the man. Then he reached for the compartment's door handle.

Before Abel could open the door, a porter, who looked as though he were still in high school, bustled past the man in the black suit and rapped on the door. Abel dropped his hand. The man turned around sharply and disappeared from view. The porter knocked again. Through the beautiful glass, Stella could see a worry line appearing on the young man's brow.

"Let him in, Abel," Stella said.

Abel's shoulders twitched. He glanced back at her, his expression clouded and uncertain.

"The door, Abel."

Abel looked back to the door and opened it with a jerk.

The porter took a step inside. "I have a telegram for Mrs. Bled. I apologize for the delay," he said in a thick French accent.

Nicky dropped his paper. "Mrs. Lawrence."

The porter looked down at the telegram in his hand. "Please excuse me. I was told that a Mrs. Bled was in this compartment.

Nicky blew out a tense breath and looked at the ceiling.

"There is a Mrs. Bled here," said Stella.

Nicky gave her a sharp look.

"Sort of," she said.

The porter glanced between the three of them, flushing and uncertain.

"I'm Stella Bled Lawrence. My family thinks…oh, it doesn't matter. The telegram's for me."

Nicky handed the nervous porter a bill and took the telegram. Abel stared out the door after the retreating porter, arms limp at his sides. Stella hesitated but then tapped his sleeve. Abel looked down at her and straightened his tie.

"Abel, who was that?" asked Stella, taking the telegram from Nicky.

Abel shook his head slightly but didn't answer.

"Who was who?" asked Nicky. "Not another old lady, I hope."

"Definitely not an old lady," said Stella, looking up from her message.

Abel met Stella's eyes, his expression sadder than she'd ever seen them, but he addressed Nicky. "With your permission, I think I'll go to the club car."

"Of course," said Nicky, already picking up another paper.

Abel slid the door open and stepped into the corridor. Then he stopped and turned back to Stella. He reached into his overcoat and pulled out a flat square package wrapped in thick brown paper and tied with twine.

"Mrs. Lawrence, would you hold on to this for me?" Abel asked.

"Of course." Stella took the package, which was surprisingly heavy.

Abel watched her tuck the package under her handbag and then left, walking in the opposite direction of the man in the black suit.

"I wonder what that was about," said Stella.

Nicky looked at her from around the edge of the newspaper. "What happened?"

"A man was looking at Abel and it wasn't exactly friendly."

"Did he say anything?"

"Nicky, he was in the corridor, but it seemed like he knew Abel."

"It's probably just because Abel's Jewish."

"Abel's Jewish?"

"You didn't know that?" asked Nicky.

"How would I know that?"

"Well, for starters, his last name is Herschmann."

"Herschmann is a Jewish name?"

"Of course it is, Darling." Nicky looped his arm around her shoulders and pulled her to him. "Where have you been?"

"Missouri."

"Well, that explains it." He picked up another newspaper and tried to withdraw his arm.

Stella snatched the newspaper away and tossed it onto Abel's seat. "No more newspapers. I'm sick to death of the news."

"If you insist."

"I do."

Nicky pulled her close again and nuzzled her cheek, pricking her with his bristly but invisible whiskers. "How shall we spend our time?"

Stella reached beside her and presented him with one of the objects that had fallen out of her handbag. "Look at this. It fell on the floor. Do you see any scratches?"

Nicky took the cigarette case from her. "Not exactly what I had in mind."

"Please look."

"I don't see any flaws," said Nicky, ignoring the cigarette case and focusing on Stella.

"Are you sure? It's for my father and I'd just die if it got wrecked."

"It's fine." Nicky handed the case back and began kissing Stella's neck.

Stella let him pull her onto his lap, even though they really shouldn't be seen like that in public. Nicky ran his hands over her while she ran hers over the cigarette case. It still looked to be in mint condition, the perfect addition to her father's collection. She checked again. The seed pearls were intact, as were the wavy enameled panels of translucent orange. So delicate. She couldn't believe her luck. A Fabergé cigarette case in an obscure jeweler's shop in Paris. The man had no idea what he had. And not just a Fabergé case, a Michael Perchin. She'd paid the asking price instead of haggling with the shop owner as she normally would have. The man had a family and it certainly wasn't a crime to not recognize a rare artist. Not many would have.

Nicky placed his hands under her suit jacket and began inching his way up. Stella wrapped the case in the thick padded velvet it had come in and picked up her mother's present. She opened a rosewood box to reveal a Fabergé vanity case, seemingly unscathed by the fall. The present cost a mint, but Nicky didn't blink at the cost, nor did he stop to admire the enamel Venus cameo at the center surrounded by fine guilloche engraving.

"What about this one?" she asked, running her index finger over the seed pearls lining the box's edges.

Nicky withdrew his mouth from her neck and looked at the case in her hand. "It's fine, I'm sure." Then he went back to nuzzling her neck while she rewrapped the case.

"Remind me to ask Abel about antique shops in Vienna."

"How many more presents do you need to buy?"

"This isn't about a present. It's a favor for Uncle Josiah." Stella waved her telegram under Nicky's nose.

"What does he want?"

"A liquor cabinet."

"Doesn't he have people to do that for him? We're on our honeymoon," said Nicky as the train lurched to a stop.

Stella again felt a prickle of intuition and shot a glance at the door. The man in black stood at the window, looking intently at her. As soon as their eyes met, the man stepped back. She slipped off Nicky's lap and picked up Abel's package, pressing it instinctively to her chest. The man glanced at the package and walked off, oozing smug superiority.

"Darling," said Nicky, "I said why can't Uncle Josiah have one of his people buy his liquor cabinet?"

Stella shifted her attention from the window to her husband. Nicky looked at her with a set jaw, making him look like a very handsome bulldog. Stella laughed and said, "Of course he could, but it wouldn't be the same as if I picked it out. You understand."

As she said it, Stella felt a twinge of guilt. Nicky didn't understand and she knew it. She also felt sure that he would soon understand. He just hadn't had enough time yet. Knowing a person for four months was hardly enough time to get used to their family. Her parents had suggested they wait to get married, since she was only eighteen, but there didn't seem to be any reason to wait. Eighteen and twenty-four were fine ages to get married. That was exactly how old her parents were when they married. Besides, Stella knew from the moment she laid eyes on Nicky that he'd be her husband. Whether he got used to her family before or after the wedding was immaterial. They'd be married in either case.

Nicky stood up and grabbed a hat box from the rack above their heads and placed it on the seat. He didn't say anything, but a muscle quivered in his jaw and Stella suspected he had plenty to say.

"Nicky," Stella sidled up to him, stood on her tiptoes, and kissed that quivering muscle. "I have to do it. He asked me. How can I say no?"

"I suppose you can't."

His lips said the words, but his eyes said the opposite. Stella didn't understand why it was so difficult for him when the answers were so obvious. You did for family and that was all there was to it. Stella was about to tell him that when the compartment opened. Stella jumped, expecting the man in the black suit to come barging in, but it was only Abel followed by a couple of porters.

"What's wrong?" Abel asked.

Stella was going to tell him about the man looking in the window again, but Abel's worried face stopped her. "Nothing. Just a bit jumpy, I guess."

"Ready to see my Vienna?"

"Absolutely." Stella handed him his package and he tucked it back inside his overcoat.

Nicky guided Stella out of the compartment with a reminder to the porters not to forget any of their bags. As she walked down the corridor, she realized how quiet it was. Only the sound of their shoes on the flooring and noises of the porters unloading their bags behind them were apparent. There were no other passengers exiting the car. When she looked into another compartment as they passed, the people inside looked away quickly and seemed to hunker down.

At the end of the car, Stella grasped the brass handrail and came around the corner to a silent train platform. She stepped gingerly down the steps and found herself holding her breath. The train station in Venice had been a riot of noise. Dozens of people smoking, eating, and talking, sometimes all at once. Venice was disgusting, dirty, and unruly, but it was wonderfully alive. Vienna felt like a funeral procession had just been through and the swastikas hanging from every possible surface didn't help the situation. Their primary colors of black, red, and white felt like an assault and Stella noticed that people pointedly avoided looking at them. Could a flag be angry? It would seem so.

Stella stepped down onto the concrete when she really wanted to turn right around and get back on the train. The few people in the station hustled by with their heads down and soldiers in brown shirts stood in a group at the far end, their steely eyes examining each traveler with suspicion. Anyone walking by gave them a wide berth. An older couple passed by, heading for the exit. They walked so fast, they looked like they were about to break into a run.

Nicky came up beside Stella and took her hand. He said over his shoulder to Abel, "When you're right, my friend, you're right."

"It gives me no pleasure, I assure you," said Abel.

Just then, the group of brown-shirted soldiers took notice of them. They formed up and marched in their direction, their movements stiff and unnatural.

Nicky turned to Stella and Abel. "You two go see if you can hail a cab."

"What about the luggage?" asked Stella.

"I'll take care of it. Just go. Go right now."

Abel nodded at Nicky and took Stella's arm. He pulled her gently toward the exit. Stella twisted around and got a glimpse of Nicky walking toward the soldiers with a big smile on his face. Abel picked up speed, his long fingers squeezing her arm. Stella looked up at him, surprised to see a sheen of sweat on his broad forehead.

"We shouldn't have come," he said.

CHAPTER 3

Stella emerged from the bright lights of the train station into nighttime Vienna with Abel's hand still squeezing her arm. It was only seven o'clock, but it felt much later. The sky was completely black with a sprinkling of stars and the traffic on the road ahead of them was light. A chill wind ruffled Stella's hair and she turned up the fur collar on her coat as she turned to Abel. The way he stood in the doorway, a jagged bit of light cut across his face, concealing his lower jaw and illuminating his eyes. His head remained still, but his dark eyes darted around the street and buildings. Stella looked also, but she couldn't spot anything interesting.

"Abel, what are you looking for?" she asked.

"A cab."

Stella pursed her lips. A cab. He was not looking for a cab. Unless cabs could be found halfway up the side of a building. "Tell me another one."

Abel's gaze shifted to the far end of the street and his grip tightened on her arm to the point of pain. "There's one," he said. "You'll have to hail it."

Stella had never hailed a cab in her life. Men always hailed them for her. Even if she was alone, there was always a stranger ready to raise his arm for her. "Me? Why me?"

"Please, Mrs. Lawrence. Just go down to the curb and raise your hand," said Abel.

Stella started to object, but Abel gave her a gentle push down the wide concrete stairs.

"All right, all right," said Stella, turning around. "I'm going, but I don't see why I should."

"Please, Mrs. Lawrence."

"It's Stella." Then she clamped her mouth shut, spun around, went to the curb, and raised her gloved hand even though her mother would've been appalled. Ladies didn't hail cabs. Just why that was so, Stella couldn't say.

Maybe ladies didn't hail cabs in America, but apparently, they did in Austria. A black Daimler taxi rolled to a stop in front of her. The vehicle was an older model, very upright and square, but it gleamed like it was brand new. An elderly driver leaned across the seat and smiled through a spotless window. Stella's tension seeped away. This was what they needed, friendliness and a clean taxi to sweep them away from the miserable station into a more reasonable section of the city. She grinned at the driver and opened the rear door. "Can you wait just a minute?"

The driver frowned as he glanced past her. Light sparkled on his stubbly five o'clock shadow and made him look jolly in spite of his fierce expression.

"Do you speak English?" asked Stella.

The driver shrugged. "A little."

"Can you wait?"

The driver leaned farther forward and looked out his passenger side window. "Is he with you?"

Stella looked back at the train station, expecting to find Abel facing her, but he wasn't. He was looking in through the station doors under the enormous white swastika that had been a fixed to the old, elegant station. One might as well paint that hideous symbol on a Monet. It couldn't have been more out of place. Abel glanced up and

Stella had a brief but frightening vision of the swastika falling off and squashing him.

"Abel!" Stella called. "Hurry! I have the cab!"

He didn't turn around.

"Abel! Don't stand under there!"

Just then, Nicky emerged. He spoke to Abel and they trotted down the stairs.

"Excellent, darling," said Nicky. "You got the cab."

"You make it sound like you weren't sure I could do it," said Stella.

Nicky glanced over his shoulder at the train station. "I didn't mean to imply that." He gestured to the taxi's door. "Shall we?"

"I'll have you know I can do lots of things. Things you'd never imagine. I'm very accomplished."

Nicky grabbed her by the shoulders and planted a swift kiss on her lips that almost knocked her hat off her head. "Yes, you are. Let's get going." With that, he spun her around and pushed her into the taxi. The driver's frown grew deeper. He said something low in German and then glared at Abel as he started to get in.

"I don't think I can take all three of you," the driver said.

"Oh, yes, you can." Nicky handed him a German bill and pulled Abel in behind him.

Abel shut the door and said, "Hotel Blechhammer."

The driver looked to Nicky, who nodded. The driver shrugged and tucked Nicky's bill into his breast pocket. As they pulled away, Stella shifted in her seat, ready to let Nicky have it, when something caught her eye. The man in the black suit exited the station and took a drag on a long cigarette. The burning ember glowed bright against the gray stone building as he watched them pull away. Stella wished the swastika would fall on him, but of course, it didn't. As her mother always said bad things never seemed to happen to bad people and Stella was quite certain that he was bad, though she couldn't say exactly why. He'd done nothing more than look at them, but there was ill intent in that, she was certain.

Stella faced forward and grabbed Nicky's hand. "What were you doing in there?"

"In the train station?" asked Nicky.

"Yes, in the train station."

"Nothing, darling."

"Don't give me nothing. I saw you go talk to those soldiers."

"Don't worry about it." Nicky didn't meet her eyes. "I wanted to ask them their favorite sites."

Stella dropped his hand. "Why would you do that? Abel's a native. He knows everything there is to know."

"It's been a long day. Let's drop by the hotel. I'll instruct them to retrieve our luggage, and then we can get some dinner. What do you say?"

An overly cheerful expression settled on Nicky's face. She could ask all night, but he wasn't going to give her a real answer. Stella crossed her arms and looked out the window. Nicky and Abel began talking about dinner and their itinerary. Would they see the Hofburg or Schonbrunn palace first? Should they have schnitzel at Figlmüller that night or just grab something at the hotel? Stella listened at first, noting the men's inane conversation, so unusual for them. But nothing they said felt relevant to recent developments and she ended up paying little attention to it. She focused on the buildings they were passing instead. The word "Jude" was written on several shop windows, often next to a painted star. A few storefronts had shattered windows and those garnered most of her attention. The German words painted on the doors made her bite her lip. She had no idea what they said, but something about them, their size, the way the letters were scrawled, told her they were nasty. They weren't in a bad section of town either. The buildings were well-kept and highly orna-mented. It seemed every other block had a ruined storefront. Some had boards nailed over the gaping maws, but others were bare. A couple of times, Stella saw people climbing in through the broken windows and carrying out items.

As these sights passed her by, Stella began feeling more than hearing the men's conversation. They kept prattling away, saying nothing of importance, but each sentence made Stella more uneasy. They never talked like that. They were usually quite stingy with their words. Stella always thought they hoarded them in case they might need them later. It seemed now they were employing every unused word they'd tucked away. Since when did Nicky care about seeing an opera, much less which seats were best? She hadn't known him very long, but she'd never heard him say the word 'opera' before. Now he was going on like he lived for the stuff.

A group of soldiers in brown shirts marched down one street, passing some men clearly robbing a store. They did nothing. When the taxi passed by, the soldiers gave her hard looks with narrowed eyes. She felt sure she was being evaluated for something, but she couldn't imagine what. They couldn't see enough of her to determine whether she was pretty or not. Plus, she was in the taxi with Nicky. The sight of him usually stopped any interest straight away.

"Abel," said Stella. "Why are there so many soldiers in town?"

The men stopped talking, but neither replied.

"Abel?"

He looked straight ahead. "As you know, we have lately been annexed by Germany. These things don't always go smoothly."

"Something must be gumming up the works. Did you see all those busted up stores? They look like nice places, too."

"These things happen," said Nicky. "Now about dinner."

Stella spotted a word painted on a car. She'd seen it several times on buildings. It was scrawled in red. "What's scheiße?"

Nicky coughed. "Nothing, Darling. Don't worry about it."

"Nothing? It's written all over the place," said Stella. "Abel, what does it mean?"

Abel didn't answer immediately, his eyes downcast. Stella couldn't help staring at the sheen of sweat glinting in the dim light on his broad forehead. It was beginning to drip and so out of character. She'd never seen him sweating, not even in Italy's unrelenting heat. It could've been her imagination, but he appeared sadder than usual. Perhaps he was coming down with something or just tired. It had been a long train ride.

"Are you feeling all right?" asked Stella.

"I'm very well," said Abel without conviction. "Here we are."

The taxi pulled up in front of the hotel. The driver jumped out and opened Stella's door. Abel went to open his door, but Stella reached across Nicky and grasped Abel's arm.

"What does it mean, Abel?" she asked.

Abel looked into her eyes. He hesitated but then seemed to resign himself. "It means excrement, Stella."

She let loose of his arm. "Oh." Then she brightened. "You called me Stella."

Abel patted her hand, slid out, and stood with his back to them, facing the hotel. Stella took the driver's offered arm and stepped out of the taxi. The Hotel Blechhammer rose before her in its old-world perfection. All its windows were intact and gleaming. A doorman bustled up and greeted them in German, then quickly switched to English.

"We have a room booked, but our luggage is still at the south station," said Nicky.

"What name can you be registered under, please, sir?" asked the doorman.

"Lawrence. Nicholas Lawrence."

"Ah, yes, Sir. We have been awaiting your arrival. But there must be some mistake. I believe we have you registered under Bled Lawrence."

Nicky frowned. His handsome face creased into folds that didn't look possible from his normally smooth countenance. "Oh, it's a mistake all right." He turned to Abel and Stella quickly stepped between them. "Now don't be going after Abel. My father requested the room." She spoke to the doorman. "I'm a Bled, you see."

"Yes, yes, we know. One of the Bleds of the Bled Brewery in America. We've been honored with your parents' presence many times."

Nicky grumbled and Stella could've sworn she saw a hint of a smile creep onto Abel's lips.

"But I'm a Lawrence now, you understand," said Stella.

"Of course. It's a pleasure to have you both with us. If you'll come this way." The doorman gestured to the front door.

Nicky continued grumbling all the way up the beautiful marble steps toward the elaborate crystal and walnut doors. Stella knew he probably wanted to tell the doorman that he was Nicky Lawrence of the New York Lawrences. But he'd tried that tact before and it hadn't worked out for him. The average person didn't know who the Lawrences were or that they owned United Shipping and Steel. Everyone knew about Bled Beer. It wasn't as though Bled was a very common name and once you said your name was Bled, everyone was your friend. If you said your name was Lawrence, they shrugged like Lawrences were a dime a dozen. Stella wanted to tell Nicky it didn't matter if people recognized the name Bled and not the name Lawrence. People who *did* know the Lawrences utterly respected them. It wasn't so with the Bleds. Along with their notoriety, the Bleds had a strain of eccentricity and a streak of insanity that managed to show up in every generation. Of course, she'd tried this tact before, too, and it hadn't worked out for her either.

The doorman pulled the door open with a flourish and Stella stepped through the doorway into the sumptuous lobby. She paused and took it all in. The woodwork, the enormous chandelier dripping with crystals, and the paintings, old German masters mostly, were just as her parents described. Although it was a five-star hotel, the Hotel Blechhammer had a familiarity to it that made her feel cozy, like her parents were there with her. She could never say that to Nicky though. He wouldn't understand how she missed them. His family, while eminently respectable, hadn't sent them as much as a post card.

Nicky nudged her and Stella stepped forward, smiling. Her heels tapped daintily on the inlaid marble floor with Nicky walking close behind her. Even his heavy footsteps sounded displeased. When they reached the desk, Nicky introduced himself and the female clerk blushed. Stella smiled. That should do it. The clerk didn't care about last names. Nicky would be fabulous if he were a Ford.

"Welcome, Mr. and Mrs. Bled Lawrence. We have you booked into a suite on the fifth floor. Is that satisfactory?"

Stella saw Nicky's shoulders tense, but he never stopped smiling at the pretty clerk. Nicky nodded and signed the large, tasseled guestbook.

The clerk forced her eyes away from Nicky and gave a sneaky grin to Stella. "How is Miss Myna enjoying her tour?"

"You *do* know my parents well." Stella switched to an Austrian accent that exactly mimicked the clerk's intonation. "Our tour is magnificent. I have worn out many shoes."

They laughed together. Nicky didn't laugh. He stared at his wife. "What was that?"

"Oh, nothing," said Stella. "Myna is my family nickname."

"Because…"

The clerk continued to smile and said, "Miss Myna is a perfect mimic. All the Bleds have told us so."

Nicky frowned and looked down at Stella. "No one told me."

"I'm not that good," she said quickly.

Abel leaned on the desk. "She is very good. Do the accent of the rail clerk in Venice."

"I don't think so," said Stella.

Nicky raised an eyebrow at Abel. "How do you know?"

"Yeah," said Stella. "How do you know?"

Abel's eyes ceased to be sad for a moment. "I heard you in Paris, speaking to the Moroccan."

Stella lowered her eyes. "Oh."

"He could not believe his ears. As well with the Roman who made your shoes."

Nicky looked at Stella's shoes, kid leather kitten heels with fabulous silk bows. "What about those shoes?"

"Abel knew a specialty shoe shop and he took me."

"When?" Nicky had a hint of hurt in his voice and Stella wasn't sure why. It wasn't as if he had an intense interest in shoes, especially women's. She doubted that he'd noticed that she wore shoes, much less what they looked like.

"When you had that meeting with those importers. The the…"

"Montalcini family," said Nicky. "I forgot about my meeting. What did you say to the shoemaker?"

"She charmed him," said Abel, his eyes growing sad again as he straightened his coat and glanced back at the door.

Nicky caught the look and said, "We should go up. Good evening, Abel."

Stella and the clerk glanced back and forth between the men. Stella failed to comprehend the sudden change in tone. The clerk did and she said with a wise tone, "It would be best to go now." She was looking at Abel, her eyes becoming as sad as his.

"What?" asked Stella.

"Nothing, darling," said Nicky as he rubbed her back like she was some kind of nervous pet.

"Why do you always say 'Nothing' when I ask what's going on?" She stepped away from his hand and glared.

"I don't."

"You do."

"I nearly forgot," the clerk said, looking below the desktop. "A telegram for Mrs. Bled Lawrence."

Nicky dropped the pen, which made a loud clink on the glossy desktop. "Really. How unexpected."

The clerk handed the telegram to Stella. Abel, who'd been standing back, came forward. He asked the now bright red clerk about the luggage. She managed to drag her eyes away from Nicky, called someone, and arranged for the luggage to be picked up from the station.

"Aren't you going to open it?" asked Abel, gesturing to the telegram.

"Maybe later," said Stella with a glance at Nicky's stern face.

Abel nodded and glanced at his watch. Stella might've been mistaken, but she thought she saw his hand shake.

"Have you decided about dinner?" he asked.

"I think I'd like to stay in," said Nicky. "And I imagine you'd like to get home, wouldn't you, Abel?"

"I'm at your disposal."

"I say we call it a night." Nicky eyed Stella. "Unless your parents have arranged our dinner for us."

"I've no idea." Stella tucked the unopened telegram away in her handbag where it couldn't cause any more trouble.

"That settles it then," said Abel. "I'll be here at nine tomorrow morning, as usual, and we'll begin the delights of my beautiful Vienna."

The men shook hands and Stella said goodbye. She stifled a yawn and took Nicky's arm. His shoulders relaxed and he brushed a rogue curl off her forehead. "We both need some sleep, especially Miss Myna."

Stella double-checked to see if he was irritated, ready to battle about nicknames or telegrams, but he merely yawned himself, so she nodded. He led her to the elevator behind the bellhop. The feeling like she was with her parents came back with a vengeance as she looked around at the chandeliers and smelled the fresh flowers in ornate vases. It was just like they'd described and the staff knew her. They had nothing to do with the soldiers in the station, the nasty graffiti, or Abel's sad eyes. The hotel cast a spell and she couldn't wait to have a good night's rest.

It wasn't a sound that awakened Stella. It was the light and the smell. A dull orange glow and cigarette smoke filled the room. And there was something else mingling with the cigarette. A scent unfamiliar and even less appealing than the cigarette smell. Stella wrinkled her nose and wondered where she was. The ornate chandelier hanging over the foot of the bed caught her eye and she remembered. The hotel in Vienna. She focused on the chandelier and its curving, elegant lines. It looked even more beautiful in that odd orange glow. She slid her hand under the thick down comforter toward Nicky's side of the bed, only to find it cold and empty. She rolled over and saw her husband standing bare-chested by one of the windows. He had a lit cigarette in one hand and the other one held back the heavy damask drapery, allowing the orange light to filter in.

Stella sat up. "You're smoking."

Nicky glanced at her and then back out the window. "I am."

"I didn't know you smoked."

"I don't, normally." He continued to stare out the window, the light defining his muscular body and making him appear hard and sinewy. His face had been transformed into an older, angrier version that she didn't know existed.

"Why are you smoking now?"

"I think Von Rath died," said Nicky.

"Who?" asked Stella, throwing off the comforter. She padded over to him and tentatively touched his shoulder.

"The man who was shot in Paris."

"What makes you think that?"

With a sharp movement of his head, Nicky indicated the window. Stella stepped forward and wrapped her right arm around Nicky's warm waist. He put his arm over her shoulder as she peered out into a world she didn't recognize.

"What is that?" she asked. "A fire?"

"Yes."

Stella stared out the window as Nicky had done, but couldn't make sense of what she was seeing. It couldn't be one fire. The orange glow was everywhere. Different points around the hotel seemed brighter than others, but she couldn't pick out one particular blaze.

"Where is it?"

"Everywhere," said Nicky, reaching around Stella and snuffing his cigarette in a silver ashtray. It had three butts in it already.

Below their window, a group of young men ran down the street, carrying clubs and torches. They busted their way into a building across the street. A few minutes later, windows exploded on the third floor, spraying the street with glass. Stella watched as books, linens, and pieces of furniture were thrown out the windows. A man ran out of the building. Two of the young men chased him down the street and out of sight.

Stella dashed to the telephone next to the bed, ringing the front desk with shaking hands. No one picked up and she stood there, waiting and watching Nicky, who lit another cigarette. She wanted to smack it out of his hand and stomp it into the lush carpet. Why was he standing there so calm, so uncaring?

Someone finally answered in German, but Stella ignored that and just began speaking. She thought she'd scream if she didn't get it out. "You have to call the police. There are men breaking into an apartment across from our room. They just chased some poor man down the street," she said.

The person on the phone didn't reply immediately, but Stella could hear him breathing, not calm breathing. He sounded like he'd run up five flights of stairs.

"Do you understand English?" Stella asked.

"Yes, madam, but there's nothing we can do."

"Well, you can call the police, for starters."

"The authorities have been contacted," he said.

"When?"

"Quite a while ago, madam."

"Where are they then?" she asked.

"I couldn't say."

Nicky walked over, took the phone out of Stella's hand, and hung up. He pulled her to him, saying softly, "There's nothing we can do."

"I don't understand. Where are the police? If there are fires everywhere, why are there no sirens? Where are the firemen? They do have firemen, don't they?"

"Yes, darling."

Stella pushed him back. "We should call the police. Maybe the front desk didn't really do it."

"It won't do any good."

Stella stared at him. She was about to argue when faint shouts came from outside their windows. She ran to look out and saw a group of men, ragtag civilians and several soldiers, herding five men down the street. Every few feet they'd be hit or kicked. One man with snowy white hair was hit so hard he fell to his knees and had to be dragged along by the others.

Stella grabbed Nicky's arm. "You have to do something. They're beating up an old man."

Nicky sighed. "I can't interfere."

Stella shoved him aside and tried to open the window. Nicky

pulled her away and gave her a little shake. "What are you going to do? Yell at them? That's the SA."

Stella tried to twist out of his grasp. "We have to do something."

"Aren't you listening? That's the SA, Hitler's troops. They wouldn't do this, if they hadn't been ordered to."

Stella stopped struggling. "What about the cops?"

"Cops can't stop an army, even if they wanted to, which I doubt."

Nicky let go of her and she returned to the window. More people were running in the street. Glass glittered on the pavement from dozens of broken windows. The orange glow burned brighter, so that it almost felt like dawn, but a horrible dawn, one with no sun, no hope.

"So, they're burning things and beating people up. The SA, I mean," said Stella.

"They're in charge, I imagine."

"What are they burning?"

"Synagogues, schools, businesses. Whatever they're ordered to, I suppose."

"Synagogues? This is about the Jews then."

"Of course."

"Why do you say it like that? You make it sound like you knew this would happen."

"I didn't know *this* would happen, but my father told me to steer clear of the Nazis. You remember how he tried to talk us out of coming to Europe. This is why."

"My father didn't say anything," she said.

"He didn't want to worry you or your mother, but your father is as aware of the Nazis' aggression as my family."

"How did he know anything about it?"

"We have contracts with the German government. They've been inquiring into our employees' backgrounds. They don't want to have any dealings with Jews."

"I hope your father didn't go along with that."

Nicky watched a fire truck roll slowly down the street past some young boys lighting fire to the belongings that had been thrown into the street. "He rearranged the names. He said it was none of the Reich's business who we employ. We'll probably pay for that. The Nazis aren't stupid. One of these days, they'll figure out Donald James is really Simon Goldblatt."

"Abel is a Jew."

Nicky raised an eyebrow at her. "I know. I told you."

"They're attacking Jews and Abel is a Jew." Stella swallowed hard. Her dinner threatened to come back and go splat on the floor.

"There's nothing we can do."

"Stop saying that."

"It's true."

"It's not true. Call Abel and tell him to come here. He'll be safe with us."

"I tried earlier. There's no answer at his flat or his shop."

Stella and Nicky stood facing each other with the awful orange light illuminating them. Nicky touched her cheek and rested his other hand on the back of her neck, but she shook it off.

"Try him again," she said.

Nicky nodded and picked up the phone. It took another long while for the front desk to answer and even longer to get connections to Abel's home and shop. No one answered in either case. When Nicky hung up, Stella went to her dresser. She rooted through three drawers before she found the slacks she was looking for. She laid them on the bed and went to the armoire to find a blouse. Nicky sat on the bed and watched her, his brow furrowed.

"What do you think you're doing?" he asked.

"Getting dressed," she said.

"Why?" His brow furrowed deeper.

"Somebody has to go out and find Abel."

"You can't go out there."

"Oh, really?" Stella laid her blouse on the bed and crossed her arms. She'd heard other people in her family talk about this feeling she was having. The feeling that she just had to do something whether it was right or wrong or even made any sense. She had to find Abel and bring him to where he'd be safe. Uncle Josiah would understand.

She cringed a little to think that this might be why people considered him certifiable.

Nicky unfolded her arms and wrapped her in his. He ignored her stiffness and her glare. She let him move her, all the while knowing she couldn't be swayed. She would help Abel, with or without Nicky's consent.

"I'm not a coward, if that's what you're thinking," he said. "I'm practical."

"I'm not," said Stella, still stiff in his arms.

Nicky laughed, a soft half-hearted gesture. "You're a Bled."

"What else would I be?"

He held her back from him by the shoulders. "I thought you'd be a Lawrence. But I guess your family has been right all along. The best I can hope for is a Bled Lawrence."

"What does that mean?" Stella narrowed her eyes at him. If he said anything bad about her family, she was ready to let him have it. The Bleds might not be eminently respectable, but they had other qualities equally valuable, like ingenuity and loyalty.

"It means we're going to find Abel," he said.

Stella pitched herself into his arms and kissed him hard on the lips so that he staggered backwards. They fell onto the bed, a tangled pile of young, slim limbs. He kissed softly down her neck and she began to think he was trying to change the subject, so she reached over and turned on the side table lamp.

Nicky grinned at her. "I wasn't doing anything."

"Yeah, right." Stella grabbed his trousers from the chair he'd laid them on and Nicky took off his pajama bottoms as a loud knock echoed through the room. Nicky and Stella both jumped and then locked eyes with each other. Another knock came, louder than the first.

"Mr. Bled Lawrence," said a man's voice, soft and pleading. "Please open the door. This is the hotel manager, Mr. Klum."

A chandelier-rattling knock came after Mr. Klum's last word and Stella knew it wasn't the manager doing the knocking.

Nicky put on his trousers, threw back his shoulders, and walked to the door. "What in the world is it, Mr. Klum? Don't you realize the time?"

"Please, Mr. Bled Lawrence. If you don't open the door, they will kick it in."

"Who?"

"The Schutzstaffel. They want to interview you immediately."

Nicky turned to Stella, who stood by the bed wearing only her panties and clutching her negligee to her chest. "Put your dressing gown on. I have to let them in."

CHAPTER 4

Stella peered around Nicky's shoulder as the SS officer stalked into their room. Unlike the other soldiers she'd seen on the street, he wore a formal uniform with a belted black jacket and dark pants. He didn't turn and acknowledge Nicky and Stella. He looked about the room and then made a sharp gesture over his shoulder. Three other soldiers came in. They were in their shirtsleeves and all four had the Nazi swastika on an armband on their left arms. The officer said something in German and his men began opening the armoire and looking under the bed.

"Hey," said Nicky. "What the hell do you think you're doing?"

The officer turned slowly and Stella found herself holding her breath. When he faced them, she tried to let out the breath but couldn't. Maybe it was the authority the uniform conveyed or the malevolent smile on his pale, narrow face that frightened Stella or perhaps it was the combination that made him the worst creature she'd ever beheld. Whatever it was, its power didn't last long. Anger followed the fear and she met his icy stare without blinking and let out the breath.

"Going somewhere?" the officer asked.

Another man entered the room before Nicky could answer. He

was short and plump with what must've been a normally jolly face, but was at that moment fixed into an odd frightened smile. His navy blue suit was rumpled and his tie askew. "Mr. Bled Lawrence, I'm terribly sorry for this intrusion."

The officer shot him a stern glance and the man clamped his mouth shut.

"Who are you?" Nicky asked the officer.

"Where are you going?"

Nicky took a step forward. "Answer my question."

"You are demanding?" The officer's smile grew wider. "You are in no position to demand anything. It has been reported that you have been traveling with a Jew by the name of Abel Herschmann."

"What's your point?" asked Nicky.

"Where is he?"

Stella stepped from behind Nicky. "Even if we knew where he was, we wouldn't tell you."

"Stella," said Nicky under his breath.

"Don't Stella me," she replied.

The officer made another gesture at the door and a blonde woman walked in. She was tall and rather attractive in a manly, stern kind of way. She wore a uniform similar to the male officer's, except with a skirt and a pair of clunky heels.

The officer said something in German to her and she grabbed Stella by the arm. She pulled back, but before she could wrench her arm away, Nicky calmly took the woman's arm and peeled her fingers off. He pushed the woman away and maneuvered Stella back behind him.

"You must be out of your mind," Nicky said to the officer.

"On the contrary, it would be best if your wife were to wait outside," said the officer.

"It would not," said Stella as she stared at the woman from around Nicky's bare shoulder. She looked as though she might try to wrestle Stella out of the room at any moment.

"My wife isn't going anywhere. Tell me what you want and get out," said Nicky.

"I want Abel Herschmann."

"He obviously isn't here."

"Obviously." A series of shouts drew the officer's attention to the window. He went over and looked out. "But you know where he is."

"No, we don't," said Stella.

The officer turned back to the room and the woman edged closer to Stella. "I think you do."

"We don't," said Nicky. "Now get out."

"You've been telephoning him. Several times this night, but you never spoke. Now I find you going out. Do you expect me to believe you have no idea where he is?"

"I don't care what you believe," said Nicky. "Abel isn't here and we don't know where he is."

"I think you do," he said.

"Would we keep calling his office, if we did?" asked Stella, her tone much like her father's when he was negotiating with an uncooperative distributor, forceful but eerily calm.

Two of the soldiers moved in and the woman grabbed Stella's arm again, dragging her from behind Nicky. The small, plump man in blue suit rushed in front of Nicky and Stella, just as Nicky was drawing back to punch someone, anyone, including the woman. He spoke in rapid German. All Stella caught was their names and America. He said America several times. The officer made a sharp gesture and the woman dropped Stella's arm.

"Do not attempt to leave this hotel until we give you permission. Do we understand each other?"

Nicky put his arm around Stella. "I understand you well enough."

"Good."

The officer said something to the others under his command. The men left readily, but the woman hesitated. She glared at Stella, did an abrupt about face, and walked out. The officer nodded to Nicky and Stella and left them standing there with the little man who began visibly shaking.

Nicky clapped him on the shoulder. "Mr. Klum, I presume."

"Yes, Mr. Bled Lawrence. I apologize. I don't know what to say. This night. So unexpected."

"You don't need to apologize. I suspect you saved our bacon a minute ago. I thank you for that.

Mr. Klum pulled a limp handkerchief from his pocket and mopped his face. He signaled for them to be quiet and looked out the door for a moment. "They're gone," he said as he closed the door.

"But they'll be back," said Nicky.

"I'm afraid so. You must leave Vienna as soon as possible."

"We can't abandon Abel," said Stella.

"There's nothing you can do for your friend. If they don't find him tonight, they'll be back for you," said Mr. Klum.

"Why do they want him?" asked Nicky.

"I don't know, but Peiper wouldn't have come here himself if your friend wasn't very important. You must leave."

"We're not leaving Abel," said Stella.

Mr. Klum gazed at Stella for a moment then turned his attention to Nicky. "Sir, you must think of yourself, your wife, your future. You are from famous American families, but they don't care who you are. They want him, more than they value you. If you are still here when they come back, they'll arrest you both."

Nicky tightened his grip around Stella. "They can't arrest us. That's crazy."

Mr. Klum nodded. "I agree, but it will happen." He gestured to the window. "Look what they're doing now. Why not arrest a couple of prominent Americans if it gets them what they want?"

"Our families would never stand for it," said Stella.

"By the time they know, it will be too late. They'll separate you and send you to these camps they have. Accidents are common in those places. People go in and often do not come out."

"What do you suggest?" asked Nicky.

"We are not leaving Abel here," said Stella.

Nicky turned Stella to face him. "I'm not letting you get arrested. We're getting out of here now."

"Not now," said Mr. Klum. "They're attacking people randomly all over town. You'll have to wait until morning. There are guards on all our doors. You'll have to go to the roof and walk five buildings to the east. It's the Hotel Kirsch. The roof access door will be propped open. Exit through the back door and get to the train station."

"What about you?" asked Nicky. "If they find out you helped us, you'll be in one of those camps."

"My brother is a high ranking official in Munich. He'll take care of me."

"He's a Nazi?" asked Stella.

Mr. Klum shrugged. "My brother is ambitious. He wanted his business to grow. The party is the only way to do that."

"The price of doing business," said Nicky.

"Yes. Now pack light. Only what you can carry easily. You have to be on a train before they know you're gone. I'll send your luggage to Hawthorne Avenue in St. Louis."

Nicky shook Mr. Klum's hand. "Thank you."

"Perhaps someday you will return the favor. That is how the world works, is it not? Besides I don't like the SS coming into my hotel and bullying my guests." Mr. Klum smiled and opened the door. "It's bad for business."

He nodded to them and slipped out the door. Stella watched as Nicky bolted it behind him and went to the armoire and started tossing things on the bed.

Stella crossed her arms. "You're not really going to do what he said, are you?"

"I'm not. We are." He put on a shirt and stuffed a couple others into Stella's smallest valise. "Start packing."

"I'll pack, but I'm not leaving Vienna without Abel."

"Neither am I." Nicky put his watch on and knotted his tie into a perfect Windsor knot. "We'll do as Mr. Klum suggested with a slight detour."

Stella raised her eyebrows. "Detour?"

"We'll find Albert Moore."

"Abel's business partner? Why didn't I think of that?"

"That's what you have me for."

38

Stella folded a silk blouse and placed it neatly on the bed. "Nicky, the Germans found us. Won't they find Albert, too?"

"Albert's the son of a British Ambassador. Even the Germans wouldn't be so bold as to arrest him."

Stella smiled and began packing in earnest.

CHAPTER 5

$\mathcal{T}$he sun blinded Stella when she stepped onto the roof of the hotel. She shielded her eyes and turned in a slow circle, seeing pillars of smoke rising in every direction. She began to count but became discouraged when she passed thirty. So much destruction and for what? Nicky tried to make her understand that this was punishment for the death of Von Rath, but that made no sense to Stella. You punish the guilty, not random people in another country. Nicky kept saying that was the way the Nazis thought and one didn't have to understand it to accept it. But Stella had to understand and she couldn't accept it. There had to be a point to this wanton destruction because revenge was stupid and caused more problems than it solved and as Nicky said the Nazis weren't stupid. They were up to something and it was bigger than Von Rath.

Nicky silently gazed at the smoke and winced at a woman's wail somewhere behind them. He grabbed Stella's hand as if she were the one wailing and held it tight before taking her to the east toward the Hotel Kirsch. He carried their small valise and she her handbag. They were indeed traveling light with the sounds of the city coming to life drifting around them. Horns honking. The smells of breakfast cooking mixed with the smell of smoke. Stella kept listening for the sound that never came. Sirens. With all that smoke, it was unnatural to have the air undisturbed by that familiar and somehow comforting wail. Stella missed it. She missed the sensible authority it would've announced. The silence said nobody cared and it angered her.

They climbed over the last dividing wall and found the access door propped open as Mr. Klum had promised. Nicky yanked the heavy door open for Stella and followed her onto the dimly lit staircase. Surprisingly, the stairs only went down one flight. Stella hesitated with her hand on the rough-hewn door labeled five.

"I guess this is it," she said.

Nicky reached past her and grabbed the door handle. Stella stepped back and he pulled the door open. They walked into a hallway with red carpet and baroque wallpaper. About a dozen people stood in the hall. A hush fell over them as they turned to stare at Nicky and Stella.

"Incredible view," said Nicky. "You really should try it."

"View?" said one man with a heavy French accent.

"Of the city," said Stella. "That's the access to the roof. You can see what's going on."

The group nodded and started toward them. Nicky held the door open for them, smiling broadly. Once the group started to go through, he wheeled Stella around and pushed her to the end of the hall.

"Where are we going?" asked Stella.

"Servant's staircase." He pointed at a door labeled Privat.

They ran down the stairs to the first floor and slowly opened the door with a Two on it. It opened into a kitchen prep area. Stella looked at Nicky. Should they go in or not? He shrugged and pushed open the door. A couple of cooks looked up at them in surprise. Nicky waved and marched through dragging Stella behind him. They went through a door labeled Eingang, which put them in the actual kitchen.

"Now what?" asked Stella as several waiters and a chef stared at them. She smiled back, not knowing what to do.

"Look for Ausgang," said Nicky.

"What's that?"

"Exit."

Stella pointed to the far left. "There's one."

Nicky nodded to the chef. "So sorry. We're lost."

They walked through the kitchen, passing trays of pastries and fruit. Stella considered swiping one since they hadn't eaten yet but thought better of it with the chef's hard gaze still on her. Nicky led the way through the door into the alleyway behind the hotel. It was the best-looking alley Stella had ever seen, freshly swept without an ounce of trash or dirt anywhere.

"Where does Albert live?" asked Stella.

"About a block from Abel's shop. Let's try there first." He pulled a small hand-drawn map from his pocket. Stella recognized the handwriting as Abel's. He liked to draw his own maps for them. Nicky had quite a collection from Italy, especially Venice. No city could be as confusing as Venice. Abel must've drawn them ten maps for Venice alone.

Nicky took her hand again. "This way, I think."

"That's not very reassuring."

"You want to look at the map?"

"Not a bit," said Stella. "Lead on."

They kept to the alleyways at first, but when they ran out, Nicky led them onto a main street. Few people were out and those that were kept their heads down and avoided making eye contact. They were in a nice section of town with beautiful well-kept buildings. Stella kept looking at the windows on either side of the street. Shutters were bolted. Shades were drawn. No one was opening up to view the new day. She wondered, as they hustled past, what the people inside thought about what had happened. Did they think they were safe with their shutters and shades? Stella had certainly thought she and Nicky were safe before the knock on their door. The thought of the SS officer standing in their hotel room ready to arrest them for absolutely nothing made her queasy. They had to find Abel right away and go. For once, she didn't care where.

"Only a couple more blocks," said Nicky.

"Thank goodness," said Stella. Her feet were already starting to hurt. She should've worn more practical shoes, but she didn't own any.

A man crossed the street in front of them. He wore a Nazi armband and had a badge pinned to his chest. He was staring at them as he approached and Stella's stomach flip-flopped.

"*Sie dort!*" the man yelled.

"Be calm," said Nicky under his breath.

"I'm fine," said Stella.

The man stopped in front of them and began yelling in German. He pointed at them both. Stella assumed he was raving about her furs and Nicky's expensive coat. Nicky took a casual stance and let him yell, making Stella marvel at his cool exterior. All that guttural yelling made her hopping mad. She suspected it was designed to frighten her or at least make her cringe, but it didn't. She wanted to slap him.

When the man paused to take a breath, Nicky said, "Do you speak English?"

The man jerked back and the color drained out of his face. "American?"

"Yes." Nicky brushed a lock of hair off his forehead. "Have we done something to offend you, sir?"

"I need to see your identification."

Nicky passed him their passports and the man scrutinized them for a good two minutes, squinting and flipping the pages. When he handed them back, he waved them away. Nicky shrugged and walked past the man, who was scuffing his feet in the dirt.

Stella squeezed Nicky's hand. "We got away."

"And we're not wanted by the SS yet or he would've tried to arrest us."

"Did you see how he was looking at our passports? I don't think he could read," said Stella. "He probably didn't know who we were."

Nicky grinned down at her as she trotted to keep up with his long strides. "Well, I guess that's bad news for him, but still good news for us."

They rounded a corner and found themselves stepping on reams of paper. The sidewalk and street was covered with books, papers, and broken furniture. Nicky bent down and picked up a ledger. He thumbed through it and snapped it shut.

He pointed at a shop across the street with broken windows and a door hanging by one hinge. "Abel's shop."

Neither of them moved. Stella clung to Nicky's arm, barely noticing the people walking by and giving them a wide berth. Stella couldn't think. She'd seen the other shops, torched or otherwise destroyed on the walk over, but, for some reason, she hadn't thought that Abel's shop would get the same treatment.

"Come on." Nicky skirted the worst of the mess and approached the large broken picture window. He looked in the window while Stella stood beside him with tears rolling down her cheeks.

"Abel will be so upset," she said.

"I think Abel has bigger things to worry about."

"But this is his work. All his books, his maps, his correspondence."

"You stay here. I'm going to look in the back. I think that's where his apartment is," said Nicky.

Stella nodded and took the valise from him. She stood there on Abel's papers with her wet cheeks, feeling many eyes upon her from the apartment windows and slow-moving cars crunching Abel's furniture. She glanced back and caught sight of people peeking at her from behind curtains and underneath hat brims and she wondered what they thought of her in her shearling coat and expensive Parisian hat standing in front of a destroyed store.

Nicky came back out, his shoulders bowed and his eyes on a couple of picture frames he held in his hands. He passed one to Stella.

"Everything else is destroyed," said Nicky. "They even cut the safe from the wall."

"This is it?" Stella stared down at what was left of Abel's life. A picture of a young woman with waist-length braids. She sat on a bench in front of a studio backdrop, smiling over her shoulder at the camera.

Nicky took the valise from Stella and handed her the other picture, a young man in a German Army uniform.

"What should we do with them?" asked Stella.

Nicky opened the valise and Stella wrapped them in one of his silk shirts. "That'll do it. Let's see if we can locate Albert."

They walked past a pair of gossiping neighbors, two rotund men whispering together. They watched as Stella and Nicky walked by. Stella met their stares and dared them to say anything. When she didn't back down, they dropped their eyes. They knew Abel, she was sure of that. Maybe they were even friends of his. He probably had them over to play cards or had lunch in their kitchens. Now all they would do for him was whisper in front of his shop.

Once they cleared the debris from Abel's, they passed another shop torn apart and just past it, a synagogue smoldered. The roof had collapsed in on itself and the joists were pushed down together like a crushed ribcage. Someone had dragged some pews into the middle of the street and set them on fire, where they still smoldered. The remains of books and papers lay half-burnt in the ash, a few words in Hebrew remained, hardly a full sentence. The wind kicked up and blew a cloud of embers against the buildings across the street. Nicky hurried Stella past as fast as he could. When she looked up at him, she realized he wasn't looking around like she was. He kept his eyes straight ahead. His jaw was clinched and he didn't bother to avoid the shattered glass. Stella tried to pick her way around it, but it was impossible. Glittering shards coated the street and sidewalk. It wasn't all from the synagogue. That block, in particular, had dozens of broken apartment windows. Whole dining room sets and libraries had been tossed out. A bed lay broken and twisted in the middle of the street with a large red stain marking the pavement beside it. Stella looked up to see a fourth-story apartment with its windows broken. A long unrelenting scream emanated from it and bounced off the building almost like the sirens that Stella had never heard. The sound reached into Stella's soul and seared it with grief. She couldn't tell whether it was a man, woman, or child, but the sound, that soul-searing sound, would never leave her memory. It would always be there lurking just under the surface of her serenity.

"Nicky," said Stella. "Did you see that?

"Let's just go."

"But that screaming. Shouldn't we—"

"Darling, please." His eyes were fixed on a spot a block down. Whether he saw the bed or not, whether that scream had hurt him the way it hurt her, he would never want to talk about any of it. His face, in all its hardness, told her that.

A few minutes later, they arrived at Albert Moore's ritzy address. The whole block appeared to be untouched. Maids in crisp white aprons were out sweeping bits of ash off the residential hotel's front walk. Nicky led Stella past the maids, who looked at them from under lowered lashes. The doorman opened the door after giving them the once over. Stella didn't know if it was their attitude or the cut of their clothes, but the doorman spoke to them in perfect English.

"May I direct you, sir?" he asked.

"You may indeed," said Nicky. "We're looking for Mr. Albert Moore. Is he at home?"

The man hesitated. His gaze slid to the left and he eyed the street for a second. "This may not be the best time for a visit, sir."

"Why is that?" asked Nicky.

"Mr. Moore has had many visitors in the last few hours. I believe he is indisposed."

"Then he's home," said Stella.

The doorman looked at her. "As I said it may not be the best time, madam."

"The apartment number, please," said Nicky.

"C on the third floor, sir," said the doorman. "I'm quite certain Mr. Moore will not be expecting visitors such as yourselves. Perhaps the lady should stay here?"

Nicky turned to look at Stella, but she let go of his hand and marched through the open door into the lobby. He caught up with her at the elevators.

"Stella, I know you don't understand, but he was trying to say that Albert isn't the kind of man a lady visits," Nicky said with his hand on her elbow.

"I understand," she replied.

"Then you'll stay down here and I'll talk to him."

"No."

"No," he repeated incredulously and Stella smiled. 'No' felt good. She hadn't uttered the word in all the months she'd known Nicky and she'd missed it. To be fair, she hadn't had a reason to say no and he'd never said no to her either. She supposed married people said no to each other, but she never thought she'd be one of *those* wives. She expected to get what she wanted and she expected Nicky to want to give it to her. Her mother said that Uncle Josiah spoiled her and he agreed with the caveat that she deserved spoiling since she did whatever her father asked of her. Mostly. She'd learned the business of brewing and the importance of art, which was all her father, the intimidating Aleksej Bled, cared about. Uncle Josiah's interests were much more varied and infinitely more interesting.

The elevator dinged and the doors opened. Stella tried to step in the tiny wood-paneled box, but Nicky held her back. "Stella, be reasonable."

"Same to you," she said as she pulled her arm from his hand and stepped in the elevator. "Are you coming?

Nicky got in and they rode in silence to the third floor. It wasn't hard to spot Albert Moore's apartment. The door hung open and papers littered the floor in front of it. They stopped at the door and Stella felt her mouth drop. So much for an ambassador's son being untouchable. The apartment looked like it'd been attacked by wild dogs. Furniture lay upended amidst broken glass and scattered books and papers. The reek of alcohol seeped out the door like a low-lying fog.

"I guess it wasn't Albert's character he was worried about," said Nicky.

Stella stepped through the door. "Hello, Mr. Moore!"

"Come in," called a voice from a back room. "Why not? Everyone else does."

Stella picked her way around a collapsed liquor cabinet and splashed through a substance that smelled like very old oranges. "Mr. Moore, it's Mr. and Mrs. Lawrence. We're Abel's clients."

"I'm in the bedroom. If you don't mind, come back."

Stella took her time, not sure if she wanted Nicky to object or not. She was equally unsure of what she would do if he did. First, it was hailing cabs, then climbing around on rooftops and now going into a strange man's bedroom. Her mother would have a fit.

Nicky stepped in front of her and entered the room first. When Stella came in, she took his hand and waited for the small man bending over a suitcase to turn around.

"What can I do for you?" he asked, still with his back to them.

"We're trying to find Abel," said Nicky.

"Don't bother."

"How can you say that?" asked Stella.

"Very easily." The man turned around. His face was black and blue with the left side so swollen it looked ready to burst. A crusty blood-stain covered a good portion of his handmade linen shirt. "Abel's gone for good."

CHAPTER 6

*A*lbert sat on the floor with his back propped against the wall, his thin wrists resting on his knees. His right hand held a silver whiskey flask that shook when he raised it to his mouth for a sip. Stella watched a dribble escape his swollen lips and she gave him her handkerchief before he could wipe it with his sleeve.

"Pardon me," he said. "I can handle my liquor. Usually."

Stella sat down on the remains of Albert's bed, never taking her eyes off him. Swelling contorted his features and two fingers on his left hand were bent to the right. The whole hand had the color and shape of a rotting eggplant. His other hand remained shaky but untouched. The long fingers, almost ladylike in their proportions, gripped the flask. Stella couldn't imagine how he'd been able to withstand the beating as well as he had. He probably weighed less than she did.

"You're sure they haven't arrested Abel yet?" Nicky paced the width of the room, his hands thrust deep in his pockets.

Albert tried to shrug and grimaced at the attempt. "I could be mistaken. They were beating me at the time. And if Abel hasn't been arrested yet, I can't imagine it will be long. I'm the only person who would've risked concealing him. And yourselves, of course."

"If they have arrested Abel, where would they take him?"

"My neighbor said a place called Dachau. Unless they have something special in mind for him," said Albert.

Stella leaned forward. "Why would they?"

Albert took another drink and tried to get to his feet. Nicky went over and lifted him by his armpits. Albert swayed for a moment and tossed the flask on the bed. "They came after Abel last night, but I don't think it was the same as the other Jews. It wasn't a punishment for Von Rath. They want something Abel has or something they think he has."

"So they were searching your place, not just destroying things pointlessly," said Nicky.

"It looked like a search to me. They went through every drawer, every cupboard," said Albert.

"Like they did at our hotel."

"Didn't they ask you for what they wanted?" asked Stella.

Albert picked up his suitcase. "They just kept asking me where Abel was. Where he might hide. I got the impression they didn't think I knew anything about whatever it is but thought Abel might've stashed it here for safekeeping."

"So you're just going to leave?" asked Stella. "Can't your father do something for Abel?

"I've contacted my father. He'll go through diplomatic channels to try to find him."

"You don't sound very confident," said Nicky.

Albert stopped at the door. He turned slowly to face them, pain draped over every inch of his body, a shroud over a corpse. His voice came out low as though he could hardly bear to say the words. "They beat me. Like a dog. Like it was nothing. I'm Viscount Finley of Bickford House and the son of a British ambassador. Would you ever have imagined they would beat me for information?"

"Not for a minute," said Nicky.

"I never expect to see Abel again. It pains me to say, but it's true."

"What do you mean?" Stella got to her feet. "He can't just disappear. He has a family, a business, and clients. It's not like no one will notice."

"You're correct, Stella," said Albert. "People will notice. They just won't say anything. No one will admit this, but people, Jews mostly, have been disappearing. And no one will say anything because they're afraid they'll be next. First, it's the Jews and the synagogues. Maybe next it will be the Catholics and the cathedrals."

"Where are you headed?" asked Nicky.

"The Westbahnhof."

"You need a doctor," said Stella.

"I need to get out of this city before they decide to question me again."

"We'll take you," said Nicky.

"That isn't necessary."

Nicky raised his eyebrows at the shaking Albert, who gave a weak smile and handed Nicky his suitcase.

They followed Albert out of the apartment and into the elevator. He continued to shake but walked without assistance. Stella walked beside him and Nicky behind, poised to catch him in case he fainted. When they reached the front door of the hotel, the doorman stood frozen to the floor with his hand on the door.

"Mr. Moore," he said.

"Good day, Jorge," said Albert as though nothing unusual had happened.

The doorman opened the door. His face drained of color, a plaster mask of chalky white. Whatever he thought had happened to Albert, it wasn't as bad as the reality.

After they passed through the door, the doorman said, "Mr. Moore, I'm sorry. I didn't realize."

"Didn't want to realize, I expect," said Albert, looking around at the now bustling street. "Not an uncommon affliction these days. Call us a cab, will you?"

The doorman found them a cab but didn't speak again. Two round spots of color burnished his cheeks. Those spots reminded Stella of a clown's makeup. She never cared for clowns, never found stupidity very funny.

Cars, carts, and people packed the area around the Westbahnhof. The cab had to stop so far away that Stella couldn't spot any trains or the building. The driver spoke to Albert in German. He gestured to the crowds of women flowing around the cab, clutching handbags and small children. Very old men and teenage boys mixed in the crowd. No one was talking or even looking at each other. Their faces showed no emotion, at least no emotion that Stella recognized. After the night before, she would've expected crying, maybe even wailing, but the people carried themselves with a quiet dignity without the slightest feeling registering on their faces. Perhaps they were not so much frightened as shocked. Stella was certainly shocked and nobody had thrown her bed out a window.

Sometimes, brown-shirted soldiers would appear in the crowd. As soon as people spotted them their faces would grow even blanker as if they didn't see at all. Stella didn't know where to look. If she looked at the soldiers, would that attract attention? If she avoided looking at them, would that make her appear guilty of something? Of course, sitting next to Albert probably made anything she did irrelevant. Anyone seeing him would know something was up. During the short ride to the station, he'd grown worse, wheezing and occasionally shivering. His face continued to swell. When Stella looked too closely at him, she could see it throbbing and she wished she hadn't looked. Every glance at Albert reminded her that it could've been Nicky. They were probably closer to that nightmare than she had realized. Without Mr. Klum's intervention, what would've happened? Stella shivered when the question popped into her mind and it got her to thinking. Had the officer, Peiper, been back to the hotel to find them missing? Had he put out an order to arrest them? Stella didn't know she could have so many emotions at the same time, each one coming right after another like hail in a furious storm and there was nowhere to hide from the pounding. Shock, fear, and anger followed each other in rapid succession, drumming on her nerves and making her feel as shaky as Albert looked.

Nicky sat next to her, looking as though he felt none of these things. He peered out the window and exhaled deeply. If Stella hadn't known it was impossible, she would've thought him bored. His expression reminded her of the way he looked in Venice when arguing with the little red-faced porter. She hadn't thought much about it at the time and not at all since. But that argument had been about Abel. Nicky must've been mad, but he never showed it. He put on a mask and when he did, all a person saw when they looked at him was his beauty. Everything underneath was concealed. He was doing it just then, sitting in the cab and looking as though butter wouldn't melt in his mouth.

Stella picked up his hand and squeezed it. His palm was sweaty and hot. He squeezed her hand in return but continued to look out the window, showing nothing, much like the people passing by.

Albert and the driver conversed softly, almost whispering as though the brown-shirted soldiers could hear them if they spoke up. They'd talked continually since they'd gotten in the cab. The conversation made Stella nervous. She felt like a little child with her parents talking over her head, assuming she was too stupid to understand. Of course, she *was* too stupid to understand. Her mother had engaged many language tutors over the years, but Stella had stubbornly refused to learn any language after having Mr. Valentin attempt to ram Latin in her head in what her mother called a starting language. Mr. Valentin came highly recommended and he was an excellent teacher when he wasn't drunk, which was more often then not. So Stella hadn't learned her Latin and if she hadn't gotten the first one, why bother with the others? She stuck to math and the business while tormenting her language tutors by affecting a perfect accent without saying any proper words. She'd been particularly difficult with Herr Wiesse and now she regretted it. What good was her mimicry when she couldn't understand a single word Albert and the driver uttered?

Like everything else, not understanding German didn't seem to bother Nicky. The driver honked at a small truck in front of them, shook his head, and pivoted in the seat to face them. His jowls jiggled to a stop and he looked them over.

"*Der Sudbahnhof ist besser*," he said, finally.

"*Nein*," replied Albert. He went on to explain something to the driver, who shrugged and turned back around.

"What was that all about?" asked Stella.

"We're getting out." Albert struggled with his injured hand to open the cab door until Stella leaned over him and pulled the handle.

Nicky paid the driver and helped Stella out. They joined the flow of people headed to the train station. Stella held Albert's arm as he limped along. The adults paid no attention to Albert's swollen face, but the children stared. Their big eyes trained on him, silent owls that noticed everything. They looked at Nicky quite a bit, too. For the first time, Stella thought of Nicky's looks as a bad thing. People noticed him and weren't likely to forget where they'd seen such a person. Stella looked to her right at Albert, the walking mincemeat, and to her left at her husband, Mr. Hollywood, and realized she was the least memorable of the three of them. Having been considered quite a looker herself, Stella wasn't sure what to think about this. On one hand, being forgettable was exactly what she wanted if the soldiers came looking for them. On the other hand, it was like thinking you were a genius and realizing you're the stupidest one in the room.

"I wish you had a hat," said Stella.

Nicky raised his eyebrows. "I never wear hats."

"You should start."

Albert laughed and started gagging. He hacked into his handkerchief and Stella caught sight of something vile he'd coughed up. "A hat won't do the job, Stella," he said, wiping his lips. "Perhaps a tent."

"What are you talking about?" asked Nicky.

"Stella wants to make you less conspicuous, but there's no hope, I'm afraid."

"I'm the conspicuous one?" Nicky gave Albert a slight smile. "You're beginning to look like a Macy's parade balloon."

Albert dapped at his split lip with his handkerchief. "Too true, but

54

I'm hardly the only one around here in bad condition. There's only one of you."

Stella followed Albert's gaze to a woman walking with an elderly man. The man was at least seventy and almost in as bad a shape as Albert. The woman had a bruised cheek and was dragging her right leg. The more Stella looked, the more injuries she found hidden among the stalwart faces walking with them.

"I guess I'll get a hat," said Nicky.

"It can't hurt, unless it's one of Stella's," said Albert.

Stella smiled at the thought of Nicky wearing one of her hats, but it dropped off her face when she saw a crowd of men being herded toward the train station. Soldiers whacked them with long black batons and spat words at them that had to be curses. Stella examined each face, afraid to find Abel among the prisoners. But he wasn't there and she found herself almost disappointed that he was still missing. The strain of not knowing where he was, or how he was, made her stomach hurt. If the Germans were willing to beat Albert, what would they do to Abel when they found him? What if he couldn't give them what they wanted?

"Why do you think they're taking those men to the train station? They can't all be criminals. Some of them are barely old enough to shave," said Stella.

"They're not criminals, Stella," said Albert. "They're probably Jews."

"Well, that's just silly. They can't arrest them just because they're Jews. They must've done something."

"After last night, being a Jew is enough."

"Because of Von Rath," said Nicky.

"Von Rath was just the excuse," said Albert. "They've been waiting for this opportunity. Too good to miss, I dare say. The cab driver said they're arresting all male Jews between the ages of eighteen and sixty-five."

"That's got to be thousands of people. What in the world are they going to do with them?" asked Nicky.

"The driver says they're sending them to their concentration camps. Dachau will take the most."

They came upon another group of prisoners, smaller this time. Five men stood together, quietly watching two soldiers having an intense conversation. The soldiers didn't appear to be paying much attention to them. Two of the men were bound with rope, but the others were unencumbered.

Nicky led them around the group. He kept his mask of disinterest on, never glancing at the men.

"Why don't they run away?" asked Stella, once they were out of earshot.

Nicky jerked his head toward her. His mask fell off and he appeared genuinely startled.

"They're under arrest, Stella," he said.

"So what? They should just run away. Those guards aren't paying any attention. They couldn't catch all five of them even if they tried."

"You can't just run away when you're under arrest." Nicky's brow wrinkled and he spoke in low, harsh tones. "It's not right. It's…,"

"It's what?" asked Stella. "Illegal? Who cares? Just being them is illegal."

"I doubt it occurred to them, Stella," said Albert. "I must admit it didn't occur to me to leave. I knew the SS were coming for me and I just sat and waited for them."

"Why?" asked Stella. "Why didn't you leave?"

Albert shook his head. His eyes teared up and he avoided Stella's questioning gaze. "I didn't really think they'd do anything to me. I didn't believe it was possible."

"We have to follow the rule of law," said Nicky, his mask firmly back in place. "If the authorities want to question you, you have to comply."

"You're both screwy." Stella's eyes roved over another group of prisoners, looking for Abel. "Uncle Josiah says rules are meant to be broken. Where would we be if nobody broke any rules?"

"Germany," said Albert with a wry smile twisting his grotesque face. "Never underestimate Germans when it comes to following rules."

"You wouldn't really stay," Stella said to Nicky. "That officer ordered us to stay at the hotel and we left."

"We're foreign citizens. He had no right to order us to do anything."

"What if we were their citizens? What would you do?"

Stella wouldn't have thought it possible, but Nicky's face grew more disinterested and he actually yawned. "I don't know, Stella. I don't want to think about it."

"Well, I wouldn't stay and I wouldn't let you stay either."

"You wouldn't let me?"

"No, I wouldn't. I couldn't call myself a Bled if I let something happen to you that I could prevent."

Nicky stiffened and seemed to grow taller. Stella wouldn't have been surprised to see a coating of ice grow on his exterior. "I couldn't call myself a Lawrence, if I didn't follow the law and went around doing whatever I pleased."

"That's not what I meant," said Stella.

"There's the station," interrupted Albert. "I should've listened to the cab driver. Getting a seat out of here will be difficult, even with my connections."

The crowd got thicker as the station came into view. A sturdy grey stone building rose above the crowd, looking more like a castle than a train station. The edifice should've given Stella comfort, since it'd taken them so long to get there, but instead, it made her pull back in surprise. A line of soldiers stood between them and the station. Within the circle of soldiers, hundreds of men, some in night clothes, most without shoes, huddled together in the November morning chill.

"There's so many." Stella's eyes flooded and she had to look away.

Nicky took her hand. "Don't worry. They'll have to let them go soon."

"You think so?" she asked.

"Yes. I don't see how they can keep them. It would cost too much."

Stella let go of his hand and wiped her eyes. "Do you see Abel?"

"No," said Nicky. "But we'll keep looking."

"I wouldn't expect to find him in this crowd," said Albert. "These men were taken in mass arrests. The Nazis have nothing against them in particular. Abel's another story. Let's get to the ticket office."

Albert pointed to where he wanted to go and Nicky led the way past silent onlookers. Several middle-aged men watched the guards and prisoners. They were between the ages of eighteen and sixty-five, so they weren't Jews. The men represented every status and trade. A butcher apron here and a fine suit there. They watched with mild interest and said nothing. Stella walked with Albert and Nicky through the shifting crowd around the ring of soldiers and wondered why no one was doing anything. Stella, her lips clamped shut, realized that she, too, was saying nothing, doing nothing. She felt ashamed of her silence but didn't know how to do otherwise. Getting themselves arrested wouldn't help anyone.

When they finally made it to the doors, Nicky pushed his way through. It wasn't easy. People covered every inch of the place. The subdued air outside stayed there. Crowds of people ebbed and flowed in the confined space, all yelling and pushing. Rail employees argued with people waving their passports in the air. Carts of luggage overturned and a white cockatoo had escaped from a gilded cage. It swooped over the heads of the crowd as a silver-haired woman shrieked and chased it through the throng.

"Which way?" shouted Nicky.

Albert pointed across the wide hall and shouted back, "Official travel."

Stella grasped Albert's arm and Nicky tried to make way for them. Albert gasped and nearly went down when a man and his diamond-bedecked wife rammed into him. Stella kept him on his feet, almost dragging him across the hall. Nicky saw her struggling and got on Albert's other side. He put his arm around the smaller man and charged through a group. He swatted people out of the away with Albert's suitcase and their valise, his face glowering, daring anyone to complain.

When they reached the glass door on the other side of the hall, it was locked. A man sat inside bent over a desk, studiously ignoring the clamor outside. When Nicky banged on the glass, the man looked up and shook his head.

"My passport and papers are in my breast pocket," said Albert, wheezing and shivering worse than ever. "If you'd be so good."

Nicky reached in and gave the paperwork to Albert, who pressed it against the glass. Nicky banged on the glass again with different results. As soon as the man saw the passport and papers were British and official, he rushed over and opened the door. After a tense few minutes, the man gave Albert a ticket and locked the door in their faces.

Nicky reached around Albert again and half-carried him out the exit onto the train platform. The overwhelming noise stayed inside and Stella let out a breath. She didn't realize she'd been holding it inside.

"Do you know which platform?" asked Nicky.

"Five," said Albert. "You can release me now."

"Sorry," said Nicky, letting go of Albert's waist.

Albert staggered to the left and Stella caught him. He rested against her, wheezing and throbbing.

"Are you sure about the doctor, Albert?" asked Stella. "I don't know if you should get on a train in this condition."

"I'll be fine once I'm in the club car with a good cigar and a glass of whiskey." He met her eyes. "You should get out, too. Even if you found Abel in this disaster, there's nothing you could do for him."

"At least we'd know where he is and your father could help him," said Stella.

"My father's pulling every string he has. He's very fond of Abel." Albert took Nicky's offered arm and began walking with halting steps toward platform five. "Consider it, Nicky. I have a diplomatic ticket. With that I can probably get you two on with me for the cost of a small bribe."

"Not a bad idea," said Nicky.

Stella glanced over Albert's head at her husband. "What about Abel? We have no idea where he is."

"Exactly, Stella," he said. "We have no idea where he is and Albert was our only chance of finding him."

"What about the shop?"

Albert coughed and shook his head. "It's been confiscated by the state. He'd be a fool to go back there."

"We have to be practical," said Nicky. "We might very well have arrest warrants out on us. It makes no sense to stay here."

Stella glanced around at the teeming platforms. Everywhere, people begged to get on trains. Nicky was right. It made no sense to stay when they had a chance to get away, but she couldn't make herself say the words. She looked at him and nodded.

"If you think you can get us on that train, we'd be happy to accept," said Nicky.

Stella looked away. Leaving Abel was absolutely the wrong thing to do but staying in Vienna was idiotic. The train at Platform Five sat up ahead, ready to go. Its whistle blew and they hustled forward. Nicky led them through the masses to the besieged conductor, trying to hold back ticketless passengers. The poor man's face dripped with sweat as people harangued him in five different languages. Nicky gently pushed people aside. When they got in front of the conductor, Albert held up his passport and ticket. The conductor's shoulders relaxed and he managed a weak smile. He spoke with Albert in French and then waved them down the way, politely ignoring Albert's condition.

"What about the bribe?" asked Stella. "Are we on?"

"No, we'll convince my car's porter to let you on," said Albert. "We don't want to be paying everyone on the train."

Stella nodded and watched a group of prisoners being herded down onto the gravel next to the tracks. She watched the line of men walk behind a low fence toward a row of boxcars across a small field.

"Here we are," said Albert, stopping in front of a lovely green First Class car. "Let me do the talking."

"No problem," said Nicky. "I only speak English."

"Americans," said Albert, sighing. "When will you learn?"

Nicky smiled. "I would guess never. Why would we?"

"Good point." Albert looked up as the porter emerged from the car and took his ticket. They began speaking so rapidly in German the words blended together in one long guttural phrase.

Stella put her back to the conversation. She didn't want to see the bribe, not that she had anything against bribes in general. This one was distasteful only because it took them away from Abel. They were letting him down. There was no doubt about it.

Another group of passengers walked by, clutching their tickets to their chests. She caught glimpses of the prisoners through the crowd. None of passengers seemed to notice the stunned and shivering men filing by. Stella closed her eyes and listened to Albert's negotiation. Soon, they'd be on the train, heading to who knows where. Away from Abel's beautiful Vienna that wasn't so beautiful anymore. They'd never even had a chance to really see it or to find out what Abel thought was so special. Uncle Josiah wouldn't be happy, but once she explained what happened, she was certain he would forgive her and come up with an alternative plan. One could always count on Uncle Josiah for a good plan.

A hand on her shoulder made her open her eyes. "I think he's getting somewhere, Darling," said Nicky in her ear. "It won't be long."

Stella nodded but didn't trust herself to speak. Everything inside her said not to go. Everything except her head. She stared out into the crowd, unseeing, until a quick movement caught her eye. She focused on the movement and saw an arm wave at her. At first, she thought she was seeing things, but no. It was Abel standing next to a boxcar, staring at her with such intensity her knees went weak.

CHAPTER 7

*S*tella pushed her way through the mass exodus and stood on the edge of the platform. A German man grabbed her arm and tried to pull her away. She shook him off and jumped, landing on the jagged white gravel and falling to her knees. The fall stung, but less than it would've if she hadn't been wearing her cushy fur coat. She struggled to her feet with her heels sinking into the rocks.

The prisoners stared at her as she ran down the fence toward the rusty boxcar. Abel watched her with his hand on another man's shoulder. He and the men around him were wearing pajamas under their coats, their breath rising in frozen funnels from their lips. Stella could see their bare feet through the gaps in the fence, some tinged blue. The men held back, but they were almost to the boxcar, being prodded by uniformed guards. The men in front of Abel climbed in. Some prisoners hung out of the door, helping the others to climb in and watching Stella run with red-rimmed eyes.

When she reached Abel, she grasped the fence and he reached over it, cupping her cheek in his ice-cold hand. He'd never touched her before, not even to help her out of a cab or onto a train. She looked into his sad eyes, still gasping but reveling in this new connection between them.

"They don't know who I am yet," Abel said in a low voice.

"They don't?" Stella took his hand and warmed it between hers.

"I was picked up at random, but they'll realize who they've got soon enough."

"The SS came looking for you at the hotel. Why do they want you so badly?"

"It's not me they want, Stella. Will you do something for me?"

"Of course, anything," she said.

Abel put his hand inside his overcoat and removed the package he'd entrusted her with the day before on the train. He placed it in her hands and she tucked it inside her coat. The men behind Abel jostled him forward. He glanced up at the boxcar and then back at Stella.

"Take it to my family. I wrote the address on the wrapping." He took her hand again. "Don't be tempted to trade it for me."

"You mean if we gave it to them, they'd let you go?"

"No, but they'd say they would. They'd say anything. Nothing's more important to my family than that package."

"It's not more important than you," she said.

"Promise me, Stella." Abel's hand went back to her cheek and she clung to his shivering arm. "Please."

She looked into his intense eyes and swore with all her heart. "I promise."

He turned to the boxcar as a brown-shirted soldier stalked over through the crowd. The prisoners started waving and yelling for Abel to get in, their voices high-pitched and frantic. The soldier shoved Abel, ramming him into the boxcar's one metal step. Abel cried out and fell to all fours. The soldier drew back his foot and aimed it at Abel's face.

Stella reached over the fence and snatched the soldier's sleeve. "Don't you dare. Don't you dare do that."

The soldier turned to her and immediately flushed bright red to the tips of his ears. Stella glared at him but couldn't help noticing how young he was, maybe even younger than her. Someone grabbed Stella from behind. She tried to jerk away, still holding onto the soldier's sleeve and yanking him into the fence. A long arm came around her and peeled her fingers off the soldier's sleeve.

Nicky whispered in her ear. "Come away, Stella."

Two other prisoners picked Abel up and handed him to others in the boxcar. He turned and watched Nicky pulling her backwards away from the fence. Nicky pivoted around and half-marched half-carried Stella in front of him. Stella glanced back around Nicky's shoulder. Her last glimpse of Abel was of him being held by many hands and pulled backwards into the darkness of the boxcar.

Nicky jerked her back forward. "Stop looking back."

"Abel," Stella choked out.

"I know, Darling. We can't do anything for him right now but get away."

Stella pressed the package to her chest, thankful it was well-concealed under her fur. What was it? She hadn't had a chance to ask. Nicky was right. They had to get away. If she were arrested, they'd get the package, whatever it was.

"Are they letting us on Albert's train?" she asked.

"Yes, but it cost me every cent we have." Nicky veered her to the right and up a flight of steps onto Platform Five. They could barely fit on with all the would-be passengers crowded together.

"Hurry," Nicky said. "It's leaving in a couple of minutes."

The worst of the crowd was around the poor conductor, who was still being screamed at. Once they cleared his area, the crowd thinned somewhat.

"Thank God," said Nicky. "There's our car. We're going to make it."

Stella broke into a jog. They were almost there. She had the package and they were almost there.

Then she skidded to a halt. Nicky rammed into the back of her, almost knocking her off her feet.

"Stella, what are you doing?" asked Nicky.

"Back up," she said.

"What for?"

Stella indicated a woman talking to the porter Albert had negoti-ated with. "It's her. The SS woman from our room last night."

"I guess it could be," said Nicky. "Are you sure?"

Stella took another look. She only had a side view and the woman wore a green woolen suit instead of her uniform, but it was her. Stella would've known her anywhere, wearing anything. She had an aura of meanness about her that was unmistakable. The way she leaned forward toward the porter so that the man backed up and bumped into the train's stairs. She shook a finger in his reddening, bewildered face.

"I'm positive," said Stella.

They pivoted on their heels and walked with careful steps toward the station. Stella counted their steps in her head and used the rhythm to calm her breathing. Five, six, seven. Fourteen would put them past the conductor and into the crowds exiting and entering the station.

"I wish I had that hat," said Nicky.

"Me, too," said Stella.

Nicky guided her around the edge of the conductor's crowd. The train's whistle blew, making them jump and glance at the train. The conductor caught sight of them. His brow wrinkled and he glanced back at the train as it geared up to leave. He raised his arm and called out to them. Stella hunched, trying to burrow down deep into the coat's warm protective folds. It made her feel less noticeable, but it made no difference to the conductor who called out, louder than before.

Nicky tightened his grip on her arm. The conductor called again and then a woman's voice rang out over the platform, shrill and angry. Whatever she said made the crowd freeze and look at them.

"Run," said Nicky.

The crowd parted as Stella and Nicky rounded the end of the train and ran onto the main platform. The woman screamed again, sounding increasingly shrill and desperate. Stella glanced back and it seemed the crowd was closing in behind them. The woman screamed at the edge, but the crowd didn't part for her.

Nicky veered to the left, taking Stella with him through the open station doors. Once inside, they couldn't hear the woman screaming anymore. Nicky pushed their way through the throng and for a moment, Stella thought they might be safe. There were hundreds of people inside the station. People from every walk of life at various levels of desperation and panic. They should be able to blend in and get away. She thought that until she glanced up at Nicky's blond head bobbing well above the crowd, a lighthouse in the dark bringing all eyes to them.

New shouts behind them drew Stella's attention back to the doors they'd come in. A group of brown-shirted soldiers were searching the crowd. One looked up and spotted Nicky. The soldier pointed and shouted at them. They dodged behind a wide stone pillar. An older man in a natty grey suit and a rabbit fur fedora stepped back and eyed them while they panted and looked around frantically.

"Problem with the SS?" the man said in an odd accent that wasn't quite British. "I don't envy you."

Stella grasped his hand and gave him her most winning look. The one that melted her father's heart in three seconds flat. "Can we have your hat?"

The man winked at her and doffed his fedora. Stella took it and plunked it on Nicky's head.

"We owe you," she said.

"And I always collect," the man replied with a wicked yet charming smile.

Nicky pointed to a group of men hustling through the crowd. They almost all had on dark fedoras. Stella grabbed Nicky's hand and pulled him toward the group. The man snatched Stella's sleeve.

"Your name, if you please," he said.

Stella shook him off. "Stella Bled Lawrence."

As they melded with the crowd, Stella heard the older man call out over the shouts from the gaining SS men. "Cyril Welk, young lady. I'll be in touch."

Nicky pulled the fedora low and crouched. They moved in the crowd toward the far end of the building. Stella looked back, scanning for the soldiers. Without Nicky's blond head to guide them, they milled around, shoving passengers and shouting. The female SS officer stood at the center of the terminal. She must've been standing on something because she was several feet above the crowd. She examined the area with her ruthless eyes, her square jaw set. As soon as Stella saw her, she faced forward and crouched down herself. A piercing shriek burst out behind them. Nicky charged forward, assuming his full height. They headed to the front doors, the way they'd come in originally, but several SS men came in through those same doors, casting around for their quarry. Stella spun around in the opposite direction toward the platforms. She dragged Nicky behind her, slipping through small crevices in the crowd and darting around luggage carts. The doors were just ahead. A quick glance found the SS woman and her henchmen too far away to catch them before they exited.

Stella ran for the door, banking around a group of women and wailing children. She was so intent on the outside, she never saw the man who was standing in front of the door until they were within five feet of him. An SS officer blocked their way. His hat obscured his eyes and all Stella could see of his face was his lips clamped into a thin line and his oversized jaw. She'd never seen a man look so stern before, unless it was her father when he caught her sneaking out at night. Nicky yanked Stella back and spun her around, dragging her backwards into the group of women. Then the officer, with a precision only a military man could muster, stepped aside. Stella would've sworn she heard the click as his boots snapped together.

Stella pulled Nicky back with all the force she could gather on the slick stone floor. Nicky turned back, saw the officer standing aside, and switched directions so fast he pulled Stella off her feet. She stumbled, banging her knee, but managed to get to her feet while Nicky dragged her. They sped past the officer without a word and he never changed his stern expression.

Back out on the platform, they ran past a group of prisoners being herded with black batons. The sight gave Stella a burst of speed. She passed Nicky, looking toward where Albert's train had been on the Number Five platform, but the tracks were empty. Another train chugged away from the Number Three platform. The whistle blew and it was about to clear the end of the boarding area. Nicky and

Stella looked at each other and ran for it. They weaved around passengers, luggage carts, and an irate porter. One car was still within reach. Nicky outpaced Stella, dragging her along behind him. With a huge lunge, he grabbed the last door's metal handlebar, got a foot on the step, wrenched Stella off her feet, and tossed her onto the steps.

CHAPTER 8

Stella hit the caboose stairs full force. Pain zinged through her body, stem to stern. For a moment, she couldn't move just feel; burning pain and an icy cold wind rushing past her ankles. She suddenly sucked in a breath and opened her eyes to see grey metal so close that her eyelashes brushed it when she blinked. She couldn't think where she was. Then a second wave of pain hit, jagged knives poking her from her forehead to her knees. Someone yanked her upward by the left arm. She banged into something with her forehead and she screamed.

"Come on, Stella," yelled Nicky as she hit her forehead again. "Move!"

Her body pinned her right arm to her chest, pressing something square between her breasts. The package. All her confusion dissipated and she drew her legs in, out of the cold, and tried to gain purchase on the stairs. After several tries she got her feet underneath her, then fell to her knees on the icy metal and looked up to see Nicky's stark white face staring at her. He crouched on the top stair, his chest heaving. He had one hand holding her left wrist—so tight it was turning blue—and one clinging to the railing.

"Stella, stand up," he said between clenched teeth. "I can't hold you forever."

Stella got her feet under her and blinked as a pair of shiny black shoes appeared next to Nicky. A spate of German rained down on them and a pair of white-gloved hands reached down to pull Stella to her feet. Nicky stood up and pulled her to his chest, wrapping a strong arm around her, crushing what little breath she had right out of her lungs. Whoever it was retreated to the top of the stairs, continuing to rant in German.

"Loosen up," Stella managed to whisper. "Can't breathe."

Nicky instantly relaxed, but he kept a strong hold of her. Stella sucked in a deep burning breath and looked up at the man, middle-aged, in a blood-red uniform. He gestured at them, clearly indicating that they were lunatics. Stella wasn't so sure he was wrong.

She was about to say just that when Nicky began shaking so that his teeth chattered loud enough to be heard over the train's clacking wheels. Stella stepped back from him and found herself to be shaking as well.

"I can't understand you," she said to the porter instead.

The porter's expression changed from one of angry exasperation to one of resignation.

"Americans," he said.

Stella supposed that meant no sense could be expected of Americans. They'd do anything and frequently did.

At the word 'Americans', Nicky stopped shaking, let go of Stella, straightened his suit, and extended his hand to the porter. "Pleased to meet you. Nicolas Lawrence."

The porter nodded and shook his hand.

"We would like two seats, please," said Nicky, as if almost killing yourself by leaping on a train at the last possible second was perfectly normal.

The porter raised one eyebrow and his mouth slid slightly to the right. "You have money?"

Nicky glanced at Stella who shrugged. She didn't have a dime on her. Her handbag, still hanging off her right arm, only contained the necessities, cosmetics and her parents' gifts.

"I'm sure we can work something out," Nicky said.

The porter frowned and gazed pointedly past them. Stella glanced back at the countryside zipping past and felt her stomach flip, a nasty addition to the rest of her aches and pains.

"No need for that," Nicky said to the porter.

"No need for what?" asked Stella. "It's not like he'll really boot us off the train, right?"

Nicky turned his attention to Stella. "What do you think?"

Stella blinked. He'd never asked her what she thought before and the realization was disconcerting. She looked up at the porter, who now sported a slight smile on his thin face.

"I think he'd boot us off in a heartbeat," she said.

"My thoughts exactly," said Nicky as he turned to the porter. "But I think we can come to an understanding. Are you familiar with Omega?"

Nicky held out his wrist to the porter, revealing his watch, a 1932 Brandt and Frère Omega.

"No," said Stella. "Your father gave you that watch for your graduation."

"Considering our situation, I'm sure he'll think it was money well spent."

She glanced around. "Where's our valise? I have jewelry in there."

"I left it with Albert." He kissed her forehead. "It's the watch."

"My parents' gifts—"

He shook his head and said in a stern voice, "Aren't worth two train tickets?"

Stella understood. He was willing to give up his watch, but not anything Fabergé, period.

The porter examined the watch, pursed his lips and then gave a sharp nod. Nicky took the watch off and handed it over. The porter slipped it in his pocket and leaned back, looking in the door of the last car. He nodded to Nicky and held his hand out to Stella. "Welcome aboard."

Stella took his hand and slowly climbed the stairs, each step painful. Then she straightened her hat, still firmly on her head by the grace of her great-grandmother's enormous hatpin.

The porter opened the door and waved her through into the caboose. Several workmen dressed in grungy overalls glanced up from a card game and then quickly averted their eyes. Stella walked past the men, several rows of bunks, and bins filled with every conceivable type of gear and tool. The caboose's smell made her eyes sting with a combination of oil, sweat, and burning tar, much like the stench of her father's Dearborn Deuce roadster when it caught fire after her brother ran it into a tree. The roadster died a fiery and smelly death. Her brother had been thrown from the car, landing on his head, which was, according to everyone, the safest place for a Bled boy to land and he only suffered cuts and bruises.

Stella moved quickly, despite the pain, and opened the exit door herself, even though she knew she shouldn't. Ladies weren't supposed to open doors for themselves. She didn't know why this was so or what opening the door said about her, but at that moment, she couldn't have cared less. But before she'd gotten the heavy steel door all the way open, Nicky reached around her and finished the job.

"I could do it," she said, stepping through the door into the breezeway between cars.

"I know." Nicky waited as she struggled with the next door but didn't intervene.

Next came a kitchen car complete with chefs in stiff white hats and a long row of black stoves, piping hot and covered with multiple pans. They glanced at her and then pretended she wasn't there. It was irritating to have so many people in one day pretending like things weren't happening. The people on the street during the walk to the station, the passengers ignoring the prisoners being marched by them, shivering and miserable. No one acknowledged anything and it made Stella angry. She wanted to shake one of those chefs and yell, "You see me. Admit it."

But she didn't. She walked past, exited the kitchen car, and then entered a third car, a club car. Again, people glanced her way and then returned to normal as though nothing unusual had happened. The porter directed her to an open table and motioned for a waiter to attend them.

Stella sat down and not with the poise her mother would've expected. It was more of a plunk than a graceful lowering. She didn't know what had come over her. The Bleds did what they wanted, but they were always polite about it. Then she glanced down and saw her arm pressing the package against her chest, her hand gripping it like a miser with money. She felt a rise of relief in her chest so overwhelming, she shuddered.

"Stella," said Nicky from across the table. "What have you got there?"

For a second, she didn't want to say. She stared down at the table's gleaming wood and pressed the package tighter. It was a miracle she'd managed to hang on to it and she felt like it might disappear the second she loosened her grip. If the package disappeared, that would be the last of Abel, who himself was on a train and not in a cushy club car with a waiter either, but in a boxcar with dozens of other men headed to that awful place Albert had told them about. She'd let him down, but she still had the package, part of him, as long as she didn't let go.

A tear dropped on the table and another joined it. Nicky's hand slid over, smearing Stella's tears. She took his hand with her free one, unable to release or reveal the package.

"Stella, we're fine," he said. "Really. We'll be just fine."

The waiter appeared at the edge of their table. Stella could see him out of the corner of her eye looking all white and well-pressed.

"We haven't got any money," she whispered.

Nicky slapped a small pile of change on the table. Stella looked up at him and he grinned at her from beneath the fedora. He'd never been more handsome.

"We're not flat broke." Nicky turned to the waiter and ordered two coffees.

Stella fingered the coins. English, Spanish, and Italian in various denominations that she couldn't recall. "How much is this? A dollar?"

"More like thirty-three cents."

"Not flat broke, huh?" Stella removed her hat pin, then her hat, and ruffled her hair. She felt better with the shoulder-length locks cascading around her face.

Nicky leaned back and draped his arm over the back of the seat. "I'll wire my father for money at the first major city we get to. We'll be back in business in no time."

Stella raised an eyebrow at him. "And what city would that be?"

Nicky opened his mouth and then shut it with a snap. Stella waved his consternation away and plucked the hat from his head. His hair stood up on end like a startled porcupine.

"Now I know why you don't wear hats," she said, feeling more cheerful at the sight of her perfect husband looking ridiculous.

Nicky touched his spiky mane, snatched the hat back, and placed it on his head at a rakish tilt. "I do now."

"Men aren't supposed to wear hats indoors," said Stella, frowning slightly at her mother's remembered rule.

"I thought you said rules are meant to be broken."

Stella's frown turned into a smile. "Too true, but you can't wear that hat forever."

"Try me."

The waiter arrived back at the table with a small silver platter. He placed tiny porcelain cups in front of each of them. Next to Stella's cup he laid a steaming towel. Stella looked down at the towel and then up at the waiter's impassive face. His eyes flicked over to Nicky, who suddenly found great interest in the coins. Then the waiter tapped his cheek with two quick raps. Stella felt her cheek. She winced and looked at her fingers. A smear of blood decorated her manicured fingertips.

"Why didn't you tell me I had blood on my face?" she asked Nicky as she pressed the hot towel to her cheek and winced afresh.

"I didn't want you to be embarrassed," he said.

"You mean *you* didn't want to be embarrassed. I'm still sitting here with blood all over me whether you tell me or not."

"To be fair, you don't have blood all over you. It's just your cheek and maybe your nose. A little."

Stella got out her compact and examined her reflection in the mirror. Then she dabbed her nose, which was suddenly quite sore at being touched, and the towel had a fresh crimson stain. "I can't believe you didn't tell me I have a bloody nose."

"Well, you hit those stairs pretty hard," Nicky said, his eyes large and innocent.

"Thanks. I had no idea."

The waiter gave a delicate cough and they both looked up at him.

"Oh, right," said Nicky.

He looked through the coins, shrugged, and then gestured for the waiter to have his pick. He took several coins and bowed.

"Wait," said Nicky. "Where are we headed?"

The waiter didn't blink. Maybe passengers asked where they were going all the time or like the porter, he considered Americans to be idiots from the get-go. Stella figured they must look like idiots whatever their nationality, considering the way they got on the train, her bloody face, and the fabulous thirty-three cents they had to their names.

"Prag, Deutschland." The waiter turned to leave, but Nicky asked, "what do you mean *Deutschland*?"

The waiter let his gaze rest on Stella's face and jutted out his square chin in a small but pointed gesture. "All will be the Fatherland soon."

"How soon?" asked Nicky.

A larger chin jut accompanied another, "Soon."

"What about the Munich Agreement?"

The waiter's expression was the same as if Nicky had said he believed in fairies, sprites, and things that go bump in the night.

Nicky scooped their scant change up and said, "Never mind. I get it."

The waiter bowed and left before they could ask any more stupid questions.

Stella rolled the word 'Prag' over her tongue, imitating the waiter's sharp intonation at the end. "Praack. Praack." Of course. Her father had said that word. His pronunciation wasn't perfect though, not being a Myna, like his daughter.

"I thought Prague was in Czechoslovakia," said Stella.

"Not for long, I guess. He meant to warn us. The Nazis must have already infiltrated the capital. We won't be safe there."

"Well, I bet that's not right in any case," said Stella, thinking of Abel's package still snug under her coat.

"What's not right?" asked Nicky.

Stella hesitated. She looked into Nicky's open face and immediately felt like a terrible, hateful wife. There should be no secrets between them. That was one of her mother's tenets of marriage and one of the better ones, too. Not like the stupid 'never go to bed angry' advice. Stella had already gone to bed angry several times. Nicky hadn't noticed. But still, it was useless advice. 'No secrets' was sound.

She dropped the towel on the table and leaned forward. "Abel gave me something."

"I know. I saw you tuck a package inside your coat."

Stella deflated a little. So much for being a loving, wonderful wife sharing secrets. She didn't even have any secrets to tell. At least, none that he would want to hear. "Oh, fine."

"You're mad because I saw the package?" he asked.

"Not exactly, but anyway, he asked me to take it to his family."

"Please tell me his family isn't back in Vienna."

Stella opened her coat and let the package slide onto her lap, revealing the address.

"No," she said. "Paris."

CHAPTER 9

The train lurched forward and Stella's drooping eyelids popped open. Nicky slept next to her with his head propped against the window and his hand on her thigh. He emitted high-pitched snores like someone squeezing a rubber duck way too hard. The fedora still sat on his head, tilted at a drunken angle and threatening to fall off. The few people left in the club car didn't seem to notice Nicky's snores. They either read books the size of concrete blocks or slept themselves.

Stella tried to sleep, but each time her eyes closed, she saw Abel in the boxcar, felt his cold hand on her cheek, and heard him saying that the package was more important than him. Each time brought a fresh anger bubbling up from a forgotten place that contained every nasty word ever said to her, every evil deed she'd heard about or witnessed. Those thoughts kept her on edge with one hand on the package at all times and the other on Nicky, snoozing without worry or pain, instead of getting the rest she so desperately needed.

Nicky's head bonked against the window as the train lurched again and he sat up, clutching her thigh and looking around like he expected the bogeyman to be sitting across the table. "What happened?

"Nothing," Stella said. "Just another stop."

"How many is that?"

"No idea. A lot."

"We must be taking the scenic route. I thought we'd be in Prague hours ago." Nicky stretched and straightened his hat with a quick look out the window.

The sky showed off in streaky bits of light, a child's careless drawing that turned out to be a masterpiece. The blues, yellows, and oranges blended together beautifully and reminded Stella of herself and Nicky. Some things didn't seem like they should go together and turned out to be more beautiful when blended.

"Did you ever see such a sky?" asked Stella, while wondering if Abel was seeing nothing but bars.

"It'd be better if it was over Czechoslovakia," said Nicky.

Stella put the package in Nicky's lap and placed his hand on top of it. "Maybe it is. I'll check on the way to the ladies' room."

Stella rose to her feet, exactly the way her mother would've wanted, like she had a book on her head and an overfull cup in her hands. Perhaps it was silly to fall back on her mother's training, but it made Stella feel put together, like she didn't have a bruise the size of a cabbage rose on her cheek or a swollen nose. She glanced back at Nicky to see if he noticed her elegant ways in spite of the day's travails, but he sat with the package held up, examining it for clues to its contents. She didn't know why he bothered. They'd looked over every inch at least a half dozen times and still had no idea, other than it was probably a book.

Stella walked to the front of the club car, trying not to limp, and glancing at a gentleman reading a book with prose so dense it surely was meant as a punishment. The waiter bustled up to direct her to the ladies' room as if she hadn't been there three times before. He opened the club car door and led her through the breezeway to the sleeping car where the facilities were. He opened the door at the same time as the door at the other end was being opened by a porter. Behind the porter, Stella caught a glimpse of a uniform, brown with knee-high boots. Stella bolted sideways through a curtained-off area meant for the staff. She tripped over a bucket and mop and pressed her back against the wall facing the corridor.

The waiter stood still as a rabbit before a hound, his eyes large. Stella couldn't speak. She shook her head and mouthed the word *please* in every language she could think of. When he recovered, the waiter shifted his gaze from Stella to the end of the car. Stella watched a wary consternation settle on his features. His impassive expression quickly replaced it. He pulled the hem of his immaculate white jacket so that it made a snapping noise and reached up to yank the curtain closed. Stella heard him stride away, saying something in German.

When Stella figured he must be at the other end, she peeked around the edge of the curtain. The waiter shot a glance over his shoulder at her and then directed the soldier into a sleeping compartment. When the soldier moved, he revealed a man standing behind him. Stella almost gasped out loud. It was the man in the black suit from the train to Vienna. As soon as he disappeared into the compartment, she jumped out from behind the curtain, yanked open the back door, and ran across the breezeway to the club car.

Nobody in the car had moved. They sat as if frozen in the positions she'd left them in. The readers hadn't turned a page and Nicky still held the package up, peering at the names. Names they'd never heard Abel say but were now vitally important. Raymond-Raoul and Suzanne Charlotte Sorkine of the Marais in Paris.

Those mysterious names and the men in the next car made Stella's chest feel like it was being put through her friend Mavis' clothes wringer as she walked down the aisle. The Bled family laundress had escaped half-starved from Ireland so she knew how to run. Mavis's knowledge would've been terribly useful just then. She'd have known how to avoid the authorities. She'd done it quite a lot in Ireland.

Stella didn't have any of Mavis' smarts, just instinct, and that wouldn't be enough to escape the Nazis. She just walked, her heels making staccato drumbeats on the parquet floor. Her heart felt so constricted in her chest she wondered how it continued to beat at all.

When she reached Nicky, she pushed the package down into his lap. "That man from the train to Vienna is in the sleeping car."

"Who?"

"The man in the black suit on the train to Vienna. I think he was following Abel. He's in the sleeping car."

Nicky handed Stella the package and slid out of the booth. He walked to the club car door with a casual swinging stride. Stella followed him, feeling like she'd been wrapped in tight bandages from head to foot. Try as she might, she knew there wasn't anything casual in her walk and fear must be radiating off her, hot as a bonfire.

Nicky took a quick look through the small glass pane in the door and spun around. He marched Stella back down the aisle to their table. He grabbed their coats, jammed his hat on his head, and pressed Stella's hat into her hands. Stella wanted to ask what he'd seen, but she was afraid to speak in case she roused one of the sleepers or distracted a reader from their tedious book. Nicky turned and marched her to the other end of the car and out the door onto the breezeway.

"What are we doing?" asked Stella.

"Jumping."

"Are you crazy? We can't jump off this train. It's suicide."

"Hobos do it all the time," Nicky said, buttoning his coat and throwing hers around her shoulders.

"That's your argument? Hobos do it? Can't we just hide until the next stop?"

"He wasn't alone. That female SS officer was with him. You still want to stay on this train?"

Stella didn't think her chest could get any tighter, but the thought of that woman being on the train made it almost impossible to breathe. She shook her head and gave Nicky the package. He put it inside his waistband and cinched his belt tight. Stella pinned her hat on, put her handbag over her arm, and then buttoned her coat. Nicky opened a small access door and stuck his head out.

"It's not too bad," he said. "An embankment and a grassy field."

Stella stood on her tiptoes and peeked through the small window into the club car. Nicky pulled her away and pressed her against the small wall next to the access door.

"They're in the club car," she whispered.

"I'll go first. Remember, bend your legs, and don't think about it." With that, Nicky flung himself out the door.

Stella stuck her head out and watched him roll down the embankment.

"Don't think about it. Don't think about it," she chanted to herself.

Stupid advice. Even worse than don't go to bed angry. But she positioned herself on the thin metal ledge, trying to follow it. The wind burned her left cheek, whipping away any sense. The night had grown darker since she last looked. The beautiful colors had been replaced with angry slashes of black and grey. Into this darkness, Stella launched herself, not thinking of anything. Her fear blocked out everything, except the tiny light of Nicky, shining away and waiting for her somewhere in that darkness.

CHAPTER 10

Nothing in Stella's life turned out the way she expected. Not her marriage, not her honeymoon, and certainly not the jump off that train. She expected terror, bone-crushing pain, and Nicky's comforting arms at the end. She only got terror right. She remembered to bend her legs so they took the impact without any bone crushing. But instead of rolling down the embankment on her side, she flipped ass over teakettle. It seemed to take a while, too. She even had time to cuss Nicky out, using the words her father's chauffeur spat when he thought no one was around. Then she landed in some cold muck instead of Nicky's warm arms.

She lay on the ground, feeling her feet sink into the muck and staring up at a thousand stars. They peered at her with cold perfection as the sound of the train disappeared with a quickness that surprised her. How fast had they been going? The more she thought about it, the less desire she had to move, even though her feet were turning into chunks of ice and her shoes had to be ruined. Her aching body and icy feet reminded her she was still alive and she rejoiced in that happy fact by letting the pain come for a long visit. Without it, where would she be?

"Stella." Nicky knelt beside her, his form silhouetted by the thin sliver of the moon.

"Hello," said Stella.

"Can you move? How bad is it?"

"I think it's fine. No harm done, unless you count my shoes."

"If you're fine, why are you just lying here?" Nicky's voice went to a higher pitch.

"Seemed like the thing to do."

Nicky sat down next to her head and buried his face in his hands. "I thought you broke your neck."

"My mother says we Bleds have hard heads, so I guess we have to have strong necks to hold them up." Stella felt a little laugh bubble in her chest and she released it into the night air, a tinkling sound, happier than any other laugh she'd ever made.

"Don't make jokes. I thought you were dead."

"I'm fine. My neck is fine. My head is fine." Stella patted her head to illustrate the fact and discovered her hat still perched on her head, a little askew but intact. She fluffed her hair and repinned it with great-grandmother's pin and scooted over next to him. His body began to quake at her touch and his face was still concealed by his hands. He loved her. She'd never questioned this fact before. She'd never thought about it at all. She'd just assumed, but now she knew. He did really love her. She wasn't just some fancy he'd taken and made an imprudent marriage with. She felt such a wave of relief, she knew that she must have been worried about it all along and not realized.

She put her arm around his wide shoulders. It didn't quite reach so she patted his back. "I'm fine."

"We jumped off a train."

"Yeah, great idea," she said with a smile.

He dropped his hands and stared at her, two creases forming between his eyes.

"I mean it," she said. "I would never have thought of it on my own. If we hadn't jumped, we probably would be arrested right now, and she'd have the package."

"It'll probably take them a while to figure out we're not on the train anymore. By then, it'll be too late." He wrapped his arms around her and pulled her to his warm chest. The ending she was looking for. They stayed like that for a few moments until Stella couldn't take her frozen feet a second longer.

"So, what do you think?" She pointed to her shoes. "Is this Austrian mud or Czechoslovakian mud?"

"I think it's all German mud now. We'll have to ask them." Nicky pointed into the distance at a group of lights.

He stood and gave Stella a hand up. A chilly wind blew her hair in her face as she stood, squishing the mud out of her pricy shoes. The bottom of her was so cold and disgusting that she looked up to escape it for a moment. The clouds crept across the sky, cloaking the moon and hiding its slight glow. The darkness that lay between them and the lights seemed velvety and foreboding. There was a message in it, but what? Stella couldn't remember a time when she'd experienced such blackness. It felt heavy and thick like she wouldn't be able to get through it without a shovel.

Nicky squeezed her shoulder and placed something in her hands. The package, intact and mud-free.

"I lost my hat," he said. "I'm going to take a look for it. Why don't you start walking?"

"I'm not going into that alone." Stella pressed the package to her chest and grabbed his hand.

"Into what?"

"That blackness. It's so dark it feels like it will never be light again."

"I didn't know you were afraid of the dark," he said.

"I'm not, but there could be anything out there."

"Like werewolves?" Nicky might've smiled at her. The darkness coated him so thickly she could barely make out the curve of his cheek.

"I don't believe in werewolves, but Nazis, they're another story. They could be anywhere, looking for us."

"They are everywhere or at least they plan to be. Stay here. I want that hat."

Stella waited, counting the lights and wishing the stars were brighter. The clouds left the moon and revealed Nicky hunched over and searching several yards to her right. The moon hid behind some clouds almost before Stella could blink. She waited with her eyes trained on the spot where Nicky had been, although she could no longer make him out. He returned a few minutes later, the fedora pulled low. He took her hand and they began stumbling across the field toward the lights. The more steps they took, the farther the light seemed.

"I'm surprised you care about that hat," said Stella when the silence began getting to her.

"Well, you said I needed one and this particular hat got us out of a jam. Maybe it's good luck."

"I didn't know you believed in luck."

"I believe in luck like you believe in werewolves."

"We're a fine pair. It seems we'll believe in anything."

"Stella?" Nicky's voice took on a somber tone. She looked at his face but couldn't make out the nuances of his expression.

"What?"

"I think we have to consider giving the SS the package."

Stella wrenched her hand out of his. "We do not."

"Be reasonable. Have you thought about how that woman came to be on the train?"

She hadn't, but she didn't want to say so. "What's your point?"

"We left her in Vienna. Yet there she was on our train. She never would've been able to catch up with us on another train or with a car."

"So how did she do it?"

"Had to be a plane."

"So?"

"They sent one of the few people in Vienna that could recognize us on sight to catch us and they sent her in a plane. Whatever's in that package must be very important. How far will they go to get it?"

"I promised Abel. Would you have me go back on that promise?"

"What did Abel say, exactly?"

"He asked me to take the package to his family." She paused, trying to decide how much to say.

"What else?" asked Nicky.

Stella sighed. She had to tell him. No secrets. Not about this anyway. "He said not to be tempted to trade the package for him."

"Then they'd let him go."

"He said they'd lie to get it, but they wouldn't let him go."

"Maybe they would. He could be wrong," he said.

"He said nothing was more important than the package. Not even him."

"That cinches it. We have to open it."

"We can't do that," said Stella. "It's like opening someone's mail. It's even addressed."

"You're a Bled," said Nicky. "Since when do you worry about rules?"

"Since when don't you?"

"Since the Nazis nearly beat Albert to death in the name of getting that package. It's obviously what they wanted. After everything that's happened, I've no doubt they'll kill to get it and now *we* have the damn thing. I don't think they're going to stop chasing us just because we've made it inconvenient."

Stella clutched the package to her chest. She'd promised. She wasn't a person who made many promises and she kept the ones she did. Still, the weight of Nicky's logic rested heavily in her chest, heavier than the overwhelming darkness and much scarier. How much should she sacrifice to keep her promise? Abel, Nicky, herself even?

"There's that man in the black suit, too." Stella didn't know why she brought him up. He could only make things worse, but she couldn't help herself. All her worries seeped to the surface and slipped past her lips without her willfully allowing it. "I think he was following Abel on the train to Vienna."

"I'm not worried about him," said Nicky, tripping over something.

Stella caught him by the arm. "Why not?"

"Abel told me about him in Venice. He's a rival historian. Historians aren't exactly dangerous characters, are they?"

"He is, if he's with that SS woman."

"I suppose you're right and they did put him on the plane, too. Why would they do that? Why him?"

Stella stopped short. "Wait a minute. You knew about him before the train. You knew and you didn't tell me?"

"It was nothing for you to worry about."

"You said the Nazis were nothing for me to worry about. Maybe if you'd have told me what was going to happen in Vienna, I wouldn't have wanted to go."

Nicky tightened his grip on her hand. "Darling, I didn't know."

Stella shoved him hard with her hip and he stumbled away into the darkness. She yelled after him. "I think you did know. You just thought I was too silly to understand."

She stomped away, kicking and tripping over a multitude of mysterious objects. Nicky caught up to her and snagged her sleeve. "Come on, Stella."

She shook him off and hurried ahead toward the lights. She yelled over her shoulder, "And we're not opening this package. I don't care what happens."

CHAPTER 11

The town sat on a small hill, a sad group of low stone buildings with windows glowing yellow in the dark. Stella was unable to make herself walk up the gentle slope. The town hardly seemed worth the last few yards. She had blisters on her feet the size of thumbtacks, and she was so tired she wasn't even mad at Nicky anymore. According to him, the distance between the railroad tracks and the lights was about three miles. Stella had never walked three miles in her entire life, much less with icy, swollen feet in the dark.

"Darling," said Nicky, touching her sleeve. "I think there's a barn over there."

"A barn?" Stella could barely remember what a barn was. Her head felt thick, like the thoughts in it were swimming around in mud and unable to get to the surface.

Nicky steered her to the right and began pushing her forward toward a ramshackle outbuilding with an assortment of pitchforks leaning against the side. "Come on, Darling."

"Why are we going to a barn?" she asked, surprised she could form the question.

"It's only for tonight."

Stella planted her heels, her brain clear, mud washed away in a tsunami of indignation. "If you think I'm sleeping in a barn, you must've forgotten who you're married to." She spun around and stuck a finger in his chest. "Let me remind you."

"I didn't forget, believe me, but we can't go to a hotel. The barn is our best option."

"A barn is no option at all," she said. "Why can't we go to a hotel?"

"First of all, I doubt this stink hole of a town has a hotel, and second, we have no money to pay for it."

Stella looked down at her hands clutching the package and her handbag. Her hands looked a lot worse than the handbag with the bruises and mud. Even though her handbag was delicate, it had somehow survived unscathed. But she wished she'd chosen a more expensive bag. Even the town rubes might recognize a Louis Vuitton and let her trade it for a night in whatever they had that passed for an inn.

Nicky rubbed her shoulders and leaned down, pressing his cheek against hers and knocking her hat sideways with the brim of his fedora. "Don't cry. It won't be so bad."

She snapped her head around to face him, staring at him with clear eyes and an intensity that made him back up a few inches. "I'm not crying. I'm trying to figure out what we can trade for a night in a bed instead of a hayloft."

"I haven't got anything else. I don't think our remaining ten cents are going to do it."

Stella looked back at her hands. Her engagement ring and wedding band winked at her in the dim light, but that was out of the question, just barely. She had her coat, but it was winter and she needed it.

Stella shook her head and was about to say she was stumped when she felt a slight tug on her earlobes. "My earrings," said Stella. "We'll trade my earrings."

She reached up and felt the diamonds, a rather boring design. Only her mother would pick princess-cut diamond studs without any style to them at all. Stella had stuck them in her ears in Italy and simply forgotten they were there.

"But they were a gift," said Nicky.

"So was your watch."

"I thought you liked them. You never take them off."

"Only because I forgot they were there and my mother likes them." Stella turned and started up the hill. Her whole body ached and the hill grade seemed to grow larger beneath her feet just the way Alice in Wonderland felt after she drank the bottle labeled DRINK ME.

"All the more reason not to trade them," said Nicky, hurrying to catch her.

"My mother will understand."

"No, she won't. She's your mother."

"Well, my father will then."

"I don't know about that. Trading my wife's earrings for a night in a fleabag hotel isn't going to make me look very good. Your father isn't so sure about me already."

Stella glanced up at him. Nicky's face was clouded below the brim of his fedora and she felt sure he would've pulled it lower if he could've. "What makes you say that?"

"Stella, the man thinks I'm useless. I've heard him call me 'pretty boy' at least half a dozen times."

Stella put the package under her arm and took his hand. "This whole debacle proves you're neither of those things."

"Darling, this has to be the worst honeymoon in history."

"It's not that bad. My father will probably like you after this."

"That's crazy," Nicky said, squeezing her hand.

"Probably, but just don't say crazy in front of Uncle Josiah. He really is cracked."

"Great. He's the only one that liked me."

"My father will like you soon enough."

"I don't understand," he said. "I'm not taking good care of you."

"He'll like you for what you're doing for Abel. It means you're more like us and less like them."

"Them?" he asked.

Stella let go of his hand and swept her arm wide in front of them. "You know, everybody else. There's us and there's them."

"I didn't know the world was so divided." He pointed up ahead at a building with a tiled roof and a swinging sign. "Do you think inn means the same to them as it does to us?"

Stella squeezed his arm and smiled in spite of the cold, the mud, and the blisters. She loved his asking. "Sure, why not?"

They trudged up the remainder of the hill to the door and Stella dropped the iron knocker twice. After a few minutes, a woman wearing a stained apron and a pair of shoes laced with twine answered the door. She looked them over with mute surprise and closed the door in their faces.

"What now?" asked Stella. "She didn't even say anything."

Nicky shrugged and reached to lift the knocker again. Before his fingers touched the iron, the door swung open again. This time, a smiling man, also in an apron, gestured them inside. The room he brought them into was meant to be an entrance hall, but felt more like a used furniture shop. Piles of broken pieces lined the walls, which were whitewashed and undecorated. Despite the broken furniture, the room was neat and clean, but with the smell of old boiled turnips drifting around. Stella caught a glimpse of an eye peaking through an open door, but as soon as she looked, the door closed.

"Welcome, welcome. You need room," he said in understandable, but halting English.

"How did you know we speak English?" asked Nicky.

The man shrugged and swept his arm up and down indicating their dress. "Americans."

"Why are we so obvious?" asked Stella.

"Have you seen yourself?" Nicky turned to the innkeeper and said, "Yes, we'd like a room, but we have a complication."

The innkeeper's brow furrowed at the word 'complication'. Stella didn't know if it was because of the word itself or because he didn't know it.

"What is *complication*?" the innkeeper asked.

"We had an accident and I've lost my wallet."

Stella stepped forward. "But I have a very nice earring. It will bring a nice price."

The innkeeper leaned in and Stella realized the turnip smell was coming from him. She tucked her hair behind her ear, tilting her head toward the man. His mouth went down into a furious frown like an old trout and he nodded. Stella removed the earring and handed it over without the slightest guilt. The innkeeper indicated the other ear and Stella shook her head.

"What are you doing?" whispered Nicky.

She pointed to the earring in the innkeeper's hand. "That one's for the room." Then she touched the other one still in her ear. "And this one is for dinner, hot baths, and breakfast. We'll need our shoes cleaned, too."

"Just dinner," said the innkeeper.

Stella laughed.

"Dinner and one bath," he said. "You share."

"These are one-carat diamond earrings. We're not sharing anything but a bed."

"How I know diamond?" The innkeeper dropped his smile and took on the wily, intense look of a stalking cat.

Stella pointed to the window glass. "Try it out."

The innkeeper went to the window and ran the earring over a small section of glass in the corner. Stella saw him swallow hard and she smiled.

"What else you got?" he asked, looking at her fur rather closely.

"Not a thing. These earrings are more than you make in a year," Stella said. "Am I right?"

A tiny flicker in the innkeeper's eye told her she was correct. She crossed her arms and waited. He crossed his arms, too, and tapped his foot. Nicky looked back and forth between them. He seemed about ready to say something when the innkeeper threw up his arms.

"Deal," he said, shaking his head and grinning.

"I'll give you the second earring after dinner and the rest of it," said Stella.

The innkeeper grinned wider until his rough, dry lips began to crack and bleed. He led them to a narrow staircase with split risers and a handrail shined by years of use. Stella followed him at a distance, fearing he would trip, fall down the stairs, and flatten her.

Nicky came up behind her. His warm tweedy scent competed with the innkeeper's turnip smell in an oddly complementary way.

Nicky ringed his hands around her waist and held her back for a second. "I wouldn't have minded sharing a bath."

"Shh," whispered Stella as she glanced back.

Over Nicky's shoulder, she spied the innkeeper's wife at the foot of the stairs, looking at them, expressionless, but threatening nonetheless. Put her in the black SS uniform and she would've given Stella nightmares.

Nicky followed Stella's gaze and his smile faltered. He froze for a moment and then pushed her gently up the stairs.

"Remind me to lock our door," he whispered in her ear.

CHAPTER 12

Stella sat on the bed swathed in a moth-eaten blanket with her hair drying into a curly halo as Nicky sank into the round tin basin that passed for a tub. A grimy oil lamp cast a yellow circle, turning the steam rising around Nicky in a caressing fog. Stella hid a smile behind her hand as she watched him settle into the basin, grunting and scooting about until he finally ended up, much as Stella had, with his knees up around his ears.

"This never happened," he said, grimacing at her.

"If only I hadn't left the camera with the luggage," said Stella, pressing her generous lips into a thin line.

"I'm serious."

"You look like someone put you in there with a shoehorn."

"It feels like it, too. This water smells odd." Nicky sniffed his hand and wrinkled his nose.

"I know. It smells like a hot spring. It's probably good for us," said Stella.

"Good for us like that soup?" He pointed at two cracked bowls on the dirt brown dresser.

"You don't like turnips?"

"I've never had one before and I never will again."

"I had no idea you were so picky." Stella lifted one of her shoes off the bed next to her. The innkeeper's wife had cleaned them, but the calf leather would never be the same.

"I'm easy to please," he said.

"Oh, really? Mister I-hate-turnips-there's-no-running-water-and-the-bed's-so-small-I'll-have-to-sleep-on-top-of-you."

Nicky grinned and held out his dripping hand. "The last one wasn't a complaint. Don't you want to get in? It's nice and hot."

"If I got in, there'd be no water left," said Stella.

"That's okay with me."

"Just wash," said Stella, slipping on her panties and wishing she had a spare pair so she could wash them out.

Nicky squirmed around. "I think I'm stuck."

"Oh, you are not. You're just trying to get me closer."

"I could be stuck."

Stella rolled her eyes and put on her slip while Nicky stood and sniffed the cracked cake of soap the innkeeper had given them. The lye soap reminded Stella of her grandmother who washed her face with the stuff every day and swore it kept her looking young. She was still a beauty, so Stella had given her face a good scrub. The soap smelled good to her, clean and earthy. Evidently, Nicky didn't agree. He grimaced as he rubbed the light brown square across his taut belly. After he finished washing, he rinsed himself with a pitcher from the nightstand. Stella tossed him her ratty blanket and he reluctantly dried himself. "Haven't these people heard of towels?"

"They haven't heard of toilets, so I doubt it." Stella fluffed her hair in front of the mirror above the nightstand. The silver backing was flaked and cracked, giving Stella a glimpse of her future when she, too, would've seen better days.

"The sooner we get out of here, the better," he said.

"I agree. I don't think the wife likes us very much."

The thought of the innkeeper's grim wife made Stella tuck her knees up to her chest and give them a squeeze. Nicky watched her as he got dressed, worry written on his handsome features until a loud knock on the door made them both jump. Stella wrapped herself in the damp blanket as Nicky slipped on his pants and then opened the door. The innkeeper's wife glowered at them from the doorway, holding out a small cracked plate with two rolls on it.

"Thank you," said Nicky, taking the plate.

As the woman turned away, Stella thought she spied a wicked smile and before Nicky could close the door, the innkeeper rushed up, grinning as usual. "You like?"

Nicky glanced at Stella. She had no idea what he was referring to, so she nodded.

"I bring more water. You soak feet. Have roll," he said, nodding like he had some sort of affliction.

"No, thank you," said Nicky. "The bath was enough."

"I bring you tea. No, no. Americans coffee, right?"

"Right." Nicky looked at Stella again, who tried to keep her face neutral.

"You rest. Rest. I bring coffee."

The innkeeper bustled away and Nicky closed the door. He stood for a moment, fingering the rolls, and then turned around. "We have to get out of here, right now."

"You mean this very minute?" asked Stella, licking her lips in anticipation of coffee. Her favorite thing.

"Who offers coffee at this time of night? He's acting weird and the wife smiled." Nicky set down the rolls and finished dressing.

"It's almost morning and maybe she's just happy." Stella really wanted that coffee.

Nicky handed her the rest of her clothes and bit a roll. Between bites, he said, "Does she strike you as a person who's ever happy for a *good* reason?"

Stella didn't respond but said a silent goodbye to her coffee and sleep. She got dressed, pinned her hat to her head, and gave herself the once-over in the mirror. She looked decent and even felt decent, if she ignored her panty situation and lack of coffee.

"We're in the middle of nowhere. What do you think they're up to?" she asked as Nicky opened the tiny window and stuck his head out into the darkness.

"There's probably a phone in this town somewhere. I bet they sold us out to the SS. My father was warned about that. The Nazis rely on ordinary people selling out their neighbors."

"Selling them out for what?" she asked, getting queasy.

"Money, protection."

"What do the Nazis want to know? You're talking about ordinary people."

Nicky handed her her coat. "They want to know who their enemy is."

"Like…"

"Socialists, Jews, Gypsies."

Stella slipped on her coat and said, "Enemies," under her breath. Abel was an enemy. It was such a general term. It took away his humanity and made him nothing more than a thing. A thing to be hunted and she realized that he had been hunted as they were now. That made them enemies, too. She didn't feel like an enemy. She felt like herself, not something hateful and bad.

"Stella, come on." Nicky examined the top half of the window and pressed his palms against edge. The wood creaked and popped. "I think I can get this pane out. Give me a hand."

"You want to climb out that little window? That doesn't sound very Lawrence-like." Stella stuffed the other roll in her mouth, grabbed onto the window edge, and pulled.

"But it's very Bled-like, wouldn't you agree?" he asked.

"Absolutely. See, you are one of us," said Stella.

"My father will be so proud."

They pulled together and the wood holding the window in place splintered and gave way. Nicky looked out the window again and then lifted Stella onto the sill.

"You first," he said. "And I'll take the earring."

"Are you serious? They probably called the SS on us."

"We're not criminals, no matter what they think. We made a deal," he said.

Stella handed Nicky the earring and he dropped it on the nightstand. Stella squeezed through the window, grabbing an outside ledge.

She dragged her legs through and stepped onto the roof of the back porch. Nicky passed the package and her handbag to her through the window. Stella gave her eyes a second to adjust. The village had no street lamps, but there was a hint of dawn in the east and she could see reasonably well by the light of the full moon. She went to the side of the roof, put the package's twine and the handbag's strap in her teeth and then climbed down a rickety lattice attached to the porch.

Creeping to the edge of the building, Stella peeked around at the front entrance. There was no one there, but in the distance, Stella spotted three long black cars. Their glowing headlamps bounced as they raced over the country road. They weren't the kind of cars that would be found in such a village. They'd be lucky to have a tractor. She turned around to find Nicky climbing onto the lattice, which made a snapping sound.

"Just jump," Stella hissed.

"I don't want to jump."

"You jumped off a train, for crying out loud."

The lattice groaned in response and Nicky jumped backward, landing on his feet initially but tumbling onto his rear in the weeds.

Stella ran over and offered a hand. "Are you okay?"

He took her hand and stood up. "Fine," he said. "Damn, I ripped my suit."

"Never mind that," said Stella. "You were right. They're coming."

"How do you know?"

"There's three black cars driving this way like they're chasing Capone. What do you think?"

"I think run." Nicky grabbed her hand and raced into the village, stumbling through back alleyways and down narrow roads flanked by falling-down cottages and piles of stinking trash. They ran until Stella had no idea where they were or what the point was.

"Wait," she said, yanking Nicky to a stop and resting against a stone wall with little plants growing out of it and a pool of fetid water at its base. "What's our plan?"

"This is it," Nicky gasped. A light came on in the small window next to him.

"What? Running? We can't run all the way to Paris."

"I don't know what you want me to say, Stella."

She didn't know what she wanted him to say either. She wanted a way out. There had to be one. What would her father say? Or Uncle Josiah? Stella put the package and her handbag on her chest, crossed her arms over them, and rested her chin on her handbag's gold clasp. Through the bag's beaded fabric she felt her lipstick case, pillbox and other cosmetics. The corner of something sharp poked her wrist. She opened her bag and spied two wrapped packages, her parents' gifts.

She smiled up at Nicky. "Let's buy a car."

"Are you wacky?"

The window curtain moved to the left and a pinched face surrounded by masses of grey hair peered out at them. Stella grabbed Nicky's arm and pulled him down a dark alleyway.

"Have you seen any cars?" she asked. "I wasn't paying attention."

"By buy, you mean steal, don't you?"

"I do not. I mean buy. We still have my parents' presents. I forgot about them."

Nicky pulled his arm out of her grasp. "That's going too far. The earrings were bad enough."

"We have to get out of here," said Stella.

"I'd rather steal a car."

Stella tilted her head and raised her eyebrows at him. "Did you really just say that?"

"If we sell your parents' presents, I have no hope with your family. Those things are irreplaceable."

"So are we," said Stella. "Now, did you see a car or not?"

Nicky paced back and forth in front of her. "Yes, but it had to be twenty years old. It probably only goes twelve miles an hour."

"Which way?"

Nicky took her hand and led her back in the direction they'd come from. The dingy run-down buildings were becoming clearer as the sun started to come up in earnest. Several villagers peeked out of windows at them and then snapped curtains back in place. A young woman stepped out on a doorstep and was pulled roughly back. The door slammed and Stella heard a bolt slide into place.

"Everybody knows about us," she said.

"Looks like it, but at least they're not trying to apprehend us with pitchforks."

"It's early yet," Stella said with a smile when Nicky glanced down at her. "Where's the car?"

Nicky pointed at a low open-sided shed. Stella squinted and managed to make out a dull grey car with a heavily-dented fender. Nicky ran them over to the left side and yanked open the car door, feeling inside. "Thank God. The keys are in the ignition."

Stella opened her purse and plucked out the first package she touched. It was her mother's Faberge vanity case and she felt sick when she felt its weight in her hand. "We could buy six cars for the price of this."

"Not today." Nicky took the case out of her hand and placed it on a worktable next to a rusting wrench. "Get in."

He opened the door and Stella scooted across the cracked leather seat. Nicky got in behind her, started the car, and backed out of the shed. A man wearing rough pants and a woolen shirt ran out the door next to the workbench and began screaming at them. Stella pointed at the workbench as Nicky changed gears and cranked on the wheel. They sped down the alley, knocking over wooden crates and causing dozens of lights on the street to come on. Heads poked out of windows watching them pass, each face ghastly in the headlamps. They reminded Stella of the death masks they'd seen in Italy. They had about as much warmth and animation.

"So much for a quiet getaway," said Stella.

"It could be worse," replied Nicky.

"Don't say that."

"Why? It could be."

"Because if you say that, it will get worse. Uncle Josiah taught me that," said Stella, bumping into the door when Nicky made a quick turn into another alley.

"You said Uncle Josiah's cracked." He turned again onto a wider street. A man crossing the street ran to get out of the way and more solemn faces appeared at the windows.

"He is, but not about war and we're at war," said Stella.

"Oh, no," said Nicky.

"What?"

"Up ahead."

Stella leaned down and saw a pair of bright headlamps turning onto the street well ahead of them. She tumbled into Nicky as he made another turn, grazed the side of a building, and knocked off a side mirror. Stella screamed and clutched the seat.

"Quiet, Stella," yelled Nicky.

Stella clamped one hand over her mouth and braced the other one against the dashboard. She glanced back as they cleared the town, producing billowing dirt clouds behind them on a road so rough that it made Stella's teeth rattle.

"They're behind us," said Nicky from between clenched teeth.

The speedometer read nearly forty kilometers per hour and the smell of burning oil invaded the cab. Stella looked back again. The sedan was gaining. It was a long, glossy black affair with bug head-lamps. She could make out two silhouettes in the front seat but couldn't tell if it was the female SS officer or not. Stella's stomach became queasy and her mouth filled with saliva. If that woman got ahold of them, especially after the merry little goose chase they'd been leading her on, it would be very bad. Albert's face flashed before her, bloody and bruised. That could be them and worse. They actually had what the SS wanted. Stella's hand fell upon the package and she closed her eyes.

"Get down!" screamed Nicky.

"What?" said Stella, her eyes popping open.

"Get down!" Nicky grabbed Stella's shoulder and roughly pushed her down onto the seat.

A sharp, shattering sound startled her and Stella stared at a small hole in the dashboard. Nicky jerked the wheel to the right and one of the backside windows shattered.

"They're shooting at us!" screamed Stella.

"I know," said Nicky, following up with a string of curse words so unusual Stella wasn't sure whether they were real or he just made them up in the heat of the moment. "Hold on."

"What's happening?"

"Tunnel."

Stella stuck her head up and saw a stone wall whizzing by Nicky's window. "What tunnel?"

"Up ahead under the railroad bridge. Yes. I think I can just about make that." Nicky flashed a devilish grin at her. "Hold on."

Stella glimpsed a bridge dead ahead with a narrow arched tunnel under it before Nicky pushed her head down. A couple of bullets pinged off the car's trunk and one shattered the other back window.

Stella screeched and grabbed onto Nicky's leg as he heaved the wheel to the left, gunning the engine. She slid across the seat, ramming her feet painfully against her door, and they were in the darkness of the tunnel for a second then out into the morning sun again. Stella barely blinked before the sound of crashing metal exploded behind them. Stella squeezed her eyes shut and waited for the car to fall to pieces or at least for it to stop. But it didn't stop, and Nicky let out a whoop that didn't sound remotely Lawrence-like. She opened her eyes and saw him grinning so wide it seemed the edges of his mouth would reach the brim of his fedora.

"What happened?" she asked.

"Take a look."

She peeked over the seat, afraid a bullet would go whistling by her face, but instead saw the sedan crashed into the side of the tunnel they'd come through. Flames flickered under the hood and a man dressed in a black uniform emerged from the wreck. He ran down the road after them with his pistol held out, firing, but they were far out of range.

"How did you know what to do?" she asked.

"I used to race my brothers in my father's cars when he was out of town on business. It didn't hurt that this piece of crap car can't go very fast and has a short wheel base. That swell sedan had every advantage on us."

"How can being better make them crash?"

"They were simply too long to make such a tight turn fast and too stupid to know it."

"Oh, I see." Stella didn't see and she didn't care. Other things were more pressing. "They were shooting at us."

Nicky's face went somber. "I know, Stella darling."

"Whatever's in Abel's package is worth shooting us for."

"I know you don't want to open it, but—"

Stella cut him off. "We have to open it."

CHAPTER 13

"This is ridiculous," said Stella, picking at the knot on the package. "What was Abel thinking? This has to be the worst knot in the history of knots."

Nicky kept his eyes on the road. He'd taken off his fedora, mindless of how his hair stood up in tangled bunches. "Leave it. We'll have to wait until we have a knife or scissors."

"I don't want to wait." Stella pursed her lips and in a spurt of frustration bit the knot, tugging on it with her teeth.

The knot wouldn't give, and she dropped the package on the seat next to the fedora. Now that they'd decided to open the package, she could hardly stand it. What was worth killing them for? She opened the glove box and touched the sharp edge of the metal door. She held the package to the edge and rubbed the thick twine encircling the package against it. It barely frayed the stubborn twine. She swore under her breath and tore away a strip of the paper, only to find well-worn oil cloth beneath it.

Nicky watched her with a sly smile dancing on his lips. "I don't want to wait either, but knowing what's in the package doesn't change our current situation. The border's coming up in five miles. There's bound to be guards and I'm sure they've been notified about us."

Stella stared at the uneven road ahead of them, lit with the morning sun so that Nicky could see all the potholes, crevasses, and rock. He tried to avoid them the best he could, but it was impossible to miss them all. The ancient car creaked and groaned, slamming their teeth together and occasionally jolting violently for no reason that Nicky could see. That the car had a full tank of gas and a small gas can strapped to the truck was a miracle for which Stella thanked God repeatedly between her prayers for Abel. She'd never been much for praying before, but her mother was quite devout. It was probably one of the reasons people called her a saint. Stella tried to follow her example, but it was hard to go to mass multiple times a week when there was so much fun to be had.

Just then, Stella wished she had her neglected rosary, which had been left tucked away in a corner of a suitcase in Vienna. Her mother would be horrified. She was never without her rosary. Stella had caught her counting the polished beads when her father was raging about some mess or other that Uncle Josiah had gotten himself into. Perhaps that was why mother remained so saint-like and calm. Perhaps the rosary was a cure-all.

Since Stella didn't have her cure-all, she rhythmically tapped Abel's package and said her ten Hail Marys, her Glory Be, and then Our Father. She repeated the sequence perfectly for the first time in her life. Usually, she was still on her Hail Marys when her obedient brothers had moved on. She'd have to skip to avoid her mother's beady eyes calculating how much she'd dawdled.

Stella let the rhythm of the rosary soothe her, craning her neck from side to side to try to ease the increasing pain in her neck. They'd been bouncing along forever and she ached all over. Her nose had swollen to embarrassing proportions and her face was asymmetrical with the cuts on one side. Nicky reached over and brushed a curl off her forehead. She winced at his touch, not wanting to be the battered bride she'd become but the pretty girl he loved to look at.

Stella opened her handbag and took out her compact, eyeing her reflection with distaste. It was worse than she imagined and she imagined it quite bad. There was a town at the border crossing. If they had to persuade someone to help them, she needed to look her best, and the current situation wasn't up to snuff. As Stella feared, the cuts from her impact with the train stairs had started to turn a nasty shade of purple. The rest of her face looked like she'd been scared pale.

She dabbed powder on her bruises, then rooted around for her mascara, but she must've left it in her makeup case back in Vienna. All those expensive cosmetics, her hats, and the clothes from Milan and Rome were gone. A fresh wave of nausea rolled over her. She knew it was stupid, but if she had to be on the run, she at least wanted to be presentable.

Stella took all the things out of her handbag, one by one, and laid them on the seat in case she'd missed the rouge. At the bottom, shoved to the side was an envelope addressed to her in black type. She removed it and ran her fingers along the edge.

"What's that?" asked Nicky.

"The telegram I got in Vienna the other night." Stella pressed the envelope to her lips. It seemed so long ago. She closed her eyes and pictured the beautiful hotel lobby, the desk clerk handing her the telegram, Nicky's irritation, Abel standing beside him unbruised, that horrible night not yet begun.

"What does it say? I'm guessing another purchase request? What is it this time, a tiara, sixty-eight bottles of wine?"

Stella glanced at him to gauge his mood, but he didn't appear as irritated as she expected. The skin under his eyes sagged, shadowed with fatigue, a golden god weary of mortals' doings.

"I don't know," she said. "I never opened it."

"Why not?" He looked at her, the first sign of interest during the long hours on the road.

Stella ran through several responses in her head but found herself too tired to conceal anything. "I thought it would make you mad."

He chuckled and put his eyes back on the road. "It probably would've. Seems stupid now. Open it and let's see what your esteemed family has to say."

Stella lifted the flap with her fingernail and pulled out the fragile paper. "It's from my father. He wants us to go visit Hans Gruber."

"Who's Hans Gruber?"

Stella tapped the paper against her lips. Hans Gruber. Hans Gruber. All at once, she could appreciate the sunlight shining in her window. The placid cows lowing from the side of the road became lovely and remindful of hope. She and Nicky weren't sitting in an almost stolen car with empty stomachs and no money, on their way into the arms of the SS. It really was beautiful country they were in. Stella hadn't noticed before. She pivoted on the seat and threw her arms around Nicky, kissing him hard on his bristly cheek.

"What's that for?" he asked.

"Hans Gruber."

"Again. Who's Hans Gruber?"

"My father's friend. He's a brewer in Austria near the German border. He'll help us."

"Sounds good," said Nicky, patting Stella's leg. "Except he's an Austrian brewer and we're in Czechoslovakia, or whatever it's called now."

"Maybe we can drive over the border somewhere."

"Maybe. I didn't want to tell you this, but we're almost out of gas. I'm praying we can make it to the border."

"So we'll ditch the car and walk across. That'll be easier."

"It would be, but then we'll be on foot," said Nicky.

Stella bit her lip and eyed a small town in the distance. A long train with red and grey cars snaked out through the rolling hills. The thought of Abel being shoved into one, weak and injured, came back to her with a jolt. Had the Nazis discovered who he was yet? If they had, what did they do to him when they realized he didn't have the package anymore? She shook her head, trying to lose those wretched thoughts. Hopefully, he wasn't on that boxcar anymore. And maybe, just maybe, Albert was wrong. The camps might not be that bad. But as that thought crossed her mind, the image of Albert's swollen face appeared unbidden in her mind, and she knew it wasn't so. The thought of the camps loomed over her like the nightmares of her childhood, the ones she couldn't quite remember upon waking. Her father would sit on her bed and stroke her hair. He'd tell her she was afraid of nothing, that the terrible darkness she feared wasn't real. She was an adult now, feeling the same terror, but without her father's comfort. Now the camps were real and not knowing what Abel was enduring made her terror complete.

"Abel's on a boxcar," she said.

"I know, Stella darling."

A little light of an idea flickered around her as they got closer and she saw men bustling around the train, loading cars. "We could be on a boxcar."

"I won't let that happen. I'll die before I let them put you in a boxcar." Nicky gripped her leg tighter, his jaw set and hard.

"No, I mean you said hobos jump off trains all the time. They must jump on them, too. We could get on a boxcar and ride into Austria."

Nicky made a low considering sound in his throat. "I thought of that, but I hate the idea of you on a boxcar under any circumstances."

They rode in silence, both of them scanning the approaching village for signs of the SS. Nicky turned onto a side road and entered the town in the residential section. Unlike the last village with the treacherous innkeepers, the streets were clean and swept without trash heaps and repulsive smells. The houses were all made of the same grey stone but were larger with freshly painted shutters and lace curtains. Nicky parked behind a Mercedes coupe next to a large three-story house with green shutters.

"Quick," said Nicky. "Get out. We'll leave the car here. Hopefully, nobody will notice it for awhile."

Stella grabbed her handbag, her hat, and the package, sliding out the door after Nicky. He walked them across the street behind a trellis covered with thick grape vines. Stella put her hat on and tucked the package under her coat.

"I'm ready," she said.

"Where does Gruber live?" asked Nicky.

Stella pulled the telegram out. The town name had seventeen letters put together in a way that seemed wholly illogical. "Hofbrau something or other."

Nicky leaned over her, looking at the telegram. His reddish-blond whiskers glinted in the sun and he still smelled of the homemade lye soap.

"All right. Here's the plan." Nicky rubbed his chin whiskers with his thumb and forefinger, making a sound like sandpaper on wood. "We'll go into the station to find out how to get to Hofbrau whatever, and then we'll hop the first train going into Austria."

"Do you think—"

He grabbed a fistful of her fur coat and pulled her close. He kissed her, his lips softly pressing against hers and his whiskers pricking a ring around her mouth. "Are you happy we have a plan?" he asked, his warm breath flowing onto her lips.

"Very happy." She tucked the telegram back in her handbag, forgetting her question.

Nicky grasped her hand and led her out onto the street, assuming his old mask of indifference. They went down alleys, avoiding the main thoroughfares. Several people saw them, but they seemed preoccupied and didn't give Stella or Nicky a second look. Nicky kept them headed in the direction of the train station, confidently making turns without appearing to think about it. Stella had no idea where they were in relation to the station and she let her mind wander to her family. Her telegram was safe in her handbag and even though her father hadn't touched it, it felt like a talisman all the same. Her father had reached out to help them, to point her in the right direction, as he had all her life. The thought made her smile as her mind automatically switched to Uncle Josiah. According to her parents, he was a bad influence, one that they couldn't contain or control. Her beloved uncle lived his life according to his own rules, rules that changed depending on the situation. Stella and Nicky turning hobo would undoubtedly delight him. Despite Uncle Josiah's intense love of German brewers, his hatred of the German military was equally intense. They spent a good deal of time trying to kill him during The Great War and he took it personally.

And in Uncle Josiah's case, it was personal. He was an ace, flying first for Britain and then for the United States after they entered the fight. He had seventy-two confirmed kills in the air and quite a few on the ground, too. He'd been shot down twice, was captured, and escaped. He'd never forgiven the German military for their audacity in shooting down a Bled. How dare they!

"Why are you smiling?" asked Nicky.

"I was thinking about Uncle Josiah," Stella said. "He does love an adventure."

"I wouldn't call this an adventure."

"It most certainly is."

Nicky frowned down at her. "You understand that we could be killed?"

"Uncle Josiah says that every great adventure begins with equally great peril."

"He really is cracked. I doubt your parents share that opinion."

Stella squeezed his hand. "My father was just as adventurous in his youth. Mother, too."

"I find that hard to believe."

"Doubt all you want. My mother and her sister ran away when they were sixteen and seventeen."

Nicky's eyes went wide. "Ran away to where?"

"Florida. They wanted to see palm trees so they pooled their pocket money and took a train to Miami all by themselves."

"How much pocket money did they have?"

"Grandfather doted on them. Still, it took them a couple of months to save up and they bought a car when they got there."

Nicky's grip on her hand tightened. "Tell me that they hired a chauffeur."

"They drove," said Stella.

"Your mother and her sister drove a car in…what kind of car?"

"That hardly matters. My point is—"

"I never had a chance of making you a Lawrence," interrupted Nicky. "I had no idea your family is so…"

"Independent?"

"Sure. Let's call it that."

As they crept through the streets of that foreign village, Stella wondered where her *independent* parents were. What were they doing?

Did they know about what had happened in Vienna? Had they tried to contact them without success? Stella reminded herself that they most certainly would. They'd received telegrams from her family nearly every day no matter where they were and she sent them a telegram at each stop they made. They would know something was wrong when she didn't send one. It felt oddly comforting to think her father would be making calls and sending someone to inquire after them. He wouldn't wait and see. He wouldn't hesitate. Her father would act decisively, as always. They'd been so isolated since jumping on the train in Vienna. It helped to know someone was out there loving them instead of hunting them.

They came around a corner and Stella's heel crunched some glass. She looked down to see the pavement sparkling with broken glass. The house on their left had all its windows broken out. Two houses past the broken glass, a dark-haired woman in a flowered housedress knelt on the pavement in front of two men in suits. Stella wanted to stop walking, to turn around and go any way but that way, but somehow, they kept walking.

Nicky squeezed her hand. He stepped into the street to give the scene a wide berth. "Just walk, Stella," he said under his breath.

As they approached, the men gave Nicky and Stella the once-over, but they didn't do anything but nod. The woman kept her eyes on the pavement. She had a large scrub brush in her hands. She pushed it over the pavement in a soapy pool of reddish water.

Nicky quickened his pace and they went back up on the sidewalk. Stella couldn't stop herself. She glanced back. The woman was looking at her from between the men, her face blotched as if from a beating with eyes both pleading and hopeless. That face would remain with Stella for the rest of her life, just as Albert's and Abel's would. So would the feeling she had when she saw it, the feeling of walking away from a terrible accident without doing a thing to help.

Nicky jerked her arm. "Stop looking."

Stella turned forward again, her stomach in a hot knot. "It's happening here, too."

Nicky nodded slightly.

They entered the business district. Glass littered the street for an entire block. One shop stood out like a burnt-out carcass between the unscathed ones on either side. Several women were sweeping the glass, supervised by both men and women. This time, Stella avoided looking at their faces. She had memories enough. But she couldn't avoid the feeling on the street or the sound of muffled weeping coming from above the shops mixed with a tinny radio broadcast of a woman singing boisterous songs in German. Without Nicky's firm grip on her arm, she might've broken into a run. She had to get away from the feeling of unhappiness and danger that pervaded the street. The scene's nastiness came over her like a thick hand on her mouth, blocking her breath. When they turned off the street, she gasped and stumbled.

Nicky kept her on her feet. He walked with measured strides, never hesitating, never changing expression. "We're almost there, Stella."

The station came into view, ringed by soldiers in the brown uniforms Stella remembered so well. Nicky side-stepped her into an alley and they skirted the station altogether.

"What are we going to do?" asked Stella.

"We're going to hop that train," said Nicky, pointing at a long line of red boxcars set to travel over the border.

"But we don't know where it's going."

"It's going out of here. That's all we need to know."

CHAPTER 14

*S*tella and Nicky picked their way through the rail yard past rusting flatbed cars and stacks of railroad ties. The train's whistle blew and Nicky increased his speed so that Stella had to jog to keep up.

On a dime, he pivoted and changed direction, pulling Stella behind a rickety shack next to a set of empty tracks. He shook his head before she could open her mouth to protest. He looked through one of the wide cracks between the shack's boards. His hand pressed against the small of her back until she looked through a crack herself. Beyond the shack, past three sets of tracks, two German soldiers and another man in a stiff grey suit walked alongside the red cars. The man in the suit stooped to look under each car and occasionally made a note on the large clipboard he carried. Stella and Nicky watched until the men walked the entire length of the train. They met and conferred with another group that had apparently been doing the same thing on the other side. One of the men waved at a man in grey coveralls hanging off the engine. The engineer doffed his cap and the group walked down to the station and went inside. Steam started coming out of the engine's smoke stack, first in small puffs then big, billowing clouds.

Nicky edged around the shack, pulling Stella by the hand. He pointed to the train's last car, pulling her close and whispering in her ear. "That one. It's leaving now, but we have to find a door on the other side, so no one will see us."

Stella nodded.

"Run when I say," said Nicky, his eyes focused on the cars.

Stella squeezed his hand.

"Now," he said.

Nicky bolted out from behind the shack. He moved so fast, he almost pulled Stella off her feet, but she recovered and raced after him, jumping over a switch. Her feet barely brushed the railroad ties of each set of tracks they passed over. They skirted the caboose and passed a couple of coal cars before heading for the last car. Nicky reached for the handle, his foot rising toward the rusty metal step. Then he stopped so abruptly Stella ran into his back. His hand and foot dropped.

"What is it?" hissed Stella.

Nicky didn't answer. He pointed at the gap between the car's wooden slats. Dozens of eyes looked out at them. Solemn eyes, dry and unblinking. Stella dropped Nicky's hand and covered her mouth to stop herself from crying out. Lips replaced the eyes as the people inside shouted at them. Nicky spun around, wildly looking at the other trains. He grabbed her arm and started dragging her away.

Stella dropped her hands, her eyes on the car. "It's full of people."

"I know," said Nicky without missing a stride.

"Do you think they're Jews like Abel?"

"Yes."

The train whistle blew and Stella jerked her arm out of Nicky's grasp. "Where are you going?"

"There's another train headed over the border." He pointed at a newer train with a couple of flatbed cars containing mechanical equipment, coal cars, and a few wooden boxcars painted gray.

"We have to let them out," said Stella, turning and walking back to the car.

Nicky grabbed her arm. "We can't."

The train whistle blew again and the shouts from the car became more desperate.

"Why not? The door handle's right there."

"It's ridiculous. Where would they go? The guards are armed." Nicky pulled Stella's arm, but she refused to be moved.

"I know Abel isn't on that train, but if he was, nothing would stop me from getting him out," said Stella.

Nicky met her eyes as the train started to move. He dropped her arm and ran back to the last car. He jumped on the step, grabbed the long lever, and flipped the wooden bar over, unlocking the door. He pulled back the door, revealing the occupants, a motley group of men dressed in everything from elegant suits to pajamas. They shielded their eyes and stumbled forward toward the open door. Nicky jumped off the step and ran to the next car. He opened it as the train picked up a little speed and leapt off, running to the third. He just managed to get the handle pushed over before tumbling into the long grass as the train really got going. Men jumped off the train, pouring out the open doors like malted barley out of one of her father's mills. Stella ran around a man covered in crusted black blood to Nicky and helped him to his feet. The train pulled away and exposed them all. The SS on the platform paused for a second, staring at the chaos beside the tracks, and then began screaming and pointing their weapons. Nicky grabbed Stella's hand and dashed toward the other train. They went over another set of tracks and clambered between two boxcars of the new train, over the greasy coupling and onto the other side.

Nicky stepped onto the jagged rocks of the steep embankment, let go of Stella's arm, and slid down amidst the clacking rocks and landed at the bottom on thick grass. Stella followed him, much less gracefully. She held the package tight to her chest, using only one arm for balance. The rocks slipped out from beneath her feet and she finished the trip on her bottom, landing at Nicky's feet. Nicky lifted her up and then looked at the row of cars. Smoke puffed from the engine's smokestack in a grey twister and a man in coveralls stood on the coal car behind the engine. He had a shovel in one hand, his back to them. Shots rang out on the other side of the train amidst shouts and screams in several languages. Stella gasped and clung to Nicky's hand as she stared up at the hard, closed sides of the boxcars.

They were all solid-sided, unlike the cattle cars, and the lack of oxygen for any inhabitants reassured Stella that they were probably empty of people, unlike the other train that had already disappeared into the distance with the remains of its shameful cargo. A whistle pierced the air, for a second, overriding the havoc erupting on the other side and they made for the third to last car. Stella had to crane her neck to look up at the car's dingy exterior, looking for any indication of what it contained. The sides were blank, but she felt uneasy nonetheless.

"Don't worry," said Nicky. "It's not people."

"But it's something," she said. "It's *always* something."

"At this point, I don't care." Nicky launched himself at the embankment, scrambling up the gravel and onto the side of the car. He balanced on the metal slide at the base of the door and pushed at the door's long lever. The lock creaked and the door slid open an inch. Nicky shuffled sideways and pushed again. The door opened completely with a whine, revealing wooden crates. Nicky slipped, falling backwards and swinging out with one hand on the metal brace next to the door. Stella climbed the embankment in an effort to support his foot, but by the time she got there, he'd already recovered.

"Just a second, Stella," he said, hooking his arm around the open edge and heaving himself inside.

A moment later, he emerged, crouching down with his hand extended to Stella. He tugged her up and she stumbled across the small open area inside the car, bumping into a stack of wooden crates. The car was full of them with just enough room for the two people.

"I was right," said Stella.

Nicky sighed. "It could be worse."

"I suppose." Stella touched the side of a crate. Her hand brushed against an eagle standing on the Nazi swastika. Each crate was marked in the same way and the sight gave her a nasty chill.

"What is this stuff?" she asked.

"No idea." Nicky yanked the door and inched it across until it was almost closed. "I need something to brace it with, so we don't get locked in. Look around."

Cracks around the car's door let in just enough light for them to see. Stella blinked as her eyes adjusted and ran her hands over the shortest stacks nearest the door. "There's nothing but crates."

"How heavy are they?"

Stella put her handbag and the package on one crate and tried to lift the one next to it. "Pretty heavy." She stopped trying and her hands ran up the side of the crate. The lid shifted as she pressed against it. "Wait. The lid's not attached on this one."

She took the lid and gave it to Nicky, who placed it between the door and the wall. Stella looped her arm around his waist and placed her head against his back. He let out a long-held breath and rolled his head side to side. Stella imagined the tense muscles in his neck and wished she could put him in a bath so hot the steam would blanket their room like New England fog.

The train jerked and threw Stella into the crates. Nicky turned, grabbing her arm to steady her as the train picked up speed. Then he went to the door and looked out through the crack.

"Do you see anything?" Stella asked.

"Just the border crossing," he said. "We're over it now."

"I never thought I'd be happy to be back in Austria again."

"Me, either."

Nicky fumbled in his pocket and came up with his lighter. He flicked it and a small flame threw warm shadows around their snug hideout. But instead of feeling comforted, Stella suppressed a shiver.

"Not very nice, is it?" Nicky ran his hand over a swastika. "We're surrounded."

Stella looked down into the crate she'd opened. It was filled with cardboard boxes and one was missing. Nicky reached in and pulled out a box. He examined the label on the end with a somber face.

"Ammunition. Looks like 9mm," he said. "I guess somebody helped themselves to a box. The Nazi bean counters won't be happy."

"That's a lot of ammunition," said Stella.

"It sure is, especially if the other cars on the train are filled with it."

"Why would the Nazis need so much?"

Nicky flicked off his lighter and sat down on the crate, pulling Stella with him. "My father thinks they're going to invade Poland."

"Why would they do that?"

"Why are they chasing us across kingdom come? We have something they want. It's the same with Poland."

Stella sat on a crate and caught her hand on the sharp edge of the metal band encircling the crate. "Ouch."

Nicky flicked on his lighter again and held it over her hand. He took out his handkerchief and dabbed the pooling blood on her palm.

"What did you cut yourself on?" he asked.

Stella nodded at a wicked point coming off the corner of the crate. Nicky touched his finger to the wicked edge and picked up the package. "Sharp enough to cut twine, if you still want to."

Stella nodded and Nicky turned off the lighter. He waited a minute and then began working the twine against the metal. Stella could see his hands in a narrow slat of light, moving in short, careful jerks. The train increased speed and the car swayed back and forth in a gentle rhythm that didn't quite offset the chill of being surrounded by Nazi symbols.

Nicky made one last movement and turned to Stella, handing her the package with the twine hanging loose. "You do the honors, Stella darling."

She unwound the twine and let it fall to the floor at her feet. She unfolded the brown paper, and a very old and stained oilcloth emerged. Nicky lit his lighter and held it over the package as she unwrapped the heavy square inside. She did it slowly, half afraid that what she'd find would be extraordinary and half afraid it wouldn't be interesting at all and they'd still have no clue why the Nazis were chasing them.

When the last fold of oilcloth was pulled away, a leather cover of a book emerged, hand-tooled and clearly ancient. It was perfectly square and had a large ornate letter in the center. At first, Stella didn't recognize it and then it dawned on her.

"It's a letter G," she said.

"Open it," said Nicky. "Let's see what's worth dying for."

Stella lifted the cover. The stiff leather creaked and a musty scent rushed up to greet her as a portrait of a young woman was revealed on the first page. The portrait page was slightly smaller than the rest of the book. The handmade paper showed signs of age at the edges, but the portrait itself was in remarkable condition. The woman was drawn in red chalk with her head thrown back, gazing at rays of sunshine raining down from the uppermost left-hand corner. Her face held a beatific expression of absolute happiness and Stella couldn't take her eyes off her.

"Stella," said Nicky. "Turn the page. There has to be something better than that."

"Are you joking?" Stella didn't take her eyes away from the face. "This is exquisite."

"She's very pretty, but we still don't know what it is."

Stella lifted the portrait page with the tips of her fingers on the edge. The next page was vellum and covered with loopy handwriting in another language Stella didn't immediately recognize. Around the corners of the sheet were flowers and animals, each done in vibrant inks that seemed to glow and grow before Stella's eyes.

"I don't know about you, but this isn't much help." Nicky flicked off his lighter and the boxcar went dark.

"Can we open the door?" asked Stella. "I need the light."

"What for? It's not like you can read it."

"It seems familiar. Doesn't it seem familiar to you?" asked Stella.

"Not even a little bit." Nicky's tone grew frustrated and even in the darkness of the boxcar, Stella could feel his irritation.

"Would you please open the door? It's probably safe now."

As Stella's eyes adjusted to the dim light provided by the cracks in the siding, Nicky stood and went to the door. He pushed it open and a gust of wind made him blink. Stella scooted back on the crate and pressed the fluttering pages down as Nicky stuck his foot in the door crack. He pulled out the top of the crate he'd used to prop it open and then opened the door fully. Light flooded into the car and Stella blinked rapidly as Nicky came back to sit at her side.

The same loopy script covered the next six pages, often with the same writing on the back. Every paragraph started with an enlarged letter, beautifully colored and often with delicate flowers growing out of it. The pages didn't appear to have been written at the same time, since there were different inks used and slight variations in the script. Some sections were larger than others and in some, the handwriting tilted as if the writer were rushed. Each page had illustrations with sheep, plants, and flowers being the most frequent.

After those first pages came an assortment of sheets, some vellum and some handmade paper. They were different sizes and different batches of paper. One was covered with letters, all done in an ornate style that varied from letter to letter. It looked to Stella like an artist practicing technique. Another page had flowers growing in from the corners. They flowed across the page into a writhing mass of color. The next had sketches of a table from various angles. One had a machine with a long handle and a giant wooden screw. It reminded Stella of a grape press. She leaned over the book and examined a letter H topping a middle page.

"I knew I saw something." She popped up, flashing a dazzling smile at Nicky.

Nicky looped an arm around her shoulder and bent over the page. "What? I don't see anything."

"Look there." She pointed at the letter H. "Tiny in the corner."

"All I see are flowers."

"It's a date. The year 1432 written in Roman numerals."

"So it's medieval, but we still don't know what it is."

"I think it's a diary. Lots of the pages are dated and all these drawings and portraits, it feels personal."

Stella flipped through the pages, finding more dates and more illustrations. Three more portraits of the woman were interspersed throughout the book. The last date was 1466. She turned through the next several pages, looking for missed clues and feeling more lost than ever.

"Wait," said Nicky. "Go back."

Stella turned back to a page covered with handwriting. It didn't look any different than the other pages. "Did you see something?"

Nicky reached over, turned the page, and pointed to the back. "That's different."

Odd black type covered the back of the page. The letters were elegantly scrolled with flowing lines. Some were embossed into the page, others so faint they could hardly be seen. The same loopy handwriting made notes next to several of the letters. There were sixteen typed letters in all.

"That page was printed," said Nicky. "I wonder what the notes say."

"Let me see if there's a date," said Stella.

She examined the page and found some Roman numerals underneath the third letter.

"Look here."

Nicky bent over. "Could be a date. Pretty faint. How are your Roman numerals?"

"Not the best, but I think it's something like 1440," said Stella.

"Yes. Yes. 1452."

"Your numerals are very good."

He chuckled and stooped to kiss her cheek. "My grandfather always dated his letters that way."

"Why?"

"He thought it was funny."

Stella raised an eyebrow at him and he shrugged. "Grandfather enjoyed bothering my father. Dates in Roman numerals, letters in Latin. He loved to travel, even when he was too old to go. He'd get on a ship and disappear. Father wanted him to live with us so we could watch him, but grandfather loved his freedom. He'd write, in Latin, to say he was in Istanbul."

"Grandfather was bad," said Stella, warming to the one person in the Lawrence clan that she could truly understand.

"He was great and thanks to him, I know my numerals. He said it would come in handy. Who knew?"

"He did."

"I can't wait to tell my father. He will be steamed. Grandfather's been dead for three years and he's still winning."

Stella looked back at the book. 1452. The book was as old as it looked. "Maybe there are more dates."

"Probably," said Nicky.

They went through the book, page by page, looking for anything else out of the ordinary. They found many more pages of printed letters. Some were written over like the author was recycling, but some were left intact with notes. Near the end of the book were whole pages of printed letters in a narrow column down the middle of the page. Something about the pages kept nagging at Stella, but she couldn't grasp what they were trying to tell her. She flipped back to the first page of print. 1437. The last page of print was dated 1466. Mixed in the printed pages were printed woodcuts, ornate letters in red, black, or blue with different designs. Sometimes they had little animals like elk or dogs. In others, there were geometric designs or flowers. Gradually, the woodcuts became forest scenes or scenes of everyday life.

Stella turned back to one particular page printed with Bs. "Doesn't this look familiar?"

"It's a B," said Nicky.

"It's a special B. I know I've seen it before."

Nicky looked closer. "You've seen *that* B before?"

"You don't believe me." Stella gave him an icy glare and he bumped her with the rim of his fedora. "You couldn't have seen that B. It's not a public B."

"It was printed," she said slowly.

"Yes. So?"

"It's a printed woodcut."

Nicky yawned and scratched his bristly chin. "They did that. It's not unusual."

Stella sucked in a breath and held it. That B. That particular B.

"The colors," she said in a whoosh of breath.

"What about them?"

She pointed at one B in black with a background of red, curvy leaves. "That one. I've seen that one. This page was printed in…"

"Looks like 1456."

"1456 is right. It's exactly right."

"Right for what?" Nicky arched his back and it made a dreadful cracking noise.

"The Gutenberg Bible wasn't printed until 1455. Gutenberg's psalter wasn't printed until 1457. Of course, he didn't print it, but it was his work."

Nicky blinked. "How do you know that?"

"My parents collect art." She tapped her nail on the precious B. "This is art."

"So you think this guy invented the printing press instead of Gutenberg."

"No. Gutenberg was one of a kind. He even developed the ink that could be used in printing. He was the first to combine colors like in the Bs."

"And you know that because?"

"My father has five Gutenberg leaves framed in his study, one for each of his children, one for my mother, and one for himself. I knew this looked familiar. The artwork. The style, it's distinctive. This is Gutenberg's diary. It has to be."

"Your father owns a Gutenberg Bible?"

"Only leaves. An art dealer took one apart and sold off the sections. My father jumped at the chance."

"How much is that kind of thing worth?" Nicky asked, taking off his hat and flexing the brim.

"I don't know how much he paid. I never thought about it, but one complete bible was sold for three quarters of a million dollars a few years ago."

"Did you hear that from your father?"

"I don't remember where I heard it. You sound surprised."

"I guess I am, a little. You never seem very interested in what's happening in the world. You never read the paper."

"The paper's not very interesting."

"But art is?"

"It is to me."

Nicky placed his hat back on his head and leaned forward with elbows on his knees. "So if a Gutenberg Bible is worth that much, how much for his diary?"

"It's like anything else. It's worth only what someone is willing to pay for it."

"How much would your father pay for it?"

A page lifted up in another gust of wind coming in through the door. Stella held her thumb against the page's edge and considered the question while gazing at a riot of flowers encircling a letter C. "Mark Twain said that Gutenberg's invention was the greatest in the history of the world. Presuming we could authenticate it and find its provenance, this book is worth more than everything my father owns."

"So it'd be worth a lot to the Nazis. You could buy a lot of ammo with your father's fortune."

"I doubt they want it for selling. The Nazis are collectors."

"The Nazis?" Nicky perked up and shot a glance at Stella. "The same guys who've been terrorizing Jews and chasing us? They don't seem to have refined tastes."

"All I know is that when Germany annexed Austria, my father was upset. I heard him say to my mother that all the Austrian art might be lost to Hitler's packrats and that they have no respect. That's why I wanted to go so badly."

"I'm missing something," said Nicky. "You wanted to go to Vienna *because* the Nazis are stealing the art?"

"They haven't gotten it all yet," she said, avoiding his gaze.

"Stella, what were you going to do?"

Her pointed little chin went up. "I was going to see it before Hitler proclaimed it degenerate."

"*And?*"

"And maybe I could help," she said.

"Help with what, exactly?" Nicky's voice got tight and strained.

"People have been emigrating and trying to get their best pieces out. I have a lot of luggage."

"You were going to smuggle art out of Austria under the Nazis' noses and you weren't going to tell me?"

"I didn't think you'd agree."

"Damn straight. You saw what they are. They'd have killed you."

"I didn't know it would be like that. It was calm before."

Nicky cocked an eyebrow at her.

"Sometimes, I read the papers. The annexation was fairly peaceful. I could've done it if that Von Rath thing hadn't happened."

"Does your father know about this?"

"Of course not," she said with a sniff.

"What about your mother?"

"Don't be ridiculous."

Nicky gritted his teeth so hard Stella winced at the sound. "Uncle Josiah. He put you up to this."

She shrugged. "It was the perfect opportunity. Your family has connections to the German government and we're on our honeymoon. No one would've suspected us."

"Well, the Nazis definitely suspect us now."

"Not because of my little plan."

"I presume the art you planned on stealing belongs to Jews," said Nicky.

"Not steal. Smuggle. I would give it back once they got their passports approved. And I don't know if they're Jews. It hardly matters."

"To the Nazis, it matters more than anything else."

"Then they're idiots," she said.

"They're anything but stupid. Who were these people you were going to *help*?"

"The Rothschilds, the Block Bauers, the Kronsteiners. Uncle Josiah says Adelaide Kronsteiner has been selling off some of her collection of Dutch masters and the prices are a crime. I have a blank check. If Adelaide needs money, Uncle Josiah says to give it to her."

"Jews," he said. "Stella, your family, don't they understand how the world works?"

Stella danced her fingers down the edge of the book, soaking in the significance. "'If you don't acknowledge the rules, you aren't bound by them.'"

"Josiah Bled?"

"My great grandmother Dorthea. She was a spy during the Civil War," said Stella.

Nicky looked at the boxcar's ceiling. "I'm afraid to ask, but which side was she on?"

"Actually, Dorthea was a double agent. The rebels thought she worked for them, but she was really with the North."

"She could've been hanged."

"Well, of course. She was a spy and a darn good one, too."

"What have I married into? Nobody said anything about your family being crazy."

"Untrue. You knew all about Uncle Josiah." Stella leaned over and gave him a kiss on the chin. "Would it really have made a difference?"

"I don't suppose it would've. You seemed so sweet."

"I am sweet."

"You're a lot more than that."

Stella's heart sank. She never imagined her family or their ideas would change how Nicky felt about her. "Is it okay?"

"It has to be. I love you." Nicky settled on the floor with his head propped up on the crate beside Stella's feet. "Are you sure that book is real?"

"I can't be positive. Why? What are you thinking?"

"Those letters printed on the backs of the pages. Maybe it's a code."

Stella bent over the open page and stared at a flower coiling around a capital T. "No. I think it's real. The work is incredible. It just feels real. Nobody would use this piece of art as a codebook."

"Not even the Nazis? They're not big on respect."

Stella chewed on her bottom lip, her eyes flitting over the pages before her. "True, but Abel was carrying it. Maybe it's a Jewish code."

"Well, the Nazis do seem to think there's a vast Jewish conspiracy to take over the world," said Nicky, his lips twisting into a wry smile. "That sounds even stupider out loud than it did in my head. I don't see

Abel being a part of any conspiracy, Jewish or otherwise. He's just a historian, a good man."

"We'll figure it out," said Stella.

"Well," said Nicky, settling his hat over his eyes. "I guess it doesn't matter whether it's a codebook, a diary, or something else anyway."

"What do you mean?"

"As dear old grandfather used to say, we're in a pickle. The Nazis will shoot us on sight if we try to give up the book. If we ditch it, they'll continue chasing us because they'll think we still have it."

"We're not getting rid of the book. I promised Abel."

Nicky shrugged. "Like I said, we can't anyway."

"We'll take it to Paris like we're supposed to."

"Like a virus, all we can do is pass it on."

"It's not a virus. It's a priceless object of art and literature."

Nicky took a deep breath and settled lower on the floor. "Maybe that's all it is. Makes sense, with that historian being with them. Certainly less dangerous than a codebook."

Stella flipped back to the portrait of the young woman in red chalk. "I suppose," she murmured.

CHAPTER 15

*T*he setting sun cast an orange glow over the countryside, making it seem warm and inviting instead of what it was, filled with people who would either hunt them down or turn them in. Stella, for the first time in her young life, saw enemies everywhere, instead of potential friends. When the train passed through towns, Nicky would slide the door shut and they would hold their breath. They heard voices in German and boots crunching gravel. Both sounded terribly threatening, but no one opened the door. The train would start up again and they would be able to breathe.

After one such stop, where the voices were at the door for the longest time, tears began to roll down Stella's cheeks unbidden. She reprimanded herself for defying her father and not learning German. He would've been happy and she would've known what those Nazis were saying, but no, she had to fight the language that the entire family could speak, except for her. "I'm an American. I speak English," she'd said with her nose in the air. Her mother said she would regret it and she did, most cruelly. Stella swore to God that she would learn German if those Nazis passed them by.

Just when she thought her lungs would burst, there was a sharp tap on the car and then the train, once again, started moving. She licked the tears off her lips and said a silent thank you, cuddling closer to Nicky. He was the only friend she absolutely had to have. The rest of them could go to the devil, except Abel, of course. Abel, they would save. Somehow.

Nicky opened the door when they were well out of town and a rush of cool air fluttered the pages of Abel's book. Stella lifted her coat collar and turned a page to look at the last of the woman's portraits. It was done in pencil and captured an aging face, but it retained the happiness of the earlier works.

Stella leaned on a crate as the train took a tight turn, jostling Nicky's sleeping form. He stirred, rubbed his face, and looked at his empty wrist. "I can't get used to not knowing what time it is."

"Can't say that it bothers me," said Stella without taking her eyes from the page. Maybe if she looked hard enough, Gutenberg would tell her the answer. What was it about the book that made it so valuable to the Nazis? The more she thought about it, the less she thought it was only the intrinsic value of the art that kept them coming with guns blazing.

Nicky had no such interest. He stretched beside her. "Stop looking at that. You'll ruin your eyes."

"You sound like my mother."

"Not funny."

Stella smiled at him. "A little funny."

"Very little."

Nicky reached over and delicately closed the book. "Really. It's too dark for reading now."

Stella stared out through the open door at the countryside, sitting up straight and knitting her eyebrows together.

"What is it?" Nicky asked.

"I keep thinking there has to be more to it."

"More to what?"

"The book." She shifted on the crate to face him with the book on her lap. "They've spent a lot of time and money chasing us."

"It's one of a kind. You said so yourself."

"That's true of almost everything in the art world. Maybe there is a code hidden inside. It's a lot of effort for something they'll just stick in a vault somewhere."

"The Nazis aren't always logical. Look at what they did in Vienna. It's pointless, punishing people for nothing and all that destruction. It's going to cost a pretty penny to fix everything."

"They'll probably just charge the Jews," said Stella.

Nicky turned to her with a look like she'd just slapped him. "I hadn't thought of that."

"It makes sense though, doesn't it?"

"I'm afraid it does." Nicky touched his lower lip and his brow furrowed. "Do Jews own a lot of art?"

"I told you my family doesn't make that kind of distinction. Art people are art people," she said, a tad bit frustrated.

Nicky didn't seem to notice. He drummed his long fingers on a crate and said, "They must. You were going to help the Rothschilds. Even I know they're great collectors."

Stella pressed the book to her chest. "So?"

"So charging the Jews for what happened to them would be another way to get at their collections."

"I don't know. Sounds like something Ming the Merciless would do."

Nicky arched an eyebrow at her.

"What? My brothers love Flash Gordon. We read the strip every Sunday."

"You read Flash Gordon?"

"Lots of people do."

"I'm just trying to picture you reading about Ming the Merciless next to leaves from a Gutenberg bible."

"We read Flash in the breakfast room, not the study."

"Well, it all makes sense then. Except you're wrong. Ming wouldn't charge the Jews for his mess. He'd just kill them."

Stella shuddered and looked back out the door. "Do you smell that?"

They stood up and peered out into the growing darkness as the train began to slow down.

Nicky took a deep sniff. "What?"

"I bet those are barley fields. Don't close the door."

"I have to."

"Not this time." Stella began wrapping it in its oil cloth and paper as fast as she possibly could.

"What are you doing?" Nicky asked.

"It's time to get off. Those are barley fields. Someone's brewing in the neighborhood."

"I don't smell anything. I don't even see anything."

"There's a brewery nearby. The town must be on the other side of the train."

"What are the chances that it's Hans Gruber's brewery? There have to be dozens of breweries in Austria."

"Try hundreds, but it doesn't matter. My father's support kept breweries open all over Germany and Austria after the Great War. He's practically a hero here."

"He's not a hero to the Nazis," said Nicky.

"Brewers aren't Nazis. They're brewers. Beer before all," said Stella. "I should've thought of them before."

"Are you sure about this?"

"Absolutely. Brewers are a close-knit group. I'd trust them with my life."

Nicky frowned. "You may have to."

"We have to trust somebody sometime. A brewer is our best bet."

Nicky went to the door, looked both ways and leapt out. Stella ran to the edge and let out a breath when she saw him grinning up at her. The height wasn't nearly as dramatic as when they'd boarded. Stella handed the book to Nicky. He put it on the ground at his feet and then held his arms up for her. She crouched and sprang into his welcoming arms the way she had leapt into her father's when she was a child getting off a merry-go-round. Nicky enveloped her in his arms and she laid her head against his breastbone, listening to his heart. A chill wind brushed her cheek and she nuzzled in closer. How he could make her feel safe while they were on the run and in possession of one of the greatest finds in history baffled her, but he could, and she liked him all the more for it.

"We'd better go before someone sees us," he said.

Stella knelt to retrieve the book and placed it under her coat. Its pressure against her chest felt different now. Abel's package wasn't just a mysterious weight she'd agreed to carry but a gift she'd been allowed to share.

Nicky took her hand and they walked down the line of cars. On the other side of the train, distant shouts in German went back and forth. Nicky stopped abruptly.

"What?" asked Stella.

"I just realized that brewers are probably Jewish."

"So what?"

"Nazis here will be arresting the Jews."

Stella squinted at the few buildings on their side of the tracks. "I don't know. It's a small town, not like Vienna."

"The last town was small, too. That woman wasn't scrubbing the sidewalk because it was her job. I think it's probably happening every place the Germans control. They're nothing if not thorough. We might pick the wrong brewery."

"There's no such thing," hissed Stella.

"Do you want to lead the Nazis to a Jewish brewer's door?"

Stella bit her lip and shook her head. She hadn't thought of it like that.

"We just have to be careful," he said and they walked to the last car. Nicky made a motion for Stella to stay put and he walked around the end of the train with his practiced nonchalance. A moment later, he returned and waved her around the end.

"The SS are here, but we're in luck. They're further down and having some problems."

Stella stepped over the tracks and watched Nicky peer around the edge of the last car. He reached back for her hand and they stepped over another set of tracks. The station sat fifty yards away, casting late afternoon shadows on two groups of men facing off on the small plat-form. On one side, the SS stood in front of a group of ten men. Stella assumed they were Jews because of their disheveled appearance and because one was bent over as if in pain. On the other side, between the SS and the train stood four other men with firearms. They had their feet planted wide and there was a stubborn set look about them. One man wore a uniform different from the SS and he appeared to be the leader of the resistance. The men between the Nazis and the train had their mouths clamped into firm lines, even while the three SS officers shouted at them and waved their black batons in their faces.

"What's going on there?" asked Stella as they walked into the weeds beside the tracks.

"Local resistance. Maybe they don't like their fellow citizens being arrested for no good reason."

"Maybe we should help them," said Stella.

Nicky picked up his pace, his eyes shifting back and forth down the narrow dirt road, leading to a well-lit town in front of them. "What are we going to do? Whack the SS with your purse?"

"I don't know, but I'm tired of walking away."

"The better part of valor is discretion; in the which better part I have saved my life."

"You're quoting Falstaff to me? He's not exactly a hero, you know."

Nicky's quick pace faltered, but then he resumed his long strides with Stella trotting along beside him.

She squeezed his hand hard. "You're surprised that I know that quote, aren't you? You're a skunk."

Nicky flashed one of his brilliant smiles at her. "You're a pleasure."

"Yeah, yeah. Sweet talk will get you nowhere. I get it now. You never imagined I'd know Shakespeare and Flash Gordon."

"All right, I give. I'm surprised, but that doesn't mean I'm not pleased."

"You're still a skunk."

"But I'm your skunk," said Nicky, grinning widely. "Which way to the brewery?"

Stella surveyed the town. It lay in a small valley and seemed rather well off. The buildings were covered in cream stucco and lights twinkled in the twilight in a reassuring manner.

"I think we'll just have to take a look around. There could be more than one brewer in town."

They walked down the hill and into a residential area. The streets were silent, but unlike the other towns they'd been in, Stella found the silence comforting instead of threatening. Maybe it was the smell of dry hops flitting on the breeze or the barley fields surrounding the town. Those things reminded her of family and of long walks through fields with her father and Uncle Josiah, discussing the merits of one variety of barley over another. She could almost taste their brews, cool and mellow on her tongue.

Along with the brewing smells drifted the scents of many dinners being cooked. Murmurs came to her from behind shuttered windows along with the muffled sounds of German radio.

"This is a nice town," said Stella.

"I hope you're right." Nicky directed them onto a side street toward what looked like the business end of town. "Look, there's a restaurant. Do you think we can trade my shoes for a pretzel?"

"I don't think we'll have to. That's a brewery restaurant." She pointed at the sign which read "Wirtshaus Biermann."

"I don't think we should go in the restaurant. Too many people will see us."

"You're right. We should try the family home. It looks like the brewery is attached to the restaurant, so the family home might be, too."

Stella led the way past the restaurant and down an alley. The yeasty smell of brewing beer grew stronger and she tugged on Nicky's arm in an effort to make him go faster. It smelled so much like home that she half expected to hear her father's booming voice echoing against the walls.

They found an open archway that revealed a small enclosed court-yard paved with square stones worn smooth over time. Two of the sides were connected buildings. The rest of the courtyard was enclosed with high walls and a wrought iron gate. One building had several empty wagons parked under an overhang with large arched doors. Barrels were stacked three deep between the doors. The other building was homier with curtains in the windows and crisscrossed burnt timbers bracing the walls up to a pitched roof covered with dark green tiles.

"Should we just go up and knock?" asked Nicky, his expression doubtful.

"No, that's the back door. They use that for access to the brewery. We need the front door."

They backed out of the archway and walked alongside the wall, passing the wrought iron gate and rounding another corner. Two turrets loomed over the sidewalk with exaggerated pointy princess hats on top of them. One was open like a porch and the other was enclosed with large leaded glass windows. The front of the building was a combination of red stone, which ringed the windows and formed the foundation, and painted woodwork in red, yellow, and green.

"Wow," said Nicky. "This is definitely the front."

Stella marched up to the open turret. She had to do it fast or she'd lose her nerve, but she had no idea what she should say. She couldn't think about it. The more she thought, the more nervous she'd get. Above all, they had to appear normal, not like they were running for their lives. Nicky would look calm in front of a firing squad, but she had no such faith in herself.

They climbed the red stone stairs, so worn they had a dip in the middle, and stood in front of the door. Luckily, her stomach was empty or she'd have thrown up on the nice braided mat. Nicky lifted the knocker in the shape of a bouquet of hops flowers and let it drop with a resounding thud.

It took a few minutes, but finally, the large arched door swung open. A middle-aged woman with faded blonde hair and a silk-flowered dress looked at them with raised eyebrows. She said something in German. It amazed Stella how German could sound so different depending on the person it was coming from. This woman made German sound warm and welcoming, unlike the SS whose every word sounded like a death threat.

"*Sprechen Sie Englisch?*" asked Stella. That phrase was one of the few she couldn't avoid learning.

The woman shook her head.

Stella tapped her chest. "I'm Stella Bled Lawrence of the Bled Brewing Family. Bled Brewing in Missouri."

The woman knitted her sparse eyebrows. "Bled?"

"Ja. Ja. Bled." Stella turned to Nicky. "Do you have my passport?"

He handed the passport over and smiled at the woman, who was appraising his fine form in a frank manner. Stella opened the passport and pointed at her name.

"See, Bled. Bled Brewery," Stella said.

The woman nodded and waved them inside into a large and inviting entrance hall. Several pieces of heavy black walnut furniture lined the walls with antlers and framed newspaper articles hung above them. Stella stepped onto a thick hand-woven rug and smiled. The smell of dinner wafted around them and it made her dizzy with hunger. She dared not open her mouth or drool might slip down her chin.

"Bled," said the woman again.

Nicky and Stella nodded as a little blonde head peeked around a doorway. Pale blue eyes blinked at Stella and then the head disappeared.

"Elsa," said the woman, and the head came back.

The woman said something else in German and the little girl came into the room. She kept her head down but snuck glances at Nicky and Stella from under long, pale eyelashes. Her mother said something to her that included the name Bled several times and the girl took off at a run through another door. The mother folded her hands in front of her and waited with such patience that Stella couldn't decide whether she planned on waiting hours or minutes.

The time gave Stella a chance to give the woman a good look and she decided that she must be the brewer's wife. Her hands were large and used to men's work. Stella wished she'd taken her fancy fur off, although the woman didn't seem to notice it. She was much more taken with Nicky.

The little girl returned quickly with a big grin, pulling the hand of an enormous man wearing suspenders over a work shirt, leather pants, and scuffed work boots. He looked them over and the room swam in front of Stella's eyes. What if he didn't believe she was a Bled, or worse, what if he didn't care?

"Good evening," the man said in heavily-accented English. "My wife says you are from Bled Brewery in America."

"Yes, sir," said Nicky, removing his hat. "My wife is Stella Bled Lawrence, daughter of Aleksej Bled. She insisted we drop in to say hello."

The gruff man blushed to the roots of his thinning silver hair. He grabbed Nicky's hand and pumped it so hard he almost dropped his hat. Then he turned to Stella, who nearly stepped back in the face of such enthusiasm. "Mrs. Bled, it is an honor. Your family is always welcome here in our home." He grabbed her hand. Stella braced herself, but he only kissed it with a flourish. "Come, you stay with us here."

"Sir, we wouldn't wish to be any trouble," said Nicky.

"No, Sir," said the man. He patted his chest. "Please to call me Ernst and this is my wife, Klara and daughter, Elsa. We Biermann owe the Bled family much." He shook his head sadly. "The war. But that is over now. You stay with us."

Ernst looked at his wife, who nodded with less enthusiasm, but with the same amount of warmth. She gestured around their feet and said hesitantly, "Boxes?"

"Yes, yes," said Ernst. "Where is your luggage?"

Nicky twisted the brim of his hat. "Well, sir. I mean, Ernst. Our luggage has been lost."

"Ah, yes. These things happen. No matter." He gestured to his wife. "Klara will give you something to get you through."

Elsa darted over and grabbed Stella's hand. She pulled Stella toward a twisting staircase at the back of the hall.

"Elsa will show you your room," Ernst called out. "Then come to dinner."

Elsa led them up the staircase. She jabbered away, half in English and half in German. All Stella really understood was that she was very happy to have American guests. She brought them to a large bedroom with more black walnut furniture. The room was large and well-appointed with a dressing table and a wardrobe big enough to live in. Elsa bounded around, opening drawers and patting the bed. Stella placed the book in one of the drawers Elsa opened. When the little girl wasn't looking she locked the drawer and palmed the key. Then Stella took off her coat and hat and laid them on the bed. Elsa came over and touched them with a delicate fingertip. Stella draped the coat over the girl's thin shoulders and perched the hat on her tiny head.

"I think we found a friend," said Nicky.

"We could use one," said Stella.

Elsa took the pearl-tipped hatpin out of the hat and jabbed it at Nicky like a sword. Nicky feinted to the left, and then the right. He tossed his hat on the nightstand and led Elsa around the room in a merry chase. She giggled and thrust the pin toward him as he used the wardrobe door as a shield.

"We should've traded that pin for the night in the turnip room," he said as Elsa crawled under the door and let out a fresh stream of giggles at his surprise.

"Never," said Stella. "It's a family heirloom."

Nicky jogged around the bed with Elsa in hot pursuit, dragging Stella's fur coat behind her. "Couldn't Great Grandma have given you a chair or a clock like normal people do?"

"Could be worse. Lucien got a pistol and Ansel got a dagger."

"I should've known."

Klara appeared in the open doorway with a wrinkled brow. She said something stern to Elsa, who went to attention and formally handed over the pin to Nicky. He bowed and took it with a smile. Klara came in and gave Stella a pile of clothing.

"You change for dinner?" Klara asked.

"You do speak English," said Nicky.

"Very little," she said, blushing.

"Your English is better than our German," said Stella after she'd inhaled the wonderful scent of clean laundry.

"I try do better," said Klara.

"You do very well indeed," said Nicky. "And we will change for dinner. Thank you very much for the clothes."

"Our happiness," said Klara as she plucked Stella's hat and coat off Elsa. Then she shooed her daughter out of the room and then backed out herself, closing the door.

Stella laid the clothes on the bed and chose a cream-colored dress with red embroidered tulips on the front. It hung on her, but when she tightened the back ties it fit rather nicely. Nicky put on a clean white linen shirt and a gray flannel suit with a high band at the waist. Stella couldn't decide if he looked like he was going hunting or golfing.

"I never thought I'd be so happy to put on somebody else's clothes," said Stella, admiring herself in the full-length mirror.

"I second that," said Nicky. "Shall we go down?"

"Definitely. I don't smell any turnips, do you?"

"I don't, but you wouldn't hear me complaining if I did. I was considering selling my shoe leather before we got here, remember?"

Stella took his arm and opened the door. "I'm glad it didn't come to that. You have awfully nice shoes."

"I should. You picked them out. Never looked at the price, as I recall."

"It was Paris. You don't ask prices in Paris. If you have to ask, you can't afford it."

Stella led the way down the hall to the staircase. She swallowed as a wave of delicious smells greeted her.

"I hope we never shop in Paris again."

"I hope we do, because that means we made it there."

Nicky squeezed her hand when they reached the bottom of the stairs. Elsa ran up and grabbed Stella's other hand. She dragged her through several rooms, including a library with floor to ceiling books and a formal parlor. When they got to the dining room, Ernst and a small group of men, all resembling Ernst, stood up.

"Welcome, welcome," said Ernst in his lovely accented English.

Stella blinked away tears. Now that Ernst's enthusiasm had waned somewhat, he sounded more like Abel. His soft Austrian intonation reminded her that only a few days earlier Abel would've greeted her with the same openness and pleasure. Nicky saw her distress and squeezed her hand before answering Ernst.

Klara rushed over to escort them to their seats, her face worried. Stella smiled reassuringly at her, finally extricating Abel from her mind. Twisting herself up wouldn't help him. As Nicky said, the best they could do was get away and they were proving to be quite good as it, if she did say so herself.

She put a fine linen napkin on her lap and a young servant girl came in, placing a large tureen smelling of veal on the table. Then Ernst served each of them while keeping up a running commentary on the weather.

Klara kept a close eye on Stella when she took her first bite. The soup was a clear broth with rectangular dumplings stuffed with veal and cheese. Tears rose afresh in Stella's eyes and the sheer enjoyment of it pushed Abel firmly to the back of her mind.

"Klara, this is the most wonderful soup I've ever had," she said.

Klara blushed and thanked her. The rest of the meal matched the soup in quality and taste, from the beef stew spiced with paprika to the lovely chocolate cake with apricot jam between the layers. After the first course, Ernst couldn't contain himself anymore. He pelted Stella with questions about the Bled brewing operation despite Klara's repeated attempts to get him to let her alone.

Nicky watched Stella from across the table, often hesitating with his fork halfway to his mouth when Ernst asked a particularly complex question involving ratios or wort. Stella smiled at him and answered Ernst's questions, happy to lose herself in something she understood almost without thinking about it. Ernst served several of his brews and was anxious for her to sample and give her opinion. They were all excellent, but the best was a hefeweizen. Ernst's yeast struggled just the right amount and there was a hint of banana. Stella complimented his precision and the brewers all beamed when Ernst translated her assessment.

When dinner was over, Stella excused herself to lie down while the men went to the smoking room. She climbed the stairs with the swiftness of a two-ton elephant, her brain clogged with exhaustion, beer, and rich food. The bed invited her to lie down for just a moment, but she managed to open the drawer and get the book before she complied.

Without even taking off her shoes, she flopped back on the bed and fell into a deep sleep with the book on her chest, her arms crossed over it. It seemed only seconds before the book was lifted away. She managed to open her eyelids enough to see the person taking it was only Nicky, and then she fell back asleep. When she woke again, the room was dark except for a lamp on a small desk she hadn't noticed before. Nicky sat at the desk, hunched over with a fountain pen in one hand and a fingertip poised over the book.

"What are you doing?" Stella asked, her nose peeking over the edge of the thick down comforter.

Nicky started and turned to her. He had an ink smudge on his chin and he looked more studious than she'd ever seen him. She didn't even know he could look studious. He didn't have that kind of face.

"I figured out the language," he said.

Stella sat up. "You know what it's written in?"

"I don't know why I didn't recognize it immediately," he said. "It's Latin."

"You know Latin?"

"I studied it in school. Didn't you?"

"What use is Latin? Since we were tutored at home, we studied what was useful for the business." In Stella's case, she studied nothing at all. Her brothers were much more compliant. They seemed to think they had to impress their father. Stella never had that sense. She knew brewing, backward and forward, and that was enough.

"I can't say I'm good at Latin or that it's ever been useful before, but I found an old book of translations in Ernst's library."

"What does the book say?"

"It starts when Gutenberg's living in Strasbourg and training to be a goldsmith. There's a lot about techniques, I think. Remember, this is a rough translation."

"Nothing that makes it particularly valuable to the Nazis?"

"I've only done the first page."

"Do you think Abel could read it?"

Nicky leaned back. "He speaks five languages. It's possible."

"I wonder how he got it?"

"He's a historian. I suppose he must know people."

"And those people know he has it. They must've told the Nazis," said Stella.

"I think I know why Abel said not to give it up, even for him."

Stella raised her eyebrows. "It does have a code then?"

"Maybe. It's going to take forever to translate it. But listen, Nazis aren't great lovers of books, are they? He probably thought they'd burn it."

"No. I don't buy it. They wouldn't spend all that time and money just to burn it, unless there's something in there they don't want people to know about."

Nicky gazed down at the book, rubbing the pen between his thumb and forefinger. "If there's something to be found, I'll find it. Eventually."

"You get right on that." Stella got up, yawning, and changed into a nightdress worthy of her Victorian great-grandmother. She padded over to the desk and kissed Nicky on the back of the neck. He mumbled something as he wrote on the pad next to the book. Nissa.

CHAPTER 16

*L*ate the next morning, Stella and Nicky followed Ernst and his brother Johannes past huge copper kettles with workers analyzing gauges to what she thought was a tasting room. Johannes called it something else. Neither he nor Ernst could figure out what the translation might be. Ernst finally threw up his hands, laughing, and invited them to take a seat at a long wooden table while Johannes rustled around behind an enormous bar that ran the length of the room.

Ernst put a dozen tasting glasses in front of them and Johannes brought bottles of beer. Johannes pressed his thumbs under the metal wire of a bottle stopper and the ceramic plug popped up with a satisfying fump. He tilted a glass and poured the beer from a good six inches above the rim. It transformed into lovely golden foam inside the glass with just a little beer pooling at the bottom. He poured three more beers into four glasses each.

"I've never seen anyone pour a beer like that before," said Nicky.

"It's the proper way," said Stella. "Americans don't do it much."

"Your family does, yes?" asked Johannes.

"We do, but only at home. If we did it that way in the tasting rooms or restaurants, people would think we were wasting their time."

"People hurry in America?" asked Ernst.

"Usually," said Nicky, who fingered the lip of the glass in front of him as if he couldn't imagine why that was.

"Here in Austria we don't hurry, but we use our time well as we will now," said Ernst as his face grew sober.

Stella glanced at Nicky, whose finger stopped moving on the glass.

"We do not wish alarm you," said Johannes.

The beer grew in the glasses as the foam diminished. Stella waited for Nicky to say something, but he sat silent, his implacable mask in place.

"Should we be alarmed?" asked Stella.

"Not at the moment. They don't know you are here," said Ernst, inching a glass toward Stella's hand. "Drink, now."

"Who's they?" asked Nicky, breaking his silence.

"The party. The SS," said Johannes with a frown.

"Don't worry. We don't tell them you're here," said Ernst.

"Did you know about our situation last night when we knocked on your door?" asked Stella.

Ernst shrugged. "We had idea of who you are. When they came for the Jews, they tell everyone they looking for two Americans, man and woman. They say you are dangerous criminals."

"Why did you ever let us in?" asked Nicky.

"They say the same thing about Jews," said Johannes, his dark blue eyes squinting in anger.

Ernst sipped the beer in front of him and licked his lips. "We wouldn't have let you in, but Klara said you were Bleds. The SS didn't say that."

"We're not criminals," said Nicky, taking a sip of his beer.

"It doesn't matter if you are," said Ernst. "You're Bleds."

"Just to be clear, we're not criminals or Bleds." Nicky downed the rest of the beer. "We're Lawrences. Me by birth. Stella by marriage."

The brewers nodded, but Stella could tell they were still Bleds to them.

"You like?" Johannes gestured to Nicky's glass.

"It's excellent," said Nicky. "Ernst, Johannes, I'm sorry we put you in this position."

"We were trying to get to Hans Gruber, but we were stuck," said Stella.

"Hans?" Ernst perked up. "You know Hans?"

"Not personally, but he and my father are great pals."

Ernst stroked his chin, his face brightening. "We will get you to Hans. He has great pull in the party. He will fix your problem."

"When you say party, you don't mean the Nazi party, do you?" asked Nicky. His mask remained in place, but there was a tiny twitch in the corner of his mouth.

"Yes, of course."

"Of course," whispered Stella. If Hans was a Nazi, maybe they shouldn't go there after all. Her eyes met Nicky's and she could tell he was thinking the same thing.

"It is business," said Johannes with a slight curl of distaste on his upper lip.

"One must do what one must do," said Ernst, handing Nicky another glass and looking pointedly at Stella's.

She lifted her glass obediently, as if her father had given her the look, and took a sip. The beer was mellow on the tongue with hints of clove. "Very nice."

"You're in the party," said Nicky.

It wasn't a question, but Stella wished he'd made it one. Saying it that way made it so final, so real. They were staying with Nazis.

"We're party members. One must to do business. We all understand," said Ernst.

Johannes grimaced and Ernst gave him a sharp look.

Nicky turned to Johannes. "Business is not always easy. My family has contracts with the German government."

Johannes grumbled.

"My brother does not approve of joining the party," said Ernst.

Johannes reddened. "If they tell us who to employ, they tell us how to brew."

"It did not happen," said Ernst, banging his glass on the table.

"It did."

Nicky and Stella glanced around in confusion. Stella wasn't sure what they were talking about anymore.

"One of our workers was arrested," said Ernst.

"He's Jewish?" asked Nicky.

"He is."

"Did they put him on a train?" asked Stella, thinking of Abel.

"No." Johannes smiled.

"Our cops, as you might say, stopped them," said Ernst.

"I think we saw that at the train station," said Nicky.

"We should've stood with them on the platform. Samuel did nothing."

"We have a business to protect," said Ernst.

Johannes downed another beer and stalked from the room.

"My brother," said Ernst. "He doesn't understand these things will pass."

"I hope you're right," said Nicky.

"I'm right. What else could it be? It cannot stay this way."

"How will you get us to Hans?" asked Stella, not sure what they should do, but it was the only plan they had.

"I drive you myself when the SS and brown-shirts leave town." He shrugged. "A couple of days. They give up on the Jews soon. Like Johannes say, they do nothing."

Klara called for Ernst from some distance away in the brewery. He excused himself and they waited with cool glasses in their hands.

"This is quite a situation," said Nicky.

"You said that on the train to Vienna," said Stella.

"I did, didn't I?"

"This is all my fault. I should've listened. If I had, Abel wouldn't be in that camp and we wouldn't be here."

Nicky reached across the table and took her hand in his. "There's more than enough fault to go around. You're the least culpable as far as I'm concerned."

"I knew you were worried and all I cared about was our stupid grand tour." Tears pricked her eyes, shame burning away in her chest, a forever flame.

"You cared about more than that."

Stella looked away from her husband, remembering the smoke, the screaming, and the blood in the street. "I thought I could save some artwork and have a little adventure. I never thought the Nazis would hurt anyone."

"I bet a lot of people are saying that right now. I should've told you what I knew. Hitler has a particular hatred of Vienna. I knew the situation would be bad after Von Rath."

"For the Jews, you mean," said Stella.

"Mostly, but hatred has a way of spilling over, although I never imagined we'd have the SS knocking on *our* door in the middle of the night. I thought...I thought we were special."

"No one's special to them," said Stella. "Do you think Abel had any idea? He tried to get us off the train."

Nicky finished another beer, a doppelbock dunkel that smelled of molasses even at a distance. "He didn't try that hard. He told me he was worried about a crackdown on the Jews, rioting and the violence that usually accompanies it. I never got the impression he was personally afraid. Unlike most people, he planned for the annexation and its aftermath."

"How'd he do that?"

"He became invisible. He sold his half of the business to Albert, closed his accounts, and kept absolutely nothing in his name. He moved everything to Swiss banks."

"Too bad it didn't work."

"It did work. He became Albert's employee and Albert filed paperwork saying he was irreplaceable. That, combined with the fact that he had nothing, kept the Nazis at bay. If it wasn't for the book and Von Rath's murder, he'd probably have been fine."

"So he never said anything about the SS being after him?"

"I don't think he knew. There was that historian, but I think Abel thought he could handle him."

"Following us on the train was pretty creepy. I wonder how long he was following us."

"I first saw him in Paris."

"When in Paris?" Stella sat up straight.

"About the time Abel started wearing the overcoat."

The image of Abel enveloped in his coat bloomed in Stella's mind. She knew that coat so well, the beautiful stitching, the tortoise shell buttons. "I sometimes wondered if he slept in it."

Nicky stroked Stella's hand. "Abel put that coat on and I never saw him without it again."

"Abel had the book under that coat on the train to Vienna. Do you think he wore the coat to hide it?"

"Probably."

"So he must've gotten the book in Paris. That's when he started wearing the coat. Maybe he got it from his family. They live in Paris. Why in the world would they give him the book, knowing where he was going?"

"They didn't know. He didn't know. We were all over the place. We didn't stick to the itinerary."

"So it is my fault." Stella looked down and rolled the beer glass between her palms.

"If you're going to say that, you have to say it's Abel's fault, too. He could've told us what was going on."

"I suppose so, but I don't want to say it's his fault. What do you think he was going to do with the book?"

"He mentioned Gaspard, a cousin in Greece. Maybe he was just a courier. We were supposed to go to Greece after Italy."

The sound of footsteps echoed around the room. Stella and Nicky turned to look at the archway, expecting Ernst or Johannes returning. Instead, the serving girl from the night before walked in carrying a large tray with two beer steins. She stopped short when she saw them. The steins rattled on the tray and the color drained from her face. Nicky opened his mouth to say something, but she turned on her heels and fled.

"That doesn't look good," said Stella.

"I should say not." Nicky stood up. "Ernst has been gone too long. He doesn't strike me as an inattentive host."

Stella's chair made a loud scraping squeal as she stood. The sound set her on edge and it wasn't a far trip. She was a rabbit now, always ready to run. But maybe it was nothing. It was about time for something to turn out to be nothing. They went to the door and looked out into the brewery. The big copper kettles gleamed alone. Nicky turned her around and they went by the kettles past the main staircase.

"Where are we going?" asked Stella.

"Servants' stair."

"How do you know where it is?"

"My brother Charles taught me to always have an escape plan." Nicky flung open a small inconspicuous door and pushed Stella up the narrow stairs.

Stella hurried up to the third floor. "What was Charles escaping from?" she asked between gasping breaths.

"Fathers, mostly," said Nicky, leaning forward and pressing his ear against the third-floor door.

"I don't hear anything," said Stella.

"Neither do I. Let's get the book first, and then we'll figure out what's going on," said Nicky, opening the door.

Stella ran down the hall ahead of him, pulling the key out of her pocket and going straight to the nightstand, her tongue dry and fat in her mouth. She unlocked the drawer and almost sank to her knees in relief at the sight of the book lying just the way she'd left it.

Nicky picked up their hats and coats. "Just in case."

"Are you as scared as I am?" asked Stella.

"I refuse to think about it." Nicky ushered her into the hall and looked both ways.

He guided her to the main staircase and looked over. He shook his head and shrugged. Stella pointed at the windows that overlooked the courtyard. They walked down the hall, their heels making sharp exaggerated sounds on the hardwood floor. Nicky reached the window a step ahead of Stella. But before she could look out, he yanked her to the side of the window.

"What?" she asked in a whisper.

"The SS and they've got Ernst."

Stella clamped her hand over her mouth. Then she ducked under the window and came up on the other side.

"Careful," said Nicky.

Stella peeked out through the lace curtain. Behind the wagons in the courtyard were two shiny black sedans and one truck. A dozen brown-shirts were climbing out of the back. They scanned the area with weapons at the ready as if they were hunting master criminals.

Ernst stood in front of the sedans talking to a couple of SS officers. Next to a sedan stood the historian and the female SS officer. Her hat was pulled low and Stella couldn't see her eyes, but she was sure those hard, beady things were darting around like the viper she was, looking for some sign of them. The historian leaned on the sedan, his hands in his pockets. Ernst raised his hands, not in a gesture of surrender but as if he didn't know what they wanted. One of the SS started past him. Ernst stepped in front of him, shaking his head. In one fluid gesture, the officer raised his baton and backhanded Ernst across the face with it. He went down, writhing in the dirt.

"Oh my God," said Stella through the lace.

The officer kicked Ernst in the ribs as he jerked on the ground. The historian leapt forward, shouting something, but the female SS yanked him back. They argued while the other officer kicked Ernst in the stomach.

"Stella, you run. I'll turn myself in," said Nicky.

"You both run." Johannes appeared out of the servants' stair.

"They're beating your brother for information about us," said Nicky.

"It's too late. He already told them he doesn't know anything about you. If they find you here, that lie is enough to send all of us to a camp." Johannes pulled Stella away from the window. He pushed her into the servants' stair and grimly directed her downward.

CHAPTER 17

*J*ohannes led them into the bowels of the house through boiler rooms, workshops, and storage areas. They emerged on the other side of the brewery in a smaller courtyard. A pair of brown draft horses with blond manes and fetlocks stood in the middle at the head of a sturdy wagon loaded with brand-new barrels. A slight man with his cap pulled low waited at the head of one of the horses, his hand on the bridle.

"Samuel," said Johannes. Then he continued in German.

Samuel went to the seat of the wagon and retrieved a hammer. He gave it to Johannes and nodded at Nicky and Stella. She wanted to say she was happy he didn't go to the camps, that someone had the strength to stand up to the SS for him and the rest of the town's Jews, but nothing would come out.

"We put you in these barrels," said Johannes.

Stella turned from Johannes and saw the two barrels on the end had their tops askew.

"Will we be able to breathe?" she asked.

"We won't seal you in."

Nicky helped Stella up onto the backboard of the wagon. At first, she wasn't sure if she'd fit, but up close, the barrel was more than big enough.

"What's the plan?" asked Nicky.

"Samuel will drive you to Hans Gruber's brewery. It will be several hours, but you should be safe in barrels."

Samuel climbed onto the backboard next to Stella. "Please to get in. Must hurry."

Nicky lifted Stella and she sat on the edge of a barrel, holding the book with one arm. He held her elbow as she swung her legs around and dropped inside. Nicky stuffed her coat in and carefully handed over her hat with its pin glinting in the sunlight. She looked at Johannes' grim face and opened her handbag.

"I'm so sorry, Johannes," she said, reaching out to hand him her father's gift, the Faberge cigarette case. "Please take this. It's quite valuable. You can pay for Ernst's doctor or something."

Johannes shook his head. "They will search all the property. If they find a trace of you, it will be very bad for us."

Stella withdrew the case. "We'll pay you back. Someday. I promise."

Johannes directed Nicky to get in the other barrel. "I fear we will need your help. My brother doesn't believe, but there will be another war."

Johannes gestured for Stella to crouch down. She squatted and took a deep breath as if it would be her last. She looked out from the darkness of the oak cask.

Samuel leaned over with the lid in his hand. *"Viel glück."*

The disk came over slowly like an eclipse of the sun, leaving Stella in blackness. Then the hammer struck the lid twice. Stella reached up and steepled her fingers against the wood and pressed. The lid held but gave just enough to hold down the rising panic in Stella's chest. Outside, the hammer struck again, twice, she assumed on Nicky's barrel. A slow minute passed before the wagon jerked forward. Stella lost her balance and fell against the side. She maneuvered her coat underneath her for padding and settled down with her legs folded up underneath her. The wagon began to move with a gentle sway, a rocking chair rhythm that soothed her frazzled nerves. She tried not to think about the SS seeing the wagon and running up to pull her barrel off to shatter in the street. She reminded herself that they were just another wagon. Nothing special about them at all. Nothing to raise the alarm. Samuel would be a common enough sight and since the local police had stood up to the SS to protect him, she hoped he wouldn't have any more problems.

After some time, her breathing slowed and she wondered how Nicky was doing. She had plenty of room, but he'd have his knees around his ears. Hours like that would be quite painful and she wished they could talk. He could reassure her or maybe she would reassure him.

Stella wrapped her arms around the book and leaned against the side of the barrel as the swaying increased. She thought about her promise and began to go through the German she was supposed to have learned. Some came back quite easily. *Ich bin. Du bist. Er ist.* She'd had to recite that so she knew it in spite of herself. Then there was the German her parents spoke. They weren't German or Austrian, but they said German was the language of beer and they must know it. Her mother always said to her father when they were going out. *"Du gefällst mir."* Stella supposed it meant I love you, but it started with 'you', instead of 'I'.

She whispered the words until she thought they had made it out of town. Then she let her mind wander. The SS would still be searching Ernst's house and brewery for them so she didn't let it tarry there. She went to the first time she saw Nicky, smiling at her from the corner of his mother's cottage. She knew she would marry him in that perfect instance and that everything would be wonderful. And it was. Until they arrived in Vienna. Best not to think about that. She just kept thinking of Nicky's face. The swaying rhythm and the darkness sapped Stella's energy and her eyelids drooped. There was no reason to keep them open anyway and she soon fell asleep.

Stella awoke when the wagon hit a rut and her barrel knocked against Nicky's barrel and the back of the wagon. If the backboard hadn't been in place, it might've fallen off. She braced her arm against the side in case of another rut and rubbed her forehead where it'd struck the wood. Another bruise to add to her collection. Her nose still hurt from where she'd struck the train steps and now her legs ached with cramps. Several of her blisters had popped and her stockings had damp oozy spots on the heels and toes.

Once the wagon's rhythm was restored, she tried to get herself into a more comfortable position. The only one she found comfortable was so unladylike, Stella blushed to assume it. She couldn't imagine what her mother would say about her sitting with her legs crisscrossed, even if she was inside a barrel. Of course, Stella reminded herself that her mother would never imagine her in a barrel in the first place, so she should do what she liked.

She hiked up her skirt, shifted around, and crossed her legs. "Sorry, Mama," she whispered. "It had to be done."

Then she pulled her skirt back down as far as it would reach over her knees, as if someone could see her in Klara's tulip dress, sitting like a five-year-old. She smoothed the tulips on her chest and wondered if Klara had embroidered them herself. Then she jolted upright with her hand still poised on her chest. She was wearing Klara's dress. That meant her clothes were at Ernst's brewery and Nicky's clothes, too. If the SS found them, they'd have proof that the family concealed them. She thumped the palm of her hands against the top of the barrel. It lifted, letting in a sliver of light. She could get out, but what good would it do? They couldn't get back in time to warn Ernst. The SS would've already searched the house. She settled back against the side of the barrel and cried into her hands. Tears coursed down her cheeks and dripped off her chin. She could see Ernst and Johannes being shoved into a boxcar, both of them as badly off as Albert had been after his encounter with the SS. There was no use trying to talk herself out of this one. It was her fault. If they hadn't shown up on Ernst's doorstep, the SS would've had no reason to bother the family. And now they were headed to Hans Gruber's home, bringing their plague of misfortune with them.

The book lay in her lap. Its edges bit into her thighs and she ran her hand over the stiff brown paper. Abel thought the book was worth his life. That was his choice to make. She wasn't sure he was wrong. Books mattered, whatever the Nazis might say about it. Art made humans human and not just art that followed a party line, but art that challenged with its beauty, enlightened with its insight. Gutenberg changed the world with his invention. The book lying on her lap was the art of his soul, an entrance into his mind. How much was it worth and who else would have to pay to keep it safe?

She'd made a promise, a blind promise, as it turned out. But she wouldn't undo it if she could. She'd never have said no to a friend. If he'd told her what was in the package and what it meant, she'd still have taken it. But her 'yes' was hers alone and now she'd involved others. Ernst was suffering for her promise, and Johannes and Klara. She couldn't bear to think of little Elsa. Why had she seen Abel at the train station in Vienna? Out of the hundreds of men, why had her eyes found his face? Her mother would say it was God. Her father would say it was luck. But it amounted to the same thing. She'd seen him. And once she did, the book became her burden.

The wagon rolled to a stop and Stella's stomach lurched. Were they at Hans' home or had some lucky SS patrol spotted them? A minute later, the lid of her barrel lifted with a groan and she blinked up at the soft light raining into her cocoon.

"Mrs. Bled?" asked Samuel, looking down at her tear-streaked face. "What has happened?"

Stella wiped her cheeks, clutched the book to her chest, and held up her hand. Samuel hauled her to her feet and pain shot down her stiff legs.

"You have illness?"

"No, Samuel. I'm fine." Stella shielded her eyes until they adjusted. She heard a creak of wood and Nicky's voice came out of his barrel, distant and strained.

"Help me up, Samuel, will you?"

Stella dropped her hand and saw Nicky emerge out of his barrel. He held Samuel's hand with both of his and nearly pulled the smaller man in. Nicky wobbled and fell against the side. His face contorted in pain, his hair dark with sweat.

Stella reached out and touched his shoulder.

"Stella?" he asked, his eyes still closed.

"Yes. I'm here."

"Are you all right?"

"I'm perfectly fine." She turned to Samuel. "If you'll help me, we can get him out together."

Samuel took the book and placed it on another barrel. Then he lifted her onto the edge without the slightest trouble. She swung her legs around and stood next to the barrel. Her legs were quite wobbly and while she waited for them to steady, she looked around. Samuel had stopped the wagon in a small copse of trees just off a narrow dirt road. It was twilight and the dim light gave the countryside an indistinct and bluish cast. They could've been inside an impressionist painting, all soft and flowing. It was a lovely area. A large building a mile distant suggested a brewery, low hills surrounding it with a cozy majesty.

"I think I'm ready now," said Nicky.

Samuel and Stella braced Nicky's arms and he kicked a leg over the rim. Then he managed to get the rest of him out on his own. He still wobbled but soon began to look stronger.

He clapped Samuel on the shoulder. "I'm not going to lie to you, my man. That was a miserable experience."

"It was the best way to conceal you," said Samuel.

Nicky reached into Stella's barrel and fetched her hat, coat, and handbag. He handed them to her and watched with concern as she put on her coat and concealed the book underneath.

"I'm fine. Really," she said.

He pulled her to him. "You're tougher than you look."

"So are you."

"Did you just insult me?"

"Not at all. How would your brothers do stuffed into a barrel?" asked Stella.

"They'd never get in. One has claustrophobia and the other wouldn't want to muss his hair."

Stella kissed him on the cheek. "That's just my point."

"What's next, Samuel?" asked Nicky.

Samuel pointed to the building in the distance. "Hans Gruber's brewery. Coming in a barrel would be strange. You agree?"

"Excellent choice," said Nicky. "There's enough suspicious about us without arriving in barrels."

Samuel helped Stella off the wagon. He suggested they ride on the front, but they both wanted to walk. Stella went up to one of the horses and walked beside him with one hand on his warm neck. Samuel apparently didn't think he should ride when they were walking and came to the head of the horses and took control with a short lead rope, walking in silence. Nicky bent and stretched as he walked. His knees creaked and he groaned like an old man with gout. When they'd covered half the distance to the brewery, Stella decided to speak up. She could hardly bear to tell them about the clothes, but she couldn't pretend she didn't know.

"Samuel," she said. "You should consider staying here."

He glanced over at her with a raised eyebrow under his worn hat. "Why, Mrs. Bled?"

"Johannes said there could be no evidence of us in the house or they'd be sent to a camp." She gestured to the tulip dress. "We left our clothes in the guest room. I didn't realize it until it was too late."

Samuel nodded and kept walking. He said nothing, but Stella thought she saw his shoulders droop and his steps falter.

"I'm so sorry, Samuel."

He shrugged his shoulders and didn't look back at her again. "Nothing to do now. Klara maybe burn clothes. Maybe not."

Nicky ran his hand up and down her back. This comforting gesture brought fresh tears to her eyes. Nicky handed her one of Klara's crisp handkerchiefs.

"Dry your eyes, Stella darling. It wouldn't do to show up with a tear-streaked face."

Stella nodded and wiped her eyes. "Won't you stay, Samuel? I can't bear it if you're arrested because of us, too."

"I have a family. I must go back to them."

Stella couldn't think of a response. Samuel had left his family with the SS on the brewery doorstep to help them and now he had to go back to face the consequences. If the SS discovered they'd been at the brewery, they might figure out Samuel had helped them escape. Nicky looped his arm around her shoulders. They walked the rest of the way to the brewery in silence. The temperature dropped and Stella shivered despite her fur coat. The shadows loomed larger on the brewery and it wasn't until they were upon the structure that Stella realized how big it was, three times the size of Ernst's place. The ancient stone walls spanned the length of a city block. To one side, a bell tower and an enormous squat tower rose above the walls. Stella would've thought it was an abbey if she hadn't known better.

Samuel led the horses onto a cobblestone drive and they circled the building toward the tower. The horses' hooves clopped against the stones, making hard, hollow sounds. With each footstep, Stella found herself more fearful, afraid to knock on Hans' door, knowing the trouble they surely brought with them. She was afraid not to knock at the same time. But what else could they do? They couldn't go back.

They turned and walked under a large archway. The arch turned out to be a tunnel, and the wall surrounding the brewery wasn't just a wall. It was as thick as most houses. The tunnel wasn't lit and smelled of dirt and moss. It felt protected and safe like nothing else had since they arrived in Vienna. Stella's steps faltered and Nicky said, "What's wrong?"

"Nothing," she said and straightened up. If Samuel could return home to face the SS, she could surely knock on her father's friend's door.

They emerged in a courtyard much like Ernst's, only larger. A stable sat on one side. The horses whinnied and stomped their feet when they heard the visitors. Samuel's pair tossed their heads and whinnied back. He turned them toward the stable and looped the lead rope around an iron ring fixed to the wall. Stella and Nicky followed him across the courtyard to a set of double-wide stone stairs that led to a huge arched oak door with a black ring on it. Next to the door were two posts with ropes dangling from them. Samuel yanked on one of the ropes and a loud clang rang through the courtyard. Nicky jumped and Stella clutched her heart.

Samuel smiled a weary smile and yanked the rope a second time. "Hans hear his bell. Only he come for this bell. Knocking not loud enough."

"I guess not in a place like this," said Nicky as he glanced around at the buildings that surrounded the courtyard. On further inspection, they didn't match. The styles varied like someone stuck on additions whenever it suited them and they made little effort to keep a cohesive look.

Samuel rang the bell a third time and after a few more minutes, the door swung open. A man almost as tall as the door stepped out. He was as skinny as he was tall with a hawk nose and a bottle-green smoking jacket with a silver ascot knotted at the neck. Thinning silver hair swept back from his brow as if there was a strong wind blowing in the still and silent courtyard. He looked down at them with an expression so solemn he made Abel's sad expression seem ebullient.

Samuel took his hat off and said, *"Guten Abend, Herr Gruber."*

But the man wasn't paying any mind to Samuel. He was staring at Stella. She looked him in the eyes and stepped further into the light the open door cast.

"Stella?" he said.

She barely nodded before he bear-hugged her, knocking her hat onto the back of her head and sweeping her off her feet. Her ankles banged into each other as he swung her back and forth, a human pendulum. Then he set her down gently and took her face in his hands. A smile wreathed his face and Stella laughed out loud to see such an expression on his formerly stern face.

"Where have you been?" he asked. "Your father is frantic."

"I can't believe you recognize me," said Stella, still bubbling with laughter and relief.

"I'd know that face anywhere. You are the image of your mother. Her only gift to you, according to your father."

"He says I inherited her face and his soul."

"I don't doubt it. Your father always speaks the truth."

A gentle cough came from behind her, reminding Stella that they weren't alone. She backed out of Hans' hands and turned to Nicky.

"Mr. Gruber, may I present my husband, Nicky Lawrence of the New York Lawrences."

Hans took Nicky's offered hand and pulled him into another hug. Nicky was so startled he didn't open his mouth except to emit a whoosh as Hans squeezed the air out. Hans released him, all smiles, and turned to Samuel.

"Ah, my old friend, I shouldn't be surprised that it is you who deliver such a pleasant surprise." He shook Samuel's hand but didn't hug him.

Samuel glanced behind him at the wagon. "I must go."

"Not tonight. Stay and we will have a celebration."

"No. I must get back. I might get there before they know I'm missing," said Samuel.

Hans face darkened. "So it is not all good news."

"I'm afraid not, Mr. Gruber," said Nicky.

Samuel turned to Stella and Nicky. "You're safe now."

Nicky reached inside his breast pocket and took out his card. "We owe you, Samuel. And I don't say that lightly. If you need help with anything or anyone, you can count on my family."

Samuel nodded and took the card. He looked at it for a moment as if he were memorizing the words and numbers. He handed it back to Nicky. He exchanged a solemn look with Hans and then shook hands with Nicky and Stella before he returned to the wagon. He waved once and drove out of the courtyard through the archway whose darkness swallowed him at once.

"We have much to discuss," said Hans. "You have no luggage, I presume."

"We have nothing," said Nicky.

"We'll fix that." Hans opened the door wider and waved them inside.

Stella glanced back at the archway. The hoofbeats from Samuel's horses faded to nothing and she swallowed a lump in her throat. Nicky took her arm and she let him guide her through the doorway. Once inside, a wave of goodness washed over her. The smell of braised cabbage, roasted meat, and wood fires tickled her nose and brought a rush of saliva into her mouth. She hadn't realized how hungry she was.

Hans led them through a wide stone hallway. Stella expected to be greeted by a sumptuous room filled with beautiful antiques and delicate tapestries. Her parents had visited Hans several times and their descriptions didn't match what she was seeing. The walls were lined with barrels interspersed with several desks. Piles of paper and ledgers concealed the desktops and each barrel had a piece of paper lying on top.

"Please excuse the mess," said Hans. "This is our office area where we fill special orders and conduct most business. Samuel knew not to bring you to our main entrance." Hans smiled at Stella. "But perhaps you appreciate the business better than the beauty."

Stella smiled back but didn't trust herself to answer. She didn't want Nicky to know how involved she was in her father's business. He hadn't asked any questions yet. She wasn't sure how he would take it when he did. As far as she could tell, Nicky's mother spent her time attending tea parties and having her feet buffed.

Nicky cast her a puzzled look and then asked Hans, "Are these barrels all special orders?"

"Yes. We brew specialty beers. These barrels contain Samichlaus, our strongest brew, aged one year. We're filling Christmas orders. It's a busy time." Hans opened another arched door and ushered them into a library. Shelves covered the walls from floor to ceiling. Two rolling ladders of ornate carved walnut graced either side of the room. Stella touched the hissing serpent that extended off the handrail of the nearest ladder.

"Gorgeous," she said.

Hans smiled wider. "You have your father's eye."

Stella glanced past him to an elegant French empire desk. Above the shiny bird's eye maple hung a much older tapestry.

"Gobelin?" she asked, certain of the answer and of the piece's era.

"Yes. A new acquisition. Seventeenth century, as I'm sure you know."

"I thought it must be new. My father didn't mention it and he certainly would have."

Nicky coughed and shifted his feet. Hans glanced at him and immediately directed them to another door, smaller but of better quality. Stella guessed this was a door to the rest of the main house.

"You've chosen a good time to arrive," said Hans. "I'm hosting a party tonight with several dignitaries. I'd like to introduce you after you've freshened up. I'll just go tell them dinner will be slightly delayed."

Nicky stopped short when Hans said the word 'party'. Stella barely took notice of his change in attitude. She stepped eagerly forward. A party. Champagne. Food. It was just what she needed, a chance to be herself again. The Stella who existed before Vienna.

Nicky grabbed her arm and rocked her back on her kitten heels. She shot him a look over her shoulder and was surprised to find him looking at her with such stern intensity.

"What?" she asked under her breath.

"Party member," Nicky answered.

An icy shiver ran down her arms and she wobbled a bit as she turned toward Hans. She raised her hand and opened her mouth, but before she could stop him, Hans swung open the door. A rush of chattering German voices filled the library and Nicky yanked Stella out of the view of the open doorway. Hans stared at them with an open mouth.

A man's voice came through the door. "Herr Gruber."

Nicky and Stella jumped behind the door. Hans opened it wider, pressing them between the shiny walnut and books on Greek mythology. He answered the man in German. They conversed for several minutes as the icy shivers left Stella's arms, spread to her chest, and settled in the pit of her stomach. The voice was familiar and that couldn't be a good thing. Nicky stood behind her with his hands tight on her shoulders. She glanced up at him and he mouthed, "I know."

At last, Hans closed the door. He kept his palm against it like someone might try to burst in. "What is going on?"

Stella opened her mouth, but her throat constricted and she couldn't choke out a single word.

Nicky squeezed her shoulders and said, "We're wanted by the SS."

Hans' body jerked and the color drained from his face. "The SS? How is this possible?"

A loud knock rang through the library and the same voice asked a question.

"*Ein Moment,*" called Hans.

Nicky pushed Stella toward the other door to the offices.

"No. Wait." Hans rushed to a section of bookcase in the middle of the wall. He bent low and fumbled with something underneath a shelf. There was a faint click and the bookcase shifted. *The Collected Works of Shakespeare* sat an eighth of an inch in front of *The Collected Works of St. Teresa of Avila.* If Stella hadn't seen it happen, she wouldn't have noticed the difference.

Hans tugged on the bookcase and it swung out a few inches with a low groan. Nicky leapt forward and pulled the shelf all the way out. The wall opened to reveal a tiny dark room the size of a French elevator. Cobwebs and dust hung in the air and Stella would much rather have escaped through the office.

Another knock came, sounding more insistent and making Stella's heart pound.

"Get in," said Hans.

Nicky grabbed Stella and pushed her in ahead of him. A leather loop dangled from the back of the bookcase. Nicky caught hold of it and pulled it. The case groaned again and slowly swung closed. Stella fell back against the cobwebbed wall and clamped a hand over her mouth. Just as the case clicked closed, shutting out the light of the library, a voice said, "Herr Gruber, what are you doing?"

CHAPTER 18

*V*oices came through the bookcase, muted but intelligible. Stella bit her lip behind Nicky's back. The area was so tight her nose touched his jacket between his shoulder blades.

"Dr. Van Wijk," said Hans. "There you are. I'm looking for the book you mentioned earlier."

"Book?" asked the unfamiliar, accented voice. Stella guessed the speaker as Dutch.

"Yes, you remember. The Mainz diary. The contemporary of Gutenberg."

Stella squeezed Nicky's arm with her free hand. She wished she could see him, but the secret room was black. As her eyes adjusted, she began to pick up on tiny pinpricks of light around Nicky's shoulder, but they weren't enough to illuminate anything.

"Peiper is looking for you," said the Dutchman.

"Is he?" Hans sounded disinterested and there was a scraping noise on the bookcase. "Ah, here it is. Dr. Van Wijk, when you get to my age, you can't put things off or you'll forget what you wanted."

There was silence. And for a moment, all Stella could hear was the whoosh of Nicky's labored breath. She fought the urge to shush him. The man had to breathe. But did he have to do it so loudly?

"Dr. Van Wijk, are you looking for something else?" asked Hans.

"Eyes playing tricks on me."

"What tricks?"

"I thought I saw the bookcase shift when I came in."

Hans laughed. "And I thought it was just my old eyes. Gerta tells me my depth perception is off. Yours, too, it seems."

"It must be the height of the cases or the length of the room. I would've sworn…" said the Dutchman, sounding confused and disappointed.

"I won't tell anyone," said Hans. "You still want to see the book?"

"Yes, of course. Thank you. There are very few copies of this one around."

"I know. That's why I bought it," said Hans. "Shall we go back to the party? You said something about Peiper."

The Dutchman agreed and the voices faded away. Stella listened to Nicky's breathing slow, then she slipped her arm around his waist and rested her forehead on his spine.

"Problems with the SS?" asked a low voice.

Nicky jumped, ramming Stella's head back into the wall. She yelped, but her hand on her mouth muffled the sound.

"What the hell?" said Nicky.

Something sizzled, and the smell of sulfur filled the small room along with a warm yellow light. Stella peeked around Nicky's shoulder to find a man looking back at her. He was holding a lit match and was wedged in a space carved into the wall. The space looked to be about twelve inches wide. How he managed to cram himself in there, she couldn't imagine.

"I'm sorry. I didn't mean to startle you." The match flame wavered with the man's breath.

Nicky's left arm shot out. He grabbed a fistful of the man's rough grey jacket. The man blinked but otherwise didn't react. Nicky leaned toward him and the man cocked his head slightly, peering at them with ice blue eyes under a tattered driving cap.

"Quiet," the man whispered and blew out the match, leaving them in inky blackness.

Then Stella heard something getting close to the bookcase. Soft, purposeful footsteps advancing on them. Scraping sounds echoed around their tiny chamber. Books were being taken off the shelf and replaced. Stella held her breath. The Dutchman must not have bought Hans' excuse about the movement. She clutched the book tighter to her chest, feeling its edge bite into her breasts. Could he possibly find the catch that opened the case? Most of the noises came from the waist-high shelves. Maybe he wouldn't think to look lower. Then scraping sounds came from around ankle height and she clutched the book even tighter. Whoever it was had to be inches from opening the case.

Another voice spoke outside in the library. "Can I help you find something, Dr. Van Wijk?"

A woman's voice, low and lilting with a stronger Austrian accent than Hans.

"Mr. Gruber mentioned an obscure title on Mainz that he had. I'm afraid I was presumptuous in seeking it," said Dr. Van Wijk.

"Perhaps I can assist you," said the woman. "I'm familiar with all of Herr Gruber's books. What is the subject?"

Silence followed and Stella's lip twitched. The Dutchman was caught and he didn't have an answer.

"I believe it might have been a diary of some sort," said Dr. VanWijk finally.

"Mr. Gruber does not usually acquire diaries. He says people think their lives are scintillating, but they rarely are. There is one Mainz diary, however. He acquired it because of its rarity, not its subject."

The woman's voice got closer to the bookcase. "Let me see."

"Don't trouble yourself. It's unimportant," said Dr. Van Wijk.

"No, no. Here it is, lying on the shelf. Mr. Gruber must've pulled it for you himself."

"I should've seen it straight away. Thank you."

Their voices faded and after a few moments, the man struck another match. Its light flooded the chamber and Stella saw Nicky's fist still holding the man's jacket.

"I take it you weren't expecting me," whispered the man in a British accent.

"Who are you?" asked Nicky.

"I'm more interested in who you are."

Nicky raised his fist until it was pressed against the man's throat.

"Fine. I'll go first. Oliver Fip, at your service."

"What are you doing in here?" asked Stella.

Oliver shifted his gaze from Nicky's face to Stella's. "Same as you, I imagine. Hiding from the SS."

"What did you do?"

"Nothing, unfortunately."

"What does that mean?"

"It's better if you don't know," said Oliver. "I take it you're not part of the movement."

"Movement?" Nicky's arm relaxed, but he kept the man's jacket in his fist.

"I thought not. You don't look the type, but you must be vital or you wouldn't be in here."

Stella had never considered herself vital to anything and she wasn't sure she liked the idea. "I don't know about that."

"I do." Oliver blew out the stub of the match and lit another with a practiced flick of his thumb. "Hans wouldn't risk exposing me for anything less. May I have your names? I do believe I've earned them."

"Nicky Lawrence and this is my wife, Stella."

"Interesting," said Oliver. "A New York Lawrence on the run from the SS."

Stella blinked. Oliver knew who Nicky was. She couldn't believe they'd traveled all over Europe and found the one person who'd heard of the Lawrences hiding in a secret room.

"You know who I am?" asked Nicky, his voice flat and not nearly as pleased as Stella felt.

"It's my business to know."

"And what, exactly, do you know?"

"Your family is in shipping and has multiple contracts with the German government. Shall I go on?"

"Please."

"The Lawrences are conservative and quiet politically. Extremely wealthy but not self-indulgent. One of the sons, Charles, if I'm not mistaken, got a young woman pregnant when he was sixteen and now pays for the child's maintenance."

Nicky let his arm drop. "How did you know that?"

"Is it true?" asked Stella.

"It's true," he said, not shifting his gaze from Oliver. "*How* do you know that?"

"As I said, your family has contracts with Germany. It's our business to know. The Nazis know about your brother, too, by the way."

"Why would they care?" asked Stella.

Oliver smiled. "They care about everything. Every detail, every morsel of information they can use to their advantage. You might be interested to know that they don't know about the Jews on your payroll. Not yet, anyway."

"But you do." Nicky turned and knocked Stella into the wall again. "Sorry, Stella darling."

Stella wiggled closer to Oliver to make room and after a bit of maneuvering, they all stood facing each other with about twelve inches between them.

"That's better," said Oliver. "Now that you basically know who I am, why don't you tell me what you did to get yourselves in here?"

"I don't know who you are," said Stella.

Oliver looked at Nicky and straightened his tattered jacket.

"I think," said Nicky. "He's part of a German resistance movement."

"But aren't you British?" asked Stella.

"Thank you for noticing. Yes, I'm British."

"Then what are you doing in a German resistance movement?"

"I never said I was. But let me just say that resistance movements tend to be more multi-national than one would think," said Oliver with a smile. "Back to your particular troubles."

Nicky considered for a moment and then spoke. "We're on our honeymoon. Our tour guide was Jewish. He did something, I don't know what, and they think we helped him."

"Fine. If you don't want to tell me, don't tell me."

"He just told you," said Stella.

"Do you know who just showed up at Hans' little soirée? Ober-führer Peiper of the SS and a bunch of his henchmen. They make the Bolshevik army look like a pacifist movement. I don't rate that kind of hunt but apparently, you do."

"You don't know they're after us for certain."

"It has to be you," said Oliver. "Stella, you have known ties with Hans through your father. If I were the SS, this is where I'd start."

"So you know about Stella's family, too," said Nicky.

Oliver let his match go out and lit another. "I'm aware of the Bleds, mostly because they pertain to your family, Mr. Lawrence and, of course, I'm familiar with the beer. Excellent wheat brews."

"Thank you. What else do you know about us?" asked Stella, a little afraid of what Oliver might say. She imagined Nicky's father had checked out her family thoroughly, but it was one thing to know and another to hear it out loud.

"The Bleds are even less politically active than the Lawrences. They are felt to be more artists than businessmen. They have consid-erable ties in both Germany and Austria. The Nazis have reached out to the family several times in the past five years with various lucrative offers. Each attempt has been met with silence. Because of this, the Bleds are considered unstable."

Stella dropped her eyes. What did it mean to be considered unstable by the Nazis? Was it a good thing or a bad thing? Stella looked back up and found Oliver pondering her with a thoughtful expression.

"I would take it as a compliment, if I were you, Mrs. Lawrence," he said.

"So would I," said Nicky.

"What did they want from my family, anyway?" she asked.

"Influence. Bled beer is an international brand. It's good propa-ganda if the family is known to be Nazi supporters. It's really too bad that you aren't political."

"Why's that?" asked Nicky.

"The Bleds are so well-known that any side they chose would benefit."

"I didn't know there were sides," said Stella as the match put itself out.

Oliver continued in the dark. "There are always sides, Mrs. Lawrence. Soon, everyone will have to choose."

"Johannes said there would be another war coming."

"Who?" asked Oliver.

Before Stella could answer, Oliver shushed her. Footsteps fell outside the bookcase and stopped directly in front of where the three of them were hidden. She reached out for Nicky's hand, groping in the dark for his warm comfort. But before she could find it, there was a tiny click and the case opened, blinding them with light.

CHAPTER 19

$\mathcal{A}$ hand grabbed Stella's wrist and she let out a screech.

"Quiet," said the same woman's voice from before. "Do you want to get us all caught?"

"Who are y—"

The woman yanked her out of the hidden room and the men followed, squinting and shielding their eyes.

"Hurry," the woman said, pointing to a door to the offices. A man in a waiter's outfit stood in front of it. He waved to them and darted through the door. When they didn't follow, he peeked out and waved again.

Stella tiptoed as fast as she could without breaking into a run. She would gladly have run if she wasn't afraid of the noise her heels would make on the floor.

"Are they gone?" she asked the woman when they reached the door.

"No," the woman said. "And they're very suspicious."

The woman pulled her through the door and into a narrow hall off the office area. She walked with quick, efficient steps, her plain woolen dress clinging to her voluptuous figure.

"Who are you?" asked Stella.

"Gerta."

"If they're still here, why are we moving?"

"That chamber was too small. It couldn't sustain you three for very long. We had to take the chance to move you when we had the opportunity."

Gerta held her finger in front of her lips and waved them away from a door in the hall. They pressed themselves against the wall while she opened the door and took a quick look. Then she took Stella's wrist again and led her into a small sitting room. The furnishings were of lower quality than the library. The curtains and floor covering had a well-worn feel that befitted servants' quarters. Gerta motioned for Oliver to close the door behind them. When he closed the door and stood in front of it, she kicked back the rug and kneeled down to push on a spot in the center of the floor. Stella couldn't see anything special about the spot until a small wooden square popped out. Gerta pushed aside the square and felt around in the hole it left. She found a metal ring and pulled up a section of floor two feet by two feet. Stella leaned over the hole and saw a narrow ladder disappearing down into darkness.

"Where does that go?" asked Nicky.

"It doesn't matter," said Oliver. "We have to go in."

Gerta handed Oliver three candles and a pack of matches. "Don't light them until I've sealed you in."

Stella shivered when she heard the word "sealed". The only thing she heard of people being sealed into was a coffin and that was the last thing she wanted to think of as she looked down into that musty hole.

Nicky rubbed her back and said, "I'll go first."

"Be my guest," said Oliver.

Nicky tucked his matches and candle into his pocket and climbed into the hole. Once he'd disappeared into the darkness, he called out, "Come on, Stella."

Stella took Oliver's offered hand and stepped onto the ladder. It creaked under her weight and the smell of earth and mold rushed up to greet her. She held her breath as she lowered herself down into the darkness, but realized it was pointless. She may as well get used to it.

At the bottom of the ladder, Nicky's hands gripped her waist and pulled her down onto her knees and pushed her into an earthen tunnel.

"Watch your head," he said.

"Do you think there are rats down here?"

Nicky didn't answer and Stella took that as a yes. Oh, how she hated rats. The only thing worse was snakes.

"Oh my God," she gasped. "Are there snakes? What was that? I think I felt something move."

"You did. Me," said Nicky. "Stella, you have to bolt yourself together. Nothing that could happen to us down here is as bad as what would happen to us up there."

She gripped the book tighter and measured her breathing. He was right. She'd rather be where they were than where Abel was.

"I'm okay," she said. "Are we going to light a candle?"

"It's faster not to," said Nicky.

"I agree," said Oliver from behind her. "Gerta says to crawl straight ahead. It will open up after a few meters."

"How far is a meter?" asked Stella.

Neither man answered and Nicky started crawling away through the tunnel. She started to follow but realized Oliver was directly behind her and she was wearing a dress. She blushed with the realization.

"Go, Mrs. Lawrence," said Oliver.

She tugged the hem of her dress down, put her handbag's strap and the book's knotted twine between her teeth, and crawled. Something cold squished under her hand, but she swallowed hard and continued to follow the sound of Nicky rustling up ahead. The weight of the book made her jaw ache. She tried to think of another way to carry it but came up with nothing.

Then a bit of light flashed in the distance. She crawled faster and saw the end. Nicky held a lit candle in a round hole. He waved her forward. When she got closer, he put a finger to his lips. She wrinkled her nose at him. Obviously, she couldn't talk. Her mouth was full of leather and grotty old twine.

Nicky helped her out of the tunnel into an enormous open area the size of a ballroom, except that it was only three feet high. Above them were thick floor joists and wood planks. A multitude of voices and footsteps seeped through the boards.

Stella mouthed, "Hans' party?"

Nicky nodded before helping Oliver out of the tunnel and lighting both their candles. The three small flames threw odd shadows around the room and made Stella sigh with relief. Oliver motioned for them to put their heads together. "Gerta said there's another secret door in the corner."

"Which corner?" whispered Nicky.

Oliver shrugged. He squatted and looked around the room. Then he started for the nearest corner using a strange squatting walk. He felt around for a few moments and then turned back to them. He shook his head no and went to the next corner. That one was wrong as well. The third one was it. Oliver pressed on the wall and a long, thin handle fell out. He tugged on it and a small door opened. Stella and Nicky hustled over with Stella trying to keep her skirt over her knees, but she gave up after a few steps and went for speed instead.

In the corner, the conversations above them dropped to just one and Stella again wished she spoke German. Dr. Van Wijk pleaded with the German with the familiar voice. It must be Oberführer Peiper.

Oliver indicated that she should go through the door but then stopped and cocked his head to the side. Then he looked at her and the package dangling from her mouth. He sat back on his haunches and mouthed to her. "Wait."

She nodded and dropped the book and her handbag into her arms. Nicky sat with his long legs crossed, listening to the men above them almost like he could understand them. After a few minutes, two sets of footsteps clicked away from them and the conversation faded. Oliver waved them through the doorway into a smaller room and closed the door behind them with a disturbingly final thump.

Unlike the larger room behind them, light filtered down through cracks in the flooring, allowing them to see just enough. Oliver waddled to the center of the room, tossed his candle aside, and pulled a cord. Dim light warmed the area from a small yellow bulb hanging naked in the middle of the room that was still three feet high but whitewashed with a concrete floor. It felt wonderfully clean after the dirt of the tunnel.

"That's better," said Oliver.

Nicky jumped and put his finger to his lips.

"Relax. I've been here before. We're under a storage area. It's locked and only Hans has a key."

Stella dropped the package into her hands and blew out her candle. "You've been here before? But you didn't seem like you knew where you were going."

"I've never come by that particular route before."

"So there are more secret passages?" asked Nicky.

Oliver nodded. "The whole place is riddled with them. It has a long history of subversion. The Peasant's War, for example."

"Tell me they were on the side of the peasants," said Stella.

"Occasionally." Oliver waddled over to the wall and opened a box next to a pallet. He felt around in the box and pulled out a wine bottle. "Care for a drink?"

"You have no idea," said Nicky, following him and watching with satisfaction as Oliver uncorked the bottle and poured a significant amount into a jar.

Stella followed them and collapsed on the pallet with the package on her chest. "Is there anything to eat in that box?"

"Let's see," said Oliver. "I've got a tin of peaches."

"I'll take it." She sat up and placed the package in her lap.

Oliver opened the peaches and handed her the tin. The smell of the fruit amidst the dirt and spider webs made her choke up. Her face flushed and she swallowed hard. She didn't know plain old peaches could smell so good.

"Go ahead, Stella darling," said Nicky.

"No fork," she choked out.

"Sorry. We don't have any utensils, I'm afraid," said Oliver.

Stella looked down into the tin and jammed her fingers right down into the slimy liquid. She fished out a peach slice and slurped it into her mouth. Just a couple of days before, she couldn't have conceived of eating with dirty fingers and now, it seemed perfectly fine, almost natural.

She swallowed a few more slices and then looked down at the package in her lap. The book had changed her. Now she knew eating with her fingers and hopping on trains like a hobo weren't the only things she was capable of. She could do anything. Anything at all, if it were necessary to protect the book or Nicky.

She offered the peaches to Nicky and Oliver. Each man took a couple of slices and left her the rest. Oliver went in search of more food in the tunnels but came back with only a small jar of pickles.

"Terribly sorry," he said. "Usually, Hans is better about keeping the old place stocked."

"How many times have you been here?" asked Nicky.

"Too many and not enough," replied Oliver, biting a pickle and washing it down with wine.

Stella listened to the men talk about the state of Germany, the Austrian annexation, and possibility of Czechoslovakia or Poland being next on the Fuhrer's list. The conversation didn't hold her interest. Those things seemed so far away. Instead, she ran her fingers over the package, tracing the edges and remembering the details inside like they were right in front of her. Maybe she could only care about a few things at a time. Her father was like that. He loved few things, but he loved them intensely. Beer, family, and art were his loves. He resisted all temptations to love another thing. There simply wasn't room. She must be the same. She couldn't be made to care about the people of Poland and the fate Nicky feared they'd suffer. The book in her hands was too much. It blocked out her compassion. She focused on it and the people it impacted. There wasn't room for her to worry about anything else. She couldn't do anything for them. Maybe someday it would be different.

"So you want to tell me about that package?" asked Oliver.

Stella glanced up at him and he raised an eyebrow at her. She switched her gaze to Nicky as he assumed his favorite disinterested expression.

"It's nothing," he said.

"Peiper didn't seem to think so," said Oliver.

"You speak German?" asked Stella.

"Fluently. Wouldn't be much use, if I didn't."

"What did you hear?" Nicky ate another pickle, munching it slowly.

"Peiper *is* after you. I've made some powerful people angry in my day, but you make me look like an amateur."

"I never do anything by halves," said Nicky.

"Clearly," said Oliver.

"When do they leave?"

"They didn't say. I'd expect us to be down here a few days, at least. Himmler and Göring arrive tonight. They're on their way to Vienna to view the destruction. They made a detour because of you to nobody's satisfaction." Oliver spat the names Himmler and Göring. His face, usually placid, twisted briefly with distaste.

"Who are they?" asked Stella.

"Himmler heads the SS and Peiper reports to him. But it seems he's more concerned about telling Göring of his failure to apprehend you than he is Himmler."

Nicky frowned and took a large gulp of wine. "And who is Göring?"

"He collects art," said Stella.

The men stared at her for a second and then Nicky asked Oliver, "That can't be the same person?"

"Your wife is right. Göring does have a growing collection. How did you know, Mrs. Lawrence?" asked Oliver.

"Uncle Josiah knows him from the Great War," said Stella. "They were both pilots. On opposite sides, of course."

"Of course." Oliver scratched his chin and said thoughtfully. "And now?"

"And what?"

"Are they friendly? Your uncle and Göring?"

Stella let out a little tinkling laugh and was surprised that laughing was still inside her. "Not a bit. Uncle Josiah loathes Göring. He calls him a thief and a…a…showboat. That's it. A showboat."

Oliver chuckled. "That is a perfect description of Göring."

"If he's an art collector, why would Peiper worry about him at all?" asked Nicky.

"Art is Göring's hobby. I don't know what Peiper has to do with Göring. He handed the SS over to Himmler several years ago. He's the head of the Luftwaffe, among other things now. It sounds like Dr. Van Wijk answers to Göring directly. He and Peiper are rather more nervous than I would expect over a slippery socialite and her playboy husband."

Stella ignored the dig and said, "Dr. Van Wijk sounds Dutch. What's he doing working for the Germans?"

"The Nazis pay their experts well. Van Wijk is an art historian. He's concerned that Himmler is working with Göring on whatever they're doing and doesn't want to deal with Himmler at all."

Stella and Nicky glanced at each other. Oliver caught the exchange and popped a small pickle in his mouth while eying them.

"What else did they say?" asked Nicky.

"They mentioned an article which you have in your possession. Interesting that both Himmler and Göring have a stake in obtaining it."

Oliver's eyes flicked back and forth between the two of them. Stella tried to assume Nicky's look of indifference but failed, as she usually did.

"Mrs. Lawrence, what is in that package?"

"I'm not telling you, if you won't tell us why you're in here," she said.

"Excellent point."

"Did you hear that?" asked Nicky.

Both Stella and Oliver cocked their heads to listen.

"Sounds like champagne corks," said Stella with longing.

Nicky set down his jar of wine and said, "Do you have an operation happening here tonight?"

"No," said Oliver, his brow furrowed.

"You have to tell us."

"I don't have to do anything, but the answer is still no."

"Then what is it?"

"Himmler and Göring," said Oliver.

An explosion somewhere above them rocked the floor joists and a cloud of dust and grit filled the air. Stella coughed and clutched the package to her chest as another explosion went off closer than the first. Nicky crawled over as one of the floor joists fell into their hiding place, narrowly missing his head.

He grabbed Stella's arm. "Come on."

"Where?" she asked between coughs.

Nicky looked at Oliver, who pointed at the far wall opposite where the explosions were coming from. Stella followed Nicky to the wall when another explosion went off right on top of them. A chunk of flooring hit Stella in the head and she fell face down, feeling weight pile up on her back. Then someone grabbed her arm and began dragging her through the rubble. She couldn't form a coherent thought. Her head was swimming and the rest of her body felt limp and useless as an overcooked noodle. Then the next thing she knew, there was no rubble, only cool, smooth dirt. She opened her eyes and saw blackness. Someone was pulling her. His hand slipped on her arm. He adjusted his grip and kept pulling. Stella couldn't think what had happened or where she was. She opened her mouth to say she was awake when another explosion rocked the tunnel. A load of dirt fell on her, but the man kept pulling. Then he let go and she smelled burning wood and a smell she would later identify as burning flesh.

"Mrs. Lawrence," said Oliver, rolling her over. "Wake up."

"I'm awake." Her voice sounded raspy and clogged.

"Mrs. Lawrence, please wake up."

Stella opened her eyes to find Oliver bent over her. High above him were rafters. It was then that she heard the screaming and gunfire.

"Mrs. Lawrence, do you know where you are?"

"Stella."

"What?" Oliver bent closer. She could see a hint of red in his beard and the deeply carved lines on his forehead that his cap had concealed before.

"Call me Stella."

"Thank God," he said. "Can you walk?"

"I don't know. Where's Nicky?" She touched her chest. Her fingers touched the gritty tulips. She sat up, bumping foreheads with Oliver. "Where's the book?"

"Book?" he asked.

"I have it," said Nicky from the tunnel.

Stella held her hand out to Nicky as he crawled onto the bed of straw. If it hadn't been for his voice, she would never have known him. He was so grimy he looked like a coal miner and an injured one at that. His hands were bloody and he had a gash in his shoulder that was black with blood.

"I'm okay." He took her hand and placed the package and her handbag in her lap. When he smiled at her, there was blood in his teeth.

Another explosion went off, this time farther away.

"What the hell is going on?" asked Nicky. "This can't be about any of us."

"I agree," said Oliver. "An assassination attempt is more likely."

"Assassinate who?" asked Stella.

"Himmler and Göring are both supposed to be here tonight. Any number of people want to kill them, myself included."

"You said this wasn't your operation," said Nicky.

"It isn't, but we're not the only game in town, are we? Stay here. I'm going to have a look around."

Oliver got to his feet but stayed in a crouch. He headed to a low door, crushing the straw, and Stella realized they were in a horse stall. Oliver reached over the edge of the stall door and there was a clank as the bolt slid back. He pushed back his coat and slipped his hand in his pocket. He pulled out a small black pistol, checked something on it, and then looked at them.

"I won't be long," he said as he slipped out of the stall and disappeared.

In his absence, the noise outside became louder. Lots of shouts in German and sporadic gunfire. Stella drew in a deep breath. The familiar scent of clean hay refreshed her after the dirt of the tunnel.

"Don't you think we should stay together?" asked Stella.

"I don't know what I think," said Nicky.

"What if something happens to him?"

"If you haven't noticed, something's always happening to the people around us. We're not exactly good luck."

"This isn't our fault."

"I wouldn't put it past us."

"Somebody's probably trying to kill Göring or the other one." Stella slid herself over to the wall of the stall and started pulling herself up with her free hand.

"What are you doing?" asked Nicky.

Stella ignored her shaking legs and the metallic taste of blood in her mouth. "He's been gone too long."

"It's only been a few minutes."

More gunfire erupted in the distance.

"One minute is too long and what about Hans?"

Nicky got to his feet and took off his hat, revealing the only clean spot on him. His hair seemed even blonder against the grey grime and dirt from the tunnel. "This is a terrible idea."

"Then don't come." Stella pushed at the stall door and peeked out through the crack. Two rows of stalls lined a center aisle and a horse with a brilliant white blaze whinnied at the sight of her. The door at the far end of the aisle was open. Smoke seeped in through the opening, the entrance to hell. Outside, people ran past, their bodies backlit by fire. Stella ran to the door. When she looked out, she had the queasy feeling of déjà vu. It was like looking out at Vienna the night the Nazis had terrorized the city, except now she was street level and not protected by an elegant hotel.

Nicky came up behind her. "Good God."

Two dozen windows around the courtyard blazed. The building directly across from them had a huge gaping hole in the side and several disheveled people stumbled from the hole, collapsing in the rubble. Then a long grey limousine rolled up to the entrance of the courtyard. A dozen black uniformed soldiers ran past the car and took positions in front of it. The driver got out, opened the back door, and the oddest man climbed out. Stella couldn't take her eyes off him. He was tall and obese, wearing an outfit that was part uniform and part costume with a voluminous cape and a wide gold sash. The man wore rouge on his cheeks and sported tassels on his sash and a fat feather on his odd turban-like cap. He stared out at the destruction with cold eyes, one big hand on his hip and a gold and white-enameled baton in the other. He surveyed the destruction and then began shouting in German at the soldiers around him.

Nicky yanked Stella backward and pulled the stable door closed.

"What happened?" asked Oliver from behind them.

They spun around and Stella started to answer but gasped instead. Oliver's left arm dangled loose at his side. His right hand, the one with the gun, shook, whacking the barrel against his slim thigh. Ribbons of bright red streamed down his bare arm from a gaping slice on his shoulder. His pale grey shirt was in tatters with dozens of bloody holes and burn marks.

Stella ran to him and caught him just as his knees buckled. The book was pressed between their chests as she lowered him to the ground, smelling the rancid stench of burnt flesh mixed with fresh blood. Behind her, the stable door opened with a scrape. There was a shout in German and Oliver reached over Stella's shoulder. He fired behind her head and she felt the concussion vibrate through her skull. A sharp scream pierced the air and Stella glanced over her shoulder to see a soldier standing in the stable doorway spurting blood from his chest and screaming. He dropped his gun, his arms flailing in the air. Nicky shoved him out the door, then closed and bolted it. He picked up the soldier's gun, a long rifle. It was black with a wooden stock and an over-sized clip. He looked at Stella, who cradled Oliver in her arms and pressed her lips against his forehead. Nicky stood there for a second, wavering so much Stella feared he'd drop, too.

Instead, he ran over and grabbed Oliver's good arm. "We have to get out of here."

"Back in the tunnel?" asked Stella.

"I don't know." His head swiveled as he searched for an escape route.

They both screamed as Hans burst out of a stall. His hair stood on end and there were a multitude of bloody holes in his right cheek and neck. He coughed violently as he dropped beside Stella and took hold of Oliver around the waist. "There's another way."

CHAPTER 20

*T*he wall of the tack room closed behind them with a grinding shudder. Stella felt along the wall, listening to Oliver being dragged in front of her and her own ragged breath.

"Lay him down here," said Hans. "We're clear of the door."

Oliver groaned as the dragging stopped. Then there was a click and a sizzle. Hans stood over Oliver holding a lighter. The glow burned intensely at the center and faded out slowly in softly defined rings like the Madonna's halo glow. Nicky knelt by Oliver's side, the soldier's gun lying at his feet. He pressed a sopping red handkerchief to Oliver's shoulder and blood ran rivers down his hand soaking his cuff.

"You'll have to hold the lighter," Hans said, clicking it off and pressing it against Stella's chest.

She held the lighter high as Hans had and flicked the wheel with her thumb. She'd seen a million men do it, but the lighter didn't light. She tried again and again.

"I can't get it," she said.

"Give it to me," said Nicky.

Stella shivered at the feel of his blood-soaked hand on her leg. He stood beside her and took the lighter out of her hand. He flicked it on easily and flooded the hidden corridor with another warm halo.

Hans untied the knotted belt on his smoking jacket. "Help me tie this around his shoulder, Stella."

"Why?" She asked while easing Oliver onto his side.

Hans slipped the belt under Oliver's shoulder, looping it under his arm and tying it. "To cut off the blood. It's called a tourniquet." He tightened the tie. Oliver's eyes opened and he barely suppressed a scream before he went limp.

"Tourniquet," Stella whispered, imitating Hans' accent.

"You haven't heard of it?" Han's sat back and removed the handkerchief, watching as the blood stopped flowing.

"No reason that she should," said Nicky. "Stella hasn't been to war."

Hans glanced up. "But you have?"

Nicky shrugged and the halo bounced up and down in time with another explosion outside. "There are accidents in shipyards. I've seen them used. Usually on legs though."

"You worked in the shipyard?" asked Stella.

"My father required me to start at the bottom. I was nine when I started working for Mr. Short in tools. My job was to collect and hand out chits."

Stella glanced up at her elegant husband and his expression was as impassive as ever, even with blood and dirt all over him. It appeared that there were things he'd neglected to tell her, too, but she doubted that he'd consider them even. He was a man. She was a woman. Her family wouldn't think that made a difference, but she was quite sure his would.

"The tourniquet has worked." Hans replaced the bloody handkerchief and fumbled with his jacket before turning to Stella. "Reach into my pocket. There's a box. I can't get it." He held up his hand, slick with Oliver's blood.

Stella handed him Abel's package and felt around inside the damp pocket. She found a slick leather case and pulled it out. Hans wiped his hands on his velvet jacket without much effect and took the box in his blood-soaked hands.

"You'll have to help me again, Stella," said Hans.

"With what? You said the bleeding stopped."

"Come over next to me."

Reluctantly, Stella crawled over beside Hans and sat on her haunches. Her mother would be horrified. She wasn't allowed to sit like that as a five-year-old, much less as an eighteen-year-old married woman. Stella smiled a grim smile, banishing the genteel Francesqua Bled from her mind. Those old lessons were worse than useless now.

"What's in the case?" she asked.

"A couple of small miracles."

Stella glanced up at Nicky and he shrugged, bobbling the halo again.

Hans checked the tourniquet and tightened it a little more, causing Oliver to groan. Then he lifted the handkerchief. Stella's hands shook and an odd kind of quiver started in her chest when she saw the wound up close. It was a grinning mouth, exposing the meat and bone of Oliver's shoulder, but it had only a little blood in the cavity. Hans tugged off his cravat and pressed the fresh fabric to the wound. Then he pointed at the box by his knee.

"Open it and remove the metal container," he said.

Stella couldn't tear her eyes away from the cravat and the blood that had pooled under Oliver's shoulder. She shook and stared, hearing Hans but not listening to him.

"Stella. Now," said Nicky as he jerked his gaze to the door. People were running through the stable, shouting in German. They held their breath until the German faded away.

"Stella, please," said Hans.

She jerked to attention and grabbed the case. She nearly dropped it when she tried to undo the tiny brass clasp and Hans let out a gasp for good reason. The metal container wasn't alone in the box. One side had the metal box and on the other side were two cardboard boxes with official labels. One said Prontosil Solubile and the other Eukadol

"Open the metal box," said Hans in a calm low voice.

Stella popped it open and it was her turn to gasp. The box held a glass syringe encased in metal and a collection of needles. She held it out to Hans. "Oh, no. You take it."

"Your hands are cleaner," he said.

Stella looked down. Her hands couldn't have been dirtier. She'd climbed through a dirt tunnel and eaten peaches with her bare hands. "I don't think so."

"Stella," said Nicky. "You have to do it. I'm holding the lighter."

"But Hans…" She trailed off as she saw Hans' hands shaking and not from fear. He was in pain, a lot of pain.

"What am I doing?" she asked.

"First, get the flask out of my breast pocket. There isn't much schnapps left. We'll have to hope it's enough."

"Okay," said Stella with a slight smile. "Am I supposed to drink it? I don't care for schnapps."

She was rewarded with a larger smile from Hans. "Pour it on your fingers to sterilize them."

The schnapps smelled like it was made purely of over-ripe peaches and just the scent was intoxicating. She poured the small remaining amount on her fingertips and rubbed them furiously. "That's not enough to sterilize anything."

"You needn't worry about it too much. What you're doing will protect Oliver. Now, screw on the smallest needle."

That was easy enough, if one didn't think about what was obviously coming next.

"Done," she said.

"Get an ampule of Eukadol and snap it open."

Stella bit her lip and looked in the little case. "Can't he have the aspirin first?"

Oliver moaned as if to answer her query.

Nicky leaned over her. "Aspirin?"

"There is no aspirin," said Hans. "Open the box of Eukadol."

"But it says Bayer right there." Stella pointed at the Prontosil box.

"Bayer makes other things other than aspirin. The Prontosil, for instance."

"Prontosil isn't aspirin?" asked Nicky.

"Aspirin is aspirin," said Hans. "Eukadol will ease his pain."

Stella wanted to give Oliver an aspirin so badly. Aspirin came in tablets, not scary syringes. But she opened the Eukadol box and found five little ampules of clear liquid. She emptied her mind. She couldn't think. Thinking was bad. Doing was good. Good and necessary. Oliver opened his eyes and watched her, bleary and cringing in pain. She had to give him that stuff and hoped it helped.

Stella followed Hans instructions, drawing the liquid into the syringe and pushing the needle deep into the meat of Oliver's shoulder. Any normal person would've cried out in agony, but Oliver gritted his teeth in a fierce grimace.

"He may need another dose," said Hans. "In the meantime, you will give him the Prontosil."

"What is this stuff?" asked Nicky. "I've never heard of it."

"Eukadol eases pain and Prontosil cures septicemia and gangrene."

Nicky and Hans discussed the recent invention as Stella prepared the syringe again with Prontosil and injected it. Oliver was much more relaxed and murmured a thank you.

"Move his arm," said Hans. "Let's see how he feels."

Oliver reacted but very little, only moving when Stella put pressure on his arm. Still, he didn't look good. There was an amazing amount of blood on the floor and all over them. Those German medicines sounded like a gift from God, but they couldn't replace his blood.

Oliver's face became slack and his breathing shallow. Stella watched his chest, expecting each rise to be his last, despite the medicines. Hans lifted his cravat off of the wound and sighed in relief. "He's clotting, but his hand is cold and blue. Loosen the tourniquet."

"Are you sure?" asked Nicky.

"His arm needs some blood or it will die." Hans reached for the tourniquet with shaking hands, but Stella beat him to it. She eased the knot open and a small amount of blood flowed into the wound, but the hand pinked up nicely.

"That looks better," said Nicky. "Hans, how do you know how to do all of this? Where did you get the medicine?"

"My dear Mr. Lawrence, I went through what you call The Great War. I wasn't a young man but I went when the Fatherland called. I survived when so many friends did not. I swore that I would never again be without medicine. I would never watch young men die in agony for want of care. When Oliver came, I knew I had to be prepared. I only wish I'd gotten my pack of bandages, but Peiper was suspicious and I didn't have an excuse to disappear again." He paused and looked at Stella and Nicky. "There is another war coming. We all must be prepared."

"I know," said Nicky. "My father said we won't be involved this time, but I saw Vienna. We will have to come to Europe's aid."

"The party is coming for us all," said Hans. "Their ambition knows no boundaries. Other countries are asking for Germany to help so we must invade."

Nicky snorted. "Czechoslovakia asked for them to annex the Sudetenland?"

"Of course. And Poland will need us next. After that, all of Czechoslovakia," Hans said wryly. "It is only beginning. Soon, the Führer will turn his eyes west to France and who knows."

"Britain," said Nicky.

"And Belgium and The Netherlands. They all need us, you see."

"My father didn't say that."

"The world is not listening."

The men looked at Stella as she removed the needle from the syringe and wiped it on her blouse. It was the cleanest thing available. "My father only talked about the art that they've been confiscating. My mother and Aunt Florence are particularly worried about the Klimts. He's their favorite. I guess my family isn't listening either." Stella felt remarkably ignorant and angry. Uncle Josiah should have known and he should've told her. Abel would be safe. She never would've risked him, not even for a thousand Klimts.

"Your father listens," said Hans, looking more and more weary. "Help me off with my jacket."

She put everything back in the leather case and slipped the jacket from Hans' thin shoulders. "How does he know?"

189

"I told him."

"What about Uncle Josiah?"

"I would assume that Aleksej told him."

She could feel Nicky radiating anger above her so she didn't look up. A surge of love rose up in her chest and she didn't care what Nicky thought. Uncle Josiah had his reasons and they were good reasons, no matter what people said. He wasn't insane. He wasn't.

"Can I give you some of that Eukadol?" Stella asked after seeing the small wounds all over the elderly Hans.

"I'm better now." The bloody holes on his cheek and chest said otherwise, but Stella didn't protest. They'd have to go somewhere and carrying two men wasn't possible. Even Nicky couldn't manage it and she was practically useless in that department.

"Maybe some Prontosil. You could get an infection, too."

"We must save it for Oliver. You will give him two more ampules in six hours."

Stella held up the jacket. "What should I do with this?"

"Tear out the lining. It's silk. The velvet will only irritate the wound."

Stella stripped the lining and followed Hans' instructions in constructing a makeshift bandage and sling. She tied the sling around Oliver's neck with a sleeve lining, careful not to make it too tight.

"Now what?" asked Nicky. "That's not going to do it. He needs a doctor."

Hans lifted the hem of Oliver's shirt and revealed a bloodstain the size of a cantaloupe on his hip.

"He certainly does, but our first concern is escape. Second is a doctor."

"Escape sounds good. Any ideas?"

They stopped for a second and listened to the muffled sounds from outside. There was no longer any gunfire going on as far as Stella could tell, but plenty of shouting and crashing noises. Hans stroked his chin, his gaze falling on Stella. He was considering her, but for what, she didn't know.

"Peiper arrived in a plane," he said, finally.

Nicky leaned over above them with the lighter held high. The flame put his face in shadow beneath his hat brim. "I hope you can fly a plane? Because I can't."

"I can't either," said Hans.

"Swell. So the plane's out. You must have a car. Where's the nearest doctor?"

"Himmler's men will have all the roads blocked. Even if they didn't, all the doctors are ardent party members. They wouldn't treat him. They'd turn him in." Hans kept his eyes on Stella. "You'll have to do it."

Stella jerked in surprise. "My father knows?" she asked without thinking.

"Not as far as I know. Josiah told me," said Hans.

"Told you what?" asked Nicky.

Stella hesitated and then looked up at him. "Remember how I told you that Uncle Josiah bought the plane he flew in the Great War?"

Nicky nodded and Stella wished she could see his eyes. "Well, he taught me to fly it and others."

"He taught *you* to fly? Is he insane?"

"I'm his favorite."

"So he tried to kill you?"

"He wasn't trying to kill me," said Stella, suddenly indignant. "He just wanted me to have some fun."

"You're a girl."

"Amelia Earhart was a girl."

"And look how that ended."

"She might not be dead."

"Stella, she's dead."

"Not because she's a girl."

Hans stood up, the lines in his face deeply etched in the lighter's warm glow. "This argument is pointless. We have a means of escape. We must take it."

Nicky hesitated and then looked back at Stella. "You can really fly a plane?"

"Sure. It's as easy as driving a car," said Stella.

"You can drive a car?"

"Forget I said that." She stood, picked up the gun, and slung it over her shoulder. "Lead the way, Hans."

The plane sat at the far end of the brewery's main road. The road split the large oval lawn that was ringed with trees. Stella could barely make it out from the small storage room they'd reached through a series of passageways too complicated to comprehend. Next to her feet, Oliver lay on the floor amidst a wide array of farm implements. His eyes were open, but he wasn't talking or responding to anything but pain. He probably needed more Eukadol, but there wasn't time. They had to get out, so she didn't bother to suggest it. Hans and Nicky couldn't deal with another thing. They sat on the floor next to Oliver, drenched with sweat from the effort of carrying him through tight spaces.

"Are there any guards?" asked Hans after a minute.

"I don't think so. I guess everyone's busy," she said.

"Assassination attempts will do that," said Nicky.

"I only wish they'd been successful," said Hans.

Nicky lifted his hat and wiped his brow. "How do you know they weren't?"

"Himmler and Göring were late. The explosions went off before they arrived."

"Who was behind it?"

Hans shook his head and winced at the pain. "I don't know, but it was an inside job, as Josiah would say. My guest list included a number of high-ranking officials and party members. They were staying the night and came with luggage. They could easily have placed devices when no one was looking."

"They tried to kill their own?" asked Nicky.

"There have been several attempts on Das Führer from inside the party. But those two have their own enemies. Himmler is feared by everyone," said Hans.

"What about Hitler?" asked Nicky.

"Except him."

"Well, we saw somebody arrive," said Stella. "But it couldn't have been one of those guys."

"Why not?" Hans got to his feet, using Nicky's shoulder and a butter churn to brace himself.

"Because he was dressed like Valentino in The Sheik," said Nicky.

"That was Göring then. He's unusual for a Nazi," said Hans.

"He's unusual for anyone. Does he dress like that all the time?"

"I'm sure he'd like to."

Stella thought about what Uncle Josiah had said about Göring. "Uncle Josiah never mentioned the dressing up, but he said he was married. I didn't see a woman though."

"Emmy was not coming tonight." Hans tilted his head, squinting. "None of the wives were to be here tonight. Perhaps that is why my home was targeted."

"There's honor among thieves," said Nicky gruffly.

"Hardly," said Hans. "You'll find the party is a cutthroat business. Now that's enough rest. We'll skirt the tree line." He pointed past Stella's head at the line of slim trees, "and approach the plane from the right."

Hans bent over and took Oliver's limp arm. Nicky stood and removed Oliver's arm from Hans' hand. "I'll carry him."

"You can't possibly. It's a least four hundred meters."

"I can do it." Nicky squatted and sliding his arms under Oliver's shoulders and knees. He heaved him aloft with a grunt reminiscent of a strongman at a carnival.

Hans opened the storage room door wide, stuck his head out, and nodded to Nicky, who walked sideways out the door. Stella slung the rifle over her shoulder and went out after him into the cool night air, watching for some sign that Nicky would buckle, but he never wavered. He marched along the tree line with Oliver's head bouncing against his shoulder, his feet swinging in a gentle rhythm.

Hans had a much harder time just lifting his feet.

"Let me help you," said Stella.

"No, my dear," he said. "Conserve your energy for the ordeal ahead."

"Flying isn't an ordeal. It's pure joy."

He touched her arm. "I fear tonight won't be the same for you."

"Nothing is the same now."

Hans looked at her sadly and stumbled on a tree root. Stella took his arm against his wishes and felt him tremble. She hadn't thought about it before, but he was elderly, at least a generation older than her father. She tended to think of them as the same since they were such great friends, but Hans was an old man. The strain of the night's events could kill him.

Stella glanced back at the brewery, her stomach twisting into a double knot. Plenty of other things might kill him, too. She expected to be spotted at any moment, but the explosions were in the courtyard of the great building. Far out to the right, they were shielded from most of the activity. Huge flames danced on the rooftops, silhouetting the outline. She supposed everyone was trying to put out the flames or help survivors. They probably didn't think they had to guard the plane. Who would steal a plane? Hardly anybody could fly one. It was just luck that she could.

Stella said a silent thank you to Uncle Josiah for his leading her astray and watched helplessly as Nicky stumbled, catching himself at the last moment.

"I must help you, my friend," said Hans, pulling away from Stella.

"No, sir. I'm the one for this job." Nicky stopped to shift Oliver's weight and Stella stood on her tiptoes, patting his hat more firmly on his head.

"Don't want to lose that hat," she said. "The owner will be miffed."

"We wouldn't want that," said Nicky through what sounded like clenched teeth.

"That isn't your hat?" Hans' eyes darted around, but he maintained a conversational tone.

"No," grunted Nicky.

"A man in the Vienna train station gave it to us to hide Nicky's hair," said Stella.

"Really?" Hans straightened up and his feet stopped scraping the ground. "That's quite interesting. This gentleman wants his hat back?"

"That's what he said," answered Stella, relieved that he'd perked up. "Something about how he always collects."

Hans hesitated. "What did he say, exactly?"

"I don't know *exactly*. I think I said we owed him and he said he always collects. Something like that."

"What did this man look like?"

"Why? He was just a man in the station."

"He was a man who helped you at great risk to himself. What did he look like?"

"He was short, old, and wore a very nice grey suit. Oh, and he had an accent. It sounded kind of British, but different."

"Cyril Welk," said Hans, running his hand over his face. "I knew that hat looked familiar."

"That *was* his name. How did you know?"

"He's one of Oliver's contacts and no one has heard from him since the *Kristallnacht*. When did you see him?"

"The tenth," said Nicky.

"What's the *Kristallnacht*?" asked Stella.

"That's what they're calling the night the Jews were attacked. It means 'night of broken glass'," said Hans.

Stella bit her lip and gripped the book tighter. Night of broken glass. It was an apt description, yet it didn't quite cover what she'd seen.

"How was Cyril when you saw him?" asked Hans.

"Fine, as far as I could tell," said Stella.

They rounded the corner on the edge of the lawn and once again came into view of anyone in the brewery courtyard. The plane sat dead ahead off to the right of the brewery road. It was wreathed in the trees' shadows, but the swastika on its tail stood out plain in the moonlight. The closer they got, the more nervous Stella felt. She hadn't flown in months, not since before meeting Nicky. She'd spent hundreds of hours in the air but had only gone up a half a dozen times by herself. Uncle Josiah was usually with her. She couldn't remember any fear during any of those flights, at least nothing like what she was feeling at that moment. Uncle Josiah was an ace in the Great War and an excellent teacher. She relied on his vast experience and enjoyed flying together rather than alone. What she told Nicky was true. She was his favorite and he was hers. Who else would've defied her parents and taken her flying when she showed an interest? She was still amazed that they'd gotten away with it. All those days when she was supposed to be studying mathematics with her governess, Miss Bloom, instead were spent in flying lessons. If her mother had been paying attention, she'd have known Miss Bloom was in love with Uncle Josiah and would've agreed to anything he wanted. Stella smiled at the remembrance, but then the smile fell off her face as they approached the plane.

"That's a bi-plane, a two-seater," she said while wondering how she hadn't realized it before. Of course it was a two-seater. You couldn't land a larger craft on the narrow brewery road.

"Yes," said Hans. "You will have to fly Oliver out by yourself."

Nicky lay Oliver in the grass under the left wing. Then he groaned, arching his back and leaning on the plane's lower silver wing. "Does he go in the front or the back?"

Stella stopped five feet away, but Hans walked on and knelt beside Oliver. He took his pulse and adjusted the bandage on his shoulder.

"I can't do it," Stella said.

Hans looked up at her, his hand over Oliver's heart. "You can. Josiah said you're very talented. You're the son he never had."

"I mean I can't leave you here. Either of you."

Nicky said nothing. He stared down at the wing, panting. Hans struggled to his feet and faced Stella.

"You have to. Oliver will die if you don't and we can't afford to lose him. The only other escape is on foot through the woods."

"I can't." Stella clutched the book and her handbag to her chest. The brewery fires raged in the distance, growing brighter every minute.

"You have to," said Nicky without raising his head.

"I won't leave you."

"I'll meet you in Paris. I'll find a way."

"I never flew in the dark before. I can't do it."

Nicky straightened up and then bent over Oliver. He scooped him up in his arms and faced her. The fire's light flickered and licked at his face. He showed no emotion as he looked at her with a steady gaze.

"Front or back?" he asked.

"I can't."

"Stella, Oliver will die. I won't."

"You promise?"

A hint of a smile danced on the edge of his lips. "I promise."

"Front," she said.

Nicky laid Oliver on the wing between the fuselage and the metal struts connecting the two wings. He climbed up next to him and straddled the wire where it attached to the wing. Oliver's body started sliding sideways. Nicky grabbed a handful of his jacket as Stella ran up, dropped her load in the grass, and braced Oliver's sliding body before it could fall off.

"I'll get on the other side," said Hans.

Nicky bent around the wire and and with Stella's help, got his hands under Oliver's armpits. He heaved him up until Oliver's head was level with his chest.

"Just shove him this way," said Hans from the other wing. He held his hands out, ready to grab Oliver.

Nicky shifted and twisted, almost throwing Oliver past his shoulder. Hans lurched forward and caught hold of Oliver's jacket and dragged him over the lip of the cockpit. Nicky turned around and lifted Oliver's hips. Stella slipped the rifle off her shoulder, letting it fall by the book, and clamored up onto the wing. She bent Oliver's knees and pushed his feet into the cockpit. Hans arranged his body against the many struts inside. He tucked Oliver's hands inside his pockets and pulled his cap low on his forehead.

Hans looked past the two of them standing on the wing bent over Oliver. "You better get in, Stella. We're about to be spotted."

Nicky and Stella looked over their shoulders. A swarm of soldiers were coming around the right side of the brewery, headed for a transport truck parked behind Göring's car. Nicky reached up and took hold of the upper wing. He maneuvered Stella between himself and the fuselage. She grabbed the edge of the pilot's cockpit, stepped over the lip, and sat down with a thump.

Once in the pilot's seat, a feeling of familiarity, of déjà vu came over her. She flicked the lighting switch and touched the altimeter. The controls weren't any different than Uncle Josiah's planes. She put her feet in the petals and gave them a gentle push. They were just right, responsive and well-designed. She let out a tensely held breath and said, "Focke-Wulf Fw44."

"What was that?" asked Hans.

She looked toward his voice but could barely see him over the lip of the cockpit. "I think it might be a Focke-Wulf. Uncle Josiah said they were easy to fly, except I can't see anything."

Uncle Josiah always put a thick pad on her seat to raise her up. He often said she had no business being so tiny. For once, she agreed with him. She couldn't fly if she couldn't see.

"I need something to sit on. I'm too short," she said.

"What about that package you've been carrying around?" asked Hans. "It's rather thick."

"Nicky," said Stella. "I left the book and my handbag on the ground."

He got them for her and she slid the book under her bottom. The extra inches were just enough and she could see over the edge.

"Perfect," she said. "But where am I going?"

"I've been thinking about that," said Hans.

"Think fast," said Nicky. "They're looking this way."

"Englehof Brewery," said Hans. "They're three hundred and twenty kilometers southwest of here in Germany. The owner, Kaspar, is part of the network. He'll protect you."

"How will I find it?" asked Stella.

"Fly due west until you see a small river. About eighty kilometers," said Hans.

"How much is a kilometer?"

"A kilometer is a little over half a mile."

"That doesn't help me." Stella's chest tightened. She never was any good at judging distances.

"Hurry," said Nicky. "They're starting to get more interested."

Hans ran his fingers through his hair. "It doesn't matter, Stella. Fly to the river and follow it south until you see a very large vineyard."

"I thought you said it was a brewery."

"It's both. Pass the main buildings. To the southwest, there are open fields lying fallow. Land there."

"They're pointing," said Nicky.

"Hans, get off and stand back," said Stella with one hand on the stick and the other on the throttle.

He reached over the edge and brushed her cheek. "You are your father's daughter and your Uncle's son. Good Luck."

Hans disappeared and Stella turned to Nicky. He stood stock still, the brewery fire giving a harsh edge to his silhouette.

"Wish me luck," she said.

He didn't answer immediately. Instead, he bent over into the cockpit and kissed her. She tasted the warm tears on his lips and fought back her own.

"I love you more than my life," he whispered.

Stella couldn't answer. She could only nod.

"I'll meet you at Napoleon's tomb in three days. Noon. Don't be late," he said.

She nodded again and took her father's gift, the Faberge cigarette case, out of her handbag. She handed him the precious piece and then wrapped her small hands around his large ones.

"Find the right person and it will bring you to Paris," she choked out. "*Du gefällst mir.*"

He smiled, took off her hat, stabbed the hatpin into the crown and tossed it into her lap. Then he took off Cyril Welk's hat and put it on her head. It slipped down around her ears, warming her head immediately.

Without another word, Nicky jumped off the wing. Stella waved her arm and the prop sprang to life.

CHAPTER 21

$\mathscr{T}$he plane hit the brewery's drive with a teeth-rattling bounce as Stella squinted at the dimly lit instrument panel. The instruments were laid out in a logical pattern and felt as familiar to her as Uncle Josiah's Sopwith Camel or his O-19. The most important gauge, the fuel gauge, read nearly full.

She stopped the plane, glancing to the right and then the left. Neither direction seemed to have enough road space to take off or land, but Peiper had certainly landed. He wouldn't have landed if he didn't think he had enough space to get back in the air. If he could do it, so could she. Another glance to the right told her it wasn't an option with less than four hundred feet to a drop-off. She maneuvered the plane to face the brewery. It seemed such a short distance, but the left would have to do. If she got off the ground at the right moment, she could fly between the buildings through the courtyard.

She bit her lip and a movement caught her eye. Nicky stood beside the plane, waving and pointing. The soldiers at the brewery were running toward them full-tilt, their weapons raised. Stella eased the throttle forward. The engine ran up and she felt a surge of pleasure at its eager response. Uncle Josiah's many instructions and stories went zinging through her head. Every word he'd ever said about flying came back to her. Her hands moved automatically. The craft jerked and bounced on the rough road. Oliver's head in the student's seat banged against the side. And then Uncle Josiah's most important advice about flying lit up her brain. Pray. When things are bad, rely on your training and pray. Once she asked him, since he wasn't a church-going man, who he prayed to. He said, "Whoever will listen."

So she opened her mouth and prayed to the only god she was intimately acquainted with, Uncle Josiah himself.

"Please!"

The plane picked up speed and again bounced.

"Please help me!"

Airborne, but they were very low to the ground, rushing at the men running across the field. She pulled back on the stick, using every ounce of control she had not to yank it. They rose gracefully, headed straight at the burning brewery. It was about feel. Uncle Josiah told her that time and again. Now she knew what he meant. She stared at the brewery past Oliver's head and gauged exactly how much to pull up so that they would clear the building. A million calculations and adjustments went on in her head. She could feel what was right.

A little bit more.

Keep going.

In an instant they were over the transport truck. There was a slight shudder, but Stella's gut told her it was fine. Her plane was fine.

They soared through the gap between the buildings and up over the engulfed main section of Hans' home. Stella pictured the flames licking at their underbelly and smiled. She'd done it and it felt so natural, as if Uncle Josiah had been training her for this all her life, like he'd known she'd need the information someday.

She banked to the right and Oliver's body shifted, cracking his head on the right side. Stella looked down and saw two dozen soldiers firing at them even though they were well out of range. She fought the urge to wave and squeezed the throttle instead. As they flew over the field, she dipped her wings to signal Nicky that she was all right and saw multiple firefly lights flickering in the area where the plane had been parked. Gunfire. She couldn't make out who was who, but Nicky would have the gun from the soldier Oliver shot.

Run. Make it to Paris. I'll be there.

They soared over the trees marking the edge of Hans' property and banked again to the right, heading east instead of west like she was supposed to. She flew over the brewery and into the darkness, away from the inferno. She figured she had to go at least a couple miles before she could backtrack and head west. She didn't want the Nazis to have an easy time tracking her. The more false leads she could give them, the better.

Two hours later, the river slithered below Stella, dotted with barges and lined with small towns still in darkness. The barges saved her. Hans made the river sound easy to find, but she'd flown over it twice before spotting the twinkling lights of a large coal barge. Oliver lay in the student seat, still unconscious. At least she hoped he was unconscious and not dead. He hadn't moved in an hour and that movement was hardly comforting. It was more of a spasm than anything voluntary. She thought maybe he'd moaned at one point, but it could've been the wind. She almost hoped it was. She hated the idea that he might be semi-conscious and unable to move. The cold tortured her, but at least she was able to move and get the blood pumping. Oliver might be freezing to death. It was better if he couldn't feel it.

Her fur coat and Cyril Welk's hat protected her well enough, but her feet were numb stumps. She'd been able to rip off her silk slip, tear it in half, and wrap each of her feet up. The silk helped, but not for long. Her feet were long since numb and she feared she'd lose her toes.

Her only hope for warmth was the sun that took forever to rise. When it did, it was behind her, giving the landscape a pale rosy glow. It didn't give off enough light to warm the ground, much less the air. So Stella flexed each muscle in sequence once again. It kept the blood flowing to her extremities or at least Uncle Josiah claimed it did. It was a trick he used during the war when he flew long, cold flights. He said it also gave him something to think about other than death. It had surprised her the first time he'd told her that he'd thought about death continually during the war. Those dark, unhappy thoughts hardly matched the dashing image she had of him during his youth. The pictures hanging at her grandmother's home, Prie Dieu, showed a man without fear, grinning at the camera with his silk scarf and leather helmet. With those pictures, grandmother had framed the official correspondence she'd received from his various commanding officers. It was just like grandmother to be equally proud of her son's misdeeds, of which there were many. He'd been repeatedly disciplined by his commanders for reckless behavior and disobeying direct orders. Anyone else would've been jailed or possibly shot. But, of course, one didn't do that sort of thing to a Bled, particularly to a Bled with Uncle Josiah's record. The commanders sent letters to his mother hoping she could talk some sense into her boy. Grandmother just laughed and said Josiah could not be contained or controlled. He was a Bled to the bone and she had no influence whatsoever. Grandmother couldn't imagine why they thought she would and Stella wondered as she flexed her muscles again whether she would be so cavalier about her granddaughter's current predicament.

Stella found herself smiling despite the fact that smiling cracked her lips and hurt her frozen face in general. Grandmother was the only one in the family who knew about Stella's flying lessons. One day when Stella was fourteen, Uncle Josiah had snuck her out of her lessons for her first solo flight in the Camel, only to find grandmother leaning on the wing, smoking one of her husband's favorite Havana cigars and shaking her perfect, marcel-waved head at them. She took a big puff, blew out a series of smoke rings, and casually threatened her son's life.

"If something happens to this girl, you had better hope you die in the crash because what I do to you later will make that prison camp you were in look like a Sunday picnic," she said in her raspy low voice.

Uncle Josiah snapped to attention and saluted his imperious mother. "Never fear. Stella's safe with me."

"See that she is." Grandmother turned to Stella. "Your mother can never know. And if, by chance, she finds out, she had better never find out that I knew and let you skip your French lessons. Or is it German today?"

"French," said Stella.

Grandmother blew another smoke ring and gave her an icy glare. "Name the secret ingredient in West Country White Ale."

"Eggs," said Stella.

Grandmother's icy glare continued.

"Egg whites."

"And in what part of the process does the brewer add the whites?" Grandmother asked, her glare beginning to melt.

"The wort."

"Very well then." She kissed Stella's cheek and gave her her blessing before stalking off to her ruby-red Auburn, startling her chauffeur. Clarence jumped out and ran around the incredibly long speedster. Grandmother waved her cigar at Stella and never said another word about her flying beyond a raised eyebrow now and again.

"Thank you, grandmother," whispered Stella between blue lips.

The thought of her grandmother's largesse brought up other memories. Pictures of grandmother on an elephant in India and before the pyramids in Giza. Grandmother sneaking her a sip of wine when her mother wasn't looking, but most of all, Stella could hear her whiskey-soaked voice singing nursery songs. Grandmother's voice was unique and she made trite old songs sound original. Stella's voice wasn't unique or interesting in any way, but she sang with grandmother's voice in her head. Oliver probably wished he was unconscious if he wasn't. Like her father, she couldn't carry a tune in a beer barrel. After depleting grandmother's repertoire, she practiced her French verbs, the few she could remember from Miss Bloom. Anything not to think about Nicky, death, Abel, or Oliver. If she wasn't actively occupied, the firefight on the ground would barge into her mind and she'd begin to think Nicky was dead. She couldn't think that, not for a moment, so she practiced *aller*, *etre*, and *avoir* instead.

After a while, she let the verbs slip away and began talking. At first, it was to no one in particular and then it was to Abel. She played both parts. They discussed the Klimt paintings they should've seen in Vienna. Then Abel became her mother and Stella explained what led her to hail a cab, wear another woman's clothing, and fly a plane. Her mother became her father and they discussed the book, the Gutenberg treasure she was currently sitting on. Her father was quite pleased with her and he didn't care if she hailed a million cabs.

Stella pictured her father safe at home in his study. Hans said he was frantic. She'd never seen him frantic. Angry plenty of times, but never frantic. She tried to imagine what that would look like and failed. Uncle Josiah was a different story. His frantic would be loud and include plenty of cursing. When it was all over, she would tell them all what happened and Uncle Josiah would say he was proud. Damn proud was more likely and her mother would gasp at the word.

Thinking about Uncle Josiah comforted her and she began talking to him. She told him every reading on the cockpit instruments and gauges. She kept coming back to the fuel gauge. Its needle seemed to be moving faster toward empty. In the beginning, she thought she had plenty of fuel to get to the Englehof Brewery, but she had no way of knowing the plane's range. She chose to think it was similar to Uncle Josiah's Sopwith Camel, maybe a little better with a similar speed. If that were true, she should make it. If it wasn't, she'd better start looking for a place to land. Stella leaned to her left and peeked over the cockpit edge. It was a lot lighter out and she could make out the ground features easily. There was a small, rough road next to the river, but it twisted with the waterway and was useless to land on. Fields abounded, but she'd never attempted a field landing before and trying it in an unfamiliar plane seemed like a bad idea.

What had Hans said about the brewery? Only that it was on the river and very large. The vineyard should be a good flag, but what if she missed it? The fuel gauge was edging closer to empty. It would only be a few minutes until the needle touched the zero. How long would she have after it did? Uncle Josiah said the Camel always gave a few extra miles. A fact that had saved his bacon a few times over

France, but she had no idea what the Focke-Wulf would do. Her eyes darted around the instrument panel, and then she leaned over the edge again. The river took a sharp turn and she followed it.

"I'll wait," she said. "There has to be a better spot."

Stella looked at the back of Oliver's head. He was still crumpled to the right and unresponsive. She looked over the edge once again and saw no place for a smooth landing.

"It can't be easy," she said.

If she had to land in a field, it would be terribly rough. Oliver might even bounce out since he couldn't brace himself. She had to a find a more level surface.

The needle touched the zero almost exactly at the moment that she decided to keep waiting. The plane shuddered and coughed like one of her father's employees, the big men who smoked rank cigars nonstop.

"Oh, no! Not now. Give me some more." Stella stroked the throttle. "You're as good as a camel." Then she realized the Focke-Wulf was better. The Germans were precise. If it was designed to fly three hundred miles, that's exactly how far it would fly. No guesswork necessary.

She leaned over and looked for a good spot. The terrain had grown hilly with nothing remotely flat to land on. She'd have to turn around and try to make it back to the fields. They were at least better than hills. She banked to the right so Oliver wouldn't shift and crack his head again. When the right wing dipped, she looked down at the hills racing past. They were studded with thousands of posts and wires. Stumpy little trunks were placed at precise intervals. Grapevines.

"The vineyard!" Stella shouted.

She banked again and turned them around completely. The plane shuddered again and Stella held her breath. Hans was right. The vineyard was huge. A dozen more hills and it was still going. Then she went over another larger hill and saw a group of buildings at the water's edge. They were low and stone. Certainly not as impressive as Johannes' or Hans' breweries.

Stella flew over the buildings and saw a man in the vineyard. He wore a broad-brimmed hat and stooped over a vine. When they flew over, he stood up and watched them pass. Stella reached to adjust the mixture when the engine conked out. The needle was exactly in the center of the zero. German engineering. Perfect.

Gliding in wasn't difficult, according to Uncle Josiah. Of course, everything was easy to him as long as he wasn't being shot at. Stella spotted a fallow field with a long, straight road in the center and she wasn't being shot at, so in theory, she should be able to land with no difficulty. All she had to do was make it over the stand of trees marking the edge. She pulled back on the stick, hoping to get a little extra lift, but she'd allowed herself to get too low. She yanked back and they grazed the tops of the first trees, going lower and lower. The sound of cracking branches assaulted her ears and she hunkered down in the cockpit, holding the stick and praying to God and Uncle Josiah.

The Focke-Wulf broke through the trees, slightly twisting to the right. Stella felt the change but couldn't do anything about it before they hit the ground. The right wing sliced into the dirt and snapped with a tremendous crack. Stella grappled for the brake and that was the last thing she remembered.

"*Wer ist es?*" said a man's voice from somewhere above Stella.

"Oliver. *Er ist, aber gerade kaum lebendig.*"

Someone shifted Stella's head and she felt a cold breeze as her hat was removed.

"*Es ist eine junge frau.*"

There were sounds of someone scrambling around. Stella struggled to open her eyes. They felt so heavy, as though someone had attached weights to them. The best she could do for a moment was blurry slits. All she could see was grey and someone indistinct moving around. Something icy and wet was pressed against her forehead. The cold roused her and she opened her eyes in response.

When they began to focus, she could make out a man bent low over her, his face nearly level with hers. His skin was soft and saggy. He looked at her with dark hazel eyes under a pair of bushy eyebrows.

He smiled and removed a white cloth from her forehead that was stained with red.

"*Sie ist fein,*" he said to someone behind Stella.

The man refolded the cloth so that it was mostly white and placed it back on Stella's head. Then he reached down and held up the battered rabbit fur fedora.

"I always intended to get my hat back, Mrs. Bled, but I never expected such a dramatic delivery."

Stella blinked.

"Don't tell me you don't remember your savior in Vienna? My heart will be absolutely shattered," he said with a smile she would've considered rakish if he wasn't so old.

"You're missing," she said.

"Cyril Welk is never missing. People just don't know where I am."

CHAPTER 22

Cyril laid Stella on the grass beside the plane and covered her with an itchy wool blanket that smelled like fish. Under any other circumstances, she would've tossed the nasty thing away, but the blanket's warmth was worth it. She rolled her head to the side to look at Oliver lying on the grass beside her. A blond man she didn't know examined the gash on his shoulder, then covered it in a fresh bandage and sat back with his arms crossed. His gaze switched from Oliver's white face to Stella's.

"Can you speak?" he asked in perfect English with a soft German accent.

Stella opened her mouth to answer but found the words didn't want to come. Oliver was alive. He didn't look it, but he was alive. After a moment of struggling, she nodded her head, causing a searing pain to start behind her eyes.

"Where did you come from?" he asked.

"Hans," she said with effort.

"Hans Gruber?"

She nodded again.

He looked up at the Nazi plane and down at Oliver. "What happened?"

"Hans said someone was trying to kill a Nazi named Göring or the other one."

"Göring was at the brewery?"

"Yes. There were explosions. Oliver was hurt. We had to get him out." The effort of talking exhausted Stella and she closed her eyes. The pain in her head grew steadily worse and she wished for an aspirin or one of her father's hot toddies to dull the pain.

"Mrs. Bled Lawrence."

Stella jerked and opened her eyes.

"Whose plane is this?"

"Peiper."

The man paled. "You stole Helmut Peiper's plane?"

Her eyes slid closed. "I don't know if he's called Helmut, but he is an *Oberführer*, whatever that is."

The man touched her face and she looked into his fearful eyes. "You stole Oberführer Peiper's plane?"

"The only way," she murmured.

The man shot to his feet and started shouting orders. One boy, quite young, ran into the woods. Stella closed her eyes and when she opened them again, the boy was leading a pair of draft horses past her. The blond man took the reins and led them out of Stella's field of vision. She tried to sit up, but nausea hit and forced her to lie back down.

"Don't try to get up yet," said Cyril, squatting next to her. "You've taken a nasty blow to the head, not that it's marred you in any way. Kaspar says you won't even have a scar."

"Is he a doctor?"

"No. He was a kind of medic in the war. On the other side, you understand," said Cyril.

The plane lurched forward with a sudden screech of metal and snapping tree limbs. Stella sat up, holding her head. She almost fell back over, but Cyril caught her by the shoulders. She let him pull her to his chest and breathed in the comforting scents of pipe tobacco and castile soap with its olive oil undertones while waiting for the spins to stop. Cyril rubbed her back and she breathed deeper. Uncle Josiah carried the scent of tobacco smoke with him like a talisman against bad luck. The scent never left him. As the spins slowed and her stomach settled, Stella imagined it was Uncle Josiah there with her, smelling fabulous and taking care of things as he always did.

As she relaxed, Cyril's grip tightened. "You are quite lovely," he said.

Stella's eyes flew open and she jerked out of his arms

"What, my dear?" he asked. "I was merely stating a fact."

Stella pursed her lips and glared at him. Every instinct she had said she should give him a good smack. But he was an old man. She couldn't be going around smacking old men, especially this one. He knew Hans and she was beholden to him, at least for the moment. Besides, her head hurt, her defrosting toes were on fire, and she needed to throw up. She didn't want to fight with anyone.

"Just don't be doing anything," she said, holding her aching head between her hands.

Cyril touched his chest. "My dear, you don't think I was going to… I have a daughter your age. The very idea." He fluttered his hands about and he looked genuinely disgusted.

"You have a daughter?" Stella asked as another wave of nausea came over her.

"I do, indeed. Alexandra. She's a lovely sweet girl." Cyril smiled, appearing to be warmed by the memory of his child. But there was something else there, too. Stella tried to figure out what it was. Something with Alexandra, perhaps. The effort to puzzle it out hurt her head and she decided that it hardly mattered if Cyril really had a daughter or not.

Stella relaxed and pushed all unpleasant thoughts out of her mind. She let Cyril hold her again and watched the plane being dragged away by the horses. Kaspar led the enormous animals to the right and two other men carried the broken wing behind them.

"Where are they taking it?" she asked.

"The river," said Cyril. "It's the best option for concealing your crash."

"The river? They're going to throw it in the river?" Stella felt around the blanket. Her hands searched, but she wasn't sure what they were supposed to find. What was she missing? Her hands fluttered up to her chest and pressed against her breasts. Definitely missing something. There should be a weight, a hard-edged weight there.

The plane left the field between two trees. Stella saw a river in the distance a hundred yards or so beyond it. She closed her eyes and Abel's battered face appeared. A mirage or a message straight from her soul.

Her eyes flew open. "The book."

"What book?" asked Cyril, stroking her hand.

Stella jerked away. "The book's in the plane."

She pushed back the blanket and staggered to her feet. The field melted into a post-impressionist blur. Cyril caught her arm and forced her back down onto the blanket.

"I'll get it," he said before racing across the field.

Stella fell over on her side and closed her eyes, but the white starbursts were so sickening she opened them again. The grass in front of her doubled and blurred. Someone called her name, but she couldn't respond and her vision went black.

The room was dark, but cozy. Candlelight tickled the walls with warm caresses and all was safe and secure. Stella slid her hand under the blankets toward Nicky's side of the bed but found a wall instead. She turned her head, her hand roving over crumbling plaster as she wished her head would stop throbbing and wondered where she was and more importantly, where Nicky was.

"I am but a prophet of words. A man filled with unrealistic dreams."

Stella turned away from the wall and saw Cyril sitting in a canebottomed chair with a candle at his elbow.

"What?" she asked.

"You have good taste in books, Stella Bled Lawrence," said Cyril, his face marked with shadows.

The book lay open on his lap, its wrappings trailing over his knees like he'd opened a long-awaited Christmas gift. She stirred under the blankets, trying to get up enough steam to snatch the book away, but she couldn't move more than a few inches.

"Don't strain yourself, Stella."

"You shouldn't have opened that," she said.

"Perhaps not. But I couldn't resist. Is this beauty what got you running in Vienna?" Cyril asked.

"None of your business."

"It's my business now," he said. "You're here, aren't you?"

"Give it to me."

"I'd like to read it first, if I may."

"No." Stella pushed herself upright. Her head swum a little, but she felt much better. "Give it back."

"Didn't your parents teach you to share?" He gave her a wink and ran his fingers sensuously down the edge of the book's pages.

She crossed her arms. "Are you flirting with me?"

"I'm gratified you noticed."

"Give me my book."

"So it's yours?" he asked, turning a page.

Stella hesitated. The book wasn't hers, but the look on Cyril's face told her she was in deep waters. If the book wasn't hers, it could become his.

"It's mine," she said.

"I think not. If someone in your family had a complete work by Gutenberg, it would be your father."

"How did you know it's by Gutenberg?" Stella asked.

"I can read." It was Cyril's turn to hesitate. "But you can't, can you? Read Latin, that is."

Stella didn't answer. Instead, she reached over and gently pulled the book off his lap and onto hers. She pressed its familiar weight to her chest and felt complete again. With the book, she felt stronger, like she knew what she was supposed to be doing.

"Have you heard from Hans?" she asked.

"No, but the assassination attempt was reported on the radio. They called it a gas explosion."

Stella swallowed and held the book tighter. "Any word about my husband?"

"None. But word has filtered down about the SS moving through the east from Hans' brewery. No one knows what they're doing. I would assume they're looking for Peiper's plane, but why east?"

"I flew east to give them a false trail," said Stella. "Are you sure there's nothing about Nicky? They didn't take any prisoners?"

"For a *gas explosion*? No. That would not be public. We can't make any inquiries. It's never wise to look too interested in State affairs. Excellent decision in flying east. They'll waste time searching Austria when you're in their own backyard. Taking Peiper's plane was less wise."

"I told Kaspar it was the only way to get Oliver out. How is he?"

"He'll lose some toes, but Kaspar says the cold may have saved his life. It slowed his bleeding. How are you acquainted with Peiper?"

Stella lay back on the bed, too tired to conceal anything anymore. "He interviewed us in Vienna."

"Peiper interviewed you personally and you weren't arrested? Impressive. Was it about the book?" Cyril leaned back in his chair and propped his feet up on Stella's bed.

"No. It was about our tour guide, Abel."

Cyril tapped his lips with his forefinger and narrowed his eyes at Stella. "Peiper was interested in your guide? How intriguing. And your guide is Jewish, I assume."

Stella gave him a sharp glance. "That doesn't matter."

"I think it does. The book isn't yours, so perhaps it belongs to your guide. He was important enough to the Oberführer that he was searching for the man himself."

"I said it doesn't matter."

"You know the book is by Gutenberg. What else do you know?"

"Nicky translated some of it. It's Gutenberg's diary."

"What else?"

"Nothing else. What else should there be?"

Stella watched Cyril's face. He looked like her brother when he'd found her Easter basket and couldn't hardly wait to tell her where the bunny had hidden it.

"Why don't you just tell me? You obviously want to," she said.

"What's the information worth to you?" He leaned forward, dropping the chair legs on the floor with a clunk, his eyes ravenous.

Stella clutched the book tighter. "Cyril, I'm probably the same age as your daughter."

"What daughter?"

"Don't play stupid."

"Why not?" Cyril asked with a sly grin. "Stupidity has served me well. No one suspects an idiot."

"You should be embarrassed to play the fool."

"I use what works and that's hardly foolish."

He reached out and patted her calf. Stella looked down at his soft hand with its polished nails and French cuff. Then she saw the leg underneath it, filthy with a multitude of scratches on top of bruises that varied in age and color. Above the calf was the once-lovely tulip dress. It was no longer remotely white with imbedded dirt and splatters of blood from at least three sources. Cyril's hand started inching up toward her skirt and Stella stared as it impudently made its way up under her filthy hem, when her face curved into a smile and her long unused laugh bubbled up from the place where she kept all her happiness.

"Stop it. You are ridiculous," she said between guffaws.

Cyril pulled back his hand and laughed along with her. "You aren't the first woman to say so."

"And I won't be the last, if you keep that nonsense up."

"I had to try."

"Why?" asked Stella, wiping her eyes. "Look at me. I'm hardly enticing."

"You underestimate yourself."

"The only thing I'm underestimating is your craziness and I'm a Bled. I know crazy."

Cyril laughed so hard he had to grasp the edge of the bed to brace himself. "Yes, you should know better. I've read your family's dossier. How many times has your Uncle been arrested for drunken disorderly conduct?"

"Fifty-three." Stella fell over and clutched her stomach. "Never convicted though."

The room's door swung open with a creak and Cyril stopped laughing the instant he saw the woman standing in the doorway. She was a tiny figure, the size of a twelve-year-old boy, with iron grey hair in a tight bun, wearing a flowered housedress cinched at the waist with a man's belt. She looked at Stella with a bird-hunting-a-worm intensity and then switched to Cyril, who jumped to his feet and held up his hands. The woman began speaking rapid-fire German. Cyril returned fire, but Stella could see he was getting the worse end of it. The woman shook her finger in his face and grabbed his shoulder. Cyril tried to get away from her but only succeeded in dancing in a circle.

The woman maneuvered him over to the door and kicked him through it with a sturdy boy's shoe. She slammed the door in his face and Cyril started yelling through it. The woman yelled back and pounded on the door as if she was trying to get in instead of trying to keep Cyril out.

"I'll be back, Stella," yelled Cyril. "Hildegard will take care of you."

The woman, presumably Hildegard, made a rude gesture to the door and turned to face Stella, who sat up and looked for a weapon. Hildegard threw up her hands and rolled her eyes. She spoke to Stella in German without pausing for breath. Stella could only stare at her and clutch the book. Hildegard turned on her heels, flung open the door, and looked out both ways. Then she yelled something down the hall. In a minute, two young women in braids and rough men's clothing tromped in carrying large buckets. They dumped them into a galvanized tub in the corner that looked like an oversized mop bucket. The women kept bringing buckets until the tub was half-full and then left, closing Stella in with Hildegard who had never stopped talking the entire time.

Then she jerked the blanket off Stella's feet and unwrapped the bandages that covered her toes. Stella recoiled when she saw the white and yellow patches that covered her feet. Hildegard kept talking while she pulled a small green packet out of her pocket. She opened the packet, produced a pin that resembled Stella's great grandmother's hatpin and, without hesitation, jabbed it into Stella's big toe. Stella shrieked and tried to yank her foot away, but Hildegard held it firm in her tiny hand and for a moment was quiet. Then she rubbed Stella's toe, working it like she was milking a cow. Then she began speaking again. The words came just as rapidly, but with a satisfied tone. She rubbed her thumb on Stella's toe and held it up for her to see. A bright red smear decorated it. Stella assumed this was a good thing since the woman smiled. Stella smiled back, hoping there would be no more toe jabbing in her future. Happily, Hildegard put the pin back in its packet. She put her hands on her hips and lectured for a few minutes. Stella sat on the bed, holding the book and wishing Cyril would come back, although he seemed more afraid of Hildegard than she was.

When Stella didn't respond to the lecture, Hildegard stomped her foot, grabbed Stella's ankles, and pulled her to the edge of the bed. She bent Stella over and unbuttoned the back of the tulip dress before Stella could open her mouth to protest. She grabbed Stella by the shoulders and lifted her to her feet as easily as she would a small child. She gave Stella a stern look, accompanied by about half a million German words, and took the book out of her hands. She placed the book on the bed with a firmness that said now that is that. Then she took Stella's dress by the hem and pulled it over her head, leaving her in her brassiere and panties. Now she shook her finger in Stella's face, gesturing to her mostly nude figure. It took a second, but Stella finally realized what she was being chastised for. She pointed at the floor where her poor little Parisian shoes were lying, covered in dirt. Next to them were the remains of her slip. The woman snatched up the silk rags, gave Stella an evaluating glance, and decided to forgive her for her lapse in decorum. She dropped the slip bits, spun Stella around, unhooked her bra, and started yanking on her panties. Before Stella knew it, she was up to her chin in the tub and the woman was scrubbing her hair with a bar of soap that smelled like lilacs.

A knock on the door echoed through the small chamber and a woman said in a small, timid voice, "*Hallo?*"

"*Ja*"

The door swung open and one of the young women from before crept in carrying a tray loaded with dark brown bread, a hunk of creamy soft butter, and a beer stein filled to the brim. The young woman set the tray on the bed, nodded to Hildegard, and crept back out the door. Hildegard said something that came across as highly critical. The young woman must've been Hildegard's daughter. Only a mother could sound so wholly dissatisfied with such a nice-looking girl. Stella opened her mouth to tell Hildegard that being a mother didn't come with the right to criticize every single thing a person did, but Hildegard, being a mother, must've sensed a protest. She put her hand on top of Stella's head and shoved it under the water. Stella came up sputtering and without a thought to mother-daughter dynamics. Hildegard gave her the soap and indicated it was time to wash the rest of herself. She also made it clear that she wasn't leaving for the sake of privacy. Stella pointed at the door, but Hildegard shook her head and snorted. Then she let out some German that Stella was almost certain she understood. Hildegard was saying she was fussy and spoiled with that I-had-it-terrible-when-I-was-a-child look on her face.

Stella grimaced and Hildegard crossed her arms.

"Fine," said Stella, rocketing out of the water.

A good deal of water sloshed on the floor and Hildegard threw her hands up at the sight.

Stella held her arms wide and ignored the burning pain in her feet. "Do I look spoiled to you?"

Hildegard said something dismissive and went to a small cupboard and got out several rags. Stella started scrubbing herself the second Hildegard's back was turned. She ran the soap over her chest and belly. Even she was amazed at her own condition. Cuts, bruises, and scrapes covered every inch of her. Certainly not the body of a spoiled woman. She possessed the body of a woman who could hail cabs, escape in beer barrels, and survive plane crashes. Her mother would be shocked and probably would take to her bed for a week when she found out. The thought was oddly satisfying.

Stella sat down as Hildegard mopped up the water. When she finished mopping, she lifted Stella out of the tub by her shoulders and rubbed her down with an old cotton sheet like she was a lathered mare. Then she dressed her in a man's dress shirt and pants. Both were high-quality and hand-made. Stella suspected they'd been pilfered from Cyril's wardrobe.

Hildegard sat Stella on the bed, handed her a piece of bread smeared with pale yellow butter, and stomped out of the room. Stella sat for a moment before she took a bite. She half-expected Hildegard to come back and put it in her mouth for her. But she didn't come back and Stella ate her bread in blissful silence. The bread was nutty and warm and the butter sweet with a hint of honey. As Stella ate, she began to be light-headed. Her body had almost forgotten about the pleasures of food, especially food so simple and rich.

And after a few minutes, a soft knock on the door interrupted her pleasure.

"Stella," said Cyril. "Is it safe?"

"Hildegard's gone, if that's what you mean," said Stella.

Cyril opened the door and peeked at her through the crack. "That's exactly what I meant."

"Come in. Do you want some bread? It's delicious."

"It had better be. Hildegard made it. It wouldn't dare be otherwise. But no, thank you. I've eaten," he said, taking his seat on the chair next to the bed. "How are you feeling?"

"Better," said Stella, yawning. "Any news?"

"Nothing yet."

"When can I leave?" she asked, finger-combing her hair with her free hand.

"You're anxious to go?"

"I'm afraid to stay. Everywhere I go, disaster follows. Besides, I have to take the book to Paris. I told Nicky I'd meet him in three days. I've only got two days left."

Cyril nodded as he contemplated her, his eyes roaming over her face and figure. The look in his eye should've bothered her, but she found she didn't mind. Her mother would've ordered him out of the room for looking at her like that, but her father and Uncle Josiah would've laughed. Stella found her feelings fell on the side of laughter. Besides, she had bigger things to worry about. Paris in two days was no easy feat. She needed Cyril.

He shifted in his chair, clearly settling in for a while. "You want to tell me about the historian?"

"I thought you said you hadn't heard anything," said Stella.

"I haven't. Oliver woke up. He said there was a Dutch historian with Peiper."

"Then you know as much as I do." She took a big bite and washed it down with a dark hoppy beer that she wasn't familiar with. She'd have to ask about the style for her father. He'd want to know.

"Has he seen you?" asked Cyril. "In person?"

"He was on the train to Vienna. I guess he was following us," she said.

"You mean he was following your guide. Peiper wasn't there?"

"No, he wasn't. Why?"

"A lot of people want to get their hands on that book. Van Wijk was willing to team up with Peiper to get it. A dangerous proposition if there ever was one. And it seems Himmler and Göring are in the picture." Cyril paused and touched her knee. "I'll take the book to Paris. It's the least I can do after you risked your life to save Oliver."

"I'm going to Paris. I told you. I'm meeting Nicky."

"Fine. We'll travel to Paris separately. I'll carry the book."

Stella put down her bread. "Why would you do that?"

"It's better that way. I know I don't look it, but I am rather skilled in these matters. Why does the book have to go to Paris?"

"I promised Abel I'd take it to his family."

"The Sorkines are his family then." Cyril stood up, knocking his chair back several inches. "He had no right to ask that of you."

"Who was he supposed to ask? He'd been arrested. They were sending him to a camp."

"He shouldn't have asked you," said Cyril, his voice rising.

"Why not?"

"Because he knew what the book meant and you didn't."

"The book's a treasure. What more is there to know?"

"That's not why they want it."

"Van Wijk is a historian. Of course that's why they want it."

"I doubt Van Wijk knows."

"Knows what?" Stella was now yelling. She could hear someone moving outside the door, but she didn't care.

"Peiper will burn the book."

"That's crazy. It's a historic treasure. Priceless."

Cyril slumped into his chair. "The Nazis burn books."

"Not that book," said Stella. "It's art. They collect art."

He shook his head. "Only a certain kind of art, the kind Hitler can understand. Anything that doesn't fit his ideology burns."

Stella thought of the burning synagogues in Vienna and said, "The book doesn't support anybody's ideology. It's Gutenberg's diary. It has to do with the first printed bible."

"It also has to do with Gutenberg's life. He was a German, perhaps the most famous German of all time, inventor of the world's greatest invention."

"You'll get no arguments here," said Stella.

Cyril shifted in his chair and blew out a breath. "I suppose you must know what you're dealing with." He hesitated and then said, "Gutenberg was a great man. He was also a man who loved and married a Jewish woman. It's all in the book. Her name was Nissa."

"Nicky wrote down that name. I didn't realize she was his wife." Stella picked up the book and opened the cover to the red chalk portrait that had so entranced her the first time she'd seen it. The lovely woman with the beatific expression. Nissa. "My father said Gutenberg was never married," said Stella.

"It must be one of the best-kept secrets of all time," said Cyril.

Stella stared at the portrait, memorizing the lines and soft strokes. "They wouldn't burn it. They couldn't. Nobody could see this and throw it in a fire."

"There's no better way to keep a secret than to destroy it," he said.

"I don't understand why they would want to."

Cyril leaned forward and touched her hand. It was an aching touch. A touch that longed to be more. "I can see you don't. You'll just have to trust me on this. It matters. The Nazis are bent on purging all the Jews from Germany. This book," he said. "This little book would hinder their cause. If Gutenberg loved and valued a Jew, why shouldn't the German people value them? They can't afford for their people to ask that question. Even worse, it would focus the world's attention on Germany and its policies. People might start thinking about the Jews in a different way. That's the last thing they want."

"They could just lock it away," said Stella.

"And they could just leave the Jews alone, but they won't. Their hate is focused. It cannot be diverted. I'll carry the book to Paris."

She shook her head, her damp curls pitter-pattering her cheeks. "It's my responsibility. I gave my word."

"They'd kill you for it."

"Doesn't your word mean anything to you?"

"It depends who I'm giving it to," said Cyril.

Stella closed the book and wrapped her arms around it. "Promise me you won't take it from me."

"I promise." Cyril met her eyes. "Do you believe me?"

Stella nodded. She did believe him, though she would never tell a single soul why. She'd seen that look in men's eyes before and it was too precious to be discounted. She handed him the book. "Will you read it to me?"

Cyril took the book and opened it to a place about a fourth of the way in. Stella lay down and tucked a pillow under her head as he began reading in a hesitant way that grew stronger as he contin-ued. He read of Gutenberg meeting a young woman in an apothe-cary shop. He spoke of her smile and how her interfering maid refused to let them speak. Nissa was half his age and a Jew, but that didn't matter to Gutenberg. He pursued her, breaking off his engagement to another woman and doing everything he could think of to persuade her father of his worthiness. He had his family tree drawn on vellum, not so subtly reminding the gentleman that he was from a patrician family with connections. Gutenberg was a member of the goldsmith guild and he had loyal and discreet friends in the organization write Nissa's father letters praising his status and good character. The gentleman wasn't convinced and pressed Gutenberg about his need to keep the marriage to his daughter a secret, a plan of which he did not approve. It was clear that the marriage would hurt Gutenberg's business prospects if the marriage was discovered, but it was a risk he was willing to take. Nissa's father was not.

It wasn't clear how the marriage came to take place. There were only hints of Nissa herself making it come about through some sort of threat. Gutenberg praised his wife's ingenuity and said that Nissa was the woman with whom he would find great success. She was steady and sensible as well as a beauty.

"And what did he say about himself?" Stella asked. "He was a patrician and a goldsmith. Anything else?"

Cyril turned the book toward her and pointed to a specific line. "Johannes Gutenberg was uncommonly honest and accurate about himself."

"What does it say?"

"I am but a prophet of words. A man filled with unrealistic dreams," he read.

Stella yawned and said, "Nissa was the secret of his success."

"He believed so."

The more Cyril read, the more Stella understood the man. Through his words, Gutenberg became alive for her, a real person and one not so different from herself. He knew the moment he saw Nissa that she would be his wife. He knew the same way Stella had known about Nicky. People called that love at first sight, but to call it that was to diminish the feeling which went well beyond looks and far into character.

Cyril glanced at Stella as he read. His voice was strong and warm with emotion, especially when he read about Nissa's beauty and her clever invention of the inks that Gutenberg would later use to print his bible. They shared a passion for art and a talent for it. It was

Gutenberg himself who drew the portraits of his wife, but it was she who drew the sketches of the printing press.

Stella flexed her painful toes and closed her eyes. "So no one ever knew."

Cyril lifted her limp arm and slid the book under it. "No. People found out."

Stella's eyes opened to slits. "Who knew?"

"The Catholic church and others."

"The church," Stella repeated.

Cyril bent low over her, blowing the rich scent of tobacco in her face. "Go to sleep, Stella Bled." He kissed her dangerously close to her mouth and then rested his lips in her hair for a moment.

"Lawrence," she said. "Stella Bled Lawrence."

"Of course," he said, standing up and going to the door.

"Children?" whispered Stella, already half-asleep.

Cyril opened the door and looked back, his brow folding like an accordion. "What was that, my dear?"

"Did they have children?"

"Yes. They most certainly did."

Stella cuddled down and pressed the book to her chest, whispering, "Abel."

CHAPTER 23

The next morning, Stella sat in the corner of a large room with low blackened beams and a well-swept dirt floor. Hildegard had swathed her in blankets and insisted she eat a brötchen with a thick slab of butter in the center. Saying she wasn't very hungry made no difference to Hildegard. Stella would eat and endure a painful examination of her feet while she did it.

After Stella had choked down two large *brötchen* and a small tankard of crisp white wine that Hildegard seemed to indicate would help her feet, Kaspar came in with some unfamiliar men and Cyril.

Kaspar nodded to her and went to a table in the center of the room. Hildegard went after him, haranguing him and gesturing like a Southern Italian. They went on arguing for nearly an hour, only pausing for Hildegard to fill everyone's tankard.

Stella couldn't understand Hildegard at all and only caught a word or two of what Kaspar said, useless words like '*nein*' and '*sie*'. She did detect a note of panic in his deep voice. She'd heard it in her father's during prohibition when it looked like their small bootlegging operation might be uncovered by federal agents. It never was, being well-concealed in the factory basement beneath their new operations of powdered milk and dye manufacturing.

The one thing Stella knew for certain was that the argument was about her. Cyril's worried face backed up her intuition, but he said nothing and kept well away from the storming Hildegard.

After the argument, another couple of men came in. They stomped their feet and shook off sparkling drops of rain that clung to their heavy jackets and caps. They greeted Cyril and nodded to Stella before bending over the table with Kaspar. Their fear wasn't nearly so well-concealed. Beads of sweat formed down their domed foreheads and upper lips as they glanced at Stella in an inscrutable way that she now recognized as distinctly German. Angry and admiring. Two expressions she didn't know went together until she met Wilhelm and Erich. She gathered that they were brothers and were in disguise, not that it did much good. Their rough farmers' clothing couldn't hide their pale skin and long, aristocratic fingers that had never known a callus. Her father and uncles were more roughened and they were rarely in the fields.

Hildegard looked them over and was obviously not satisfied. She bellowed out the door and one of the girls hustled in with a platter. Hildegard whipped off the cloth that covered the platter and began haranguing the girl, who ran back out.

"What was that about?" Stella asked Cyril.

"Bad cheese."

Kaspar smiled at her and said something. Stella caught 'Hildegard' and '*käse*'.

Hildegard smacked Kaspar on the arm and he laughed. "*Dein käse ist geworden.*"

"*Nein.*"

"*Ja.*"

Cyril said to Stella, "Her cheese is bad. I've had it. It's turned." Then he translated what he said to Kaspar, eliciting smug looks. Hildegard crossed her arms and nodded at Erich.

The men wiped their grins off and began examining a map that Erich rolled out on the table, holding it down with a couple of bricks. Cyril came to stand next to Stella. He'd been keeping his distance all morning and seemed uncomfortable to be close to her. She wasn't sure if it was something she did or something he did, but he wasn't happy at all.

Wilhelm pointed at something on the map and Kaspar barked at Hildegard, who marched over and put a heavy hand on Stella's shoulder. She snarled something in German that made Stella queasy with nerves.

"What's going on?" Stella asked Cyril.

He didn't look at her. "They're arguing about what to do with you."

"What do you mean? Why do they have to do something with me? I'll just leave. I have to go to Paris. If I can just borrow some money, I'll be out of their hair."

"It's more complicated than that, my dear," he said.

Kaspar rolled up the map, gave some orders to the other men, and turned to Stella.

"Peiper is having a house to house search performed and they're headed this way. If you or Oliver are found, we'll all be exposed."

Stella raised an eyebrow despite the stinging it caused. "Exposed as what?"

The men merely stared at her and then began speaking in German again. Hildegard frowned and pointed a bony finger at Cyril. He blushed and straightened up, insisting about something.

"Who are you people?" asked Stella, raising her voice to match her brow. "I know what Oliver is. He told me. Are you spies, too?"

"We are not spies," said Kaspar. "We resist."

"And what are you resisting?"

"The party."

"The Nazis?"

"Yes."

Stella glanced over at the map on the table and the line of weapons stacked up along the wall. They were doing more than simply resisting. Stella knew about resisting. She resisted lessons, curfews, and the clothes her mother picked out. Resisting didn't take an arsenal. This was something more like a revolution or a mutiny.

"How's the *resisting* going?" she asked.

"Well. Until last night." The men frowned at Stella and she lifted her hands out of the cocoon of blankets. "Those explosions had nothing to do with me or Oliver."

"Yes, but you stole the plane and led them here."

"I had to. You saw Oliver. He would've died."

"Yes, but this complicates our operations," said Kaspar.

Stella reached down and patted the book on her lap for reassurance. "Well, spot me a few bucks and I'll get out of your hair. Can't you hide Oliver in a wall or something?"

"Hildegard and I have found a plan. There is a family of Swiss nearby. They have been helping Jews to escape. They may agree to help the two of you."

Stella sat up. "Who are they?"

"We will not say. Secrecy is vital," said Kaspar. "Why do you wish to know?"

"I have a friend. He was arrested in Vienna. I may need to smuggle him out if my family can't use their connections."

"Who is this person?" asked Erich in English for the first time.

"Abel Herschmann."

"A Jew?"

"Yes, and he's the one Peiper is really after," she said.

"But they have him. Why follow you?" Erich and his brother frowned as the sweat on their brows increased.

Stella managed to keep herself from glancing at Cyril. He hadn't told them about the book and she didn't want to give it away. "They don't know they have him. He gave them a false name, I think."

"And why would he do that?"

"I'll take her," said Cyril.

"You're to return to London," said Kaspar.

"I'm taking her. It's the least we can do for Hans."

At the name Hans, Hildegard gripped Stella tighter to the point that she winced but didn't dare pull away. Hildegard asked Kaspar something and he responded with several sentences about Hans.

"What's that about Hans?" asked Stella.

Everyone stopped talking when she said his name. Kaspar turned away and spoke over his shoulder to her. "We've just had word this morning. Hans is dead."

He said something else, but Stella stopped hearing him after the word 'dead'. Hildegard lifted Stella to her feet, gave her a fierce hug, and then sat her back on the stool.

"Are you sure?" Stella whispered.

"It was on the radio. They said he died in the fire," said Kaspar.

Stella let her tears trace rivers on her cheeks. "But you don't believe that's how it happened."

"No."

"Why would they lie?"

"Hans was important to the party and to Germany. He was a very popular brewer. To reveal that he was against them, would be inconvenient to their cause."

Their cause. There were those words again.

"What about Nicky?" Stella could hardly force the words out. If Hans was dead, what chance did her husband have?

"Nothing about any Americans." Kaspar turned around. "I don't know if we can get you to Paris even with the Swiss family's help."

"I told you I'll take her," said Cyril more strongly.

"It is too big a risk. Hildegard is a better choice."

Hildegard heard her name and began letting them have it. Stella almost wanted to know what was going on, but thoughts of Hans flooded her mind. She wondered if her father knew yet and what he would say when he found out that she'd been there, that it might be her fault. She started sobbing at the thought of her father's grief. She dropped the remains of her brötchen and covered her eyes. Someone parted the blankets and took the book off her lap. She wanted to protest but couldn't stop the huge shuddering sobs that racked her body. Cyril whispered in her ear, lifted her off the stool, and guided her out of the room. Hildegard kept up a running argument while they walked, but Cyril hardly answered. When they got to the room, he steered Stella through the door, blocked Hildegard, and closed the door in her face. Hildegard yelled outside the door for a minute and then stomped down the hall.

Cyril lowered Stella's hands and put the book in them. "I'll get you to Paris. Hildegard cleaned your dress and left you some cosmetics to cover your bruises. We'll go as soon as you're ready."

Stella nodded and watched him leave, only to be pounced on by Hildegard who was lurking in the hall. He closed the door to argue with her and Stella stood in the middle of the room, holding the book and feeling frozen and heavy. Hans was dead. She kept telling herself that, but somehow, the more she said it the less convinced she got. She began to think there was a mistake. She would get to Paris. Nicky would be there and he'd tell her it was somebody else who died.

She made herself move toward the bed. The tulip dress lay across the blankets, clean and ironed. The stains had been washed pale, but so had the tulips. They were an odd pink instead of their brilliant red and some of the stitching had come loose. She set the book next to the dress and began to undress, whispering a prayer. This time to her mother.

"Smile, Stella." Cyril led her into the train station with a fuming Hildegard attached to her side. The two escorts had argued continuously on the trip into town and from what Stella gathered, Hildegard was winning. Cyril wanted the lady to walk behind them like a servant, but she wouldn't budge. Hildegard held on to Stella as if she were her last nickel and Cyril was out to steal it.

"Uh-huh," murmured Stella.

"Remember, you're happy," he said with a distinct edge.

Stella fixed a smile on her face that was neither convincing nor genuine, but it was the best she could do. There was such a swirl of emotion rotating through her body that she had to remind herself to smile every few minutes. Only the thought of Nicky waiting in Paris kept her going. She refused to think of anything or anyone else. There'd be time enough for that later.

They found a ticket booth at the far end of the station and Cyril charmed the girl behind the counter into giving them seats in first class for the price of second. Stella smiled her approval and started to feel better. Maybe this was a good idea, not a disaster in the offing.

As Cyril handed over a stack of cash, Hildegard squeezed her arm and gave her an oddly blank look, cocking her small head to the side. Then Stella heard it, the sound of hard boot heels striking the floor behind them and getting closer. Stella patted the older woman's hand and they both looked straight ahead, not acknowledging the man who stood behind them so close that Stella could feel his breath on the back of her neck.

"*Guten Tag*," said Cyril with an American twang as he pocketed the tickets the counter girl gave him.

He turned around and smiled broadly at Stella. The man behind her stepped to her left and addressed Cyril in German.

"What was that?" asked Cyril. "Do you speak English?"

"I must see your passports, sir," said the soldier.

Stella swallowed hard and took Hildegard's hand. The sight of the man's black uniform made her feel faint.

"Sure. Sure." Cyril handed over three passports and picked his teeth with a toothpick.

The soldier examined the passports one by one. He seemed suspicious, although Stella couldn't see why. The passports were newly minted by Kaspar but appeared months old and well-used.

The soldier thumbed through the passports a third time and then turned to Stella. She met his brazen gaze before his eyes dropped to the V between her breasts. Hildegard saw that look and went crazy. She waved her little finger in his face until the man turned red and begged Stella's forgiveness.

"How long will you be traveling in our country, Miss?" he asked hastily.

Stella took a breath. She remembered Nicky's expression when under pressure and adopted it. She wasn't worried, not in the least. In fact, she was completely disinterested in everything going on around her.

"About a month, I think." She turned to Cyril. "Is that right, Uncle Bob?"

"It is, darling," said Stella's new Uncle Bob.

"He's your uncle?" said the soldier with a doubtful look.

Stella glanced past him and yawned. "Uh-huh."

If he didn't buy it, Stella wasn't sure what they would do. The plan was simple. Cyril said she was to be like *The Purloined Letter*. They'd put her out in plain sight. He swore the Nazis wouldn't expect such a bold plan. Stella only agreed when word came that the SS was searching for a plane and two *men*. Part of her smarted that they assumed the pilot had to be a man. It was logical but still an insult.

The two men exchanged a look that was both sly and knowing. The soldier gave a slight cough and said, "Have a nice trip with your *niece*, sir."

Cyril winked at him and Stella felt slimy. She clutched Hildegard's hand and could feel the tension radiating out of her guardian. Hildegard growled deep in her throat and gave Cyril a look like she was ready to flay him alive. Stella had no doubt that she was capable of doing just that, but Cyril laughed and doffed his hat to the soldier before leading them away.

Hildegard said something which Cyril ignored as he pointed them toward Track Six.

"What was that all about?" asked Stella.

"New plan. You're my mistress."

Stella stopped short and Hildegard gripped her tighter. He continued to smile and leaned in, brushing her cheek with his lips.

"Don't make a scene. Remember, I'm Bob. You're Lorena. We're on a romantic trip posing as uncle and niece."

"That is disgusting. You're taking this too far."

"You want to get to Paris or not?" He pulled back and removed Hildegard's hand from hers, saying a few quick words in German. Hildegard narrowed her eyes at him but stepped away.

"Don't think of it as a chore. I'm really not so bad, am I?" he asked.

"You're getting worse all the time," said Stella.

"Try to enjoy it." He tucked his hand behind her neck and kissed her full on the lips. "I will."

"Nicky will kill you."

"Nicky will be grateful that you're alive, as am I," said Cyril.

"Have you heard of karma?"

"I have, but I'm not worried," he said with another kiss. "Come now, my little pudding pie. Let's get to our compartment."

Cyril hooked his arm around her waist and started walking her to the platform. Stella glanced back at Hildegard, who had a look on her face like she'd just been punched in the kidney.

"You'd better watch yourself," said Stella. "Hildegard doesn't look too happy."

"She likes me."

"I can tell."

"All women love me."

"Present company excepted."

"You'll love me by the end of this." Cyril's hand slid down Stella's back to rest on her rump. There was a loud smack and his hand jerked back to her side.

"That woman is a menace." His grimace turned into a smile when the porter approached them.

Cyril handed over the tickets and made inane conversation about Rhine wines. The porter told him which car their compartment was in and led them down the long platform. Stella's shoulders relaxed and she started feeling like pretending to be a mistress wouldn't be so bad as long as it got her to where she wanted to go. Hildegard stiffened beside her as they walked and there was a slight hiccup in her gait. Stella looked over at her chaperon and was surprised to see her with a relaxed expression on her face. She'd transformed. She somehow appeared almost servile, which was, of course, the part she was meant to play, but Stella never really expected it of her. Hildegard's eyes darted over to Stella and then trained on a spot dead ahead. Stella followed her eye line to a car up ahead. Two SS officers were climbing down out of the car. Cyril tightened his grip on Stella and increased his swagger.

"No fear," he said.

"None," said Stella as she kissed his cheek.

Cyril blushed and Hildegard coughed behind them. The cough got the SS officers' attention. They turned with crisp movements to face them, their hats pulled low on their brows and their arms stiff at their sides. Cyril raised his arm in a greeting, but they didn't respond. They only waited until the trio had stopped in front of them.

"Hey there," said Cyril with a fabulous twang that made Stella inwardly cringe. "Sure are a lot of you boys around today."

"Identification, please," said the one on the right.

"Again? Well, I guess I must. When in Rome." Cyril turned to Stella. "Ain't that right?"

Stella nodded, not trusting herself to speak. One officer inspected their passports while the other squinted at Stella. He stepped forward, his eyes roaming over her Parisian hat and fur coat. They were still looking a bit rough, even after Hildegard's thorough cleaning. Stella just prayed he wouldn't notice her wrecked shoes. They were a dead giveaway that something wasn't right, but she could hardly wear men's shoes and they hadn't wanted to risk shopping. So there they were, her poor Parisian heels with peeling leather and shredded ribbons, a red flag if there ever was one.

The officer nudged his partner, who took a closer look at both Stella's passport and her. A grim smile flickered over the officer's thin lips, then he took her arm and directed her back to the station.

"What do you think you're doing?" asked Cyril, grabbing her other arm.

The officer didn't get a chance to respond. Hildegard jumped in front of him, throwing her hands in the air and lecturing the officer with such ferocity that Stella wasn't a bit surprised by the bright red tint that colored his cheeks. Hildegard kept it up until he stepped back and waved them past. Cyril helped Stella up the stairs into the car, followed by a triumphant Hildegard.

At the top of the stairs, a young man about Stella's age with shaking hands and a lip he couldn't stop biting peeked around the door to the car.

"Hey there," said Cyril.

The young man tried to look past them and then frantically waved them aboard. "*Ja, ja. Beeilung!*"

It wasn't until he dashed down the stairs and looked out onto the platform that Stella realized he was a porter. He leaned back against the rail and sighed with a hand on his chest. And it really was on his chest. His tunic was missing and four buttons had been ripped off his shirt. There was a ruddy bruise on his cheek and blood in his left nostril. He closed his eyes and whispered, *"Mein Gott."*

Stella squeezed past Cyril. "Are you all right?"

The porter's eyes popped opened as there was an angry shout in the distance and the train whistle blew. *"Enschuldigung."* He looked out onto the platform again, paled, and shooed Stella back up the stairs. "Go. Go."

"What's happening, young fella?" asked Cyril.

The porter's eyes went shifty. "Nothing, sir."

"Doesn't sound like nothing," said Stella.

"There was a…a… The *polizei*, they believed one of our passengers was…it is nothing."

"There is a lot of nothing with the *Schutzstaffel* these days," said Cyril.

"In truth, they were *Gestapo*," said the porter and he jogged up the stairs, straightening his shirt and cuffs. "May I have your tickets, please?"

"Gestapo, you say?" said Cyril. "I haven't heard of them. What do they do?"

"They secure the Fatherland."

"The Fatherland needs a whole lot of securing then."

"Your tickets, sir."

Cyril handed over their tickets and the porter apologized for any inconvenience they might have endured. He'd assumed a casual air, but he wasn't nearly so good at it as Nicky. It wasn't until the train whistle blew again that his breathing slowed down and he stopped shaking. He did show them to a lovely compartment upholstered in red and offered newspapers, which Cyril declined. He bowed on his way out and Stella said, "You'll want to get some ice on that or the bruising will be worse."

"Yes, ma'am," said the porter with all the normal formality. "I will see to it."

Cyril tipped him generously. "Do you have another uniform?"

"Yes, sir."

"I'd get yourself settled before our next stop. Those Gestapo don't play games and they seem to be all over the place."

The porter nodded and left. Stella leaned out the door, watching him walk down the corridor. He discreetly knocked on another compartment door as he passed by and the door slid open. A matronly woman opened the door and looked out. She ducked back in the instant she saw Stella.

"There's a lot going on in this country," said Stella.

Cyril drew her inside, closed the sliding door firmly, and bent low to look out the window.

"That gave me a turn," he said. "I didn't expect the station to be quite so well covered."

"What's the Gestapo?" asked Stella.

"The Secret Police."

"They don't seem so secret."

"What they do to people is," he said.

Stella sat on the left seat, enjoying the luxe fabric and cushions. She'd never appreciated cushions before, but she would thereafter. "Oliver said Peiper was SS, but maybe he's Gestapo. They seem worse."

"It's hard to say which organization is worse, but I will put my money on the Gestapo," said Cyril. "They are technically part of the SS though."

"Of course they are."

Cyril made a move to sit next to Stella as the train began moving, but Hildegard grabbed him by the ear and steered him over to the right side. Then she took the place next to Stella and crossed her arms. Stella smiled at her and removed her hat. The thing was in remarkable condition, considering it was a flighty little thing meant for looks alone. Stella jabbed her grandmother's hatpin in the crown and slipped off her coat, allowing the soft folds to encircle her hips.

She laid the book on her lap and traced the Paris address with her finger, trying to ignore the bloody handprints Hans had left on the brown wrapping paper, but she failed as sadness heavy as a horse settled in her chest. She closed her eyes, hoping the tears wouldn't come when several shouts rang out, high and panicked. Stella shot up and looked out the window. One of the Gestapo ran next to the train. He waved his arms and yelled. Before she could see anything else, Cyril shoved her back into the seat and looked out himself.

A couple seconds later, he sat down. "Gabriele Griese," he said.

"*Mein Gott*," said Hildegard.

Stella glanced back and forth between the two of them. Cyril rubbed his chin and looked out the window and Hildegard sat back on the cushions like she was angry at them.

"Who's Gabriele Griese?" Stella asked.

"Don't worry," said Cyril. "She's nothing to do with you."

"How do you know?"

Cyril carefully moved the rabbit fur fedora and placed it on his knee. Then he spoke to Hildegard in German and stroked the crown of his hat.

"The train isn't slowing," Cyril said, smiling at Stella. "She failed."

Hildegard said something about Munich and Cyril nodded.

"Will you tell me what's going on?" asked Stella.

Cyril ignored her question and looked out the window. "I don't understand what she's doing here. I last saw her in Vienna. All that misery should've kept her there, feeding like the beast she is."

"You saw this woman in Vienna?" asked Stella. "What does she look like?"

"Pretty until you see her soul," he said while plucking at a speck of lint on the hat's brim.

"Is she in the SS?"

Stella's question brought Cyril's attention back to her.

"In a manner of speaking, she is. She's what you might call a jack of all trades. She wears the uniform when it suits her superiors."

"Does she work with Peiper?"

"On occasion," he said slowly.

"Then you're wrong. She has everything to do with me," said Stella.

"You don't even know who she is."

"There was a woman with Peiper the night he came to our hotel. She was scarier than he was, if you can imagine."

"Plenty of women are in the SS." Cyril shook his head.

"You saw her in the train station, right? About the time we met?"

"Yes, but..." Cyril trailed off and then turned to Hildegard and they spoke for several minutes.

"Did anyone see you when you looked out the window?" asked Cyril.

"I don't know. It was only for a second."

"Then we'll proceed as planned." He leaned forward and touched Stella's knee. "You must do exactly as I say. Never allow yourself to appear alarmed or confused."

Stella thought of Nicky and said, "I can do that."

"Good." Cyril sat back and ran his handkerchief over his forehead.

Hildegard nodded at her and opened her handbag, pulling out a half-finished sock and knitting needles. She began knitting at a furious pace. The noise reminded Stella of Uncle Josiah's ticker tape machine. That awful, endless clatter put her on edge and Hildegard's needles did the same. She wanted to run out of the compartment or snatch the needles out of Hildegard's hands. She opened her mouth to tell her to knock off that racket when she saw her face. Two spots of hot pink shone on Hildegard's cheeks. Her eyes glistened as they stared at the opposite seat instead of at the needles which moved at such a speed they were a blur.

Stella closed her mouth and looked back at Cyril. "What's wrong with Hildegard?"

"I should've kept you-know-who to myself. The woman upsets her," said Cyril.

"She's more worried about her than Peiper?"

"With good reason. She and Peiper have captured several of our people over the years. Peiper's prisoners usually make it to trial. Hers don't."

Stella hugged the book to her chest. "Please tell Hildegard that I'm sorry she's involved."

Cyril spoke to Hildegard and she laid down her needles. She put a rough hand on Stella's shoulder and German became a lyrical, soothing language when she spoke.

"She says you shouldn't be sorry," translated Cyril. "She knows what things are worth and so should you."

Hildegard put her hand on the book and smiled.

"She thinks the book is worth it," said Cyril.

"You told her about the book?" Stella stared at him. "How could you?"

"I can't hide things from Hildegard. She's more persuasive than a priest in the Spanish Inquisition. Peiper could use her, come to think of it."

Hildegard took the book out of Stella's arms and untied the string. She folded back the paper and then the oil cloth. She held the book between her small, well-worn hands and smiled down on it, speaking softly.

Cyril translated. "Who are you doing this for?"

"Abel," whispered Stella.

"*Nein*," said Hildegard.

Even Stella knew what that meant.

"*Ja*," said Stella. Yes being one of the few words she knew.

Hildegard clasped Stella's hand and placed it on the book's ornate letter G.

"Abel," Stella insisted.

"*Nein*," said Hildegard. "Nissa."

"Nissa?" Stella stared at Hildegard, not sure if she heard right. Nissa was dead and gone. There was nothing to be done for her. Stella blocked out the thought that the same might be said of Abel.

Hildegard spoke, her voice choked with feeling. Cyril translated her words with equal emotion.

"She was forgotten once. We can't let her be obliterated for all time. Gutenberg more than loved her. He needed her. She sketched his ideas. She created his inks. Without her, there would've been no printing press." Hildegard patted the book. "He admitted as much. I'm doing this for her."

"I'm doing this for Abel," said Stella without hesitation.

Cyril told Hildegard what she said and the older woman took Stella's face in her hands. She kissed her cheeks and gave a small chuckle before speaking again.

"Two reasons. Same result," translated Cyril.

Hildegard handed Cyril the book and gave him several sharp commands.

"She wants me to read," he said.

"Good idea," said Stella.

Cyril opened the book to Nissa's portrait and gazed at it for a second.

"So, why are you doing this?" asked Stella, indicating Nissa's picture. "I assume it's not for a dead woman or my friend."

Cyril looked up from the portrait, his eyes hot. "I'm doing it for you. Don't you know that?"

Hildegard shushed him and Stella averted her eyes.

"What would you have me read?" Cyril asked after a moment.

Stella kept her eyes on the window, afraid of what she might see in Cyril. "Read about the church. How did they find out about Nissa?"

"That was Archbishop Adolph Von Nassau. I'm afraid the book doesn't say how the Archbishop found out about Nissa, only that he did."

"Good enough," said Stella.

"We are discovered," read Cyril. "I am ruined. The Archbishop must decide in Fust's favor and the work is lost."

"Who was Fust?" asked Stella.

Cyril replied, not looking up from the book. "From what I gather, some sort of moneylender. He sued Gutenberg over a loan." He scanned the page. "If my translation is correct, the lawsuit was a type of blackmail. Fust threatened to reveal Nissa as his wife."

"I don't understand how everyone didn't already know about her. They had children. They must've lived together."

Cyril shook his head. "Nissa stayed in her parents' home. They were in ghetto."

"Ghetto," said Stella, mimicking Cyril's accent. "That doesn't sound good."

"It was the Jewish section of Mainz, a place where they could be contained and controlled." He said it in an even, rather aloof tone, but Stella could see in his eyes that he didn't like it.

"Sounds like something the Nazis would be all for."

"They are. Shall I continue?" he asked.

Stella thought for a moment. "Maybe it was Fust who told the archbishop and used the information to sway the case."

Cyril turned the page. "If that's what happened, Gutenberg doesn't mention it."

"Keep reading," said Stella.

"He demands five hundred guilders for his precious silence. I have it not to give," said Cyril.

Stella settled more comfortably on her seat and leaned over to place her head on Hildegard's shoulder. Hildegard reached up and patted her cheek, knitting again at a less frantic pace. The clicking, instead of irritating Stella, soothed her with its constant rhythm that seemed to match Gutenberg's steady description of his downfall. Cyril read on and on through Gutenberg's losses as the train sped toward Munich and the women listened to how love created and destroyed a genius.

CHAPTER 24

*L*ovely billowing clouds decorated the sky over Munich. Stella watched them from her seat as they drifted above the car in great swirling curls. She wanted to stand and take a peek at the city but didn't dare. Instead, she put on her coat and pinned her hat to her hair, adjusting it until it sat at the perfect angle to show off her cheek bones and large eyes.

"Are you listening?" asked Cyril.

Stella tweaked the brim and heaved a sigh. "You aren't really saying anything."

"I'm telling you what to expect."

"No, you're not," said Stella. "You're telling me to be calm and follow your lead. You're not telling me what's going to happen."

Cyril finished wrapping the book back in its paper and oil cloth. "It's better you don't know."

"Then stop going on about it." She plucked the book off his lap and tucked it away under her coat.

"Do you have your cosmetics?" he asked.

"Why?"

He tapped his lips with his forefinger and squinted at her. "Perhaps some lipstick and rouge would improve the situation."

She narrowed her eyes at him. "What's wrong with my situation? I used that theater makeup."

"That bruise on your cheek is showing again. We're lucky your hat covers the cuts on your forehead. And you're still limping."

"I am?"

"Slightly." He eyed her face and ran his fingers and thumb along his jawline.

"What?" asked Stella.

He did one more circuit of his jaw and then said, "I'm thinking the more you stand out, the more you'll fit in."

"I can limp more, if you like." She stuck out her leg and put the back of her hand against her forehead. "Oh, my leg. Oh, my leg."

Cyril grimaced at her. "Please be serious. Your life, *our lives*, depend on you presenting the correct image."

"The limp makes me stand out. What more do you want?"

"You must belong in the part you're playing. In my experience, mistresses wear plenty of lipstick and rouge. They don't limp."

Stella gave him a crooked smile. "Your experience?"

"My experience of other men's mistresses, of course," he said with a growing, lecherous smile.

"Of course." Stella opened her handbag and found her lipstick at the bottom.

Hildegard grumbled when she saw the lipstick, but she didn't say anything. Stella smeared on a healthy amount of her favorite color, oxblood, and rouged her cheeks to a rosy glow, concealing the bruise once again.

"How's that?" she asked.

"Infinitely better," said Cyril.

Hildegard regarded Stella's new face, frowned, and put her knitting needles away. She sat ramrod straight with her small feet dangling as the train slowed down. She hadn't said much since Cyril started reading. After a few pages, she'd begun snoring with tiny baby-like snores that made Stella and Cyril smile.

A sharp rap on the door announced a visitor and the compartment door slid open. The young porter in a fresh uniform stuck his head in, speaking to Cyril but looking at Stella. "We're arriving in Munich, sir."

"Thank you kindly," said Cyril, back in full American twang without missing a beat.

The porter nodded at Stella and lingered for a moment until Cyril flipped him a coin and shooed him out the door.

"That is a good example," said Cyril.

"Of what?"

"Of you standing out."

"I was just sitting here," protested Stella.

Cyril shook his head as the train wheels squealed. "You weren't and you know it. You charmed that boy without a word, the smile, the tilt of your hat. Do that out there."

Stella tried not to look bewildered. She really was just sitting there. She smiled. Of course, she did. One smiled when a person came to tell you information you needed. It was only polite. For lack of any good response, she stood up, but Cyril waved her back down.

"We're wealthy tourists in no particular hurry," he said and they waited for the train to come to a complete stop before getting up.

Stella kept examining her feelings for some hint of nervousness but couldn't find any. When she thought about how nervous she'd been before arriving at Hans' brewery and flying the plane, she felt curiously empty. Perhaps she'd used up all her fear, and calmness was all she had left.

As soon as the train shuddered to a stop, Hildegard shot to her feet and yanked back the compartment door. A man in the corridor jumped aside and bumped into the door opposite. Hildegard told him off like he'd startled her. He backed away and let her herd Stella out of the compartment and down the corridor in front of him. Cyril chuckled as they walked off the train onto the platform. Enormous pillars dwarfed them while holding up a network of girders that were oddly delicate in comparison. The delicacy didn't extend to the swastikas hanging below them. Stella couldn't imagine why there had to be so many when one would have done the trick. The Nazis were in control. Who needed to be reminded of that every five seconds?

Cyril spun them around, looking for the station and finding it a couple of football fields away down the tracks. The building was unimpressive compared to the soaring heights of the glassed-in platform.

Other passengers bustled past them and Cyril looped his arm around Stella's waist and checked his watch. Hildegard checked hers as well and without glancing at each other, they began walking toward the station. Cyril walked on her right side and Hildegard slightly behind her to the left.

No one was paying them any attention, but Stella suddenly felt as though several spotlights were trained on her. It was all so open and unprotected. She cocked her head toward Cyril and smiled broadly. "So far, so good."

"It's only just begun." Cyril opened the station door and the nervousness she was missing jumped back into her stomach with a queasy heave.

The last time she'd been in a station that large was in Vienna. She half expected Gabriele Griese's shrill voice to ring out the alarm at any second, but instead, Cyril ushered her through the door to a teeming but orderly station. No one was yelling or begging for tickets. Prisoners weren't being queued up and headed toward boxcars to oblivion. It looked perfectly normal and to Stella, quite foreign. She'd forgotten people could be normal, even German people. They weren't all like the brown-shirts in the streets of Vienna. They were just people living their lives, probably unaware of the strife if it didn't affect them.

Cyril guided her around a newspaper stand covered in screaming headlines. All the papers were in German and the prominent word on each edition was *Juden.* It was similar to the word she'd seen scrawled across storefronts in Vienna. There was some kind of reference to money and quite a lot of it. What had she said to Nicky? "They'll probably just charge the Jews." Was that actually happening? It was inconceivable but most everything that had happened to them had been.

Stella bent close enough to Cyril to smell his musky aftershave and said, "Does *Juden* mean Jew?"

Cyril took the chance to sneak a quick kiss. "Yes," he murmured, his breath hot on her lips.

"What's with the mo—"

Hildegard said something in a harsh tone and came up beside Stella. She jerked her away from Cyril and marched her toward a group of school boys wearing brown uniforms. The boys had swastikas on their armbands and stood at attention with fixed, hard expressions on their young faces. Their eyes were bright and excited. Wherever they were going, it was the greatest thrill. Stella couldn't imagine her brothers standing at attention and marching around. She'd never seen them stand still for three seconds put together.

Hildegard executed her own military maneuvers and wheeled her around the boys. Cyril caught up and took Stella's other hand. His palm slipped against hers, warm and moist.

Stella leaned her body into his and whispered, "This doesn't seem like the plan."

"I never question Hildegard. It isn't good for the health," said Cyril as he pointed at an exit door.

He checked his watch and glanced up at the departures side of the huge schedule. He nodded and guided them to the other side of the station toward a set of large arched doors. Hildegard cut Stella off and went through first. She paused, going into a coughing fit which ended with her hacking something up into a handkerchief. Stella stared at her for a second but then remembered she was supposed to expect everything and everything was normal. She patted Hildegard on the back and murmured comforting sounds. Cyril whipped out a cigar and lit it. He ignored Hildegard's coughing as he surveyed the rows of trains like he owned them.

"Come on, girls," he said loudly. "We can't be dillydallying around here all day."

He led them toward the platform at the end. There was a scattering of officers in the black uniform of the SS but also some brownshirts milling around. None of them appeared to be looking for anyone. Stella smiled and sashayed down the platform, even though her feet were burning and a fresh headache was blossoming in her head. None of that mattered. It was just pain. Stella was playing a part, a part that would get her to Nicky. That was important.

The more Stella smiled, the more she began to feel her role and started enjoying being a spectacle. Her mother had warned her against being a spectacle all her life. Stella was never quite sure why being noticeable was so bad, but she was beginning to get the picture. It felt good. Grinning at strange men, wiggling her hips, and licking her lips. Every one of those men smiled back and appraised her figure, although it was mostly concealed by her coat. They looked all the same. She was the one who was special. Powerful. Just what Cyril ordered. She was right out in the open.

Cyril kept up a running commentary on the sights they would be seeing and coiled his arm around Stella's waist, nodding at the other men with a knowing smile. When they reached Platform Six, his grip tightened. Stella made sure not to show this change in her face. She kept up her smiling as she looked for the cause of Cyril's tension. Then she saw her. A woman approached from the end of the platform, flanked by an older man in a natty grey suit and an older woman wearing a shapeless woolen coat and a severe bun. They were all remarkably familiar, especially the woman wearing a calf-length lambskin coat. Soft brown curly hair lay on her shoulders and her lips were dark red. Stella felt like she was looking in a mirror, except the woman was missing a hat.

The woman didn't meet Stella's eyes. She swung her handbag, almost identical to Stella's, with every step. She smiled and swished her hips seductively and Stella found herself imitating the woman's toothy grin and exaggerated movements. The man at her side kept up a loud commentary in French as the wind gusted up and blew leaves and debris across the platform. They were headed straight for Stella, Cyril, and Hildegard. They made no move to step aside or skirt around them. Stella leaned to the right, but Cyril and Hildegard held her firm.

Something made a sizzling sound behind them. Stella's steps faltered. Cyril's arm tightened around her, pressing her forward. Then an explosion rattled the platform. Stella jerked around as a cloud of black smoke blew over them. Hildegard wrenched her arm and faced her forward, still walking. The woman and her companions advanced on them with determination. At the last second, the woman was released by her companions. Cyril and Hildegard dropped their arms. The woman grabbed Stella and for a second, they were nose-to-nose. Their eyes met. The woman was older than Stella with lines at the edges of her eyes. She spun Stella around and gave her a gentle push as another explosion went off somewhere beyond Platform Nine. Stella's arms were taken up again. She looked to her left and Cyril gave her a quick glance. She turned to her right and it wasn't Hildegard there, but the woman's companion was now holding her hand. Behind them, she heard Hildegard's voice haranguing someone, and then a small cry. Stella glanced behind her. The other woman was on the ground in a faint with Cyril's double and Hildegard bent over her. She was now wearing a hat. Cyril jerked Stella forward and they walked into the growing black cloud.

Stella coughed and stumbled.

"Steady," said Cyril.

Soldiers and civilians ran past them toward the area of the second blast. Cyril produced a handkerchief and pressed it over Stella's nose and mouth. The new Hildegard let go of Stella's hand and staggered. A brown-shirt caught her before she went down. Cyril yelled in French, something about *ma mère*. He pointed down the platform and took the woman from the brown-shirt, who ran to where he pointed. Cyril swept the new Hildegard up in his arms and started down the platform. He shouted at Stella in French. She stared at him and then ran to catch up.

"Take off your hat," he said from between gritted teeth.

Stella took off her hat and stuffed it under her coat with the book. She followed him with her hand on the woman's forehead. They went past the station. People were running and screaming. Stella flashed back to the Kristallnacht. The burning wood. The ash in the air. She saw Nicky's face tight with a cigarette between his lips. Abel's pleading eyes. His cold hand on her cheek. Albert's face swelling and throbbing. Stella started shaking. Her teeth chattered. She tried to clamp them together, but she couldn't make them stop.

"Ne vous inquiétez pas, mon amour. Ma mère va bien se passer," Cyril said loudly to Stella.

Then under his breath, he said, "Two."

Stella looked up ahead. Platform Two had an engine belching smoke, ready to depart. They turned to walk beside the train and Cyril placed the woman's feet on the ground. They continued together, the woman growing stronger with every step. She reached up and released her bun. Greying brown hair cascaded onto her shoulders and she looked down. When the woman looked up again, she was wearing small glasses and lipstick. She was transformed in the time it took to walk ten steps. Stella forced herself not to stare and to remember her part.

A porter came out of a dining car and approached them. He spoke German and Cyril switched his language to something Stella didn't recognize. It had a singsong kind of rhythm to it. Perhaps Swedish. Whatever it was, the porter didn't speak it. The two of them went around and around for several minutes until another explosion went off and the porter ran toward it. Cyril caught Stella's arm and pushed her onto the dining car steps.

"Go," he said.

Stella jogged up the steps and into the car. It was empty with all the places set for dinner service.

"Keep going." Cyril pushed her from behind.

Stella looked back and saw no one behind Cyril. "Where is she? The other woman."

"Her assignment is complete." He flashed her a pair of tickets and a wad of cash.

They left the dining car and went through two first class cars. Stella had to push her way past dozens of people roaming the corridor. One extremely fat Belgian cornered her in the second first class car by the porter's post.

"Were you out there, my lovely lady?" he asked in a thick accent.

Stella didn't know if she was supposed to speak. Nobody said anything about her speaking, but Cyril had been separated from her by an old lady who spilled her enormous handbag in the corridor and he would've had to step on the contents to get to her. He looked up at her from under the rabbit fur fedora. His face was tinged pink and she couldn't tell what he wanted her to do.

"I…I was on the platform," she said.

"Ah, an American," he said, drawing closer.

Oh, no. He'll remember me.

"Yes," she said.

"So many Americans traveling in Europe these days."

"Yes."

"Did you see what happened on the platform? They tell us nothing," said the Belgian.

"There was an explosion and lots of smoke. I don't know what it was."

"Your face." His breath smelled like crème de menthe and his waxed mustache shone in the dim light of the corridor. "Your face is quite familiar. Perhaps you have been in the newspapers?"

Stella swallowed. "No. No, I'm just Lorena."

Had they given her a last name? They must've, but she couldn't remember it.

"Just Lorena." The Belgian winked at her and backed away as Cyril hurried up.

"I see you've met my niece." Cyril extended his hand to the Belgian, who took it by the fingers and gave them a slight shake.

"Your niece?" The Belgian laughed, holding his belly like a ball.

A new porter came down the hall, shooing people into their compartments. Stella expected him to ask them for tickets, but he didn't. Cyril edged her away from the Belgian, past the porter to the next car. He opened the door and ushered her through.

Stella stopped short after entering the dark, cozy interior. "This is a sleeper."

"I know."

"Look." She turned around to face him with her one free hand on her hip. "Why can't we be in a regular compartment?"

He looked over her shoulder to check for other passengers. "We are lovers. We need a bed."

"One bed?"

"It's the compartment that they bought."

"The other couple? The other us?"

He tried to push her back into the sleeper, but she wasn't having it. "Yes. Please, Stella. We will attract the wrong kind of attention."

"Has that other couple taken our place on the other train?" she asked.

"Yes. If they are stopped, the SS will find a pair of native Germans.

"Is this train going to Paris?" asked Stella.

"Of course, and if my calculations are correct, you have one day left or would you like to get off and look for another way?"

Twenty-four hours to Nicky. There was no way she was getting off that train.

CHAPTER 25

*S*tella lay, warm and safe, cuddled up under a pile of downy blankets imprinted with the Wagons-Lit logo. She'd been awake for awhile but wasn't quite ready to face Cyril, who'd been obliged to spend the night on the upholstered bench wedged in the corner instead of in bed with her where he much preferred to be.

She preferred that he leave her alone, so she read by the dim glow of the tulip lamp above her head, preferring that over thinking about Nicky. Was he alive and free? Did he make it to Paris? Those thoughts were simply not helpful the way a good book always was.

Flipping the pages turned out to be louder than she realized and a voice intruded into her imaginary world.

"So you liked it?" said Cyril.

Stella gritted her teeth, but she supposed asking a question was better than him slipping under the covers. Cyril had done that several times under the guise that the porter might come and he ought to find him properly in bed with his *niece*. The porter never came, but Cyril was kicked, punched, and hit over the head with Gutenberg's priceless diary. Stella instantly regretted using it, but it made an effective weapon and was none the worse for it.

"Stella, I know you're awake."

She peeked at him over the satin edge of the blanket and found him already sipping tea from a tiny cup. He looked older in the dawn. The bags under his eyes had a purple cast and the loose skin on his cheeks seemed to sag a little more. Not for the first time, Stella wondered who he really was. She assumed Cyril wasn't his real name since he was purported to be a spy. Looking at him, rumpled and exhausted in the corner, she thought it less likely than ever. Still, there he was, helping her escape the SS, all the while looking like an English professor or a librarian. Perhaps that was his cover, forever looking like he wanted a nap.

"What are you looking at?" Cyril asked, a shaggy brow raised.

"You, of course. I'm trying to understand why you're here."

"And what is your conclusion?"

She smiled at him and threw out a line just the way he liked, accent and all. "I do not get on at all. I hear such different accounts of you as to puzzle me exceedingly."

Cyril straightened up and ten years fell off his face. "I can readily believe that reports may vary greatly with respect to me and I could wish, Miss Bled, that you were not to sketch my character at the present moment, as there is reason to fear the performance would reflect no credit on either."

"But if I do not take your likeness now I may never have another opportunity," said Stella.

"I would by no means suspend any pleasure of yours," said Cyril. But unlike Mr. Darcy in *Pride and Prejudice*, the little spy wasn't cold in the least. His passion glowed through any disguise he might choose to put on.

"Not many men take the trouble to read Austen." Stella was getting good at ignoring that familiar glow. She only hoped Nicky would do the same. Husbands were known to be fussy about that sort of thing.

"It's part of the job description," he replied before finishing off his tea.

"Reading Austen?"

"Reading everything. You're rather more well-read than I expected."

Stella sat up and crossed her arms. "For a brewer's daughter, you mean."

"For anyone. I didn't mean to insult you."

"Well, you did. I may not have done my mathematics or studied Latin, but my father has a huge library and I've read most of it. The English stuff, anyway."

He bowed his head to her and said, "I apologize. You always exceed my expectations."

"It's time you raise them then."

"I will do so," he said. "Since your father's library didn't include my book, you'll have to add to his collection."

"Your book?" she asked.

"The one you were reading all night."

"Oh, right." Stella pulled a book out from her little nest, its stylized cover instantly making her smile. The snow-capped mountains in blue, green, and black were peaceful, even with dragons flying around them.

"In a hole in the ground there lived a hobbit," she said with a smile. "It seems like a children's book."

"But it's not," said Cyril. "And I have it on good authority that there will be more tales coming from Middle Earth."

"Do you now?"

Cyril stood up and slipped on his jacket before straightening his tie.

"Come on," she pleaded. "Do you know the author? Are you the author? Are you J.R.R. Tolkien?"

He bent over and planted a warm kiss on her forehead. "Far from. Tolkien is a professor at Oxford and I'm…"

"Yes?" she asked more eagerly than she wished to.

"And I'm your uncle," he said with a rakish grin. "We'll be arriving in Paris soon. Coffee?"

"I'd rather have answers."

"I'm afraid only coffee is available to pretty young women who ask too many questions."

Stella held out *The Hobbit*. "Then I'll have a café crème."

Cyril waved away the book. "Finish it. I think you'll find that you have much in common with Bilbo Baggins."

"If I'm Bilbo," she said with a sly grin, "who are you in the book?"

"It depends on the scene."

Stella held Cyril's arm firmly as they exited the Gare de Lyon station and walked straight into a flock of fat, grey pigeons. The birds fluttered into the air, swirling around Stella's head in a flurry of wings and beaks. She dropped Cyril's arm and backed away from the torrent, waving her arms and squealing.

Cyril laughed so hard he bent over and slapped his fedora against his chest before using it to wave away the birds. "You are a remarkable woman. Braving the wrath of the SS. Crashing planes. Hardly a misstep in the face of multiple smoke bombs, but pigeons are too much."

Stella ducked as the last of the pigeons flew over her head and then scowled at him. "Pigeons are dirty and you said those smoke bombs were child's play."

"And so they were. Much ado about nothing. Full of sound and fury, signifying nothing."

"Enough Shakespeare," said Stella with a slow eye roll.

Cyril knew most of the bard's works by heart and he had no trouble reciting them word for word. He was also fluent in Dickens, Tolstoy, and Lord Byron. Stella's only respite during their final hour on the train was a poker game with chocolate squares for chips. The game distracted Cyril quite well from both his reciting and his attempts at seducing Stella until she broke down and ate all the chocolate.

"You like it," he said.

"I like not fair terms and a villain's mind," quoted Stella.

"You think I have a villain's mind? After everything we've been through?" Cyril bent his face close to hers.

"I do," she said.

"I never see thy face but I think upon hell fire."

"I inspire visions of hell," said Stella. "That has to be the worst compliment I've ever gotten."

"You're not thinking of it in the right way. It is the greatest compliment I could give."

"You are a villain."

Cyril swept his arm across the broad streets of Paris. "It is a far far better thing I do today than I have ever done."

"Not planning on going to your rest today, are you?" asked Stella.

Cyril smiled. "Not today. Too much to live for."

Stella looked away. "How far is Napoleon's tomb?"

Cyril's face fell. "We don't have to go there now. It's barely morning. We have plenty of time."

"He might be early. I don't want to take a chance of missing him."

"Stella," said Cyril, his face falling into sad folds. "You should prepare yourself—"

"He'll be there." Stella looked at him, fear growing in her belly.

"Yes, I know. Just don't expect too much."

"What's too much? Have you heard something about Nicky?" Her skin felt afire like the time her brother convinced her to put a spoon in a light socket.

"No, no." He patted her arm. "It's just that—"

"Good. Let's go."

Cyril paused to let a speeding taxi careen by. Then he walked her across the street between cars, taxis, and multitudes of pedestrians. Just being in Paris made Stella feel better, the smell, the wrought iron balconies, and all the proud people not hunched over in fear. Nicky was there or soon would be. She could feel it. Everything would be fine.

They walked past a number of bakeries before Cyril spun Stella around and insisted they go in one. He looked over each pastry and chatted about which ones he'd had and how they tasted. Stella stood behind him. The man behind the counter kept sneaking peeks at her. Stella shuffled her feet and tried to keep a pleasant expression on her face. She knew she should probably converse with Cyril and keep up the pretense of a couple on a pleasant holiday, but she couldn't manage more than monosyllabic answers to his many inquiries.

After an interminable speech on the intricacies of producing perfect pâté à choux, Cyril bought her an enormous buttery croissant and declined anything for himself. They walked until the smell of fresh coffee rolled over them, warm and comforting. Cyril enticed her to the café emanating the delicious smell, a quaint little place on the corner with half a dozen tables outside. Stella started to walk in, but Cyril pulled out a chair well in view of everyone on the street.

"Shouldn't we get out of sight?" she asked.

"There are a million people living in Paris. No one will notice us unless we behave oddly like sitting inside on a sunny day."

Stella bit her lip but sat anyway. She was so used to hiding it seemed unnatural to sit out in the open.

"Smile, Stella," said Cyril.

Stella fixed a pleasant look on her face and looked around. The street was nice enough. Working class and well-kept. She kept looking for something and not finding it. It took her a moment before she realized what it was.

"Of course," she said. "This is France."

"Pardon?" asked a waiter, arriving at their table in time to hear her speak out loud.

Cyril waved Stella's words away and spoke to the waiter in heavily-accented French. The poor man had to wait through Cyril butchering his native language while ordering a café noisette for Stella and a café noir for himself. The waiter nodded politely, but Stella could see the pain and exasperation in his eyes. He left with a quick almost military turn and went into the café.

"As you were saying," said Cyril.

"I was looking for the destruction I saw in Germany and Austria, but this is Paris. No Nazis."

"Oh, they're around."

257

"They are?" asked Stella, taking a quick scan of the street.

"Certainly. The same way I am, as are my American counterparts, and others, I assure you."

"You never did say exactly who you are."

"Didn't I?" he asked, his eyes wide in mock surprise.

"No, you didn't, and I suppose you won't. And you didn't answer my question from earlier either. How far to Napoleon's tomb?"

Cyril's expression didn't become sad this time. He was all confidence when the waiter returned with their coffee. Stella threw back her café in two quick gulps, searing her tongue in the process. Cyril ignored her rush, settled back in his chair, and took a small sip.

"Cyril," said Stella. "Drink up. We've got places to be."

"I suggest we go to the Marais first."

"Why in the world?"

"You have a delivery to make."

Stella had almost forgotten about Abel's book with her thoughts swirling around Nicky and the noon deadline. "I suppose we could. If you think we have time."

"You don't want to unburden yourself?" asked Cyril.

Stella took a bite of her croissant and flaky bits rained down on her dress. They stuck to the fur of her coat and covered a good deal of Bilbo's Misty Mountains now tethered to Abel's package with thick twine that Cyril had gotten from the porter. She flicked the flakes off one by one and pondered Cyril's question. She did want to keep her promise to Abel, but she'd become quite attached to the book. It'd been her constant companion through everything. She'd rarely had it off her person so that it'd become like an appendage. The thought of it being gone left her feeling hollow. To not be able to see it every day, to never view Nissa's portrait or hear more of Gutenberg's words. The only thing she had to compare it with was the loss of Nicky. Being away from him was like being hungry all the time and never being fed.

After a minute, she finally answered. "I want to do what I must."

"Interesting way to put it," said Cyril. "Like wanting to have a surgery because you'll die if you don't."

She ran the tip of finger around the rim of her coffee cup, keeping one hand firmly on the books. "Don't you have a quote for that feeling? You're usually full of quotes."

"O look, look in the mirror. O look in your distress. Life remains a blessing. Although you cannot bless."

"That's not Shakespeare or Dickens," said Stella.

"W.H. Auden."

"Really? I've never heard it before."

"It is as yet unpublished."

"It makes me feel like I did when my great-grandmother died. I knew I should find a way to be happy again, but I couldn't for a long time."

"Auden does that to people."

"You sound like you know him."

Cyril finished his coffee and watched the Parisians go about their business.

"Are you going to answer me?" Stella asked.

He flicked his eyes over to her, looking more professorial than ever. "Did you ask a question? You should be more precise."

"You know I did."

"One must seek the truth within—not without," he said.

Stella gritted her teeth and said, "You are exasperating."

"I'll take that as a compliment."

"You shouldn't. You're no Poirot."

Since Cyril offered no more quotes or insight into his character, Stella set her cup on its saucer hard and stood up. "Let's finish this."

Cyril followed her example although at a snail-like pace. He straightened his jacket and settled his battered hat lower on his head. Then he added up the correct amount of coinage like he'd just recently learned to count.

"Oh, for heaven's sake!" Stella seriously considered bashing him with the books again.

"I have to get the correct amount," he said.

"Just pay the man."

"I am, my dear." Cyril finally dropped a pile of coins on the table and extended his arm to Stella. She took it and with the other squeezed the books. She didn't know where the Marais was in relation to them. She never paid much attention to her whereabouts. Especially not in Paris. There was too much to see so she allowed Cyril to lead her, letting her eyes rove over the shops and apartments. It hadn't been very long since she'd been there, but she'd already forgotten the way Paris felt. The history, the love of art, of food, it was everywhere. They passed another pastry shop and she spotted Nicky's favorite almond torte and right next to it, Abel's beloved Choux Chantilly. She could see them, smiling and eating their way through Paris. Nicky would tour anything as long as there was food involved and Abel knew the best cafes, pastry shops, and restaurants next to each monument they toured. Stella thought of these things and began to pick up her pace, but Cyril held her back. "I can't hold myself back I must have a pâté à choux. What do you say to an éclair?"

"Really, Cyril. Can't we just go?"

He opened the pastry shop door, bowing and sweeping his hat low over his feet. "Stella."

"I don't want anything."

"Come in and help me choose."

Stella planted her feet. She would've crossed her arms, if she hadn't been holding the books. "I'll wait here."

Cyril shrugged and went inside. He repeated his performance at the last shop and kept a running conversation with the lady behind the counter. Stella watched him charm her into multiple samples. He nibbled each delicately and dabbed at the edges of his mouth with the tiny napkin the lady gave him. Just when Stella was about to barge in and order him to hurry it up, he purchased an éclair the size of a small loaf of bread.

He exited the shop and held the éclair up high, a conqueror of all things pastry.

"I got the largest," he said with a smile. "We can share."

"I don't want any." Stella turned on her heels and took off down the sidewalk.

Cyril caught up with her, his head thrown back in a groan of sugary delight.

"Have some. You must. It is perfection."

"No."

"There's nothing like Paris for pastries." He swept the enormous éclair under Stella's nose. "Smell it. Eat it. Enjoy it."

"Will you stop?"

"This is Paris. Enjoy the moment, Stella," said Cyril.

Stella turned around so quickly Cyril almost pushed the éclair into her chest.

"Enjoy myself? Are you joking? I don't know where my husband is. Abel's in some horrid camp. Oliver's half-dead and Hans *is* dead. I'm not enjoying myself, Cyril. I'm just trying to get through."

Cyril brushed a tear off her cheek and drew her to him. "I'm so terribly sorry. We have plenty of time. I know this city like a mistress's buttocks. I'll get you where you need to go."

He looked so crestfallen and contrite that Stella began to feel guilty. Look at everything he'd done for her and there she was, scolding him like some bitter old shrew.

"I'm sorry, Cyril," she said. "I'm worried. I'm trying hard not to be, but I am."

"I know you are. I promise everything will work out just the way it should."

"Promises, promises."

"These I shall keep." Cyril turned her around and walked her down the lovely boulevard with slow steps while hugging her to his side. "We will deliver the book and find the husband."

"We will," said Stella, feeling stouter with each step.

Cyril turned them onto another street. They walked down yet another wide boulevard lined with shops and apartments with lovely twisted wrought iron. Cyril kept walking and walking. He never asked directions or consulted a map. He just walked with purposeful steps down those boulevards with hardly a look right or left.

"How far is it?" asked Stella. "Can't we take a cab?"

"I thought you might wish to stretch your lovely legs. You've spent a great deal of time on trains of late."

"Have you seen my feet?"

Cyril glanced down. "They're lovely, if a little worse for wear."

Stella would've stomped her feet, if it wouldn't have hurt so much. "Worse for wear? I've got blisters on top of my calluses. Let's get a cab."

"I'm sorry, my dear." Cyril raised his arm and a cab came to a squealing halt a foot from him. He didn't twitch, except for a smile at Stella's involuntary yelp.

They drove through the streets, the driver honking and waving his cigarette. Stella closed her eyes, turning away from the stench. She pressed the books to her chest right next to the prickly uneasy feeling that had taken up residence inside. In a few minutes, they would arrive at the book's address and she'd hand over a treasure without any parallel. Her father wouldn't get to read Gutenberg's diary. Her mother wouldn't see Nissa's face. She hadn't even taken a picture. Her camera was back in Vienna. Once the book was out of her hands, it would be like it never existed. If Cyril was right and there were Nazis in Paris… No. It didn't matter. She'd promised. Abel's face appeared in her mind, followed by so many other faces. She'd promised and they'd sacrificed. It was too late to turn back. She knew that. So why did she feel like something wasn't right? Like she shouldn't give up the book. Like something was going to happen.

"We have arrived," said Cyril, his breath caressing her ear.

"Already?"

"It wasn't far."

The driver opened her door and doffed his cap, calling her mademoiselle and saying a bunch of things that were fired at her so quickly she was disoriented and couldn't think how to respond.

Cyril led her onto the sidewalk. "He quite likes you."

"Uh-huh," she said, spinning around. "Which way? Should we get a map?"

"It's only another block," said Cyril.

"To the Marais or to the apartment?"

"Both." Cyril settled his fedora on his head and wrapped her hand around his arm, walking much more slowly than before. Stella squeezed his arm and scanned the buildings around them. They were nothing like what she remembered. They must be in a different section of the Marais. The shops and apartment buildings were rather staid and middle class. The Marais had style, but there was nothing out of the ordinary there, except perhaps the noise. There was a great deal of noise coming from the streets ahead of them. They advanced another block and a faint smell joined the noise. It scurried up the street and swirled around Stella.

"Do you smell that? What is that?" All of it was becoming familiar, but she couldn't quite place it.

They turned another corner and an enormous market came into view with people crowding the convergence of two streets, piles of crates, and hand carts blocking their way. Stella jerked her arm away from Cyril. "This isn't the Marais. I know the Marais. This is Les Halles. Abel brought us here."

Cyril took her hand and refused to release it when she tried to jerk it away. "I thought you might like to do some shopping."

"Shopping?" Stella twisted her hand in his grasp. "You should stop thinking. It's not working for you today."

"And you should start. Wouldn't you like a new hat or a new dress before you see Abel's family? And Nicky, of course." He dragged her through the crowd to a long row of rickety stalls with tin roofs.

Stella gazed at the cheap cotton dresses blowing on wire hangers between stalls with piles of onions, fresh fish, and ox tongue.

"You thought we'd buy them here? What kind of impression are we trying to make? I'd smell. Bad, in case you're wondering."

Cyril took her arm and led her deeper into the throng. "They may not be of the quality you're used to, but they're free of blood stains, and I hate to admit that we do have a budget."

Stella recognized the word 'budget'. She'd never used it herself or had it applied to her. But Cyril kept smiling at her and nodding. He gestured to dresses that weren't hideous or too far out of style, but the more he smiled, the worse the prickly uneasy feeling got. She couldn't account for it. A new dress, even a cheap one, was a good thing. She should be grateful. She should be happy. She shouldn't be having the nervous suspicion she always got when her brother gave her a winning smile right before he put a snake down her dress.

"Stella," said Cyril, "do you object to a new dress and shoes?"

From the look on his face, she knew she couldn't object. It would be absolutely wrong thing to do. So she ignored the feeling and let him lead her deeper into Les Halles with a terrible feeling growing in her gut.

CHAPTER 26

*C*yril bullied his way into yet another cheese stall through a crowd of arguing Frenchmen, who threw their arms around like they were pitching baseballs. Stella followed Cyril, dragging her feet and dodging lit cigarettes. When she reached him, the cheese seller handed him a small stick with a sample of runny light brown cheese on it. It was so pungent Stella could smell it, even when it was in his mouth.

"Did you try the cheeses the last time you came?" he asked.

"No."

The cheese man handed Cyril another sample. He held it up to the light and admired it as it oozed down the stick toward his fingers.

"Did you know the French have over four hundred different types of cheese?"

"No."

"Try this." Cyril pushed the stinky cheese stick past her lips when she opened them to object.

Stella jerked her head back, but a good smear got on her tongue. She saw the cheese man watching her from behind his high counter with the studied indifference only the French could convey. It was everything she could do not to spit it out and punch Cyril in the face.

It would be an insult of unbelievable magnitude and they might not make it out of the stall alive.

"Oh my God, Cyril," she gasped when she trusted herself to speak.

"Have you ever tasted anything like it?" Cyril asked.

"No. I should kill you."

Cyril turned to the cheese man and nodded. With the help of big hand gestures, he ordered about a quarter pound of the horrible cheese and had it wrapped up. When they left, the cheese man nodded and favored them with a brief smile. Cyril led the way back into the throng of shoppers. He stuck the package of cheese in the cloth bag he'd purchased along with a loaf of bread riddled with roasted garlic, a pound of prosciutto, three pears, and a live white mouse because it was cute. The stink emanated from the bag and the mouse squeaked louder. It made Stella gag and feel bad for the mouse. She wasn't sure the poor thing would survive. The cheese could probably be used to kill roaches.

"Did you know they have over a hundred goat cheeses alone?" asked Cyril.

"Fascinating." Stella tried to wave the stink away, but somehow, that made it worse.

Cyril stopped and glanced around. "Do you smell that?"

"How can you smell anything with that cheese in your bag?"

"Smells like…" Cyril tapped his chin. "Olives. I would love some niçoise olives after that cheese."

"No olives, Cyril. We've been here forever," said Stella. "What time is it?"

Cyril grabbed her arm and charged through the crowd. Stella couldn't tell where she was. They'd been through dozens of stalls. Cyril wanted to sample everything, touch everything, and they hadn't even looked at clothes yet. He darted right by a stall with dresses that were nearly fashionable toward a booth with large enamel bowls on a long table. Each bowl had a different kind of olive. Some were mixed with lemon wedges, tomatoes, or whole cloves of garlic. Stella had seen the shop before, but they hadn't gone in, since neither they nor Abel had a taste for the briny fruit.

She tugged at Cyril's sleeve. "We don't need olives."

"Everyone needs olives. Did you try the oil? It's extraordinary."

"We have to go."

"In a minute." He took her arm and steered her to the table with a man in a rough work shirt sitting behind it. He scowled at them as they approached, his swarthy face folding into demonic lines. That look would've been enough to drive Stella away, no matter how much she wanted olives, but it didn't deter Cyril.

"Look at those jars," he said, pointing to the dozens of jars on a rack behind the seller. "Those are the rarer types or specialty cured."

"Cyril."

Stella planned on saying she'd had enough. She wanted to go to the Marais right then. No more waiting. She didn't care about cheese or sunflowers or lavender. She'd take a cab by herself, if she had to. If she could fly a plane alone, she could take a cab. But before she could get it out, Cyril asked the olive seller for niçoise olives, which started a furious discussion, involving mostly gestures. So Stella sighed and adjusted the books. She'd let him have his olives, but that was it.

Then another man came into the booth. He smelled of rosemary and had a crisp, white apron wrapped around his hips. He stood next to Stella and bent over the olive bowls. He muttered to himself and rocked up and down on the balls of his feet. After the seller figured out what kind of olive Cyril wanted, he gave him a taste and turned to the man in the apron. They conversed in French and the olive seller relaxed his scowl to a mere frown. The man in the apron reached out, pointing at a bowl of olives behind the seller. Stella caught a glimpse of his watch and her eyes went wide. Doing her best not to panic, she waited for him to show her his wrist again and when he did, she confirmed it. Ten thirty. Was it possible that they'd been wandering around Les Halles for hours? They'd wasted so much time. She turned to Cyril to tell him the time when she saw him give a flick of his wrist and check his watch. When he looked at her, she averted her eyes and made no objections when he continued to sample olives for at least another five minutes before he made his choice.

He wrapped his arm around her waist and led her back into the crowds. He whispered in her ear that he absolutely had to visit the pâté seller at the far end of the market. At least that was where he thought the seller was. They'd have to look.

Stella walked with him. She said nothing. He wasn't taking her to Abel's family. He wasn't taking her to Nicky. He was stalling.

"Cyril, did you see that pastry shop back there?" asked Stella.

"Do you want a pastry?"

"They had some gorgeous petit fours. I have to try one."

Cyril wheeled her around and walked her back to the stall. He started to walk in, but she held him back.

"Can I do it myself? I really should practice dealing with the locals," said Stella.

"Indeed, you should," said Cyril.

He dropped a handful of coins into her hand without looking at them. She kissed him on the cheek and went into the booth alone. She started at the far end of the case and looked over each pastry the slow, methodical way that Cyril had shopped for everything. She could see him behind her, reflected in the glass. He watched her with his over-stuffed bag and a smile. She continued down the line, hoping, praying he'd lose interest. And he did. After a few minutes, he turned and looked out at the passing crowd.

Stella looked at the girl behind the counter and found her staring back with a puzzled expression. The girl arched one eyebrow and waited. Stella glanced back over her shoulder to check on Cyril. When she turned back to the girl, she was smiling at Stella with a knowing expression. Stella put her finger to her lips and the girl gave her a barely perceptible nod. Stella ducked behind the counter and went out through a door in the back, stepping into the alley behind the stalls. She looked both ways, put the coins in her coat pocket, and dashed down the alleyway past racks of discarded vegetables and packing boxes to an area crowded with towers of wine crates.

Stella squeezed through the towers and bumped into a bucket of rancid shrimp. She jumped away from the foul water and stepped on a dead rat. Its bones crunched under her heel and made a horrible squishing sound. A man in a butcher's apron stepped out from between a stall's canvas flaps just as Stella shrieked and danced away from the rat. He watched her with dark eyes, his mouth concealed under an enormous mustache. Stella clutched the books and her handbag to her chest, panting like she'd run a mile, which she might've. It was hard to tell in the warren of Les Halles. The butcher blinked once and pointed. Stella followed his finger. The spires of a gothic church rose over the stalls of the market. Saint-Eustache. A stoic guardian over the market's chaos.

"Thank you," said Stella.

The butcher nodded as if finding a panicked woman in a fur coat behind his stall was an everyday occurrence. Stella turned from him and ran toward the church. She expected to hear Cyril's steps behind her. She almost thought she could hear him shouting her name, but when she glanced behind her, all she saw was rotting fruit and the occasional shopkeeper.

She cleared the market and ran into the courtyard of Saint-Eustache. She leaned against the wrought iron fencing and caught her breath. Saint-Eustache loomed above, more staid and sober than she remembered from her visit with Nicky and Abel.

A shout rang out from the market and she ran east around the church, past startled tourists and almost upsetting a priest picking his teeth with his fingernail. The other side of the church was what she remembered, a renaissance beauty with all the exuberance of the age. She ran past the arched stained-glass windows and flying buttresses and looked for a cab, preferably one that could be bought for the contents of her pocket.

A red and black Renault taxi pulled up just past the walled garden at the southeast tip of the church and Stella sprinted for it across the crazed Parisian traffic with her coat whipping around behind her like a torn sail.

She made it to the cab just as a fashionable woman wearing a cherry red suit swung her long legs out of the cab. Stella panted next to the door and braced herself against it. The woman eyed Stella's torn and stained dress and her battered hat and curled her lip. She messed with her handbag and applied a thick coat of lipstick that matched her shoes. When she started adjusting the direction of her buttons, Stella grabbed her arm and yanked her out of cab. She screamed at Stella and got the door slammed in her face for her trouble.

The driver swiveled in his seat to get a look at her. He was young and somewhat handsome in spite of having one eyebrow instead of two.

"*Où?*" he asked with a raising of the brow.

"Marais," said Stella. "Go. Go now."

The driver scowled. "You are a Jew."

Stella froze. "What?"

"Marais is for the Jews." He gave her a hard look. "You are a Jew?"

She wanted to scream that it didn't matter, but instead said, "No. I'm not. Just go!"

"*Adresse?*"

She pointed frantically forward and he shrugged.

The cab began rolling and Stella looked back out the window at Saint Eustace. Cyril came running around the side. His face glowed bright red, his bag swinging wildly.

"Go! Go!" yelled Stella.

The cab driver hit the gas and they bounced off the curb. Stella sank down in the seat and hoped Cyril didn't spot her. The cab took several turns at a breakneck pace and then slowed to a more normal speed.

"You can come up," said the driver. "We have gone far from him."

Stella slid up and stuck her nose over the driver's seat back. "Are you sure?"

"Quite simply positive, Madam." He had a lovely accent that was very French, but not Parisian.

Stella came all the way up and rested her chin on the seat.

"Is he your husband?" the cab driver asked.

"Not hardly."

"Your lover?" The driver waggled his large eyebrow at her in the rearview mirror.

Stella laughed and shook her head.

"You are…not upset by this chasing."

Stella thought about it for a second as the cab wormed its way through side streets and back alleyways. "I suppose I'm not."

"This is common for you?" he asked.

"Being chased?" Stella asked.

"Yes."

"Happens all the time."

"I'm pleased you choose my cab."

Stella sat up straighter. "Why?"

"You're the most exciting thing to happen to me all day."

"Glad to help."

"What is your address?"

Stella didn't know how to say the address, so she stuck the books over the seat and the driver read it off the packaging. He nodded and started pointing out various sights. It was all Stella could do to nod politely and fake an interest.

"What time is it?" she asked when the driver paused for breath.

"It is five of eleven, Madam."

Sixty-five minutes until the meeting with Nicky. Maybe she should've gone to the tomb first. She hadn't thought about it. The Marais was the first thing that popped into her head when she got into the cab.

"How long to Napoleon's tomb?" she asked.

"From here?"

"From the address."

"Twenty minutes." He shrugged. "Maybe thirty if the traffic is bad."

"Can you get me to the address and then to the tomb by noon?"

He shrugged. "It is possible."

"How possible?"

He flashed a crooked grin at her, filled with cigarette stained teeth and male confidence. "We do it," he said.

The cab jolted forward. Stella fell back against the seat and the books slid off her lap. She snatched them up and wrapped her arms around the bundle. If the driver couldn't have heard her, she would've spoken to it. She would've said silly things to Gutenberg's diary, but things said from the heart. She would miss it, despite all the trouble it caused. It was beautiful and magical and worth everything Abel thought it was worth. She couldn't say these endearments because the driver was listening and looking in the mirror. He watched Stella press her lips to the package but didn't comment.

After a few minutes, he stroked his chin and said, "Does that man, not your husband, know where you are going?"

Stella looked up, surprised. "Yes."

"We stop a block away. It is possible he arrive before you do."

Stella gave him a sharp look.

"It is only possible. I go fast."

Stella nodded and craned her neck to see herself in the mirror. Not too bad. Considering. She adjusted her hat and pinned it to her hair with her grandmother's perfect pearl pin. She touched the pearl and thought that at least she'd managed to hold on to that. Then she brushed at the wrinkles in Klara's dress. It was hopeless. After all it'd been through, it was no more than a rag, although a well-fitted one. It would have to do. If Abel's family was anything like him, they'd understand and never even question her appearance. She did wonder what they would say when she showed up on their doorstep clutching their family's most prized possession and bringing news of Abel's arrest. If they were like Abel, they probably wouldn't say much. They'd quietly take the book with all its secrets and once again bear the burden they'd been guarding for centuries.

The cab stopped on a side street and the driver turned and hooked his arm over the back of the seat. "We're a block away, as I said." He pointed out the front window. "You go to corner café and turn right."

"Thank you," said Stella, pulling the coins out of her pocket.

"I stay here," said the driver with a wink. "You come back and pay. I take you to the emperor by noon."

Stella poured the coins back in her pocket and got out of the cab. She stood on the cobblestone sidewalk and adjusted her collar against the wind whistling up the street. The Marais felt like an entirely different city than the Les Halles area. It had a style about it that the other area lacked, rundown but still aristocratic with gorgeous seventeenth-century façades and enormous doors made for carriages to drive through. Stella walked past a twelve-foot-high door painted a peeling rusty red with swags of rowan over the top. Next to it was an apartment building with an equally colorful door and a gargoyle door knocker hanging by one nail.

The café on the corner screamed disreputable and she half-expected Uncle Josiah to amble out of the door with a whiskey in one hand and an even more disreputable woman in the other. He'd been the one to insist she go to the area and try something called hummus at the tiny restaurant called Chez Madeline or Marie or something with an M. Abel had been very surprised and the restaurant was adorable with seven tables, a real mom and pop affair. The food was an education, but Abel never said it was in the Jewish quarter and Stella wondered if Nicky knew. Of course, he probably did and thought she was too young and silly to mention it to. Well, who was young and silly now? Not Stella. Not anymore.

She turned right and walked by several more apartment buildings in better condition. Abel did say the area had been in decline since the revolution when the aristocrats got the boot, but there was still money in the Marais. The cobblestoned street got rougher on her feet and she began picking her path more carefully. Every wobble made the blisters burn and just when she felt like parking away from the building was a dreadful mistake, an incredible building rose up on the opposite corner. It reminded Stella of a compact palace with creamy stone and a turret with a black dome perched on top. She checked the address on the package and sure enough, that was it.

It was exactly the kind of place that she wanted Abel's family to live in. The wrought-iron balconies were perfect with curves and flower boxes. It looked safe and safety was what they needed.

She jogged across the street, ignoring her screaming feet, to a big oak door and knocked.

No doorman greeted her and she knocked again. There were doorbells with no numbers or names, just letters. She could just start pushing them, but that was terribly impolite. Another thing she'd have to edit out of the story for her mother's sake. Mother would think she should have a proper introduction, as if she had time for that. She pounded on the door instead. It wasn't dignified, but it was effective. The door swung open and a powerful feeling of dread came over her.

"Hello?" she called out. "Is anyone here?"

No answer and the feeling didn't dissipate.

"I shouldn't go in there," Stella said to herself and then ignored her own advice, walking down the grand entrance hall toward a small elevator and the end of a curvy staircase with a well-worn rail. To banish the feeling, she practiced what she would say to Abel's family, but with every step, she got more and more nervous. She hoped they wouldn't think she'd abandoned Abel in Vienna. She dreaded telling them of the last time she saw him. Those many hands pulling him back deep into the boxcar. She tried not to think of that image, preferring to focus on the more pleasant picture of Abel sitting on the tufted green cushions in the last train compartment they'd shared. She liked that picture, that sweet man with the sad eyes.

She rounded the corner to walk up the steps and found a man sitting halfway up the flight with a steak clapped over his left eye. His swollen and misshapen left hand rested on his knee. The fingers were bent to the right. Stella froze and stared at the man's hand. Her chest constricted and her heart hurt. She couldn't breathe. She couldn't turn around. Those fingers. Broken. Just like Albert's in Vienna.

"I told you. I don't know," said the man in a soft southern accent.

Stella swallowed and somehow squeaked out, "Don't know what?"

The man jerked his head up and dropped the steak on the stair with a bloody splat.

"That was you calling?" he asked. "I thought it was her."

"Yes. What happened to you?" asked Stella, still staring at the fingers and wishing them to be straight and normal.

"You're an American. Thank God. Help me up."

He extended his undamaged hand, smeared with blood, but Stella didn't take it.

"Who did this to you?"

"Didn't give their names."

Stella tore her eyes away from his hand and looked at his face. He matched Albert, probably blow for blow. His eye was swollen shut and lumpy knots decorated the left side of his face. Although none of his wounds were purple yet, they soon would be. Stella spun around and walked back down the hall. She forced herself not to break into a run.

"Hey! Wait a minute," called out the man. "Don't leave me here."

Stella glanced over her shoulder. The man stumbled down the hall after her. He had the steak over his eye and flailed his broken hand in an effort to maintain his precarious balance. Stella looked back at the door and took a couple more steps.

"Please! They're coming back!"

Stella wheeled around and ran to him, hooking his bad arm over her shoulders and wrapping her free arm around his waist. He gasped when she squeezed his ribcage and muttered an expletive so vile he made Uncle Josiah sound like a grandmother.

"You have to hurry," said Stella.

"This is hurrying," he said.

"Don't make me leave you."

The man grimaced and doubled his pace so that they made it to the door in a reasonable amount of time. Stella tucked the books under her chin and opened the door, and then hid the book away under her coat as she maneuvered the man outside.

"We have to hurry," she said.

They walked several steps up the street. The cobblestones were much worse going back and beads of sweat formed in Stella's armpits, rolling over her ribcage. The man coughed. A red mist exploded from his lips and blew into Stella's face.

"I'm sorry." He gagged and spat a good amount of blood onto the cobblestones.

"Never mind," said Stella. "Hurry."

They made it to the top of the street and turned left. Stella had hoped the cab driver would see them, but he had his newspaper open and she could only make out the top of his head.

The man coughed again and stumbled.

"Almost there," said Stella.

"You know who did this to me, don't you?" he asked.

"I do, if they're German."

"Damn krauts. Who the fuck are they?"

Stella kept her eyes trained on the cab. Half a block to go. "Describe them."

"A bunch of guys and a woman, pretty, but mannish."

"Gabriele Griese. Was there a man? An officer. Scare the socks off the devil type."

"No uniforms and they all scared me. She was the worst though. Enjoyed it."

"Do you know the Sorkine family?" Stella asked.

"Yes," said the man as he wheezed, spraying more blood on the cobbles.

The driver lowered his newspaper and sat in the cab staring at Stella and her new burden. His mouth hung open and for a moment, she thought he would drive away and leave her. Instead, he jumped out of the car and ran over. He took Stella's place and she ran to open the cab door.

"What happened?" asked the driver.

"I'm not sure," said Stella.

"Me either," said the man as the driver eased him into the back seat.

Stella got in on the other side. Her thoughts zigzagged back and forth between the book and Nicky. The driver got in and swiveled around to face them.

"Blood cost extra," he said.

"Go. Now," said Stella.

The driver shrugged and started the cab. "Where to now? Doctor?"

"Embassy," said the man.

"Napoleon's tomb," said Stella.

"Your friend says embassy," said the driver.

"He's not my friend. Napoleon's tomb. Go."

The driver put a cigarette between his lips and struck a match on the dashboard. He inhaled and blew out a smoke ring. "Who is he?"

"I don't know!" yelled Stella. "Go!"

The driver turned around and wrenched the gearshift around. "Americans. Always in hurry."

He did a neat three-point turn and started back in the direction they'd come. A shout rang out behind them. Stella looked back and saw Gabriele Griese standing at the corner. She pointed and screamed at them as the cab rolled away.

"Go!" Stella yelled at the driver.

"What is happening? I want no trouble."

"She's trouble. Go!"

The driver hit the gas and Stella hit the seat back. Her jaws snapped together and she bit her tongue. She twisted around and saw several men, not in uniform, run up the street behind them. One drew a pistol.

Stella grabbed the man and pulled him down on the seat. The back window shattered and the driver yelled out a long string of French that sounded like curse words in any language.

"Who are you?" asked the man. His steak fell off his eye and slithered over the edge of the seat onto the floor.

"Stella Bled Lawrence. Who are you?"

"Roger Morris. Really, who are you?"

"I told you. Stella Bled Lawrence."

"As in Bled Beer?" Roger's head started to go up.

"Keep your head down," said Stella.

The cab took a sharp turn, and they slid to the right across the seat into the door.

Roger gasped. "Oh, God."

Stella's face was inches from his. Blood pulsed in the damaged tissues just the way Albert's had. Stella looked away and swallowed the bit of blood from her torn tongue.

"You can come up," said the driver.

Stella helped Roger sit up. He leaned against the door, wheezing and muttering, "Oh, God."

She picked up the steak, brushed off the dirt, and carefully placed it back on his eye.

"Who pays for glass?" asked the driver, not an ounce of friendliness left in his tone.

"I will," said Stella. "Just get me to the tomb on time."

"What happened? Why are *Boche* shooting at you?"

"What's a Boche?"

Roger wheezed and squeaked out, "Germans."

"How do you know they're Germans?" Stella asked the driver.

He blew out a long stream of smoke and sneered. "You see them. No style."

"You're right about that, but I don't know what happened."

"You tell me or I turn around and let them have you. Boche have no taste, but they pay and their money is good."

"Not as good as Bled money," said Roger.

The driver raised an eyebrow. "Bled?"

"You've heard of Bled Beer, right? She's a Bled."

"A real Bled? Where is proof?"

Stella showed him her passport and he smiled, the cigarette dangling from his lower lip.

"You pay double. No, no. Triple."

"Fine," said Stella. "Just get me to the tomb."

"A real Bled." A hint of a smile crossed Roger's lips. "Finally. Some good luck."

Stella turned her attention out the window. "I wouldn't count on it."

CHAPTER 27

*C*abs, cars, and pedestrians crowded onto the noontime Parisian streets, stopping the cab at what felt like every five minutes or so it seemed to Stella. The driver kept up a good pace with special maneuvers that included driving on sidewalks and the other side of the road. People shook their fists and one lady at a vegetable stand lobbed a tomato at them. The remains lay smeared across the hood like a body had been dragged across it. Stella held onto the driver's seat back and kept a close eye on his watch. The minutes ticked away faster than the miles and Stella began to feel they'd never get there.

Roger sat back with his injured arm over his chest. Stella could hear him wheezing. The sound had been reminiscent of Albert, but Roger was getting worse. The seat fairly vibrated with his trembling.

"How much farther?" she asked the driver.

He shrugged. "We get there."

"That's not what I asked you."

"Ten minutes."

Stella reluctantly turned to Roger, who had his eyes trained on her. They'd grown larger over the course of the drive and his expression resembled her brother's after he'd fallen out of Uncle Josiah's big oak tree and had the wind knocked out of him. Her brother looked like he thought maybe he'd never breathe again, and a similar fear radiated off Roger. Sweat plastered his dark hair to his forehead and the swelling extended itself across his face to the right side. His nose, never a delicate feature, took on a large bulbous shape, and two black eyes were developing so rapidly that Stella could see the color grow darker if she looked for more than fifteen seconds. But worse than the color and swelling was the breath that came out of swollen lips with rattling slowness and there was a sort of clicking in his chest.

Stella reached across the seat to his knee and patted it. "It will be fine."

"My chest hurts," he said.

"Did they kick you there?"

"More like stomped."

"What did they want from you?" she asked.

"They were mad the Sorkines weren't home. They kept asking me questions, but I don't know them that well."

"How well do you know them?" she asked.

"They're sort of my patrons."

Stella opened her coat and pulled out the books, running her fingers over the worn edges of Abel's package. "Do you know Abel Herschmann?"

Roger covered his mouth, went into an explosive coughing fit, and then wiped the bloody sputum on his pant leg. "Never heard of him."

"Please tell me you know where the Sorkines went?"

"Sorry. No idea. I was just happy to have a nice place to hang my hat for a while." Roger glanced down at the paint splotches on his pants next to the bloody smear. "Starving artist."

"The Sorkines didn't tell you anything at all?"

"Did they tell me I was going to be beaten to a bloody pulp? No."

"What are they like?" Stella asked. All she could picture when she thought of them was Abel's sad face.

Roger spewed and red droplets hung like dew on Stella's fur. "Nice people," he managed to wheeze out. "They wouldn't have left me there if they knew."

The driver held up a mostly clean handkerchief and Stella used it to mop up Roger's mouth. "Nobody thinks it will happen until it happens to them." Stella grabbed the seat back as the driver made another sharp turn. "I can't believe they're gone."

"What is that?" Roger pointed at the books.

"Just a package I was supposed to deliver."

Roger touched the package reverently, as if he knew what it contained. "Whose blood is that?"

"It's a collection," said Stella.

He looked up into her battered face. "Yours?"

"Mine, others, and now yours."

"They don't want the Sorkines," said Roger.

"No?"

"They were searching for something. It's that package. Has to be. You look like you've been through hell."

"Compared to you? I don't think so," said Stella, a sting of fear going through her body. "When did the Sorkines leave, exactly?"

"About two hours ago." Roger reached up and pulled a tooth out of his mouth. They stared at it as the blood rolled onto his fingers. "What is in that package?"

"It's better if you don't know."

"I'll take your word for it."

"Good. Did the Sorkines seem worried or was this a planned vacation?"

Roger tucked his tooth in the tattered pocket of his vest. "No. Last-minute. They called and said to hurry. A family emergency."

"You really have no clue where they went?" asked Stella. "Anything will help."

Roger looked down.

"Please," said Stella. "I'm saving your bacon here."

"They didn't tell me anything."

"But…"

"But they left a list of train times. I recognized the schedule."

Stella grabbed his arm. "Where are they going?"

"I don't know for sure, but it was the schedule for trains to Italy."

"Venice," gasped Stella. "Of course."

"How did you know?" Roger shifted and gasped, going the color of butcher paper. "Oh, god. My chest hurts."

"I'm sorry," said Stella. "Don't—"

"*Sacré Bleu!*" yelled the driver.

"What?" asked Stella.

The driver puffed on what was left of his stubby cigarette. "Boche find us.'

"Oh, shit," moaned Roger.

Stella swiveled around and looked out the windows. "Where, where?"

She didn't spot the Germans but shot pinged off the trunk and she pulled Roger over. He cried out, bloody foam bubbling up on his lips.

The driver took a hard right and hit something. Stella saw flowers fly past the windows as she and Roger bounced around in the back seat. She tried to hold him down, but it just made him cry out more.

The driver snarled. "I lose them. You pay?"

"I'll pay! I'll pay!" shouted Stella as she tried to keep a grip on the seat and the books at the same time.

The tires squealed and the driver turned left. "I know shortcuts. Stupid Boche."

Stella rolled off the seat and sat on the floor in front of Roger. She put the books on her lap and braced Roger so he wouldn't slide off the seat. The rear passenger window shattered and glittering shards of glass rained down on them to stick to Roger's sweaty face.

"You were right," he said.

"About what?" Stella asked.

"You're not lucky."

Stella nodded and brushed the glass off Roger's cheek. Several tiny shards lodged in Stella's fingers and palm. She started to pick them out, but the driver turned and she had to grab Roger, driving the glass deep into her hand. When her hand left his arm, a blood stain remained on his sleeve.

"I lost them," said the driver.

"Thank God," said Roger, closing his eyes.

"*Fils de salope!*"

"What?" yelled Stella.

"Son of a bitch," said Roger.

"Boche are stupid cabbages," said the driver, then he laughed. "I have idea."

Stella peeked up over the edge of his seat. "What's your idea?"

The driver turned into an alley and Roger slid across the seat. Stella grabbed his thigh right before he whacked his head on the door.

"What are you going to do?" she asked.

The driver just grimaced with the lit cigarette stub clamped between his yellow, crooked teeth. The narrow alley barely had enough room for the cab. He avoided trash bins and old ladies by mere inches. Gabriele Griese's car was too far back for them to get off a reasonable shot, but they were gaining.

The driver hit the brakes and the Germans zoomed towards them. Stella saw Gabriele Griese behind the wheel, her eyes trained on them with intense maniacal joy. The driver hit the gas and they leapt forward toward a wooden overhang that jutted into the street. The driver shifted to the left to avoid it and Gabriele Griese followed suit. At the last second, the driver pressed the gas pedal to the floor and they lurched forward and left a five-foot gap between the cars. The driver jerked the wheel to the right and Griese did the same. The cab took out the two wooden beams that held up the overhang. The small wooden roof crashed down, bounced off the back of the cab, and fell directly into Griese's path. Griese swerved and ran into a metal trash bin that shattered her windshield. She fishtailed and rammed into the back of a restaurant.

The cab sped away from the smoking wreck and Stella prayed it would explode, but it didn't and a man stumbled out of the passenger side. He fired his pistol at them, but the shots went wild since he was wobbling around like a drunk.

"*Dégage!*" The driver made a rude gesture in the rearview mirror.

"What happened?" asked Roger.

"We hit an overhang and it flew into the Germans' car. Then they hit a wall," said Stella.

"Serves them right, bastards," said Roger. "I hope they croaked."

"At least one's alive, but we can always hope for a brain hemorrhage."

Roger tried to reach out with his injured hand and pulled it back with a grimace. "I like the way you think."

Stella helped him upright and scooted over next to him. He closed his eyes and leaned against the window. His shuddering stopped and he seemed to deflate a bit. Stella put the back of her hand to his forehead the way her mother did when one of them was sick. His skin was cool and clammy and his breath grew shallower.

"There we are," said the driver.

Stella leaned forward and saw the great expanse of the Alexander III Bridge before them and beyond the bridge, Les Invalides and Napoleon's tomb.

"We're almost there," said Stella.

Roger groaned. His eyes remained closed.

The driver drove onto the bridge at such a high speed that Stella cringed. He wove in between cars, occasionally crossing the center line. Once over the bridge, he put on more speed and raced through traffic on the wide avenue leading to Les Invalides. He drove around a strange oval traffic circle and headed toward the ornate gate decorated with gold. Stella looked around for some sort of guard. It didn't seem like they should be going through there, but the driver didn't hesitate. He drove over the cobblestones at an alarming speed that rattled Stella's teeth. Roger slumped over with his head banging against the window. She grabbed his wrist and found a faint heartbeat.

"Thank God," she said.

The driver grunted and glanced back at her.

"Nothing," said Stella, her eyes trained on the fabulous building in front of her.

The driver turned to the right and came to a jolting stop at the beginning of the long walkway.

"You pay me," he said with his hand out.

Stella looked at his grubby hand with its yellow-stained fingertips and then looked back at Roger. His eyes were open, but he was the color of cook's custard pie. Another casualty of the book.

"What happened?" Roger asked.

"We made it. We're at Les Invalides."

Roger tried to push himself upright and collapsed against the door.

"You're staying here," said Stella.

"I'll go with you."

"You have to get to the embassy."

The driver pivoted around and blew smoke in Stella's face. "No, no. I am *fini*. Pay me."

Stella felt in her pocket for the coins that weren't nearly enough. She clutched them in her sweaty palm and then dropped them back in the pocket. She held up her hand. The rings flashed in the sun and the driver's eyes grew large. They were exquisite and she was so thrilled when Nicky slipped each of them on her hand. Her eyes watered a little, but they were only things, just things. Nicky was waiting for her and Roger was possibly dying. They were more important. Things could be replaced.

"You like them?" Stella asked. "They're worth quite a lot."

"Your wedding rings?" asked Roger beside her, but she ignored him.

"Are they real?" asked the driver.

"I'm a Bled. What do you think?" Stella took off her engagement ring and swiped a deep scratch with the two-carat diamond across the rear passenger window.

"I'll take it."

Stella handed him the ring. "That takes care of the ride and the damage. Now let's discuss the embassy."

"No embassy," said the driver.

Stella held up her hand again. "Cartier. More than you make in a year. Two years."

The driver flicked the stub of his cigarette out of the shattered window. "Just the embassy. Nothing else."

"You drive him to the embassy and put him personally in the hands of the guards."

"Deal." He held out his hand.

Stella slipped off her ring. It came off easily like it didn't mind going and she pressed it into Roger's good hand. "Don't give it to him until you're safe at the embassy."

He shook his head. "I can't."

Stella smiled. "It's done. Someday, I'll explain it all to you."

He nodded, closed his fist, and put the ring over his chest with a wheeze.

Stella turned back to the driver. "Listen to me. You do as you promised or I'll take care of you the way my Uncle took care of the man who tried to steal my father's recipes."

The driver lit another cigarette and tossed his lighter on the seat. "What happened to him?"

Stella smiled and leaned forward. "Nobody knows."

"I heard you Bleds are crazy."

"We're a lot of things. Not all of them nice."

"I'll take him."

Stella got out of the cab and bent over the driver's window. "A friend to the Bleds is a friend for life."

The driver grinned and Stella could practically hear the bills fluttering around in his mind. He hit the gas and peeled away back through the gate, leaving her standing in front of a group of gaping tourists. Stella reddened under their scrutiny and wondered how much they'd heard.

A small man with slicked back hair and a clipboard stepped forward. He spoke in a light, almost undetectable French accent. "Were those bullet holes in that taxi?"

"Yes." Stella fought off her mother's polite teachings and ran toward Les Invalides' arched entrance as fast as her screaming feet would allow.

CHAPTER 28

*S*tella ran past the conical trees that stood guard in neatly spaced rows on either side of the cobblestone walk, soldiers stiff and watchful. Louis XIV's grand hospital was all that stood between her and the Dôme de Invalides where Nicky would be waiting. When Abel had brought them to the museum on their first visit to Paris, she got a crick in her neck from looking up at the overly ornamented entrance, but this time, she only wondered if Nicky had come through there on his way to the tomb. The arch could've been on fire and she wouldn't have paused to wonder how stone could burn.

She passed through the great doors into a dark stone corridor. To her right sat a large desk with several lamps on it. Their yellow glow attempted to illuminate the cold stone expanse and failed. Stella ran up to the girl who sat behind the desk wearing an enormous rough woolen coat and a sour expression. Before the girl could ask for the entrance fee, Stella dug in her pocket and tossed the coins on the desk. The sour girl jumped up and shouted, but Stella zipped past the armed guards standing on either side of the fifty-foot stone arch that opened to the courtyard. She ran past startled tourists and tripped on the knobby cobbles that paved the entire expanse. She fell forward and caught herself just before she hit the grey stones. A man rushed toward her, but she left him in her dust as she raced across the court-yard that seemed to get longer the more she ran. Stella panted and brushed a curl out of her eyes, looking everywhere for Nicky in case he was trying to catch her before she crossed the courtyard. But she didn't see him, only chilly tourists on a pilgrimage to view the emper-or's tomb.

Up ahead, the entrance to the soldier's church rose in a much more ordinary fashion. Stella ignored it, except for one glance up at the statue of Napoleon glowering down at her from his arch above the door. Stella stopped short once she was inside to straighten her hat and coat in an attempt to look somewhat respectable as she hurried past a couple of men in smart suits looking out into the subdued chapel. Captured enemy flags hung limp in the still air above the cornices and the silence seemed to highlight Stella's labored breathing.

She kept expecting Nicky to step out from behind a column and wave her to him, but her only company were the little old ladies hunched in random pews. They gave Stella evil looks as she rushed past without a care to how much noise her heels made against the marble floors.

She walked as fast as she could toward the enormous glass window behind the altar. Inside the glass, glorious pillars of the royal altar twisted up to a balustrade celebrating the Sun King. Those pillars were Abel's favorite part of the whole place and a wave of sadness pushed at Stella as she once again pictured him standing at their base, staring up at their perfect balance and musicality. She tore her eyes away and skirted the soldiers' altar and passed from the austere beauty that belonged to the soldiers into the world of the royal chapel. She rushed past two generals' tombs to the altar that was so ornate it looked like it ought to collapse under the weight of its own glory.

Stella took a deep breath and glanced right and left. Nicky wasn't there, standing next to either of the huge mournful statues that flanked the green marble opening to the stairs, so she dashed down the wide steps and came to a halt when she ran into a clump of elderly tourists starting to navigate upward. Beyond their greying heads, Napoleon's sarcophagus sat under the dome, impossibly huge and gleaming dark red. Stella squeezed between canes and shopping bags to walk through the door under the golden cherub's head and glanced around the crypt. A couple stood across the way and chatted beside a colossal statue on one of the many pillars. Their voices rang off the marble walls and floor, sounding both musical and frightening.

She turned to the right and walked the ring around Napoleon's tomb, passing behind the statues. Her shoes made small clicks against the marble and her eyes darted everywhere. She walked around the tourists, who glanced at her and went back to their conversation. She knew if she just kept walking, Nicky would come. He wasn't dead in Austria like Hans. He wouldn't leave her alone with the book and nowhere to go. He wouldn't. She kept walking and looking. She passed behind the twelve statues again and started another pass when she caught sight of someone looking over the balcony above. A flash of a tall figure in dark clothes.

Stella sprinted around the circle, dodging people and ignoring her burning feet. Up she went, pushing past the elderly tourists, clutching the books to her chest.

"Pardon! Pardon!"

They didn't pardon her. They cursed her. A couple might even have spit, but she didn't care. She cornered around the altar and emerged into the church under the magnificent dome. People wandered around, peering over the balcony down into the crypt, but none of them were Nicky. Maybe he just meant the whole church when he said Napoleon's tomb. She dashed left into a side chapel to find Marshal Foch's impressive sarcophagus alone. She circled the black pediment with the WWI soldiers holding Foch's coffin on their weary shoulders high above her and caught a glimpse of a dark figure passing into the corridor to the next chapel.

"Wait!" she cried out, but the figure didn't turn.

She dashed through to Vauban's chapel and found it empty as well. A strange feeling of something not being right came over her. Nicky wouldn't hide from her. The very notion was ridiculous. He must just be in another chapel. Perhaps he was a little late. That was okay. He would get there. He would.

She stepped past the entrance toward Vauban's tomb with the great engineer reclining on his own black coffin flanked by two goddesses when the feeling got much, much worse. She knew without a doubt that she shouldn't go in there. She spun around to dash back to Foch when a body stepped in front of her. She almost ran into the dark-suited chest before skidding to a halt. Nicky! She grinned up at the face looking down at her and then jumped back, clutching the books and her handbag to her chest.

"He's not here," said the man in a soft Dutch accent. The man from the train. The Dutch historian, if Oliver was right.

Stella turned to run, but there was a click and a small snub-nosed revolver emerged from inside his right sleeve.

"Back up slowly." He said it gently like he didn't want to hurt her, but one look at his face and Stella knew that was just his manner of speaking, not the reality behind the words.

"I don't think I will," said Stella.

"I'll shoot you. Tourists or no. You're lucky I found you instead of Peiper. He would shoot you on sight." He waved the pistol and she moved backward to the sarcophagus to stand in front of the name Vauban that was done in gold on the front.

Dr. Van Wijk blocked the main entrance to the chapel and Stella shifted to the right to try and see around him. Why didn't someone come in? Where were all the tourists?

"Why would Peiper want to shoot me?" she asked.

"You stole his beloved plane, not that he requires a reason to kill," he said. "That was you, was it not?"

"What makes you think it was me?"

"Peiper caught sight of your husband fleeing alone after Herr Gruber had been shot. You were either dead or in that plane. We never found a body, so it had to be you."

"Did you kill Hans?"

"I'm not a murderer," said Dr. Van Wijk.

"Oh, really?" asked Stella, her lips twisted with sarcasm.

"I only want the book."

"What book?"

Dr. Van Wijk's forehead knotted and the revolver emerged further from his sleeve. "Don't try my patience."

"I'll try any damn thing I want," said Stella. "I've earned it."

"You stood on the shoulders of giants to get this far."

"At least I know where to stand, unlike you."

"You're not as bright as you think you are. How do you suppose I happen to be here?" He waved the gun in a short arch, indicating the chapel. "Of all the places in Paris or the world, for that matter. I'm waiting in the very place you're meeting your husband. Quite a coincidence."

Stella kept her eyes steady and trained on Dr. Van Wijk's hard face. Several people knew where she was meeting Nicky. Which one of them betrayed her?

"Don't want to guess?" The historian moved closer and lowered his voice. "Well, I want to tell you. Your little Australian spy is a very interesting little fellow."

"He's British."

"He's cooperative."

Stella's mouth fell open. "You caught Cyril?"

"Briefly. But before he escaped, he let it slip that you'd be here at noon. All I had to do was sit and wait."

"He didn't let it slip. Cyril doesn't make mistakes."

Dr. Van Wijk smiled. "That makes the betrayal complete, doesn't it? Now give me the book and I'll let you go."

"You'll have to shoot me," said Stella, struggling to keep her voice calm.

"Gutenberg is the work of my life. Don't underestimate what I'll do to get that diary." He stepped forward and Stella dodged to the side, glancing up at the war goddess. Van Wijk stood in front of science with the great Vauban staring down at him from the ages. If the historian noticed where he was or who he'd become, he didn't show it. His slim face would've been studious and sincere with any expression other than ravenous desire.

"You must think I'm stupid," said Stella.

"Not stupid. Only young and foolish."

"Better than old and foolish. You've got that covered."

He scowled. "I will have that book."

"If you truly had a passion for Gutenberg, you'd never do this. You're probably not even an historian. Historians preserve history. They don't destroy it."

Dr. Van Wijk's face reddened. He stepped forward and pressed the pistol into Stella's stomach just below the book. "You little fool. I'm going to study it. I'll devote my life to it."

"You're the fool. They'll never let you have it. You'll never even get to read it."

"Don't you listen? I'm going to study it. My work will be read by every serious scholar in the world."

Stella stepped closer to Dr. Van Wijk. The pistol's muzzle poked painfully into her gut, but she smiled up at him. "Is that what they promised you? Abel was right. They'll say anything."

"You know nothing about it. They want the book for the world, for the greater glory of Germany."

"They're going to destroy it. You'll be lucky if you get a peek."

"You're as crazy as the rest of your family. Give me the book."

"Gutenberg married a Jew," said Stella in a vicious whisper.

Dr. Van Wijk staggered back as though she'd hit him. "What?"

"Listen to me. Gutenberg married a Jewish woman named Nissa. His descendants have been protecting themselves and this secret ever since. I don't know how your buddy, Peiper, and the rest of the Nazis found out, but you know they'll never let you publish that the greatest invention of all time happened because of a Jew."

Dr. Van Wijk's face flushed and sweat beads formed at his greying temples. "Gutenberg was the inventor, not some woman."

Stella pulled the package from inside her coat. "Not quite and it's all in here. A Jew developed the ink and inspired Gutenberg. It wouldn't have happened without her. He said so."

"Gutenberg said," whispered Van Wijk.

"That's right. He credited his Jewish wife, Nissa," said Stella.

"You're sure?"

"Of course, I'm sure. This book will be the worst thing to happen to Germany since—I don't know—the last war. The Nazis will eradicate Nissa. They'll burn it."

"No," whispered Dr. Van Wijk. "It's too great a treasure. They'll just cut that part out."

"The whole thing is Nissa. She's all over it." Stella pushed the muzzle of the gun away and looked him in the eye. "What do they do with things that don't fit their vision? I've heard about the book burnings. You must've seen them. You know about the Jews in Vienna. If you truly want the world to know the depth of Gutenberg's genius, you can't let them destroy the book."

Stella untied the twine, tucked *The Hobbit* in her pocket, and unwrapped the book. Dr. Van Wijk stared at the embossed letter G on the cover and gasped as she opened it to reveal Nissa's portrait in red chalk. Then she turned to the page Cyril had shown her and pointed to the words that first announced Nissa's religion.

Dr. Van Wijk mouthed the words. Then he spoke the Latin, softly with love.

"They're his words," he said to Stella. "Gutenberg speaking to us."

"Yes." Stella closed the book and clasped his gun hand. "Don't betray him."

The revolver disappeared into Dr. Welk's sleeve. "Go. I'll cover for you."

"You won't be sorry," said Stella.

The historian nodded and a shot rang out. Blood sprayed out of his chest and splattered Vauban's name as Van Wijk collapsed and cracked his head on the swirled marble base. His revolver went skittering across the floor and bumped into the wall. Stella whipped around and found Gabriele Griese smiling at her from the chapel's entrance. She wore a smart brown suit, her blonde hair swept up into elegant coils on top of her head. Nothing about her said murderer, except her expression.

"I think you're wrong," she said, her words tainted with pleasure and malice. "He does regret it."

Several of the tourists rushed to the side entrance, but Gabriele waved her black pistol at them and they vanished without a protest. Stella stepped backward onto the slim stairs up to the tomb, slipping on Dr. Van Wijk's blood and trying not to gag.

Gabriele followed, her hard eyes fixed on Stella's face, marching up without faltering or acknowledging the devastation she'd caused.

Stella bumped into the sarcophagus. The pool of blood spread beneath her feet, a growing, living thing. Stella glanced down at it, almost surprised that it didn't lick at her feet and wind its awfulness around her slim ankles. The pool was so large, fresh, and thick, Stella could taste its metallic tang in her mouth. Dr. Van Wijk's body slipped against the cold marble and bumped into Stella's leg. It rested there, his face pressed against her calf as she shook with revulsion and the effort to keep herself from recoiling and enticing Gabriele's deadly trigger finger.

"How many is that?" Gabriele asked.

Stella swallowed a bit of bubbling bile in her throat and whispered, "What?"

"Your body count. How many have died because of you?"

Stella glanced at the entrance behind Gabriele. Why didn't anyone come? Where were the police?

Gabriele pointed her toe and swept it through the gore, making a red arc in front of her. "Don't bother looking for rescue. We control the building."

"But this is France."

"It is, for now. Soon, France will belong to the Reich and everyone knows it."

"Everyone must not include the French."

Gabriele curled her lip. "They will not be consulted. Give me the book and I may kill you quickly."

"No, you won't," said Stella, clutching the book tighter.

Gabriele laughed. Her harsh tones bounced off the chamber's walls, making Stella shudder. "You're cleverer than you look." She took another step, slapping her delicate pump in the blood. "Perhaps I'll have you destroy it yourself. Yes, that will do nicely. You'll tear out every page and light it afire. Everything you tried to protect. Gone. Poof."

"I won't do it."

"Oh, you will and it will be agony. Sweet, luscious agony."

"I won't."

Gabriele reached in her pocket and extracted a lighter. She flicked it and a flame burst from the end, causing Stella to shake more violently. Dr. Van Wijk's head slipped off her leg. He fell with a wet thump at her feet in the congealing pool of his own blood.

Gabriele extended the lighter to Stella and lowered the gun to aim at Stella's foot and cocked it. The click bounced off the walls, a dozen threats in one. "I'll start with the foot and what a lovely, delicate foot it is. So easily shattered."

Stella couldn't speak. Her eyes shifted between the lighter and the gun.

"Let's start with one page. Any page. I'm not particular."

Stella shook her head.

Gabriele's smile widened. "I was hoping you'd say that. This could take hours."

As the last word left Gabriele's lips, something hit her head from the side. Stella screamed and the gun went off, shattering a marble tile next to her foot and ricocheting to take out a chunk of the sarcophagus. Gabriele crumpled next to Dr. Van Wijk and lay still. Stella stared at her body and at the large rock that lay a couple feet away. She couldn't move or breathe. Was Gabriel dead? Why was there a rock in Les Invalides?

A man ran to Gabriele and picked up the gun next to her body. He pointed the muzzle at her bloody temple for a long second and then seemed to reconsider. He turned to Stella and she found Nicky's blue eyes fixed on her from beneath a dirty beret.

"It's you," said Stella.

Nicky grabbed her hand and dragged her away. He shoved the pistol in his long black trench coat as he passed Gabriele lying motionless on the floor and exited the chapel through the side entrance, pulling Stella behind him.

"Are you hurt?" he asked, low over his shoulder.

Stella shook her head, not even trying to open her mouth. If she did, she might start screaming and not be able to stop.

Nicky jerked her arm. "Answer me."

She shook her head again. He pivoted around with a look of rage on his face. When their eyes met, it softened.

"Are you hurt?" he asked again in a gentler tone.

She shook her head.

"Thank God."

He turned around and walked through to Foch's chapel at his briskest pace. Stella jogged to keep up. Her eyes darted everywhere. Gabriele said they had the building, but where were *they*? Was someone hiding behind Foch's black sarcophagus? It was huge and capable of hiding several men, if positioned correctly. Nicky went past without glancing at it and they left out an exit that put them in the altar section. Nicky skirted around the twisting columns, past the stairs leading to Napoleon's tomb and went between the memorials for Duroc and Bertrand to the door leading to the soldier's chapel. He approached it from the side, flattened his back to the wall and then edged his face around the door. He pulled back immediately.

"Were the two men by the brochures there when you came in?" he asked Stella.

"Yes," she whispered, surprised that she was able to respond.

"I thought so. We can't get around them. We'll have to go back the other way."

"How did you do that?" asked Stella.

Nicky pulled her to the right and looked around the edge of the altar. "What?"

"Kill Gabriele Griese."

"I didn't kill her. I wanted to, but I didn't," said Nicky. "We'll go out the front. They have men there, but they're looking out, not in."

"But how?"

Before Nicky could answer, the man with the clipboard that Stella had seen by the front gate casually walked around the altar and put his fingers to his lips. "They are searching for you. We will cover. Go to Saint Gregory."

"What?" asked Nicky.

The man gestured to the right. "His chapel." Then he spun around and began lecturing in French.

"Do we trust him?" asked Stella.

"Do we have an alternative?"

She squeezed his hand and pulled him forward. "Let's go."

They crept around the altar, crouching low and holding their breath. The man with the clipboard lectured to a crowd of tourists who had their eyes fixed on him, but their hands were gesturing for them to hurry. They dashed into the closest chamber, an empty chapel with a few statues in alcoves in the circular room.

They ran straight through and Nicky paused at the side exit, bracing himself against the pristine creamy marble with a filthy hand. The light from the great clear glass window highlighted the layers of grime that covered Stella's fabulous husband from head to toe.

Stella looked down at the hand holding hers so firmly and didn't recognize it. The formally manicured nails were broken and cracked. Black crescents of dirt marked the tips. Stella's wrist above Nicky's hand struck her as equally unpleasant. Pinpoints of blood stood out in sharp relief against her white skin and the bones stuck out, jagged like the flying buttresses of Notre Dame. It was the wrist of a starved, pained person and it didn't seem like it could belong to her at all.

"Nicky, what happened—"

"Baseball. I was a pitcher," he hissed.

"What in the world are you talking about?" she asked.

He dashed into the next chapel past Turenne's tomb and into Jérôme Bonaparte's chapel. A pair of elderly ladies wearing elegant feathered hats were huddled next to Jerome's black sarcophagus, looking like they wanted to tuck themselves into its wall niche. They held up their hands in a stop motion and gestured for them to step back into the corridor between chapels. Stella and Nicky stepped back together, and as they did, raised voices speaking in German pinged around the marble walls. A French voice argued and protested.

The ladies straightened up at a demand from the German voice. He was speaking French but in a way that made it ugly and edgy. The ladies took on haughty expressions and shook their heads no. The German insisted and the ladies glared. There was a snapping of heels and the clicks of boots walking away. The French voice said, "Merci, mesdames, merci."

Nicky and Stella watched the ladies, who waited and then walked with their patrician noses in the air to the main exit. They casually looked around and then nodded to Stella and Nicky.

They dashed to the exit, whispering their thanks. One of the ladies growled, "Boche," and something Stella recognized as an expletive.

Nicky peeked out into the main section of the church and then squeezed Stella's hand. They crept down the steps and around the large pillar beside the entrance and headed for the stunning blue and gold doors at the church's entrance alcove. One of the great doors was open, the other closed. Just inside the closed door stood a man wearing a smart black suit. He looked out the open door and tapped his foot in a staccato rhythm. His hand was in his bulging pocket, his fingers wrapped around something shoved deep down. Stella started to warn Nicky, but he already knew. He let go of her hand and pushed her against the wall. He crept along the wall, leaving Stella to watch with her hand over her mouth.

Nicky approached the man in a crouched position. He stopped within a foot, sprang up, and hooked his long arm around the man's throat. The crook of Nicky's arm pinched the man's throat and he thrashed wildly with his free arm and legs spinning in a vain attempt to get purchase on something. The one hand in the pocket remained trapped by the gun that was undoubtedly concealed there. Nicky stood straight up and lifted the smaller man off his feet. He kicked for several seconds and then went limp. Nicky lowered the man to the floor and dragged him to the corner behind the closed door. The man let out a low groan and Nicky waved Stella over.

First, she glanced back into the rotunda and saw a man coming out of Vauban's chapel. The second their eyes met, the man screamed something in German. Stella ran to Nicky at the door. He grabbed her hand and they dashed outside past the enormous columns into the bright November sunlight.

They ran down the front steps so fast that Stella didn't remember touching them at all. It seemed like they merely flew over them, propelled by fear. Once Nicky hit the fine gravel of the wide walk leading to a gate and a wide avenue beyond, he put on some serious speed. His long legs moved like pistons, covering ground like a greyhound after a rabbit with no thought about Stella hurtling along after him, her feet barely touching the ground.

There was a sharp report of a pistol and a ping off a stone bench just to the left of them. Patients in wheelchairs on the walkway tried to roll away. They screamed and ducked as another shot rang out. Nicky jolted to the right, running between the trees toward the gate. Uncle Josiah's talk of hand-to-hand combat flashed through Stella's head. Something about moving targets being difficult. They must've been nearly impossible to hit considering the speed and cornering Nicky was capable of.

But then they broke through the trees. It was open, a real shooting gallery.

"Which way?" asked Nicky.

Stella had explored Les Invalides thoroughly, but it still took her a second to think.

"Stella!"

She yanked him to the right, away from the gate. They backtracked through a decorative garden into another line of trees to emerge at a little-used gate on the Avenue de Tourville. They ran through the gate, past a man and woman with their backs pressed against the black wrought iron, and into the street. Cars swerved around them, their brakes squealing, but Nicky didn't hesitate and he didn't stop until a car skidded to a halt in front of them, blocking their path. Nicky had so much speed he couldn't stop in time. He rammed into the side of the car and cracked the window with the force of the impact. Stella hit the car just behind but barely made a dent. She staggered back and would've fallen if Nicky hadn't held her upright. The driver inside the car stared at them for a second and then began screaming at them, spraying spittle on his window in big globs.

Nicky hesitated and then grabbed the door handle. He wrenched the door open, grabbed the spitting driver and flung him out onto the street. Then he shoved Stella into the front seat, cracking her head on the roof. He got in behind her, slammed the door, and hit the gas. The car peeled out with a fishtail waggle and sped away from Les Invalides at breakneck speed.

Nicky drove through the traffic without hitting the brakes, past cars that had come to a standstill, all the drivers watching their progress with open mouths.

The street dead-ended at a cross street. The traffic on this street was still moving. Nicky cranked the wheel to the right and they skidded across the street at top speed and broad-sided a cab. Nicky kept his foot on the gas and the smell of burning rubber filled the car. Behind them, there was a loud squeal and a crash.

Stella pivoted in her seat to see what calamity they'd caused and came face to face with two passengers sitting together in the backseat. A husband and wife, from the looks of it, clutched each other, their faces drained of color and their mouths in fixed grimaces.

Stella turned to Nicky. "There are people in the back seat."

"Never mind them. Is anyone chasing us?" Nicky turned the wheel sharply and Stella slid across the seat and rammed into his hip.

"You're going to kill us," she said.

"Not today," Nicky replied with grin.

Stella kissed his cheek and looked back over the seat, past the passengers staring at her, at a car not twenty yards behind them and gaining.

"I can't tell who it is for sure," said Stella. "But someone's following us."

"It's her," said Nicky. "It has to be her."

Stella nodded as the car following them sideswiped a smaller vehicle without even trying to swerve.

"I'll lose her," said Nicky.

"She's coming up fast."

The man in the backseat shook his head like he was coming out of a deep sleep and wasn't sure where he was. "Who the hell are you?"

Stella glanced from him to Gabriele's car as it ran up on the sidewalk to avoid a parked car and grazed a pedestrian, who crumpled behind it. Then she looked back to the man who'd gotten his color back and was rapidly turning the shade of an overripe tomato. From somewhere deep inside of Stella, her mother's training kicked in. She extended her free hand over the seat and managed the smile her father and Uncle called charming.

"I'm Stella Bled Lawrence of the Bled brewing family and this is my husband, Nicky Lawrence of the New York Lawrences," she said.

The man stared at her hand and the woman said, "You can't be."

"I assure you, I am, and I'm very sorry for this inconvenience."

The man looked out the back window just as a man emerged from Gabriele's passenger window with a pistol.

"Inconvenience?" shouted the man, pushing his wife down onto the floor. "Are you kidding?"

Nicky took a hard right and they all tumbled to the left. Stella glimpsed the Seine from between the large trees that graced the bank. Gabriele was right behind them, only three car lengths back. The man sitting in the passenger window leaned forward. A shot rang out and shattered the back window.

"This is so exciting," said the woman.

"Amelie!" yelled the husband.

The wife extended her hand over the seat. "I'm so pleased to meet you. We're the Boulards. We're not society, but I've read all about your families."

"They're not Bleds!" the husband yelled from the floor of the car. "They're criminals and they're going to get us killed."

"I am a Bled, really," said Stella. "We'll make this up to you."

"You're darn tooting," yelled Mr. Boulard.

"This is so exciting," said Mrs. Boulard. "I've never met a real celebrity before."

"Shut up, Amelie! We're going to die."

Amelie rolled her green eyes and said primly, "We're not going to die, Paul. We would know."

"I know!"

"No, you don't. Please excuse my husband, Mrs. Lawrence."

"Don't apologize for me, woman!"

"Someone has to!"

"Shut up, Amelie!"

"Shut up yourself, Paul!

Stella looked back at Nicky. "Um…how're we doing?"

"Pretty good. That pedestrian slowed her down a little."

"Oh, my God. That poor man."

Nicky clenched the steering wheel. "Save your pity for us if she catches up."

"What are we going to do?" asked Stella, gripping the seat as he swerved again.

"We're going to the embassy."

"Where is it?"

He swerved to squeeze between three-wheeled trucks and said, "By the Place de la Concorde."

"Thank God you have a plan."

"Stella darling, I always have a plan."

"That makes one of us," said Stella.

From the backseat, Amelie piped up, "Paul's a financial planner. Do you need a financial planner?"

"For the last time, Amelie, shut up!"

"I'm just saying," she said.

The two of them began bickering and Stella looked up at Nicky. He had the tiniest hint of a smile on his lips that dropped off in a split second.

"What?" Stella looked back at the road that was completely jammed with traffic. "There's a bridge. Go on the bridge." Stella pointed at a low stone bridge with lovely decorative arches. The Pont Neuf.

"Excellent," said Nicky.

Gabriele gained on them. She was only two car lengths behind when Nicky crossed the center line and cut off a motorcyclist who had turned onto the bridge from the opposite direction. The motorcyclist spun around and fell in line behind them. He shook his fist and didn't notice Gabriele coming up fast behind him.

"Oh, no," said Stella.

"What?" asked Nicky.

"She's going to hit that motorcyclist."

Nicky looked in the rearview mirror and grimaced. He swerved to the right to get around a truck loaded with crates. The motorcyclist seemed to think he was trying to escape him and followed. Nicky had to touch the brakes when the truck slowed. Gabriele took advantage of the hesitation and charged ahead. She bore down on the motorcyclist and the poor fellow didn't have a clue. Stella could see her now, bent over the steering wheel, her hands at ten and two. Her focus perfect. She saw only them. The motorcyclist might as well have been a gnat.

Nicky looked in the rear view. He swerved into oncoming traffic, but had to hit the brakes and get back behind the truck when a black cab materialized in front of them. Gabriele gunned her engine, hitting the back of the motorcyclist. The bike rolled under Gabriele's car and the rider flew through the air and hit the windshield. For a second, his body blocked the window before it rolled off to the left. Gabriele lost control of her car as it passed over the motorcycle. She fish-tailed back and forth before she clipped their rear back panel and flew past them, crashing into the back of the truck. The force of the hit rolled the truck twice into oncoming traffic. Crates flew everywhere and Stella had a glimpse of Gabriele's gunman as he flew out the window and over the side of the bridge.

Nicky slammed on the brakes and they spun three hundred and sixty degrees, all of them screaming except Nicky, who never uttered a syllable. The car stopped on an edge, two tires on the pavement and two in the air. They hung there for what seemed like a good five minutes before they crashed back to all fours with a grinding crunch.

Stella clung to the seat back with the book pressed between her breasts, her eyes locked with Amelie's. Paul's mouth opened and closed in an uncontrollable spasm. He was still on the floor and held onto the seat with white fingertips.

"Stella, are you alright?" asked Nicky.

She turned to find her husband still gripping the steering wheel and his beret hanging off one ear.

"I'm fine," she said as she looked past him to Gabriele's car.

A man opened the rear driver's side door and stumbled out. He waved a gun in the air before he sank to his knees. A pile of crates blocked Stella's view into the car, but she wasn't surprised when the crates in front of the driver's door tumbled over. Nicky kicked his door open, grabbed Stella's hand, and dragged her across the seat.

"She's coming," he said, pulling her out the door.

"Amelie!" yelled Stella. "Stay down."

"I will, Stella," Amelie yelled back.

Gabriele's man spotted them the second they got out of the car. His gun arm shook, but he fired at them anyway. He sent his bullets far over their heads and blocked their way across the bridge. Nicky turned around and ran back toward the right bank. Then he stopped short and Stella ran into his back. Several accidents spanned the bridge and blocked their way across. People swarmed over the expanse and a dozen languages colored the air with anger and fear. One of them was distinctly German.

Nicky pivoted to the right and ran across the road to a large square paved with cobbles. A bronze statue of some king riding a horse sat in the middle, fenced off by wrought iron. Nicky ran past the statue toward the edge. For a second, Stella thought he was going to jump. And for a second, she was ready to jump with him. But instead of going all the way to the edge, he took a turn to a hidden set of stairs and ran headlong down them into the dank underbelly of the ancient bridge.

At the bottom of the stairs, they turned left into an archway that opened up to a lovely garden, still tinted with summer green despite the November chill. Nicky pulled Stella down the stone stairs, looked right and left, and then yanked her over to some manicured bushes and a wooden bench.

"Hide here," he said.

"What are you going to do?" asked Stella, snatching his hand before he could turn away and pressing it to the book over her heart.

"I'm going to shoot her."

"Good."

Nicky reached in his pocket and a hardness settled onto his face.

"What?" Stella whispered.

"I lost the gun."

"How?"

He stuck his hand through his pocket and showed her his grimy hand. "I forgot. It has a hole."

"Who gave you that coat?" she asked. "It's terrible."

"I found it in a trash bin." Nicky looked into the park and his eyes darted around, assessing the options. Stella just watched him. Nicky Lawrence of the New York Lawrences was wearing trash. If four months married to her did that to him, what would forty years do? Would she get the chance to find out? Gabriele Griese wasn't likely to have any mercy and she was coming. She would always be coming. Gabriele Griese would never stop.

He pulled away, but she wouldn't let go. "What will you do now?"

"I'll know when I get there."

Then Nicky wrenched his hand out of hers and ran into the park.

CHAPTER 29

Stella heard Gabriele before she saw her. High heels rapped on the stone steps and made Stella shrink into the hidey-hole between the bush and the wall. Even Gabriele's footsteps sounded threatening, angry. At the sound of them, Stella realized she was cornered. There was no place to go unless one counted the river gurgling off to her left as a viable option. And she'd lost sight of Nicky as soon as he hopped the gate into the small triangular park that sat on the tip of the island they were on. She was alone in one of the biggest cities in the world.

Then Gabriele's footsteps stopped, making Stella's heart seize in her chest. She listened as Gabriele blew out a breath and then there was a click. Stella hated those clicks. They always preceded something bad and the bad always turned out to be worse than she expected.

While Stella waited for Gabriele to make a move, a breeze blew across the island, stirring up the leaves and blowing dust in her face. She clenched her jaw but couldn't hold her breath any longer. She expelled the hot air from between tense lips, the only thing she could control.

There were more footsteps and Gabriele stepped into view. She had her back to Stella and Dr. Van Wijk's snub-nosed revolver in her right hand. Splotches of blood covered her left side, caked on her stockings and turning her blonde hair to a crusty red.

Gabriele surveyed the island and the few people there looked back. There was a young couple having a picnic on a bench, frozen with chunks of baguette in their hands and an elderly man with an ornately carved cane who'd been heading for the stairs, probably to find out what happened on the bridge when Gabriele's appearance stopped him cold.

The German yelled at them in French and Stella saw the old man's eyes flick down at her. She held her breath again. He knew she was there. He must've seen Nicky go past him. The same with the couple.

Gabriele yelled again and pointed the revolver at the old man and Stella could see a change in his expression. He'd make a decision. Stella's chest burned as she waited to hear it.

Although she couldn't understand French beyond merci and pardon, Stella understood what he'd decided. The man took on a concerned look and held out an arm. He said something that Stella interpreted as, "Are you okay?"

Gabriele yelled again, her voice shrill with frustration.

The old man shook his head and he looked back at the couple for confirmation. They nodded and began packing up their lunch hastily. The old man pointed at the bridge and pinged a dozen questions at Gabriele, so many that Stella was afraid she'd shoot him just because he was annoying. Instead, she waved the revolver at him in a way that said, "You are an idiot. Go away."

The old man and the couple hurried past Stella, ignoring her completely. Gabriele watched them go and then scanned the bridge. Stella expected to be spotted and shot at any moment. There was no possibility of escape. All Gabriele had to do was look down and to the right. And she would. Gabriele Griese wasn't sloppy.

"Hey you!" Nicky's voice came from somewhere beyond the park.

Gabriele did an about-face and stared into the park but didn't move.

"Hey, Greasy, I have something you want!" yelled Nicky and Stella flinched at the insult. That woman would shoot him on sight. What was he doing?

Gabriele snapped open the revolver's cylinder with a flick of her wrist, checked the chambers, and snapped it closed again with the confidence of a well-practiced hand. Then she stepped with her purposeful, mannish walk to the garden's gate, kicked it open, and walked down the path in the direction that Nicky had disappeared in.

Stella watched her march away and then she braced herself with her free hand against the bench. The wind kicked up, flinging leaves and debris in her face. A strand of hair blew in her mouth and as she brushed it away, she wondered what she was doing. Waiting like a fool for something, anything to happen? That wasn't like a Bled. That wasn't like Stella.

As she considered her limited options, the wind carried a shout to her. Just a tease. Not enough to know who said what or why, but it was enough to get her moving. She bent over and peered under the bench. Then she placed the book under it, out of sight. She stood up, slowly, bracing herself with the tree and glancing around to see if anyone was watching. No one was, so she stepped out from behind the bushes and looked toward the end of the island. Gabriele was halfway through the small park. Nicky stood at the end in front of a wrought iron fence, framed by a weeping willow tree. Even at that distance, Stella could see he'd assumed his practiced nonchalance. Gabriele, on the other hand, was as taut as a piano wire. She held Dr. Van Wijk's revolver out in front of her, aimed at Nicky's chest. Stella moved to the left and skirted around the park's metal fencing onto a stone-paved path that encircled the whole tip of the island. The wind blew harder once she was out of the shelter of the bench. Her coat hem danced around her knees and her hat barely hung on thanks to her Grandmother's pin. She clamped the hat tighter on her head and peered through the fence as she walked on the balls of her feet so her heels wouldn't make a sound. She could just barely glimpse Gabriele through the bushes, but her shrill voice rode the wind, carrying its venom into Stella's chest.

A low, long whistle to her left tore her attention away from

Gabriele. She looked over and saw three men, sailors in rough clothing, waving at her. They walked along the deck of a low black barge. They shook their heads and waved at her to go back. One pointed in the direction of Gabriele and made a gun out of his fingers. Stella nodded at them and touched her hand to her heart. Kind of them to warn her.

She stopped a yard from the end of the park. Nicky was facing her, his thighs against the fence. His gun was limp at his side and he could've been having a boring conversation with his accountant for all the animation he showed. Gabriele stood in front of him. Every inch of her radiated tension.

"Where is she?" Gabriele screamed, her German accent muddling her words.

Nicky shrugged.

"I'll kill you, you insolent whelp."

"Whelp? Interesting. I think I'm probably older than you," said Nicky.

"Where is it?" Gabriele shifted to the right as she screamed and Stella could see her red face and the saliva spewing from her lips.

"Be specific."

Gabriele pointed the pistol at his face, but Nicky didn't flinch. He merely raised an eyebrow. Gabriele bellowed, shifted to the right, and fired past his shoulder. Nicky stood quiet for a second and then he did it. He yawned. Gabriele screamed and fired over his head.

"Tell me! Tell me!" she screamed.

"Tell you what?" asked Nicky in his best bored voice.

Gabriele went on ranting and for just a second, Stella locked eyes with Nicky. He moved to the right and Gabriele moved with him so that her back was to Stella. Stella looked for a weapon, a rock, anything, but the smooth square stones she stood on revealed nothing. Another wind gust came up from the river. It tore at Stella's coat, wrapping it around her legs. Her hat slid over her eyes and she whipped it off her head.

"I'll kill you!" Gabriele stalked closer to Nicky and still, he showed nothing. "I'll kill her."

Nicky raised Gabriele's gun and pointed it at her. "I don't think so."

"You're scared now, aren't you?" Gabriele asked, not screaming anymore but purring.

"If that's what makes you happy."

"Happy. Happy has nothing to do with it," she said, her voice once again rising to a scream.

"I think it does. You don't care about the book. You only want the catch, the fear. Sorry to disappoint," said Nicky.

Gabriele bellowed and fired at Nicky, who dodged to the right. The bullet grazed his shoulder. He winced and touched his hand to the wound.

Stella pressed her hat to her mouth and stifled a scream. Just below her eye, the hatpin pressed against her cheekbone. She looked at the pin and slid it out of the fabric. Nicky called it lethal and it was time to test his theory. Stella closed her fist around the pin and climbed the wall behind Gabriele.

Nicky showed his bloody fingertips to Gabriele. "Feel better?"

"Who are you?" she screamed.

"You know who I am," said Nicky.

Stella climbed over the fence and eased through the bushes until she stood directly behind Gabriele.

"You are a weak American. Stupid and spoiled."

Stella raised the pin on the word 'weak'. Nicky was not weak. She held the pin high on 'stupid'. There never was a brighter man than Nicky. She drove the pin down deep into the base of Gabriele's skull on the word 'spoiled' and washed the hated word away in a gush of blood. Gabriel staggered forward and the pin slid out of her head. She walked with arms outstretched to Nicky. He sidestepped and she stumbled, hit the fence, and careened over it.

They ran to the fence and watched as Gabriele staggered to her feet, clutching her head and screaming. She slipped on the edge of the walkway and tumbled down the smooth stone embankment into the Seine. Her body went limp and the current grabbed her, tugging her under in seconds.

Stella looked down at the bloody pin in her hand, awestruck at the gore. Nicky grabbed her and pulled her to him. Then he pushed her back, took her hand, and dragged her back through the park. As they ran, the sailors began cheering. *"Vive la France! Vive la France!"* They ran along the edge of the barge with their fists in the air. Germany might try to annex France, but it would be no easy ride.

Nicky ran through the gate left open by Gabriele. Stella glanced up at the overlook. She expected to see some horrified onlookers pointing their fingers at her, but no one was there. Sirens still wailed on the bridge and on both banks. Two plumes of smoke marred the beautiful blue sky. Nicky started for the archway to the stairs, but Stella stopped him. She ran over to the bench and pulled out the book, tucking it inside her coat.

"Come on," said Nicky, but a low whistle called her from behind. The sailors had run down to the barge's stern and were whistling at them. They pointed at the embankment.

"This way," said Stella, pulling Nicky to the right.

They ran to the side of the park and realized the stone path ran all the way under the bridge. Stella blew a kiss on her bloody hand to the sailors before running under the bridge. In a second, they emerged on the other side. That part of the Île de Cité didn't seem like it should be remotely connected to the peaceful little park on the other side of the Pont Neuf. The embankment was lined with trees. Above them was a street clogged with irate motorists, trying to merge onto the Pont Neuf. Beyond the street were tightly-packed buildings, seven stories high. The perfect place to get lost in. Nicky led Stella past some trees to a narrow set of stairs built onto the embankment and said, "Ladies first."

"Stella!" a woman's voice rang out.

Stella jumped a foot and then peeked out from under the tree at the Pont Neuf. Amelie leaned on the railing and beamed down at her.

"Hotel Henri II." Amelie pointed at the right bank farther down the river. "Let's have drinks."

Stella looked at Nicky, who shrugged. Stella nodded and waved. Then she jogged up the stairs as fast as her damaged feet would allow.

If Griese was there, Peiper couldn't be far behind. Running was getting to be as natural as breathing, but it wasn't necessary. Nobody was paying them any mind, except Amelie, who was still beaming on the bridge. All eyes were on the multiple accidents they'd caused. Stella took Nicky's hand and they walked along the road.

"Is she crazy?" asked Nicky.

"Look who's asking," replied Stella. "But it's not a bad idea. We don't know anyone else in Paris."

"We don't know them."

"But they know us. A little Bled goes a long way, and we need help."

"We need to deliver the book. The sooner, the better."

"We can't." Stella squeezed his hand. "I mean, I already tried."

"I don't think I want to hear this." Nicky rubbed his forehead and ground the dirt in deeper.

"I went to the apartment and the SS had already been there."

"How did you get away?"

"Just luck. I saw a man on the stairs that had been beaten like Albert. I never made it to the apartment."

"We'll go back. Maybe they haven't been arrested."

"They haven't. They went to Italy."

"How do you know that?"

"Roger, the man on the stairs, told me. He was watching their apartment for them. He said it was a family emergency."

"I'm guessing Abel's the emergency. The last telegram he sent them was in Venice," said Nicky.

"I would think so and Abel's supposed to have the book."

"If they look for him in Venice, they'll figure out we went to Vienna instead of Greece."

"If they go to Vienna…" Stella bit her lip and rested her chin on the top of the book under her coat.

"They'll be arrested or worse," said Nicky.

"It's always worse."

They walked in silence. Stella fingered the hat pin in her hand. The blood grew stickier by the moment. She tried to find some sorry inside herself but couldn't. She wasn't sorry. Maybe if they'd known the embankment went under the bridge, they could've run that way and escaped. Stella found she was glad they didn't know. Gabriele was gone and she couldn't regret it. Abel's family was different. She didn't suppose they owed them anything, but if they didn't go after them, they would end up in the arms of the SS. That was something she knew she would regret forever.

"We can't take the book to Italy," she said.

"Agreed," said Nicky. "But what do we do with it?"

Stella grinned at him.

"Please, don't suggest the Boulards."

"Boulards? Whoever do you mean?" Her grin grew wider and she took the lead.

CHAPTER 30

$\mathcal{N}$icky sank lower into Paul Boulard's bathtub. A black scum ring already lined the tub even though he hadn't touched the soap yet. "If this works out badly, I'll blame you."

Stella lay on Amelie and Paul's bed and sneered at him through the bathroom doorway. She finished the last flaky bit of her third croissant, lay back on a fluffy pillow, and exhaled.

"I'm serious, Stella."

"It'll be fine. Paul's an excellent financial planner," she said.

"What makes you think that?"

"They're vacationing in Paris. Either he's an excellent financial planner or a criminal."

"That does not make me feel better."

Stella ignored him and enjoyed the delicious feeling of fullness only croissants in Paris can bring. She was so used to being hungry the feeling was almost intoxicating, and she was rather lightheaded. She couldn't work up an ounce of worry about the Boulards. They hadn't tried to kill them yet and Stella took that as a very good sign. Besides, they needed help and the Boulards were available. Hiring Paul as their new financial planner seemed a small price to pay.

"How much time do I have?" asked Nicky.

"I don't know. They only have to send the telegram and buy some clothes."

"I can't believe strangers are picking out my clothes."

"Amelie has good taste, you old fuss pot," said Stella. "I never knew you cared so much about clothes."

"I just don't want to look like an insurance salesman," said Nicky.

"I don't care what they pick out as long as they bring you a hat," said Stella, rolling over to smile at him.

Nicky stood up and the water sluiced off his slick body, leaving him shiny and wet. Stella's smile turned into a frown. He'd lost quite a bit of weight. Where he'd been hard and well-muscled before, he was now stringy and gaunt. She supposed he might think the same about her, but it was nothing a few croissants couldn't fix.

Nicky needed more than a few croissants. He was painful to look at. She was relieved when he wrapped himself in Paul's robe and sat on the bed. Stella rubbed his warm thigh, thanking God that he'd survived and they were together again. Nicky hadn't asked any questions about what had happened when they were separated and she hoped it would stay that way. She couldn't bear to think, much less talk about Cyril. He'd betrayed her. She couldn't wrap her head around it. Hans trusted him. So did Hildegard, Kaspar, and the rest of the resistors. How could everyone be wrong? Was Cyril a Nazi? Was he lying about everything? No. The look in his eyes, she was sure that was real. He tried to keep her from Napoleon's tomb. If she hadn't escaped him, Nicky would've been captured, but she and the book would've been safe. Or would they? What in the world was his plan?

Nicky brushed a curl off her forehead. "Feeling sick?"

"A little."

His fingers gently traced the bruises on her face. "Some of these are new. What happened?"

"I sort of crashed the plane." A plane crash was better than the Cyril situation. No question.

"Sort of?"

"I ran out of gas," she said. "But I made it to the winery."

He nodded and she could see him mentally pull back. Maybe he didn't want to know any more than she wanted to tell him.

"When did Paul say their ship leaves Marseilles?" he asked.

"Noon, day after tomorrow."

"That's cutting it close."

"Good," said Stella. "Less time for anything to go wrong."

"We don't need time for that," said Nicky. "You'd better write your letter. They should be back soon."

Stella sat down at the small writing desk in the corner and pulled out some stationary embossed with the hotel's logo. She picked up a fountain pen and tapped it gently on her swollen lip. How to begin? How much should she say?

"Stella?" asked Nicky.

"I'm okay. I just…"

"Start on the train to Vienna." He took a sip of whiskey and groaned with pleasure before holding out the tumbler to Stella.

"No, thank you," she said. "I think he knew."

"Who? Josiah?"

"Abel. I think he knew. Remember how he wanted to get off the train?"

Nicky came over with his whiskey and kissed the top of her head. "It's not your fault. Now tell Josiah everything like you always do."

"I don't tell him everything," she said.

He kissed her again. "Almost everything. You can leave out the night of the turnip."

Stella blushed and began her letter to Uncle Josiah. She did tell him everything, except certain details about the night of the turnip.

By the end, the letter was blotted with tears and regrets but also with gratitude. She thanked him for his flying lessons and for his character. It was that that had helped her most of all. She finished by asking him to guard the book as she and Nicky had and to send them his wisdom and strength. At the last second, she added a postscript. He could show the letter to her father, but not her mother. Stella would have to come up with a sanitized version of events for Francesqua Bled unless she wanted the lady to die of shame.

After Stella finished, she blew on the ink until it dried and then placed it inside the book in front of Nissa's portrait. Nicky watched silently from the bed, noting how long it took to tell her story, but he didn't comment. When she turned to him, he closed his eyes, his blond hair wet and dark against his scalp and his cheekbones jutting out under his skin. They were so sharp they appeared ready to burst through his sunburned cheeks. She picked up another croissant and nudged his hand with it.

He opened one eye and said, "You eat it. You need it more than I do."

"No, I don't."

Nicky pointed at the mirror. "Look at yourself. You look like you've been through hell."

"That's what Roger said."

"I like Roger. Now eat."

Stella ignored the mirror, took a ferocious bite and passed the pastry to him. Nicky scowled and reluctantly consumed the rest.

They lay in silence with the sun making a warm panel across their bodies until someone knocked softly on the door. After the initial jolt of intense fear, Stella blew out a breath. The SS didn't knock as though they were afraid to do so. Nicky patted her leg and got up to answer, but before he got to the door, Paul's voice rang out from the hallway.

"It's our room, Amelie," he said.

Amelie's insistent tones followed. "We can't just barge in on the Bleds."

"They're the Lawrences."

"It doesn't matter. We have to knock."

"It's our room," Paul bellowed.

"Knock, you stubborn ass," said Amelie, still sweetly, but the woman was made of stronger stuff than she sounded.

"Shut up, Amelie!"

"Don't make me come over there."

"You're already here," said Paul. "Focus, woman."

"Knock or else!"

"Or else what?"

"Or I will make peas for every dinner for a solid month."

"I hate peas."

"I know 'cause I'm focused!"

Nicky chuckled as another stronger knock followed, competing with Paul's bellowing. Nicky opened the door to find Paul and Amelie nose-to-nose and red-faced. They both jumped and looked surprised to find him there. Paul stomped into the room and was taken aback when Nicky extended his hand.

"Thank you, my man," said Nicky as Paul dropped his shopping bags and took Nicky's hand.

"What for?" Paul asked.

"For calling us the Lawrences. You're the first."

"My pleasure," said Paul. "Amelie picked these out. Try not to hate me."

Amelie pushed past Paul, jabbing him with her elbow. "That suit is the height of fashion. I don't expect you to understand."

"Good, because I don't," he said. "And he won't like that baby blue cravat, either."

"He will."

"He won't."

"You only know it's blue because I told you, you color-blind fool." Amelie tilted her pointed little chin up at him.

"Amelie!"

Nicky stepped in front of them. "How long have you been married?"

"Seventy-eight years," said Paul.

Amelie jabbed him again. "Forty years. Happy years, too."

"I'm not happy. You make me peas."

"You make me crazy. So we're even." Amelie turned to Stella. "And you've been married for four months, right?"

Stella slid off the bed. "Just about. How did you know?"

"I saw your announcement in the New York Times. You had the most beautiful dress. Absolutely stunning." She looked down at Stella's hand. "Where are your rings? I read they were from Cartier."

Stella blushed and put her hands behind her back with a glance at Nicky. He hadn't mentioned her missing rings and she'd been dreading the conversation.

"Yes, I've been wondering," said Nicky, his voice and face blank, but Stella knew that didn't mean anything.

"I...I had to trade them to get to Les Invalides." Tears, still fresh from writing Uncle Josiah's letter, threatened to overwhelm her. "I'm so sorry. I had to do it."

"Two rings for what, a taxi ride?" he asked with a slight change in his tone. No one but Stella could've detected it.

"My engagement ring for the ride and my wedding ring to get Roger to the embassy. I'm so sorry."

He tucked a curl behind her ear and kissed the scrape on her forehead. "I'd rather have you back than have you holding on to those things. Obviously, you had to get Roger to the embassy. Don't give it another thought, Stella darling."

"You don't mind, really?"

"We still have what matters."

"Speaking of things that matter." Amelie took a hat box from Paul. "I can't wait for you to try on this hat."

Amelie dragged Stella into the bathroom in a manner that reminded Stella of Hildegard. She pulled off her robe, gave Stella a satin garter belt, and waited while she put it on before rolling the soft silk stockings up her legs and clipping them onto the belt. Then Amelie handed Stella a slim skirt lined in silk and helped her zip up the back. The skirt slid down below Stella's navel, barely hanging onto her jutting hipbones.

"Oh, no," said Amelie. "It's too big."

Stella rubbed her shoulder. "It's fine. A few more croissants and it'll be perfect."

Amelie smiled and rummaged around the bags until she found a lovely pink box. She pulled a cream-colored silk blouse from it and held it out for Stella to put on. When they finished the ensemble, Stella twirled in front of the full-length mirror. The dark red suit fit perfectly and perched on top of her head was the most extraordinary hat. It was black felt, tightly fitted to the head with feathers swooping down over the side, beautifully emphasizing Stella's cheekbone. Amelie pulled a tiny bit of delicate netting over Stella's eyes and nose.

"That is perfect," she said.

"I haven't felt this good since before Vienna," said Stella.

"Someday, you'll have to tell me the whole story," said Amelie.

"I will, when it's all over."

Amelie raised a very thin blonde eyebrow. "And it's not over yet?"

"I'm afraid not."

Stella knocked on the door to the bedroom and Nicky said they could come in. Stella opened the door to find him smoothing a dark grey winter wool suit with baggy pants and slightly wider lapels. The blue cravat at his throat made his eyes brilliant and Stella clapped her hands.

"It's fabulous, Amelie," said Stella. "Truly the height of fashion."

Nicky topped the look with a new rabbit fur fedora and said, "Shall we?"

"I think so," said Stella, picking up the makeup case Amelie had bought for her. Stella had concealed the book under the powders and lotions when the Boulards weren't looking. "Do you know where the antique shop is, Paul?"

"I do and I'm sure they have exactly what you're looking for," he said.

They arrived at the shop twenty minutes later and browsed among Chippendale chairs and Louis XIV tables. Stella zeroed in on a liquor cabinet almost immediately. It sat in the back, boxed in by huge wardrobes. The cabinet was a delicate piece with inlaid fruitwood marquetry of swirling flowers and almost twig-like cabriole legs. Stella loved it, and she knew Uncle Josiah would, too. As soon as she reached for the doors, the antique dealer, Monsieur Bergère, rushed over.

He opened the door with a flourish while assessing her ability to pay a good price and pointedly not looking at her bruises. Stella had caught him at it several times, making the man redden with embarrassment. She wanted to tell him it was fine. How often did a woman who looked like she'd gone a round with Jack Dempsey show up in his shop? Never, she was sure.

Monsieur Bergère directed her attention to the veneer while he casually noted her lack of rings, which caused a slight frown. Her grandmother's pearl hatpin stuck through the front of her fabulous hat didn't escape his notice either and that got a nod.

"A beautiful piece, madam. Mahogany with inlaid fruitwood, made in the year 1850," said the dealer.

Stella ran her fingertips over the flowers. "Nicky, where are you?"

"Here," he said, coming from behind a trio of curio cabinets.

"I found it," she said. "French. 1850."

He put his chin between his thumb and forefinger. "That's it, huh?"

"You don't like it?"

"Not much to it. So delicate. Doesn't seem like Uncle Josiah at all. Are you sure it has to be a liquor cabinet?" asked Nicky.

"That's what he asked for."

"He did?"

"Yes, in the telegram I got on the train to Vienna." Stella touched his forearm. The fine quality of the wool under her fingertips reminded her of better days, easier days when the hardest thing she had to do was buy a liquor cabinet.

"At least it's not German," said Nicky.

"Amen to that," said Stella.

Monsieur Bergère shifted on his feet, perhaps sensing a sale slipping away. "This piece has a special feature." He reached inside, pushed something, and the base of the cabinet popped up. "A secret compartment."

Nicky gave a cool smile to the dealer. "How much?"

Monsieur Bergère twisted his mouth sideways as he calculated how much they would pay. "One thousand American dollars."

"I'll give you five hundred," replied Nicky.

"Seven hundred fifty."

"Six twenty-five."

The dealer held out his hand. "I'm pleased to accept, Sir."

"I'm pleased to have you accept," said Nicky, dazzling Monsieur Bergère with a genuine smile. "My man will take care of the details."

He waved Paul over and their new financial planner seemed to swell with pride at being described as Nicky's man. Stella had seen this reaction before when her father or Uncle Josiah hired someone new at the brewery. It never happened when her mother hired someone. New maids always looked like they'd rather not work in their house, living with the crazy Bleds, but they calmed down eventually. Stella didn't know if that was from the excellent pay or that the family turned out not to be quite as crazy as rumored. Her mother and Aunt Florence had tried to hire live-in help for Uncle Josiah, but there wasn't enough money in the world to get someone to live in his house where he was rumored to have stashed his lover's body under the floorboards in the butler's pantry.

Maybe Amelie and Paul didn't know about the pantry or the rest of it. Or maybe they didn't care. Of course, they wouldn't be living in like a maid. They lived in New Orleans and had been for generations, so none of the much ballyhooed Bled insanity would bother them.

Stella patted Paul's back as he passed and he gave her a joyful grin. She was happy for him. It was nice to be doing something for someone instead of causing calamities. Paul wrote the dealer a bank draft and explained that the cabinet would have to be boxed and shipped to Marseilles immediately. Monsieur Bergère had two workmen bring the cabinet to a back room filled with wooden shipping containers. The four of them watched as the workmen began wrapping the delicate legs in cotton wool.

"Wait a minute," said Stella. "Can my husband and I just have a moment alone with the piece? I want to really look it over, so that I can describe it accurately to my uncle."

The dealer hesitated but then ushered everyone out of the room, leaving Nicky and Stella in front of the cabinet.

"Are you sure?" asked Nicky.

Stella nodded. "It'll never be safe on this continent. Uncle Josiah will know what to do."

She reopened the door and looked at the floor of the cabinet. The illusion was perfect. If one didn't know the secret compartment was there, they'd have no reason to suspect. She felt around for the latch and the bottom popped up. Then she opened her new cosmetics case and removed the book from under the cosmetics that Amelie insisted that she needed to cover her bruises. Nicky handed her a piece of thick cotton flannel he'd had Paul pick up. She wrapped the book in the flannel, placed the book in the compartment, and closed it firmly.

Nicky took Stella's hand. "You're right. He'll know what to do, but how will he know it's there?"

"He's got an architect's eye. He designed his house and it's filled with secret passages and cubbies. He'll take one look at that cabinet and see that the bottom's thick for no good reason."

"Or he won't."

"We can send a telegram with a helpful hint, but I'm telling you we won't have to," said Stella.

"If you say so."

She leaned on his shoulder, feeling sad and relieved at the same time. "I do. Should we let them back in now?"

"If you're ready."

"I'm ready."

Nicky went to the door and called everyone back in. The workmen encased the liquor cabinet in the batting so that it looked like an Egyptian mummy. Then they carefully placed it in a wooden case and packed it with wood shavings. Stella's stomach twisted when they hammered the lid on, locking the book away from her for who knows how long. Trusting it to Uncle Josiah was the right decision, the only decision, really, but her arms felt empty without it cuddled up to her breast.

The workmen loaded the crate onto the back of an odd little van. It was tall and narrow and it looked as though a stiff wind would blow it over, but Monsieur Bergère assured them that it was sturdier than it looked.

Nicky draped his arm over Stella's shoulders and bent down to whisper in her ear. "It'll be fine."

"How did you know I was worried? I didn't say anything," she said.

He lifted her hat's netting with his nose and kissed her cheek. "I just knew."

Monsieur Bergère locked the van's back door and spoke to the driver in French. The driver tipped his cap to them, got in, and drove away with the van lurching from side to side and belching black smoke. Stella sighed and a furrow appeared between her beautifully penciled eyebrows. Nicky chuckled and she shot him an icy look that would've made his testicles retreat into his abdomen, if he hadn't been expecting it.

"I only have two words for you, my beloved," he said. "Explosion and crash."

"What in the world?"

He kissed her like no one else was there, like they weren't in a dank alley, aching and bruised. He kissed her like he did the first night they were together and the way she wanted to be kissed for the rest of her life.

Nicky pulled back and cupped his rough hands on her soft cheeks. "You can handle anything. Explosions and plane crashes. The SS and the occasional assassin."

Stella melted and leaned on him. "Don't forget train jumping."

"Train jumping?" asked Paul, coming up to stand beside them. "Do they have those lunatics in Europe?"

Amelie took Stella's hand. "Don't say lunatics, Paul." She gave Stella a worried look, but Stella smiled back at her.

"What would you prefer? Mental deficient? I tell you what. I saw a man try to hop a train back in thirty-three. Went under the wheels. Cut him straight in half. You'd have to be a lunatic to try it," said Paul.

"I agree," said Nicky. "Absolutely bonkers."

Stella gave him a quick peck. "Who in the world would ever have such a crazy idea?"

"A man who hasn't had coffee in six days."

Their new financial adviser clapped him on the back. "Paris is lousy with cafés. Let's go get that coffee."

"Paul, you're alright," said Nicky, opening his jacket and pulling out a silver flask Amelie had bought him. "Let's make it a party."

Paul pulled out his own flask. "Mr. Lawrence, this was meant to be."

"That's Nicky to you and I couldn't agree more."

CHAPTER 31

"More coffee?" asked Amelie.

Nicky and Paul both raised their flasks. "Don't mind if I do," they said in chorus.

"I think you've had enough. What do you think, Stella?"

Stella looked the men over and they straightened up in a failed effort to look sober. "I agree. Let's get back to the hotel while they can still walk."

"We can walk fine," said Paul as he suppressed a burp.

"Very nice," said Amelie. "Let's go. Stella and Nicky look exhausted."

"Not yet. Let's have a picture of this momentous occasion." He held up the camera he'd slung over the back of his chair by its long leather strap.

"Excellent idea, my love," said Amelie and she gave him a peck on the cheek.

Paul snapped open the leather case and adjusted some settings. The waiter got curious and came over. They ended up having an intense discussion about cameras using mostly expressions and pointing.

"Paul?" asked Amelie.

"Uh-huh?"

"Can we take the picture now?"

"He has a camera he wants to show me," said Paul.

Amelie rolled her eyes. "How can you tell?"

"I can tell."

As if to prove Paul's point, the waiter ran off to the back and returned with a spiffy new camera. It had a beautiful art deco design in shiny black with silver lines. The waiter popped it open and the lenses emerged out of the case.

"That's nice for travel," said Stella.

"It is," said Nicky. "I almost bought one for our trip."

"Then it must be expensive."

"About one ten."

"That's pricey for a waiter," said Amelie.

The waiter handed her the camera and ran in the back again. He returned with a stack of prints and they went through them one by one. They were mostly of everyday life in Paris, beautifully composed and mesmerizing in their simplicity.

"He is very good," said Stella and the waiter gave her a bow. He didn't speak a word of English, but he knew a compliment when he heard one. "Paul, can you take down his information? My father will be interested."

Paul whipped a notepad out of his pocket, but before he could write, Amelie grabbed it. "If you write it, no one, including you, will be able to read it." She had the waiter write down his information. The young man was beaming and happily ran back to get another camera, a bulky Leica. Paul and Nicky went over the camera while Amelie and Stella ordered more coffee.

When they finished their cups, Amelie ordered Paul to take a picture and the waiter, Robert, took several shots. They squeezed together in front of the window like old friends instead of new. Stella's dose of aspirin was wearing off, allowing her face and feet to hurt more and more, but she smiled like they didn't.

"Are you all right?" asked Nicky.

"I'm fine, but I'd like to lie down before dinner."

"Yes," said Amelie. "That's a good idea. The hotel should have your room ready by now."

Paul paid Robert and then bought a photo of a man and woman kissing on the steps down into the metro and arranged to have it mailed to New Orleans.

"I love it," said Amelie.

Paul kissed her. "Happy anniversary."

"This is the best one yet."

"No doubt about that." He slung his camera over his shoulder and they walked out into the Paris twilight to return to the hotel.

Stella and Nicky followed the older couple through the warren of streets to the hotel. Nicky chatted with Paul about cameras and Amelie occasionally remarked on the architecture around them. Only Stella was silent. She wanted to keep her mind as still as she had in the café. She wanted to enjoy the moment. Twilight in Paris. It was perfect. The book was on its way to Marseilles and then to America, well out of the Nazi's grasp. But Abel wasn't. They had him and they'd probably figured out who he was. Would he be tortured for information even if he couldn't possibly know where she and Nicky were? Would they kill him in retaliation? And what about Albert? Had he survived and gotten back to England?

The Sorkines were on a train to Venice at that moment, so they should be out of danger, but how long would it take them to figure out that Abel had taken the book to Vienna? Would they follow him there in spite of the Kristallnacht? Of course they would.

"Is the telegram office still open?" she asked.

"I doubt it," said Paul over his shoulder. "Do you want to send another telegram?"

Nicky put his arm around her shoulders. "There's probably an answer from your father at the hotel right now."

"I would think so," said Amelie. "The office said they would messenger any replies over."

Stella shook her head, making the feather on her hat tickle her cheek. "I was thinking about Albert. We should telegram his father."

"Who's Albert?" asked Paul.

Nicky gave them a version of how they met Albert in Vienna. He didn't tell them how badly Peiper and his goons had beaten the ambassador's son.

They turned the corner onto the street to the hotel and Amelie said, "We can walk over to the office and send a message for you."

"I'm not sure where to send it," said Nicky.

"Maybe they can help with that? The family must have an estate."

"They do. I think Albert called it Bickford House."

"Does he have a title?" asked Amelie.

"He's Viscount—" Stella tripped on a cobble. She nearly fell to her knees, but Nicky caught her before she hit the stones. "You are exhausted."

"And clumsy."

Amelie and Paul rushed back to them, full of regret for keeping them at the café so long.

"We'll get you in bed and order room service," said Paul.

"They have an excellent menu," said Amelie. "But I wish I had a kitchen. I would make you red beans and rice."

Paul patted his wife's back. "A little spice. That's exactly what she needs."

"I'm fine. Just tired," said Stella. "I'll lie down and be good as new."

Amelie hugged her and said, "Of course, you will. You're young. The healing comes quick."

Stella looked over Amelie's shoulder and stiffened.

"What?" asked Amelie as she pulled back, holding Stella by the shoulders.

"I think someone ratted on us."

They turned around and looked where Stella was looking. At the end of the dead-end street sat the hotel, its classical façade rising up on the cross street and sneering at the more humble apartments bookending it. On the street was a collection of haphazardly parked cars. They were the typical black and some had gendarmerie leaning on them smoking cigarettes and looking incredibly bored.

"That doesn't have to be about us," said Nicky. "This is a town of three million people. Not everything is about us."

Stella pulled him back into a doorway. "Look again."

He did and said, "What am I looking at?"

"The black car on the right."

"They're all black. Some are police cars, but they're mostly black."

"The one with the crumpled fender," said Stella.

"Never mind. When you're right, you're right," said Nicky.

"It's the car that chased us, isn't it?" She started to lean out, but he pushed her back. "I have no idea, but Peiper just walked out of the front door."

"Oh, my god. What's he doing?"

Paul pushed Nicky in beside Stella. "Stay there. We'll see what's happening."

"No, wait," said Amelie. "He's arguing with a man from the hotel."

"How do you know?" asked Stella.

"He's wearing a name tag and now the police are trying to haul him away. They're fighting." Amelie touched Stella's arm. "You can't go back there."

"Neither can you. I'm so sorry. I'm like Typhoid Mary, spreading my disease of bad luck."

Paul smiled down at her. "But your luck is changing."

"They're leaving?"

"No. Pauline, the lovely girl at the desk, just came out and she saw us."

Stella sucked in a breath. "That's not good."

"It is because she didn't tell the police or that Nazi and she's coming this way."

Stella held her breath until she heard the light click of heels on cobbles.

"*Pour vous, monsieur.*" A young woman in a subdued brown suit flicked out an envelope to Paul. He took it and said, "*Merci, mademoiselle.*"

"*Bon chance.*" She slipped away down the street and around the corner.

Paul and Amelie crowded into the doorway. "It's a telegram addressed to Mrs. Bled."

Nicky rolled his eyes. "Of course it is."

"Aren't you Mrs. Lawrence?" asked Amelie.

Stella took the envelope. "Yes, but my family is partial to the Bled name. They'll get used to Lawrence."

"No, they won't and I don't much care right now." Nicky kissed her hand. "What's happening now, Paul?"

Paul leaned back and casually looked down the street. "They've gone back inside. The police are taking pictures of that banged up car."

"I knew it was the same one," said Stella. "We better get out of here while the getting's good."

"Open the telegram," said Amelie. "I can't stand the suspense."

"We should go," said Nicky.

"Where?" asked Stella.

"Anywhere but here gets my vote." Nicky took her arm and asked Paul, "Is anyone looking?"

Paul shook his head and waved them down the street. They walked like they weren't in a hurry, just tourists out for a stroll until they rounded the corner and dashed down into the metro. Paul bought four tickets and they got on the next train, not bothering to see where it was going.

Stella squeezed through the throng of well-mannered First-Class passengers and found a comfy leather seat in the back. Amelie sat down with her and Paul and Nicky crowded around, blocking the view. She opened the thin envelope and as expected, it was a telegram from her father, time stamped for five hours earlier.

"What does it say?" asked Nicky.

"Hold on."

Dearest daughter

Go to Elias. Funds behind the elephant. Josiah gone to Vienna. Will recover Abel. Return home immediately. Mother in dark. Say nothing. Love, Father

Stella stared down at the telegram. She expected to be ordered home, but the rest of it...

"What is it, Stella?" asked Nicky.

She handed him the telegram and he scanned it quickly. "Who's Elias?"

"I have no idea."

Paul leaned over. "May I?"

"Of course," said Nicky, giving him the telegram.

Paul read it. "Presumably this Elias is in Paris. Who would your father trust? Only family or a friend?"

Stella shrugged. "Both. But usually, his friends are brewers."

"How many brewers are in Paris?" asked Amelie.

"None that I know of."

The train began slowing down and a uniformed man at the end of the First-Class coach called out, "Etienne Marcel. Etienne Marcel."

"Should we get off?" asked Amelie.

Nicky held out his hand to her. "Yes. I want to look at a map and see what's what."

"I thought you'd been to Paris," said Amelie, easing out of her seat.

"We had Abel with us. I didn't give directions a thought." He helped Stella up and she wobbled for a second. "Are your feet okay?" he asked.

"They're swelling a bit, but I'm fine."

They stepped off the car into a musty station and found some paper maps pinned to a board.

"Keep a look out, will you, Paul?" asked Nicky.

"Will do."

Nicky pointed a long finger at the Etienne Marcel stop. "So we're here. I'm trying to think of who my parents know. There must be someone."

"We could send them a telegram," said Amelie.

Stella's husband made a disgruntled noise deep in his chest.

"What's that about?" she asked.

"I'm supposed to be the good one. I'd hate to ruin my reputation."

Stella cuddled up to his side. "I didn't know I got the good one. Who's the bad one?"

"Charles, but only because he always gets caught."

"So you *are* the bad one."

"We're all bad," said Nicky. "Stella, didn't your parents ever mention visiting this Elias?"

She shook her head and her feather danced. "They haven't been to Paris in years and I didn't pay any attention when they went."

They all went silent for a moment, thinking en masse, until Paul said, "There's nothing for it but to telegram your father again, Stella. From what Amelie tells me, Aleksej Bled dotes on his only daughter. He won't mind."

"He won't," said Stella. "Let's find a Western Union or whatever they have here."

"Hold on a moment," said Amelie.

"What is it?" asked Paul.

"That name. Elias. It's coming to me."

Paul rolled his eyes. "Amelie, you do not know the Bled family friends."

"Quiet, Paul," said Amelie. "It's the name. Your father is Aleksej and your uncles are…"

Stella looked at her sideways. "Nicolai and Josiah."

"Those are unusual names."

"Not for Bleds. My brothers are Lucian and Ansel."

Amelie crossed her arms over her ample chest. "Elias is unusual, too. I've never met an Elias. Your father's sending you to family. Elias Bled. It has to be. He has funds for you. Family always coughs up the dough. Give me a minute. I'll get it."

"I don't know, Amelie," said Paul. "He also mentioned an elephant. I don't think there's any Bled money at the zoo."

"I'm good at this," said Amelie. "You know I am. I found John Cabot after he killed that girl."

"You were lucky."

"What about when I tracked down the thief that broke into your office?"

"The cops would've gotten him eventually."

She rolled her big green eyes. "Those fools thought it was an inside job. They were going to arrest poor Sean just because he's Irish."

"You caught a murderer?" asked Nicky.

Amelie gave him a charming but devilish smile. "I did. Don't listen to Paul. He says it's all luck."

"It is. You should do something more appropriate like—"

"Like darn your socks," she said. "No, thank you."

"No wonder we didn't put you off," said Stella.

Amelie gave her a little hug. "I like a bit of excitement." She did a little jump. "There it is. I got it."

"You got it?" asked Stella.

"Just think about the name Elias Bled."

"God help me," said Paul. "I married a crazy woman."

"Well, I think your crazy wife is on to something," said Stella. "Elias Bled does sound familiar."

Amelie elbowed Paul. "There *is* an Elias Bled in Paris. In a manner of speaking, that is."

Stella clapped a hand over her mouth. "No."

"No?" asked Nicky.

"I mean yes."

Nicky took off his fedora and ran his fingers through his hair. "You're killing me."

"There *was* an Elias Bled in Paris," said Amelie. "He died years ago."

It was Paul's turn to roll his eyes. "How do you know that?"

"It was in that book about impressionism that I read last year. Elias Bled was a major patron here in Paris."

"I'm sorry, Amelie," said Nicky. "But that isn't helpful. The man is dead."

Stella turned to the map of Paris and pointed. "There it is."

"The Seine?" asked Paul.

"No. The Pont Marie."

Amelie grabbed her hand. "I get it. Let's go." She dragged Stella up the stairs and they crossed over to the other side of the tracks.

"Where are we going?" asked Paul.

"To the Pont Marie, silly."

The train going in the other direction rumbled down the tracks and screeched to a halt in front of them. Amelie and Stella got on, followed by the men, who were looking less than convinced that this made any sort of sense.

"Why are we going to a bridge?" asked Paul.

"Because that's where it happened," said Amelie.

Stella grinned and sat down next to her. "You do know my family."

"Everyone knows about Elias Bled. It just took me a moment to remember."

"For once, someone knowing about us isn't such a bad thing." Stella quickly filled them in on the story of Elias Bled, who disappeared in 1910.

"You have a great uncle nicknamed Elias the Odd," said Nicky. It wasn't a question. He was trying to digest.

Stella shrugged. "Every family has one."

"I don't think so."

"Well, it doesn't matter. My Great-grandmother Brina kept his apartment intact in case he came back and it's still there."

Nicky narrowed his eyes at her. "Why?"

"Why not?"

He took her hand. "What aren't you saying?"

"Nothing."

Nicky looked at Amelie, who flushed. Paul elbowed her this time and she hesitantly said, "I seem to remember something about the apartment being haunted."

"Haunted?" asked Paul. "That's ridiculous."

She glared at him. "Is it? Is it really?"

It was Paul's turn to flush. "Anything's possible."

"Indeed. So Stella, what's the address?"

"Well, I don't exactly know," said Stella.

Nicky ran his hand through his hair again. "What's your plan? Are we going to wander around Paris, knocking on doors and asking if Elias the Odd is in residence?"

"Obviously not."

"Obviously."

"The apartment is on the Île Saint-Louis overlooking the Pont Marie. It can't be that hard to find."

Nicky gave her a look and they spent the rest of the ride in silence.

CHAPTER 32

$\mathcal{T}$he sixth door was the charm. Stella lifted the large brass knocker that was an odd combination of goats, dragons, and lions, letting it drop with a resounding thunk. Only that set of doors could've carried off such an ornate knocker. They were eighteen feet high, freshly painted a lovely blue-green, and had an incredible collection of carvings above the arch with a crying woman in stone at the pinnacle.

"You think Elias the Odd lived here?" asked Nicky, oozing doubt.

"He was a Bled," said Stella. "Never doubt a Bled."

"I'm learning that."

"Good." She dropped the knocker again and there was a loud click. The door smoothly opened and instead of the expected proper doorman, a boy of eleven or twelve stood in the opening, peering out at them with large grey eyes under a heavy flop of dark hair.

"*Bon soir, mademoiselle,*" he said.

"*Bon soir,*" said Stella. "Do you speak English?"

"A little."

Stella straightened up and gave the boy her best, most charming smile. "I'm Stella Bled Lawrence and I'm looking for Elias Bled's apartment. Is it in this building?"

"Elias?"

Amelie inhaled sharply and squeezed her arm.

"Yes," said Stella. "Elias Bled. Is your father here?"

The boy closed the door in her face.

"That's not a good sign," said Paul.

"Yes, it is," said Amelie. "He recognized the name. He's going to get his father."

"For God's sake, Amelie. You don't know."

"Yes, I do."

"No, you don't."

The door swung open and an older version of the boy peered out at them. "Mademoiselle, you are seeking Elias Bled?"

"See? I told you," whispered Amelie.

Stella held out her hand and the man shook it gently. "I'm Stella Bled Lawrence and I'm actually looking for Elias' apartment. I forgot the address."

He swung the door wide, revealing an elegant interior with checked marble floors and a swooping staircase with a black wrought iron bannister. He swept his cane in front of them and then leaned on it heavily. "Please do come in, Mrs. Bled. I am Jean-Baptiste Barre. I am the manager here."

Stella led the way and breathed deep the scent of good tobacco that emanated from Monsieur Barre. "I'm sorry to trouble you, but my father said I should come here to Elias."

"And Monsieur Bled is well?" asked Monsieur Barre.

"He is and my mother as well."

"They instruct you to come to Elias?" He kept his expression neutral as any good servant would, but Stella saw the doubt flicker in his eyes and so did Amelie. She squeezed Stella's arm and said, "Show him the telegram."

Obediently, as if it were her mother giving the order, Stella got the telegram out of her handbag and held it out to Monsieur Barre. A faint pink appeared on his sallow cheeks and the boy ran up to take his cane so he could reach out with that hand and take the telegram.

He awkwardly fumbled with the envelope, his left hand missing three fingers and gnarled to the point that it looked useless.

Amelie stepped in front of Stella and gently took the envelope. "Forgive us, Monsieur. We weren't thinking. Allow me." She pulled out the telegram, unfolded it, and handed it back, doing it simply and without any sense of shame or embarrassment.

"Merci, Ma'am." Monsieur Barre read the telegram with the boy standing on his tiptoes trying to see the contents. He gave the boy a stern glance and said, "This is my son, Julian. He is a great help to me."

"*Oui*," said Julian, focusing solely on Stella, who smiled at him.

"I can see that," said Stella. "Are you in training to be a manager yourself?"

"*Oui, madam*. I will help Papa and become manager someday. I am very good. I do the electric and the typing."

"You are helpful," said Amelie. "Our sons are in training, too, but they can't type."

"They must. Type is…" Julian trailed off.

"Essential," finished his father, holding up his damaged hand. "The war ended my typing. Julian became my hand when he got old enough."

"The war hurt so many," said Stella. "My grandfather's sister lost four of her grandsons."

"A tragedy for your family."

"And for so many others. May we go to the apartment?"

"Naturally, but I feel I must—"

Stella waved his words away. "Don't worry. I know all about Elias. We're family. The Bled blood will protect us."

Monsieur Barre's shoulders relaxed. "Of course, it will. I am relieved that you are aware of the situation. Monsieur Elias is…rather opinionated about guests." He gave Amelie the telegram back and took his cane from Julian. "Let me escort you to his floor." He turned to lead them to the grand staircase.

Nicky leaned over to Stella. "Is he serious?"

"About what?"

"Elias." He swished his finger in a circle around his head. "Maybe the war did more than damage his hand."

"Shush. I told you about Elias."

"You didn't say that he was 'opinionated'."

"Who isn't?"

"Dead people, generally."

Stella rolled her eyes. "It's fine. We're family."

"Not all of us," said Paul.

Stella reached back and patted his arm. "You're with me."

"That doesn't change our blood," Paul muttered.

Amelie snorted. "As if you've never seen a ghost before. Buck up, Paul. This is exciting."

They got to the stairs and Monsieur Barre said, "I apologize. The lift is under repair. We will have to take the stairs."

Stella said, "We can take it from here. What floor?"

Monsieur Barre gave them a slight bow. "Elias is on the third. Julian will be happy to escort you."

Before Stella could respond, Julian hopped up on the first stair and grinned, showing his slightly crooked but very white teeth. "I will do it."

"Excellent," said Nicky. "Lead the way."

They all thanked Monsieur Barre, who looked relieved about not having to negotiate the stairs and was trying not to show it. He nodded to them and then limped off, leaning heavily on his cane.

Julian hopped up the stairs, chattering away in a mixture of English and French. At the second floor, he said a complete sentence in French and Stella parroted it back to him. He stopped hopping and began speaking rapid-fire French at her, making her burst into laughter.

"No, no," she said. "I can't speak French. I can just sound French."

Julian tilted his head and said, "*Et bien?*"

"*Et bien,*" said Stella.

"*Je vous aime bien.*"

"*Je vous aime bien.*"

"*Allons-y!*"

Stella took his hand and said, "*Allons-y!*"

They walked up the last flight, exchanging words and laughing. Stepping off the stairs, Stella stopped talking abruptly. Julian shook her hand. "*Qu'est-ce qui ne va pas?*"

"I thought—" She shook her head. "No. Nothing."

Nicky came up beside her and looked around the circular landing. "Stella?"

"It's fine." She walked to the center of the glossy wood floor done in a glorious sunburst pattern and calmly sniffed the simple flower arrangement sitting on the rosewood table, giving her a moment to collect herself. A man wearing a heavy coat and hat didn't just walk through the door of Apartment B. That simply didn't happen. Uncle Josiah had put that image in her head with his tales of haunted Paris. "It's fine," she repeated to herself.

Amelie bent over and whispered in her ear, "I saw him, too, but let's not make a big hullaballoo about it."

Stella winked at her and spun around. "Beautiful flowers, especially for November. So which door, Julian? B?"

Julian bit his lip and nodded. "Both apartments are for Monsieur Elias." He gestured to Apartment B. "But that is his door. You can't use it."

"That's the ghost's door," said Paul.

"Apparently so," said Nicky.

Amelie shot an icy glare at them and said to Julian, "A will do very well for us. Thank you."

The boy pulled a large key ring out of his pocket and found the appropriate key, a large brass one with an elegant E in the fob. He hesitated and asked, "Yes?"

Stella nodded. "Yes."

"But Monsieur Elias, he…"

"Monsieur Elias is my great uncle. He likes me."

There was a tremendous crash inside the apartment and the door rattled. Everyone jumped, except Julian, who sighed and said, "*C'est la vie.*"

"You heard that, right?" asked Paul.

341

"Oh, yeah," said Nicky.

"I don't think we should go in there."

"No kidding."

Stella took the key from Julian and pointed it at them. "We're going in because my father told us to and there are Nazis chasing us."

Julian went stiff. "Nazis?"

"Yes." Stella patted the boy's shoulder. "We had some trouble, but it's fine. Everything's fine."

"That we're willing to go in there is a sure sign that it's not," said Paul.

"Shush up, Paul Boulard," said Amelie. "Don't scare him."

Paul gestured to the boy. "Look at the kid. He's already scared. White as a ghost. Isn't that ironic?"

"He's not scared pale," said Stella. "That's just his skin. You're not scared, are you, Julian?"

The boy started wringing his hands. "Germans tried to kill Papa."

"At least he's not scared of Elias," said Amelie.

Something shattered into a million pieces behind door B.

"Monsieur Elias wouldn't hurt me," said Julian. "But the Germans, they hurt Papa. They break his hand."

Amelie took the shaking Julian by the shoulders. "I want you to run down and tell your father that we won't stay long. Don't tell anyone we're here."

Julian stared at her, still shaking. "Papa's hand."

Stella kissed his forehead, leaving perfect lipsticked lips, and said, "I know and I'm sorry. Hurry now."

Julian jumped into her arms and gave her a fierce hug. "I will hurry. The Germans won't get you." He dashed down the curving stairs out of sight.

"Amen to that," said Paul. "Now what?"

"We go in and find that elephant," said Amelie.

It took two hours, but they found the elephant, if you could really call it that. Amelie maintained that you could. Naturally, Paul disagreed.

"It looks nothing like an elephant," he said.

"There's the trunk." Amelie pointed to a pencil-thin tube coming out of a grey lump that may or may not have had legs on an over-sized canvas that Nicky was holding.

"I don't think that's a trunk."

She threw up her hands. "It doesn't matter. We found the safe. You do think that looks like a safe, don't you?"

"You bother me, woman," said Paul.

"I live for it." Amelie turned to Stella, who was fiddling with a large dial on a black safe the size of an oven. "Any luck?"

"None. What was my father thinking?"

"He thought you'd know the combination," said Nicky.

"Well, I don't. Why would I? This is a safe in an apartment that I've never been to that belonged to an ancestor that I forgot about."

A huge crash rattled the canvases stacked against the wall.

"Stop it, Uncle Elias!" yelled Stella. "I'm tired and I'm hurt and people want to kill me. Just stop it." Tears dripped down her cheeks and the crashing abruptly stopped.

"We should've tried that earlier," said Nicky as he looked around for a place to put the elephant canvas, but it was impossible. Elias had been a failed artist and a voracious collector of art. Every wall had prints, drawings, and paintings covering every inch. When he ran out of space on the walls, he stacked up the extras against furniture or the walls. Nicky ended up just picking a spot and leaning the elephant against another five paintings.

Then he took Stella in his arms and kissed the top of her head. "You know it. You just don't know that you know it."

"I don't," she said, snuffling into his shoulder.

"You do. Your father wouldn't send us here, if you didn't."

Paul lifted a stack of etches off a settee, sat down, and put his elbows on his knees. "Who would've set the combination?"

"Elias, probably," said Amelie. "But I imagine it's been changed since." She cocked her head in the direction where most of the crashing occurred, the second bedroom. "Who stays here most often?"

"Nobody. How can they with all that banging?" Stella yelled at the bedroom.

"Someone from your family does," said Amelie. "How about your uncle? He's…"

"Unusual," said Paul helpfully.

"Yes, let's go with that."

Stella nodded and blew her nose in Nicky's handkerchief. "Uncle Josiah's seen Elias. He told me about it. Usually, he's on the bridge though."

"But he saw him in here, too?"

She blew her nose a second time and said, "He fries ham."

Paul sat back. "You mean Uncle Josiah fries ham."

"No. Elias fries ham. He does it to annoy Uncle Josiah. He doesn't care for ham and it stinks up the whole apartment. He hates it."

They looked at her with blank expressions.

"It's not real ham," said Stella.

"Then what is it?" asked Paul slowly.

She shrugged. "I don't know. Uncle Josiah says you can hear the sizzling, but when you go in the kitchen there's nothing there and it's silent. When you leave, it starts up again."

They all stared at her and didn't say anything.

"It's like with the crashing. It sounds like a thousand plates are being broken, but when you go in, there's nothing."

"I see," said Paul.

"My uncle is not crazy," said Stella.

Nicky coughed.

"You can ask Julian. I imagine he's smelled it."

Nicky kissed her forehead again. "So Josiah's been here. He could've changed the combination to something he'd remember. Is there a special date that he talks about?"

Stella sat down on the settee next to Paul and leaned on his shoulder. She felt empty and exhausted. It was surprisingly tiring to hear a spectral temper tantrum for two hours. Plus, her feet had swollen so that she wasn't sure she could get her shoes back on. She had thick stockings on, but Nicky kept eyeing her feet and frowning. She'd been careful not to let him see them in the hotel, but she had to take off her shoes with all the swelling and there was no avoiding him seeing their odd lumpiness.

"Maybe you should have another aspirin," said Nicky.

"And some food," said Amelie.

Paul reached up and patted Stella's cheek similar to the way her father would've if he'd been there. "I could use a turkey sandwich," he said. "Do they have turkeys here? I know they have geese. We've had enough pâté to last the rest of our lives."

"I don't think so," said Stella. "Abel never pointed it out on a menu and he was very thorough."

"You'll have turkey soon enough," said Amelie. "I'll go get us some nice bread and cheese."

Paul grumbled. "When am I getting turkey? They didn't have turkey on the boat over."

Amelie rolled her eyes. "Thanksgiving's two days after we get back."

"Thanksgiving!" cried out Stella. "Uncle Josiah loves Thanksgiving. It's his favorite holiday."

"Everyone loves Thanksgiving," said Paul, his eyes glazing over. "The turkey. The pies. Amelie makes wonderful pies."

"Thank you, my love," she said.

"No," said Stella. "Uncle Josiah really loves Thanksgiving. It's the day that he escaped from the Germans during the war."

"Which time?" asked Nicky.

"The first time. We have the picture."

Nicky leaned against a sculpture of a nude woman, looking amazingly studious considering where he had his elbow. "You have a picture of Uncle Josiah escaping?"

"Well, they took it right before he escaped. It's a famous picture. You've probably seen it. He's standing with a German officer who has a gun pointed at him."

"Yes, yes," said Amelie. "I've seen that. Your uncle's all beat up.

They broke his arm and his jaw. They were going to execute him for something."

"That's right. He blew up an armory and they said he was a spy."

Paul frowned. "He was a pilot. Wasn't he supposed to blow things up?"

"He was on the ground at the time. He'd crash landed, disguised himself, took his plane's ammunition, and blew up an armory. They said he was a spy."

"So he is crazy," said Paul.

"He's a hero."

"I don't doubt that," said Amelie. "So he likes Thanksgiving. Which one?"

Stella stood and searing pain shot through her feet all the way up into her hips. She gasped and sat back down.

"I'm going to heat up some water, so you can soak those feet," said Amelie.

The windows started rattling and the crashing began in the bedroom again.

"Never mind," said Stella. "We won't be here that long."

The crashing stopped and they all rolled their eyes.

"Nicky, try eleven, twenty-nine, nineteen, seventeen."

Nicky spun the big silver dial and was rewarded by a loud clank. He pulled the handle and the door swung open. Inside were three shelves. Two were stacked with cash and the center one had velvet boxes. Paul got up and said, "Well, that will get you home in style."

"We're not going home," said Stella.

"But your father said to come back immediately," said Amelie, her eyes growing increasingly worried and the banging started up in the bedroom again. "Elias, don't make me come in there! I've had about enough of your nonsense. If you can't help your niece, pipe down!"

The banging stopped.

"All right then," said Amelie, turning to Stella. "I think you should go home."

"That gets my vote," said Paul. "This continent isn't safe for anyone, least of all you two."

Nicky pulled a stack of francs out of the safe and handed them to Paul. "We have other things to consider."

"I don't know what to do." She took her father's telegram out of her handbag and read it again. "Uncle Josiah gone to Vienna. That's a disaster. They'll arrest him to get to us."

"We'll telegram your father," said Paul. "He can call him back."

Stella shook her head. "He won't stop. He never stops. Abel was arrested because of me. It's our duty to get him back."

"It's not your fault," said Amelie.

Stella waved the notion away. "And then there's the Sorkines."

"What about them?"

"They'll go to Vienna if we don't stop them," said Nicky. "They'll end up in a camp."

"You'll end up in a camp or worse, if you stay here."

A tremendous crash erupted beyond the bedroom and they all froze.

"Was that outside?" asked Paul.

Stella hobbled into the bedroom overlooking the bridge and looked out at an improbable sight. A black sedan sat in the middle of the bridge with its front end crumpled like it had hit a pole. But there was no pole. There was nothing at all. People were coming to look and a driver in an SS uniform stumbled out of the driver's side to collapse on the pavement.

"It's them," said Nicky, closing the old curtains.

"We have to get out of here," said Stella.

"How did they know?" asked Paul.

"It's a Bled apartment," said Amelie. "It doesn't take a genius."

They ran back into the room with the safe followed by Stella, who blew a kiss toward the second bedroom. "Thanks, Uncle Elias. I owe you one."

The smell of frying bacon filled the apartment as they picked out different currencies, slammed the safe shut, and covered it with the elephant painting.

"I could eat that bacon," said Paul, stuffing cash into his breast pocket.

"I think he's telling us to get out," said Amelie.

"That is the best bacon I've ever smelled."

"Because it's not real bacon. Hurry up!"

"I'm trying." Stella managed to wedge her fat feet back into her shoes, but Nicky insisted on carrying her.

"Not you, dear," said Amelie. "Paul."

Stella struggled in Nicky's arms. "I'm not an invalid."

"Don't argue. We don't have all day." Nicky squeezed past statues heading for the door that young Julian burst through. "Germans!"

"We know!" said Nicky. "Is there another way out of the building?"

"*Oui.* I take you. Papa will stop the Germans." Julian sounded strong, but his cheeks were wet with tears and he shook violently. "He's not afraid."

"He's the only one." Nicky carried Stella through the door and Julian led them to a door hidden in the paneling. They ran down the narrow servant stairs and exited the building through a storage area into a beautiful courtyard.

Julian directed them to leave through the apartment building opposite. His father had said that they should cross to the other side of the river by the Pont de la Tournelle. They would be able to find a cab to take them to the train station.

Nicky ran across the courtyard, trailed by Amelie and Paul, all of them huffing and puffing.

"Are you all right, Stella?" asked Nicky.

"For now." She had her eyes skyward, looking at the many faces tracking their escape from the safety of their windows.

CHAPTER 33

Stella walked through the Gare de Lyon with the feather from her new hat caressing her cheek and the collar on her coat turned up, not against the chill but in a failed effort to hide. People couldn't help but see her. Amelie had had her coat cleaned by the hotel concierge before they went to the antique shop and the curly lambskin and fox collar were as beautiful and eye-catching as they were when she stepped off the train in Vienna. The hat and exquisite makeup didn't help, but there was nothing to be done about it so she held her head up and met people's eyes, plastering the expression she'd seen on so many women passing by, indifference combined with confidence.

Amelie hooked her arm through the younger woman's and leaned over, smiling and warm. "You're doing it again."

"What?" Stella said with a nod at a man giving her an admiring gaze while keeping her peripheral vision on Nicky, who was walking ahead with Paul. His head was a good foot above the crowd but somewhat concealed with the new fedora.

"Clutching your chest."

She looked down to find her arm crossed between her breasts and a wave of loss washed over her again. She had to remind herself that the book was safe and better off without her.

"Habit," she said.

"You're more interesting than I ever imagined," said Amelie.

"So are you. Tell me about that murderer."

Paul frowned over his shoulder at them as Amelie launched into her story of tracking down a charming ne'er-do-well that thought killing someone for a bit of pocket money was all in a day's work. She took Stella on a trip through the humid streets of the French quarter and painted a picture of beautiful balconies covered in lush ferns and old families that still spoke French or Spanish.

They stopped at a ticket booth and Paul said, "Are you sure?"

Nicky eyed Stella from beneath the brim of his hat. She nodded with only a hint of queasiness. They would go to Venice to find the Sorkines. Uncle Josiah could take care of himself. Besides, if her mother couldn't stop him from showing up at her garden parties to terrorize the society ladies with his bawdy and wholly unacceptable humor, Stella figured she had no chance of stopping him from going after Abel in Vienna. He was Josiah Bled and as much as she loved him, protecting him was out of the question. Charming ne'er-do-wells were like that.

Paul hesitated, his hand in his breast pocket. "Venice?"

"Absolutely. The Sorkines don't know what they're walking into," said Stella.

Nicky smiled. "And the Nazis don't know they're about to meet their match in your uncle."

"Truer words were never spoken."

Paul bought the tickets, two for Marseilles and two for Venice, using the money from Elias' safe. They stood under the board and found their trains. Venice left immediately and Marseilles in two hours. Stella turned to Amelie. "There's a place to send telegrams in here."

"That's right," said Nicky. "Downstairs. Abel sent one. Now I wonder who it was to."

"Probably his cousin Gaspard in Greece to give him our itinerary," said Stella. "In any case, I'd like you two to send a message to the Englehof Brewery in Germany before you get on your train."

"What should we say?" asked Paul.

Stella considered what Hildegard and Kaspar would understand were they to get the message and what someone else would understand if they didn't. "Rabbit fur fedora is Hildegard's cheese."

"What on Earth does that mean?" asked Amelie.

"They'll understand."

"Who?" asked Nicky.

"Only the right people."

"All right," said Paul. "Rabbit fur fedora is Hildegard's cheese. Where is this winery?"

"Near Munich. I don't have an address," said Stella.

"Consider it done."

Amelie checked her watch and nervously looked up at the board. "It's almost time. We had better hurry."

"I guess this is where we part ways," said Nicky.

"Not at all," said Paul. "We'll see you off. We have time."

They hurried out of the station and onto the platform where the Venice train awaited, puffing smoke that rolled over the walkway. The four of them walked through without hesitation, weaving through a warren of carts that had already unloaded their contents at the dining car. They found Nicky and Stella's First-Class carriage, gleaming red and gold, with several wealthy passengers boarding. Paul gave Nicky all the lira they'd found, enough cash to get them by in Italy for at least a week.

Amelie hugged Stella and shivered as a bitter wind blew in from the end of the platform. "Until we meet again."

"Thank you for everything," said Stella. "Call my father as soon as you get to the States."

"I will." Amelie took her hand again and squeezed it. "I hope you find the Sorkines quickly."

"We will." Nicky shook her hand and clapped Paul on the back.

"Get off this continent as soon as you are able," said Paul. "There will be another war. This trip taught me that."

"There's nothing that we don't agree on, my friend," said Nicky. "Safe travels."

Stella hugged Paul and turned to the porter, who stepped off the train in a sleek uniform that matched the train.

"*Bienvenue madame et monsieur. Comment puis-je vous aider?*" said the porter.

"Do you speak English?" asked Nicky.

The porter blinked twice and then said, "A little. Tickets?"

Nicky gave him their tickets and he waved them onto the train, escorting them to their compartment at the end.

"He thought we were French," whispered Nicky.

"I know," Stella replied with a smile as she ran her fingertips over the elegant wood paneling and listened to the piercing whistle signaling their imminent departure.

The porter slid open their compartment and bowed. Stella stepped inside, plopping down on the tufted red velvet seat in just the way her mother never wanted her to and not giving it a second thought.

"Do you have any English papers aboard?" Nicky asked.

"*Oui*…yes, sir. Would you like them immediately?"

Nicky looked at Stella, a flicker of hesitation in his eyes.

"By all means," she said. "We need to know what's going on."

The porter turned to leave, but she asked before he could go, "Can I have some French and German papers as well?"

"Of course. I will return directly."

Nicky gave the porter several bills and the man closed their compartment. Nicky drew the curtains and set Stella's cosmetics case next to her. Then he went to the window as the train lurched and looked out. "Why do you want French and German papers?"

"It's time I start learning the languages," said Stella.

"As your family commands?" Nicky didn't look back at her.

"No," she said. "As necessity commands. The next time someone threatens our lives, I'd like to know what they're saying."

"Next time?"

"There's bound to be a next time. It's us."

"Very true." He held out his hand to her, all smiles and warmth. "Come wave goodbye to Paul and Amelie."

Stella went to the window and blew kisses to Paul and Amelie, who stood on the platform, waving like maniacs. The train chugged forward and Stella grasped the window ledge for support. A small sign passed the window and she inhaled.

"Oh, no," she said.

"What?" said Nicky.

"Platform five. Remember the train we were supposed to get on with Albert in Vienna? I hope this isn't bad luck."

Nicky took her face in his hands. "I don't believe in luck."

Stella eyed him suspiciously. "After everything that's happened, you don't believe in luck?"

Nicky stepped back and sat down, crossing his long legs at the ankles. "I don't believe because it doesn't matter. As you say, we've had some bad luck, but we've had incredibly good luck, too. It balances out, so it doesn't matter."

"Maybe you're right. Maybe luck doesn't matter."

She looked out the window past the fringed curtain at Paul and Amelie growing smaller on the platform. She pressed her hand against the glass, her heat making a fog around her fingers. She was forever saying goodbye and rarely hello. Such good friends. The best kind.

"Goodbye," she whispered.

The train picked up speed and, in an instant, Amelie and Paul were gone.

A sharp rap rattled their compartment door.

"Come in," said Nicky.

"Sir and ma'am, your papers," said the porter.

Nicky gave him another bill and he left with a short bow. The London paper on top had a screaming headline. "Göring sends envoy here in secret."

Nicky looked at it, but he didn't pick it up. Instead, he held up the little book with the dragon on the cover that he'd gotten out of the makeup case. "Have you read the inside?"

"Not the whole thing. Not yet," said Stella.

"I think you should tell me about it."

She sat down on the plush cushions and took off her coat and hat. Then she stabbed the hatpin through the crown and took the book from Nicky, who didn't wince at the vicious thrust. "It's about a hobbit."

"What's a hobbit?"

"A kind of little man with big hairy feet."

"Continue."

"The hobbit is named Bilbo and he doesn't like adventures, but he has one anyway," she said, pressing the book to her chest.

"Like us," said Nicky.

"Exactly like us, except for the feet, height, and not liking adventures."

"I don't like adventures."

"Then why ever did you marry me?" Stella asked smiling.

He leaned over to her, kissing her lightly on the lips. "You didn't come with a warning label."

"Would it have worked?"

He kissed her again. "Not a chance. So does your book have monsters? We have monsters."

Stella held out the book. "Read it and decide for yourself."

"I'd rather have you read it." He had a funny look in his eyes as he waved the book away. "Start with the dedication."

"There's a dedication?"

"Two, actually."

Stella leaned back and opened the little book. She didn't see the dedications at first. They were half hidden by the dust jacket. The first was simple.

"For Thomas
J.R.R. Tolkien"

The second wasn't.

"Things are not always what they seem; the first appearance deceives
many; the intelligence of a few perceives what has been carefully
hidden."
William Shakespeare

"Who gave you that book?" asked Nicky.

"Cyril." She couldn't stop looking at the quote. "And it's not a dedication. It's a quote and it's wrong."

"Is it?" He crossed his arms.

"Shakespeare didn't write those words." She ran her finger over the
words. "And Cyril would know that."

"Then he wrote it…to you."

"Yes. He'd know that I'd know it was wrong, too." She looked up.
"How did you know?"

"My grandfather liked the ancients, Phaedrus in particular. So
Cyril is sending you a message."

"That things aren't what they seem."

"Or he isn't," said Nicky, coming to sit beside her. "Tell me what
happened."

She leaned into him and closed her eyes. "I don't think I know
anymore."

"Then we'll find out together. No more flying off without me."

"No more stealing cars."

"Or accepting packages without knowing what's in them."

Stella elbowed him in the ribs. "Shut up, Paul."

"Shut up, Amelie. We're going to die."

"We're not going to die. We'd know."

"I know," said Nicky, imitating Paul's bellow. "There's a lot more to
the Boulards than meets the eye."

"The same as everyone else," said Stella. "Shall we read? French, German, or English?"

"English." Nicky picked up the little book. "Let's have an adventure where we can't possibly be killed."

"Agreed." Stella began to read, letting the miles click away beneath them. Italy was far away and there was still time.

The End

PREVIEW

STRANGERS IN VENICE (STELLA BLED BOOK TWO)

*T*he men had talked at first, the irrepressible chatter of the terrified, but that had long since fallen off as the minutes turned into hours. Abel said little, not even his name. His name was more dangerous than being a Jew and that was what got him in the boxcar in the first place. That and some foolish choices.

But the choices weren't only his. A young man named Herschel Grynszpan murdered a German official in Paris, not realizing the Nazis would take revenge. In truth, they were only waiting for an excuse and Grynszpan gave them a good one, but Abel never imagined it would be this bad. He didn't think the SA would attack people in the street, drag them out of their beds and beat them, or arrest hundreds of men like himself and shove them into freezing cold boxcars, many without shoes or coats. No. He never imagined that.

The old man beside him patted his knee and said in soothing tones, "We will be there soon." He said that every few minutes, whether it was for Abel's benefit or his own Abel didn't know, but there was such kindness in his voice that Abel got a pang in his chest each time he said it.

"Yes," said Abel, but he didn't think it would be an improvement.

People came back from Dachau, but when they did, they weren't the same as when they went in.

He and the old man were huddled up with fifty other men wondering what would happen next. The only options seemed to be terrible or horrific. If only he hadn't come back to Vienna. If only he'd stayed in his flat. If only he had listened. If only he had believed. It could've been different. He could've gotten away.

Instead, he'd dropped off his clients, Stella and Nicky Lawrence, at their hotel, gone to his shop, and begun answering the correspondence that had piled up in the two months of his absence. Without any inkling of what was about to happen, he'd gone to bed in his little flat above the shop only to be woken up a short time later by his maid, Lettie, on the telephone.

"Oh, Mr. Herschmann, you are there. How I hoped you wouldn't be," she said in a rush, her strong Slavic accent muddling her words.

"What is it, Lettie?" It paid to be calm with Lettie. She got excited by a late milk delivery.

"They're coming. Now. Now. Now."

"Who is coming?"

"The brown shirts. You must go now. Hide."

Abel sat on the edge of his bed with the heavy black receiver in his hand, unable to think.

"Mr. Herschmann. Mr. Herschmann. Are you there?"

"Yes, Lettie."

"You must go. Hide."

"Why?" he asked sounding thick-headed and none too bright. "What are they doing?"

"They've set fire to your churches and they are arresting men. They are beating them. Come here. We keep you safe."

The thought of his little Bulgarian maid fending off the SA brought him to his senses.

"Lettie, it's all right. I'll be fine," Abel said, but he was already up and getting dressed. "It's Albert's shop. We changed the sign, the deed, everything."

"You think they are stupid?" she asked, her accent growing stronger.

"Not exactly."

"They came to the shop looking for you. Mr. Moore, he tells them that you are traveling, but they don't believe him."

"Who came? When?"

"The other ones. The ones in black."

The SS.

Abel slipped on his shoes. "When was that?"

"Last week. Mr. Herschmann, you must go. They were very angry. They know your name. You're not just another Jew."

Not just another Jew. Lettie was more right than she knew. "Don't worry. I'll figure something out."

"You come here."

"Thank you, Lettie. I appreciate it." He hung up and tied his shoes. Was Lettie right? Did he have to go? When the SS were told that he wasn't there, he really wasn't and not due to return for weeks. He hadn't contacted anyone about going home to Vienna instead of Greece, not even his business partner, Albert Moore, whose Aryan name was painted over the shop's door. But the Dutch historian, Dr. Van Wijk, had seen him on the train with Stella and Nicky, and Van Wijk was rumored to be working for the SS. He may have already informed them that Abel was back in Vienna.

He went to the window and peered out to find his street quiet. Some windows were lit up, but there were certainly no torches or pitchforks parading down the street and there wasn't much reason to target his area. Mainly gentiles lived and worked there with just a handful of Jewish shops and homes. Maybe it was fine.

But then he caught a glimpse of light far off to the right, a faint glow over a rooftop. Abel opened the window and leaned out. As soon as he did, he smelled a hint of smoke. The fire wasn't close. That was good. It probably wouldn't reach the shop.

He waited, listening for the sound of sirens. None came, but screams did. Across the street, his neighbor Mr. Nelböck leered out at him between lace curtains. The gruff old man was a bastard on the best of days. He'd welcomed the annexation of Austria and the loss of their independence with unrestrained joy, but he'd never said a word to Abel about it.

Mr. Nelböck wasn't content to stay silent for long. Lit by a dim streetlamp, he leaned out of his window, waving a hideous Nazi flag and pointing a plump finger at Abel, who he barely knew. "Now it's your turn, you fucking Jew chiseler!"

Abel went icy with shock. What turn was he supposed to be having? Mr. Nelböck imported fine French cheese and wine. As a historian and travel guide, Abel was hardly in competition with the man.

He reached up to close the window as Mr. Nelböck began screaming obscenities with his red-faced wife trying to drag him away. Abel slammed the window and locked it with a loud metallic snap as if that could keep hatred out. He had to go. No doubt now.

And that was when his foolishness took hold. He had three choices as he saw it. Lettie was too far away so that left Albert, Stella and Nicky, and Ho Feng Shan, the Chinese consul general. Ho was a lovely man, who looked upon the annexation with horror and the Nazis, in general, with growing trepidation. He would let Abel into the consul. The two men had become good friends after crossing paths at the Café Central. He was the first to suggest that Abel take steps to protect the business by transferring his half to Albert and putting his money in a Swiss bank account. But Ho was in the embassy district, nearly as far as Lettie.

Stella and Nicky were the closest. The young honeymooners were members of prominent families and Americans, as well. He could go to them. They were his friends and Stella, in particular, would certainly help him without a thought to her own safety.

Last was Albert, his business partner and closest friend. As the son of a British ambassador and a member of the nobility, Albert was untouchable, but he was farther from the shop than Stella and Nicky's hotel. The possibilities raced through his mind. Distance, time, safety. Arrest, prison. Escape, success. Failure, loss. Albert or Stella?

He thought he could make it to Albert. On balance, it was worth the risk, just in case Dr. Van Wijk did tell the SS about Stella and Nicky. He didn't know what would happen if he were found in their room. They could be arrested. If they touched Stella…no, it didn't bear thinking about. Albert would be fine, even if he was found there. The SS wouldn't dare harm him.

Abel threw on his coat and opened his dresser. In the false bottom of the third drawer he uncovered the diary written by his ancestor, Johannes Gutenberg, wrapped up tight in brown paper and string to disguise its worth. Besides the diary's intrinsic value it also contained the inventor's carefully guarded secret. The most famous German inventor had loved and married a Jew, Nissa, and she'd been instrumental to the invention of moveable type.

Abel's family had begun to suspect that the Nazi hierarchy was aware of the diary's existence and what it said. To Abel, Van Wijk's presence on the train confirmed it. The last thing the Nazis would want was Gutenberg's secret revealed. Gutenberg was a hero, proof of Germanic superiority. A Jew couldn't be part of the greatest invention of all time. That didn't fit the Nazi dogma and what didn't fit must be destroyed.

Abel slipped on his coat and hesitated. Nothing was guaranteed. He might have to give the book to Albert or his doorman or some stranger if he were desperate. He grabbed his fountain pen and unscrewed the top. Greece or France? Paris was closer. His cousins, the Sorkines, would know how to act. Abel quickly scribbled their address on the brown paper and tucked the book into the interior pocket of his coat. He left behind his mother's jewelry and his father's precious books, taking only a wad of Reichsmarks, his passport, his parents' wedding photo slipped out of its silver frame, his favorite picture of Stella, and the diary.

Dashing out the back into the night, he'd made his way towards Albert's flat using back alleys and neatly avoiding crowds of SA ruffians roaming the streets looking for hapless victims and randomly attacking shops and homes. The sound of breaking glass and screaming accompanied him everywhere. The smoke choked him and made his eyes burn. He couldn't escape it, only ignore it as best he could. At one point, he nearly ran into a group chanting, "Burn it down! Burn it down!" in front of a synagogue and found himself cut off. It would be easier to go to Stella and Nicky, but he stubbornly stuck to his plan, taking extra time to go around the mob.

What had he been thinking? So foolish not to adapt to circumstances. Abel tugged at his pant legs, trying in vain to cover his frozen ankles. He wrapped his arms around himself and wondered if he hadn't decided to stay on his chosen path would he be safe? And more importantly, would Stella be safe?

Read the rest in
Strangers in Venice (Stella Bled Book Two)

ALSO BY A.W. HARTOIN

Historical Thriller

The Paris Package (Stella Bled Book One)

Strangers in Venice (Stella Bled Book Two)

One Child in Berlin (Stella Bled Book Three)

Dark Victory (Stella Bled Book Four)

A Quiet Little Place in Rue de Lille (Stella Bled Book Five)

Young Adult fantasy

Flare-up (Away From Whipplethorn Short)

A Fairy's Guide To Disaster (Away From Whipplethorn Book One)

Fierce Creatures (Away From Whipplethorn Book Two)

A Monster's Paradise (Away From Whipplethorn Book Three)

A Wicked Chill (Away From Whipplethorn Book Four)

To the Eternal (Away From Whipplethorn Book Five)

Mercy Watts Mysteries

Novels

A Good Man Gone (Mercy Watts Mysteries Book One)

Diver Down (A Mercy Watts Mystery Book Two)

Double Black Diamond (Mercy Watts Mysteries BookThree)

Drop Dead Red (Mercy Watts Mysteries Book Four)

In the Worst Way (Mercy Watts Mysteries Book Five)

The Wife of Riley (Mercy Watts Mysteries Book Six)

My Bad Grandad (Mercy Watts Mysteries Book Seven)

Brain Trust (Mercy Watts Mysteries Book Eight)

Down and Dirty (Mercy Watts Mysteries Book Nine)

Small Time Crime (Mercy Watts Mysteries Book Ten)

Bottle Blonde (Mercy Watts Mysteries Book Eleven)

Mean Evergreen (Mercy Watts Mysteries Book Twelve)

Short stories

Coke with a Twist

Touch and Go

Nowhere Fast

Dry Spell

A Sin and a Shame

Paranormal

It Started with a Whisper

ABOUT THE AUTHOR

USA Today bestselling author A.W. Hartoin grew up in rural Missouri, but her grandmother lived in the Central West End area of St. Louis. The CWE fascinated her with it's enormous houses, every one unique. She was sure there was a story behind each ornate door. Going to Grandma's house was a treat and an adventure. As the only grandchild around for many years, A.W. spent her visits exploring the many rooms with their many secrets. That's how Mercy Watts and the fairies of Whipplethorn came to be.

As an adult, A.W. Hartoin decided she needed a whole lot more life experience if she was going to write good characters so she joined the Air Force. It was the best education she could've hoped for. She met her husband and traveled the world, living in Alaska, Italy, and Germany before settling in Colorado for nearly eleven years. Now A.W. has returned to Germany and lives in picturesque Waldenbuch with her family and two spoiled cats, who absolutely believe they should be allowed to escape and roam the village freely.

Printed in Great Britain
by Amazon

23987320R00212